A Poker Game of Love

ALICE WALSH

This book was first published in the United Kingdom

A Poker Game of Love
by
Alice Walsh

ISBN: 978-0-9927908-1-3

[1.Interpersonal Relations - Fiction 2. Political Figures - Fiction 3. Background Setting - Fiction 4. Characters - Fiction 5.Romance - Fiction 6. Corporate organizations - Fiction 7. Conduct of Life - Fiction 8. Self-perception - Fiction 9. Friendship - Fiction]

A CIP catalogue record for this book is available from the British Library

Walsh, Alice

A Poker Game of Love / Alice Walsh

First English Edition, March 2014

Alice Walsh asserts the moral right to be identified as the author of this work

Book Design by Alice Walsh
Cover Design by Alice Walsh
Cover Image © Alice Walsh

CHAPTER ONE

It was well past midnight and she was long asleep when the sound of a text message woke her up. "I've *got* to start switching my cell phone off at night," she moaned, reaching for it on the night stand and knocking over a half empty glass of water she kept next to the lamp. *This better be worth it,* Sylvia thought, annoyed. The text was short, concise and emotionless, as all of his texts were.

"In the mood for fucking. Come over."

His bluntness irritated her a bit at first, but at a second glance she could make out that unmistakable drive and determination that made him so attractive. And another thing – after all it was her he was texting in the middle of the night on a workday. *Either a slow month or he just can't go a week without me.* Sylvia smiled at the latter, sliding her hand down her neck. What some women found rude and thoughtless, labeling it as nothing more than a "booty call", she saw as a golden opportunity to satisfy her uncanny sexual urge. *Plus, it is such an incredible ego booster*, she thought, shaking her curls. Barely having woken up she was in the mood for sex; the message really hit the spot. The more basic and primal the man was in expressing his desire, the quicker it turned her on. In that sense, James was in a class of his own as he always knew exactly what to say and how to touch her.

"On my way," she texted back.

It was already half past three. Jumping out of bed, she grabbed the first pair of jeans she could find and a blouse, threw them on, and rushed out of the apartment. She pulled out her phone and ordered a cab while waiting for the elevator. By the time it got to the ground floor a car was already waiting outside. It was a twenty minute drive to his place, something they had agreed on in order to have the distance necessary to live their separate lives, all the while benefiting from an easy visiting range for a quick getaway when needed. As the car drove down Broadway and entered Hell's Kitchen she grinned at the thought of their turbulent history – a never-ending game of cat and mouse with the exception that one of the parties was deeply misguided about its role in the constant power struggle and she knew it wasn't her. *It's good getting what you want out of life. Out of men.* she thought contentedly. *In and out, nice and clean, without them realizing it. Just letting them think they're in control. It's easier for everyone that way.*

When she came out of the elevator James was waiting at the door of his apartment. She glanced at the whiskey bottle in his hand. He had already downed almost half of it and was nervously tapping with his fingers on the wall. The bulge in his pants was a clear indication he was still sober enough for what they had in mind, which prompted a sigh of relief from her. Pulling her inside, he started undressing her hastily.

"How long does it take you to drag your ass here? When I say I want to fuck, I mean *now*."

"I came as fast as I could."

"Yeah, well, now I'll do exactly that and next time you'll hurry up if you want any foreplay. Spread your legs."

She gladly obeyed, cheering the fact he was in such a lousy mood. His anger and aggressiveness turned him into an incredible lover. It took out all the unnecessary softness, which was unnatural to their relationship. She liked it rough and James was eager to dominate. So was she, by the way, but that was something her partners weren't meant to find out. *Besides, it's a whole other level of domination, one they have no idea about. Give 'em the physical side of it if it makes them so happy. Toying with someone emotionally and intellectually – That's a whole other level of satisfaction.* Like any smart girl she knew that submitting to men was the only way to dominate them. It was a poker game of love – for one of the parties to win, the other one had to lose. Those were the rules, simple and ruthless. And if you were a skillful player and learnt from your mistakes, it paid off. Oh, how it paid off!

The sex was wild, quick and seemed more like a struggle. They had done it so many times, for so many years now that both executed to perfection each step of the routine for a fast sexual gratification. The benefit of such relationship dynamics was to have someone in their life who knew the other one well enough to make them feel better about themselves without the added drawbacks of having to put up with that person outside of the bedroom. A mere phone call or a text away – a lingering presence, a territory that had to occasionally be re-visited meant neither one of them ever had to let their guard down and get too comfortable. *Things you have to constantly work for keep you motivated*, she thought, rolling over to her side. They had barely finished when both reached for their phones and started going through calendars and tasks. There was no need for explanations, promises or tenderness; no one felt they owed the other more than what was just given.

"I've got to go. I've an early day tomorrow."

"I was going to say the same. Sorry you can't spend the night."

"It's fine."

"I'll call you."

"Don't get up. I'll let myself out."

James watched her walk around the apartment, picking up the clothes he had thrown to the ground just minutes before. It was one of the things he liked about her – she didn't suffer from any unnecessary shyness or the typical female obsession with her physical flaws. Those few extra pounds were just right. He was sick of perfect girls who made him feel inadequate, standing next to their slim frame. Fortunately, that wasn't the case with her. James knew he was too good for her. Or so he liked to believe. *What am I saying?* He was quick to correct himself. *Of course I am too good for her. I can overlook the muffin top and all, but she's all over the place. I can't have anyone who's that big of a liability in my life. The only thing she's good at is being fucked. And that's what we're doing. That's what this is. A friendly fuck, nothing more.* He finished the bottle and pulled the cover over his eyes as she turned off the light and closed the door on her way out.

She walked outside the building and hailed a cab. Ordinarily, Sylvia enjoyed the time right after they had just been together, but neither had yet gone about their separate routine. No one was chasing anyone away, no one was jumping in a fit to take a shower and, above all, she could mellow out under the touch of his firm grip on her hips and ass. However, she had learnt not to force herself on him as it rendered the opposite of the result she was aiming for. She sensed this was one of those times when it was best to leave immediately afterwards. James was all over her – on her body, in her mind and life – and so was she in his. The only thing that drove them apart was his persistent denial of the obvious truth, but there was time to deal with that. *One step at a time,* she thought, *and I can wait. I'm in no hurry.*

Behind her back a light went on in a small apartment window and a man's silhouette stood in the frame. There was a bottle in his hand. He lingered there for a while, then turned around, went to the desk and switched on the computer.

James went to the fridge and took out a can of beer. He needed something not too strong to keep his buzz going and not too weak to kill it. Sitting in the chair, he stared at the loading screen. He had practiced the same routine for years now, perfecting it to the last detail: get drunk; turn on computer; play music; log onto messenger; wait for someone – anyone – to go online, and, lastly, open every single mailbox to see if She had written. She never had and seven years of silence were more than enough to dishearten even the strongest-willed. But for a person like him, who was as fixated on the past as can be, that wasn't nearly enough. Every night was equally lifeless; each caused him the same amount of suffering, inevitably ending in the same way – with another letter sent to her silent inbox. He always passed out right after hitting the "send" button and he always regretted it afterwards, incapable of giving up on his hopes to hear from Her again. Waking up shortly after dawn, the first thing he did was reach for his guitar. The sunrise always found him in the middle of a new song recording or rehearsal of the material for the evening performance at Jazz Standard – the club where he played. By noon he had gathered just enough pieces to pull himself together and turn into his usual charming, careless, overconfident self that all his female friends found so irresistible. His night-time fragility was just a state of mind, though he ruthlessly made efforts to bring his body to the same state of decay as some sort of twisted punishment.

He was the strong, silent type or at least that was the image he had projected for years in front of his friends and acquaintances. He knew exactly what women wanted: compliments and promises. They wanted to be caressed, loved, protected, valued; given flowers and cards; they wanted to hear they were someone's soul mate. All things he used to do. With Her. *The first and, most likely, only woman I've ever loved,* James thought. *Now I'm a typical man – I come and go without caring. No man is like this until he comes across an enchantingly vulnerable destructress who trashes his soul and leaves. Afterwards all women start looking alike; equally thin, pretty, charming, good in bed, (un)interesting.* He flirted with them, pretended to be nice, took them home, fucked them and chased them away afterwards with polite excuses why they couldn't spend the night. None of them were even remotely aware there were still signs of Her in his home. A wrinkled photograph, shoved between some magazines in the desk drawer, was the visible trace. So many memories and so much pain were the invisible ones. *That's just how She was; She loved leaving traces behind. She stole my first kiss, first love and all those first things, which are remembered just because they've never been before. It's hard to amputate them from your mind. The second are less memorable, the third, the fourth…*

All the women around him resembled something of a cure. Night after night he made an effort to lose himself in the credulity of their eyes, trying to recreate his former self – unsure, excited, scared, lost and in love. It was impossible. She still haunted him in the faces of all the women he kept punishing for what She had done to him. He wanted Her to hurt without even realizing why. It seemed easier that way. *People who've been hurt like hurting others,* he justified himself.

It wasn't that his first love was fairy-tale material or that he was dating a goddess in human form, but a pattern of idealization prolonged for years had turned James's past into an almost palpable reality. He was too young and far too immature to handle the intensity of such emotions when they had started dating, and he had made the cardinal mistake of all first-time lovers and started living his life through someone else's. Love was dangerous for a young mind because something so beautiful dulled the sense of reality. In the end things unraveled as expected – he got tired of gluing his life to Hers, of building sand castles, of saying "I love you". He had to give them up to become himself. The bad thing was, having lived without his freedom for too long, he didn't know what to do with it once he got it back. His life started filling up with past presences that lingered on.

If he had a signature characteristic it would undoubtedly be his ability to see beyond what people needed and right into what they wanted. He was so full of himself, and so busy fostering the appearance of success and self-satisfaction, that while all his former classmates were preoccupied with college applications and tuition fees he was solely concentrating on enjoying himself to the full. He was young, charming and sociable with his entire life ahead of him. Things were bound to work out.

One day he woke up to the somber realization that he was twenty-seven, without any skills, with no career prospects, and not even a clear path in life. All his former classmates were getting their PhDs, climbing the corporate ladder, starting private practices or buying houses and all he could do was play the guitar. Not that it was that late to start anew, but he had spent too much time on music to just toss it aside. Seeing his friends' success made him crave validation himself, and he believed the only way to achieve anything at this point in his life was in a familiar field. Starting from scratch would only mean all those years had gone down the drain for nothing. Deep down there was also another reason – James needed that extra something music gave him. He couldn't see himself stuck at a 9-to-5 job, taking on a supportive role; he craved more. Playing satisfied his need for admiration and attention, giving him a certain *je ne sais quoi* that made him popular with the ladies for years to come. He didn't have to be exceptional at what he did, didn't even have to be that good, although there had been a time when he believed he was destined for the limelight. Disillusionment began soon after finishing high school. Faced with the overwhelming number of talented, underpaid and unappreciated musicians, he realised the field he had chosen wasn't all it was cracked up to be. In the end, it turned out women didn't have a thing for struggling jazz musicians. But by the time he fully comprehended the severity of the situation he had gotten himself into, it was far too late to head down a different path, so he just had to make do. Which was exactly what he did.

As he stared grimly at the screen, overwhelmed by the rambling thoughts, he was distracted by the sound of someone going online in the messenger. He instinctively knew it was her. She always came when he needed to be rescued from himself. He reached for the keyboard, unaware he was smiling.

CHAPTER TWO

Sylvia walked through the door of her one-bedroom, Morningside Heights apartment just as the alarm on her night stand went off. After a shower, she walked around naked, taking her time in the closet as she picked out clothes for the day. She always stepped out of the house looking nothing less than radiant, having learnt from an early age that if she wasn't the most beautiful, she could easily be the most attractive. *Which is more than enough*, she thought, holding up a Chanel blouse. Every piece of clothing and every accessory were carefully chosen to complement her curves. Her curls fell perfectly aligned, barely glazing her shoulders. Just as she was reaching for her morning coffee, her phone rang. She looked at her wrist watch. It was a quarter to eight. He was never late.

"Good morning, beautiful."

"Good morning, Stephan. Do you have anything for me?"

He laughed at her bluntness. "I have your presentation on the quarterly projections right here, kept me up three nights in a row and you know how busy I've been with the new site going live and all. You owe me big time!"

"Oh, do I now? You make it sound as if I forced you into doing me a favor."

"Come on, beautiful – like anyone can say no to you!"

"How's that *my* problem?" Sylvia chuckled. "When can I have it? My boss wants it on his desk by noon."

"I already emailed it to you, but I'd love to take you out later. Are you free for dinner?"

"I have plans."

"A cup of coffee then?"

"Can't. Listen, I've got to go now. I'll call you when I can, k? Talk to you soon, love, and thanks again. You're a life-saver."

"K, talk to y…"

She hung up, cutting him off midsentence, and quickly opened her inbox, barely glancing at the presentation. *Very nice,* she thought. *He really knows his stuff. See? Doesn't this make more sense? Why should someone like me deal with these things when there are plenty of men capable and willing to do them? If you know how to ask, of course.* She smirked. Stephan had truly outdone himself this time. The presentation was professional, concise and easy-to-follow, just the kind of thing you would expect from an IT postgraduate with a Masters in Finance. He had also written her exemplary opening and finishing statements, as well as placed pointers for all the bullet points she needed to cover. *Men are so convenient. Thank God for them. Otherwise, we'd have to do everything ourselves. And God knows women are more efficient than that. It's not like we don't have anything better to do with our time. After all, what are all your sexual partners for if not to perform an occasional service outside of bed?* She smiled.

Her femininity made her so deliciously vulnerable, fragile and desirable that it instantly drew men to her, prompting their need to assume the outdated roles of protector and provider. It was an innate quality that she possessed, although her ability to cash in on it was something she had cultivated for years. This always got her what she wanted, for she was one of those women who didn't believe in achieving anything without the help of a man. Her father was the first male figure on whom Sylvia had tried out all those little tricks that came naturally to her, to see what she could get away with. *It turned out the sky was the limit.* She lit up at the thought. Innocent batting of her eyelashes and good-girl image had gotten her a degree in Finance from Stanford, her very own 1-bedroom apartment, which she felt was in a rather "shabby neighborhood", and a first job as the personal assistant of Tim Foster, the VP of Riverdale Bank. Of course, daddy's connections, money and powerful friends had helped with all three of these things, but that was just the first phase of her plan. Now, fully settled in Manhattan, she had started crafting a web of male friends and acquaintances. Sylvia was smart and didn't fool herself – that alone gave her a large advantage in life. She knew that sex was a means of getting ahead and saw nothing wrong in exploiting male weaknesses for her own purposes. Feminism was but a vague concept to her, and she found it downright absurd that women would gladly give up the benefits of their position for the right to be considered as strong as men. She wanted to be seen as weak. She liked her door opened and her bills paid, and she wasn't willing to give up anything that made her existence more comfortable. Moving to New York and taking on this job was her way of entering the right crowd and eventually finding that Mr. Right who would offer her the financial security she knew she deserved. It was all that interested her and all she wanted. She had no interest in love whatsoever. "Love doesn't pay bills or put food on the table. It bruises hearts and shatters dreams until we're nothing but cynical bastards who account for every feeling spent and earned, frantically checking if the total on the receipt tallies. But in love it never does. Money, however, cannot tell a lie," she liked to say.

She casually wrapped a silk scarf around her neck, grabbed her Berkin and gloves and walked out. She managed to grab a taxi straight away in front of her building, and as the car drove down FDR East River Drive she flicked through her iPhone, bored, wondering who to call tonight. Finally, she settled on taking a "male break" and enjoying some female company for a change. That was another thing about her; Sylvia was well aware of the detrimental effect women could have on each other, which was the reason she kept the count of female friends to the absolute minimum of one. Her friend Tanya had proven to be quite reliable over the years, which had earned her a front-row seat to Sylvia's life. Two short texts later, they had arranged for drinks and early dinner at Trinity Place.

The tall blonde woman looked impatiently at her phone as she sipped a cocktail at the bar. It was nearing seven. *Late as usual and not even a text,* Tanya thought, looking around the restaurant, which was bursting at the seams with white-collar types trying to unwind after a long day at work. *If she's not here in ten minutes we can kiss our table goodbye.* It had been a hectic day at the publishing agency and she was getting more agitated by the minute. Just as she was finishing her drink and getting ready to leave, she saw Sylvia making her way through the crowd with men turning their heads to ogle her. Tanya was a loyal girlfriend, but as a woman it was hard for her to pinpoint what men found so irresistible about Sylvia. *I guess it's that same je ne sais quoi everyone is drawn to, but doesn't quite understand – a quality she has that everyone notices, but no one can explain.* She shrugged. Her friend was at best average-looking, but everything about her – from clothes to body language –worked to her advantage. What was even more striking was that Sylvia was completely aware of the effect she had on men. She never underestimated the power of the attention she received, regardless of the person giving it to her. Of course, higher social status automatically conferred extra "points" to an admirer, but she generally enjoyed seeing interest and desire in any man's eyes. She was only interested in seeing envy and fear in the eyes of women, however, as those were the mark of success in the female world. She approached Tanya, snatched the cocktail from her hand, drank what was left of it, and nodded her head, indicating they should sit down. Tanya stood up and they followed the waitress, who sat them at a table in the back.

"You could've called."

"Why?"

"To say you were running late."

"I'm not that late. Besides, do I ever call, even if I am?"

"Good point. What's new with you?"

"Nothing. Same old, same old."

"Then what's the problem?"

"What do you mean?"

"You call either when you have a problem or have something new to brag about. I think we know each other well enough to cut to the chase."

Sylvia laughed, putting down the menu. "You know me too well," she smiled, touching Tanya's hand. "We're practically sisters you and I," she added softly.

"A sister will call if she's running late," Tanya teased.

"Guess who I met at that event my boss dragged me to last month. You know, the Emerging Markets Investment somethin' somethin' crap."

"I envy the level of sophistication you bring to your job."

"Anyhow, after the summit there was a formal dinner and who do you think I see in the crowd? George William Huntington the Third! He comes over to chat with Tim and it turns out they're on a first name basis. Tim introduces me, leaving us to chat, which we did for a bit and…well, long story short, we really hit it off. I'm meeting him for dinner this Thursday."

"You sure move fast. I thought you were still involved with James." Tanya raised her eyebrows.

"First of all, I have never been involved with James. We just fuck. Second, even if I had any feelings for him left, you know very well that summer I spent with him in Chicago was a cold awakening as well as a dreadful preview of what my life with him would be – a 9-to-5 job to support a struggling musician, who's got his head so far up his ass he thinks he's Al Di Meola. A girl's dream come true," Sylvia winced.

"That's a bit harsh. Even for you. If he's so pathetic why are you at his place every other night for a quickie?"

"The sex is pretty decent, as are the favors in between. Never toss a guy you've slept with out of your life. You never know when and why he might come in handy."

"But you definitely don't have feelings for him anymore?"

"If I've ever had any feelings for him it was at a time when I was very young without so much as a clue as to what's important in life, or in a man. After too many readings of Cinderella every girl starts believing all that matters is for the prince to be well-spoken and generous in his promises. You know you've grown when you're more interested in what's being delivered. Compared to George, James is not even the same species."

"Do you have feelings for George then?"

"Getting a little ahead of ourselves, aren't we? I could, but you're totally missing the point." Sylvia shrugged.

The waitress approached and started placing their food on the table: two Caesar salads, two Prime Beef Medallions and Sylvia's favorite cocktail, which alone was worth coming to this place for – a sultry mixture of Tanqueray gin, Martini, St. Germain, grapefruit and lime juice.

"What *is* the point then?" Tanya asked, picking at her salad.

"The point is that George just graduated from Harvard Business School; he comes from a family heralding seven generations of politicians. His father is the current governor of New Hampshire and George himself plans on running for office someday. Everything about him screams stability. Which is what we women really want in the end. I want to know I have a man who's going to take care of me, not the other way around. I didn't work my butt off in college just so I can provide for myself for the rest of my life. It was a résumé-building exercise. Personal résumé, that is."

"Congratulations, Sylvie. Seems like, unlike most people, you're perfectly aware of what you want and how to get it."

The young women chuckled and clicked their glasses.

"I wonder how Stephan's gonna handle it. He's been in love with you since high school. Don't know what you did to the poor schmuck," Tanya said, thoughtfully.

"It's a gift, really. Anyway, Stephan doesn't need to be up to date with my love life; it's not like he's a part of it."

"But you still have a job because of him! Aren't you giving him something in return for all his hard work?"

"No. You see, that's a common mistake. If you've slept with someone a while ago and want to keep them interested you should do everything but sleep with them again. Be nice, flirt your ass off, share and ask for help, but don't give him the one thing he desperately wants. Instead, give him just enough to lead him on, to let him hope he'll find his way out of the friend zone eventually. Then again, that only works on losers like Stephan. This type of passive-aggressive shit would never work on James; sex is the only thing keeping him hooked. My point is, play your cards according to your opponent, that way you'll always be consistently ahead of them."

"Sounds tricky."

"It doesn't have to be. Unless you focus on the wrong thing. People think it's mostly about luck, and bitch about the hand they've been dealt. But luck has nothing to do with it. It's all about making the other person believe you're holding a flush even if it's just a pair of nines."

"So it's all about lying, that's what you're saying? Relationships are about honesty."

"That kind of delusional thinking is dangerous for a woman your age," Sylvia pointed out. "And not just to you. Let's go dancing. We haven't been out in ages. How does Friday sound?"

"The day after your Big Date with the top runner for Mr. Sylvia Vassilena Watson? Won't you want to stay home and doodle his name on a napkin as you plan out the wedding?"

"Nah, you can hire people to do that for you. I hate this merry-go-round from home to the office. It's depressing. What's the point of having a generous disposable income if you can't go out and splurge?"

"And in your case you don't even have to earn it yourself – that's what your loyal minions are for."

"Exactly. But even I need a night off from the hard job of being me."

"Ok, sure, whatever. But you're buying the drinks."

"Deal."

They finished dinner and pushed away the empty plates. Sylvia nodded to the waitress, who was quick to bring the check. She handed her a gold American Express card, dismissing Tanya's weak attempts to split the bill. They had an unspoken rule about the dynamics of their friendship – Tanya would always be there to offer her a shoulder, ear or presence when asked, and Sylvia would pay for the service in a way. However, throughout the years they had grown fond of each other and started to actually perceive their friendship as an honest one. In fact, it was the mere fact that they didn't sugar-coat anything and were perfectly aware of each other's shortcomings and strengths that made it possible. Tanya was permanently barely making ends meet while Sylvia was well off and happy to share what she had – after all, it was daddy who was funding her lavish lifestyle. Her job at the bank, albeit well-paid, wasn't enough to cover the regular trips to Prada, Louis Vuitton, Jimmy Choo, Christian Louboutin, Seven Seconds, Tiffany, Hermes and the rest.

They walked outside and headed towards the boulevard. In front of a cab, as they hugged each other goodnight, Sylvia slipped some cab fare into her friend's hand and Tanya gratefully put it in her pocket. What would otherwise be an extremely messed up relationship worked for them as both viewed money as nothing other than a tool. Tanya wasn't the only one Sylvia was helping out; she had done it for several boyfriends as well, although that had been back in the day when she was entirely on daddy's allowance, since it was easier giving away something she had been given herself. However, that instantly changed her opinion of the guy; she immediately lost all respect and interest (if any still left) whatsoever. With Tanya she found it charming, but also somewhat sad; sad that a woman could lack the basic female quality of getting men to take care of her. Tanya's borrowing money, which both of them knew she'd never return, only amplified her innate vulnerability, which was at the core of femininity. With men it meant the exact opposite and was a giant red flag of liability – something Sylvia didn't want in her life. Men who had once proven they were unreliable like that she filed instantly in the "TGI Friday Fun" category – something quick, something meaningless, something to pass time with.

Where some saw a cold-hearted calculating slut, there was actually a girl who had done a lot of growing up to realise she should only get something of equal or greater value for everything she gave. That was the basis of her self-respect and sense of worth.

CHAPTER THREE

James woke up with the usual acute feeling of sickness, which alcohol abuse never failed to deliver in the morning. His neck was numb from the uncomfortable position in which he had passed out. It was already midday, and the city buzz underneath his windows was becoming unbearable. Even with the shades closed, he could physically feel all the people outside. It unnerved him. He tried covering his head with the sleeping bag to avoid waking up, but without success, so he kicked the cover away, rolled on his back and stared at the ceiling, trying to recall something, anything, from the night before. *I drank a lot. What else is new? I stayed up late, waiting for her. Did she come? I think she did. Only one way to find out.* He hesitated and reached for the power button on the computer.

On his way to the bathroom he grabbed a can of beer from the kitchen to freshen up and drank it as he pissed in the sink. The barely visible trail of blood in his urine left no doubt that his drinking was getting out of hand again, but he wasn't worried as these periods came and went. James stared at his reflection in the mirror and grunted at what was staring back at him. He generally had no issues with his appearance and was quite comfortable with the way he looked. There was still something boyish in his expression, with nothing other than the sufficient amount of boredom, cynicism and exhaustion in his eyes giving away that he was well into his thirties. Despite the routine self-abuse with alcohol, sleepless nights and junk food, he was still in pretty good shape – his body being a bit on the sturdy side. It was his soul that had taken most of the irreversible damage time had inflicted, which was the main reason he tried to drink himself to death day after day, night after night.

James' main problem was that he had sacrificed everything to get where he was, but even so he wasn't anywhere near where he thought he would be by this age. Or to put it simply – he had invested far too much time, effort and energy into daydreaming about success that had never come. The irony was that, despite the downward spiral of his life, he kept on investing in the guitar as it was the only thing he really knew. He could never quite pinpoint the exact moment when playing became a burden, rather than an enjoyable way to kill time and show off in his adolescent years, but he was sure of one thing: he was trapped in a hell of his own making. One by one, friends and family had started slipping away from his life or falling out of it, as if there wasn't any room for them in it. And there really wasn't. The pursuit of success at any cost was turning into an obsession. Ambition for perfection was rendering him incapable of outdoing himself, and the necessity for admiration was crippling his ego, all of which sentenced him to mediocrity – the thing he feared the most. With time he started neglecting all social functions to a point, where the only people who lingered on in his life were those who had been there for a considerably long time, long before he had ventured into the music industry. In his case these were women he had slept with and continued to with no strings attached. Or so he would like to convince himself. The sad truth was that every relationship, regardless of the type, came with fine print, something he was bound to eventually find out.

For a while he lived a life any young single guy wanted for himself – lots of women, lots of hot sex. The only thing James hated was the mandatory buttering-up that every woman demanded before jumping into bed with a guy; it was something he found exhausting and downright irritating. "All women like to think they're special. Even the ones that aren't," he often said to his friends over drinks when they discussed their newest conquests. In his early twenties he treated it like a matter of prestige, a direct affirmation of his worth as a man with the added bonus of a serious ego booster. Women, however, possessed an innate radar for detecting men that were full of shit, and with time fewer and fewer started falling for his words. The charming, rebellious, well-read and funny Prince Charming was unmasked for the bored, lazy, inconsiderate bastard whose personality was just one short, punctuated joke after another. Maybe he was becoming disheartened with his lack of professional development to the point where it started reflecting on his social skills; or maybe it was his fleeting success with women that was making him feel inadequate; whatever the reason, James had entered a vicious circle where he was becoming more unpleasant and alienated. One by one, the names from his Big Black Book stopped answering their phones and started being unavailable too often. As a guy he recognised, without a sign of a doubt, that he was being blown off. Occasionally, someone was still up for a quick chat or an online video session during his long drunken nights, but with the years passing by, each of his former flings eventually turned into someone's present girlfriend. Only one of them lingered on, in spite of his shortcomings and their turbulent history. *Sylvia.* Her name slipped into his mind more often than before *My relationship with you has helped me through some of the most difficult times in my life and I'll never forget that. How can something that started so randomly and someone who meant nothing to me turn into such a close friend without me even realizing it? I'm glad you're in my life.*

James never told Sylvia any of these things, of course. He was far too familiar with the female psyche to risk revealing his cards. She had entered his life in the most trivial of ways. Born and raised in the same town, their fathers had worked as partners at the local police station for over fifteen years when one night, close to New Year's Eve, there was a party for the officers. If things had gone differently, James would've never approached the shy, chubby virgin, but having just suffered his first love disappointment, he found himself in desperate need of a quick ego boost. The sixteen-year old girl was a textbook case and a month later he was fucking her on a regular basis.

Angry, alone and still hurting from the rejection of the most perfect girl he had ever known, James directed his disappointment and resentment towards Sylvia – she needed to suffer as much as him. He wasn't a bad guy and it didn't bring him any pleasure to humiliate or hurt her; he was just so caught up in the spiral of his own insecurity and pain that he had nothing else to share at the time. For a long period he paid no attention to her needs, treating her like a real-life blow-up doll, a reality she perpetuated with her own behavior. Sylvia demanded nothing. She didn't pressure, ask or want anything from him; yet she was always a phone call and a cab ride away for his convenience. The years that followed, the subsequent drama and their differences, eventually erased the memory of the beginning. Sylvia had always satisfied his needs and desires and on some level James was perfectly aware of that. It was inexplicable even to him why in the few long-term relationships he had been in after they met he would eventually always find his way back to her bed. He could care about other women, maybe even try to love them, but somehow he ended right back on the phone, speed-dialing her number. He had intentionally tried to spend months not thinking about and avoiding her, but it always ended with him looking her up. Seven years had to pass before he stopped fighting and came to terms with the realization that she was the most stable thing in his life. They weren't an item, but they were pretty close to being one. The unspoken rule was that each had a life the other one wasn't a part of, but with the ringing of the phone everything and everyone else could wait.

Perhaps if he hadn't been so fixated on the way he thought his life was supposed to be he would have realised it earlier, but he wasn't highly intuitive. Even though James had grown fond of Sylvia over the years – of her loyalty, her uninhibited playfulness, insatiable lust and uncanny simplicity – he was reluctant to admit it even to himself. He continued seeing her as that awkward, needy, clingy and pathetic high school virgin and was unable to shake off the feeling he was too good for her. He never quite got over the fact that, having started with the same social background, they had ended at such different places in life: Sylvia with her own apartment in Morningside Heights due to her father taking on that promotion as Chief of Police and subsequently running for mayor of their home town of Fargo; and James living from paycheck to paycheck. He was so preoccupied with his status that he had a hard time coping with a reality that didn't revolve around him. This was the reason he was shocked to notice an attractive vixen turning men's heads on the street, instead of the girl he knew, one day when they were out. Suddenly, involuntarily, he was content to be walking next to her, grinning at the recollection that it hadn't taken him any efforts to get her into bed. *She's mine by default*, he liked to think. The attention she started receiving from other men made her valuable in his eyes. James was entertained by their jealousy and pleased he could do whatever he wanted with her body. It never occurred to him to stop and think about why she was willing to try out anything with him – from anal sex and ATM to facials and filming everything they did – they hadn't drawn the line at anything. *She must genuinely love me*, he told himself, feeling grateful that one woman, albeit not the one he had hoped for or wanted, had remained in his life. Her excessive shopping, promiscuity and superficiality, which made her a liability in his eyes, started to fade with time and the fact that the only thing they had in common was being equally self-centered and zealous started to appear as a possible foundation for a more stable relationship. Though the sex was becoming more primal, and their conversations continued to be limited to nine sentences tops, as they took little interest in one another outside of the bedroom, James started to entertain the thought of a possible future together. If nothing better came along…

She was fragile, serene, introverted and overly sensitive, which made her emotionally vulnerable. Her looks only accentuated her personality. She was petite and fair-skinned, with freckles and long dark hair. In real life he would've thought of her as way out of his league. But James knew his strengths and always made sure the game was played on his turf, putting to use his most powerful charm – his words. He spent so much time online – in chat rooms, on forums and on the messenger – that he had learned to read people quickly, going for particularly gullible girls, who spent most of their lives "in Wonderland" as he called the Internet. "Women online are the easiest prey," he said to his friends. "The only thing between you and a woman you're hitting on is her mind; but online you skip the protective barrier of the body language. In other words, you're in with fewer efforts than, let's say, if you met at a bar or something." James enjoyed the sense of detachment online communication gave him. It was real enough to make up for his lack of normal social activities, and yet distant enough to be perfectly safe. All in all, it was clean, effortless and presented a vast field of possibilities. Eastern European chicks were his favorite prey for a while. They were so starved for proper male attention that they bent over backwards at the slightest sign of any serious intentions, pretty much wetting their panties just at the prospect of a green card. This usually resulted in a pretty eventful video session. He had at least a dozen foreign names in his contact list: Russian, Ukrainian and Polish; although he generally avoided getting in touch with a girl more than once every couple of weeks. It was a thin line between them eagerly trying to charm a husband from abroad and becoming downright aggressive and pushy. James never took any of this seriously, but it provided him with consistent material for his midnight jacking-off sessions, and was an effective time-filler, especially when days seemed to drag on at a monotonous pace. It was just a bit more personal than porn to create a deceptive sense of self-worth, and a bit short on intimacy to satisfy his necessity for connecting with someone on a more intimate level. So he kept looking – in bars, at concerts, on forums, sites and streets. Until he met her in the only place he forgot to look.

James had always gone by the cardinal rule of "never swing your dick where you work". But as he realised one late September night at the jazz club, rules were meant to be broken. She was standing alone at the bar and looking at the stage, but visibly withdrawn from her surroundings. Playing provided him with the necessary time to take a better look at her and determine if he liked the whole package. Beautiful and melancholic, she was either unaware of the effect she had on men or didn't care – both equally valuable assets in his opinion. To James few things were more off-putting in a woman than an out-of-proportion sense of self-worth or desire to attract attention at any cost, which was partially the reason he was so reluctant to start a relationship with Sylvia. This pensive, introverted stranger possessed neither. The bar was full of couples and tipsy loud groups of men and women looking for a fun time, which made this girl standing alone look rather out of place. What struck him as even more bizarre was the fact that just in an hour and a half – the amount of time the first set lasted – she managed to turn down three advances with the same distant look in her eyes she had had all night. James observed as guys approached her one after the other, leaned in and quietly spoke to her, just to get a polite shake of the head accompanied by an apologetic smile. Every once in a while she looked over at Jason – his colleague on the saxophone – with a warm and loving expression and an almost unnoticeable smile graced her lips. It was clear they were involved in some way, although he found it odd that Jason, who was an unusually straight-forward and monogamous type, had never mentioned anything about this gorgeous thing. James waited until the set was over and watched him walk over to the woman and embrace her gently. To the untrained eye that would've meant defeat, but James instantly distinguished the caring touch of a brother from the forward one of a lover, so he lost no time in moving in with his agenda. He casually approached them, leaned on the bar and ordered a Jack and Coke. He stood there, slowly sipping his drink, which provided him with the perfect cover to take a better look at Jason's companion. On a second glance he saw a delicate woman dressed casually and unpretentiously, which contrasted with all of the overly-styled females around. She was wearing skinny jeans and a white tank top, dark green scarf, a black leather jacket and black flats. She either had no or very little make-up, and her luscious hair dropped freely below her shoulders.

From where he was standing James could pick up her subtle floral scent.

Looking uninterested and not cutting in on the conversation paid off as nearly six minutes after he had ordered his drink, Jason turned to him.

"I want to introduce you to someone."

"Yeah?"

"Karen. She's my little sister." He turned to the woman. "This is James, he's a colleague of mine."

"Hi," James nodded, discreetly checking her out. He was a pro at this.

"Nice to meet you."

"Karen just moved to New York and will stay with me. You'll be seeing her around the bar. Just wanted to let you know she's off limits." Jason was always as concise as could be, not wasting time with irrelevant diplomacy.

"Cutting right to the chase as usual."

"Yes, well, I know you horny dogs – always looking to add another notch on your belt."

"Whatever."

James turned and looked around the bar. He made a conscious effort to appear bored and indifferent. It was almost time for the second set and the sound guy came over, looking for Jason. The two disappeared towards the stage, but James wasn't at all into what was going on there. He slowly turned around and leaned back against the bar, glancing at Karen. *Play it cool, James,* he thought, swallowing with a dry mouth. *Don't let her see you're into her or it'll be over before it's even begun.*

"Your brother is a pain in the ass. But I guess you know that, right?"

"He can be. He's very protective of me. Always has been."

"I can see why. With a little sister like you I don't see how he can get any rest."

She laughed. "Are you implying I'm a drag?"

"No, I'm implying you're beautiful."

"What difference does it make? People nowadays will fuck just about anything."

He didn't expect her to be this blunt so early on in the conversation and it startled him a bit. *A sassy one. She thinks she's tough. Ok, darling, I can play the part,* he thought. "Even so, it makes a *big* difference. Trust me." He cleared his throat. "Gotta go work. Listen, if you ever want to talk about anything, or if you want someone to show you around, feel free to give me a call. Ask your brother for my number. I've moved quite a bit and I know it how hard starting from scratch can be."

"Thanks, but no thanks. I'm not that stupid, although I might come off as vulnerable and naïve."

"What do you mean?"

"I know how these things work. You take me out to help me get to know the city, but instead I get to know *you* and since you're the first man I went out with, you automatically gain an advantage over any others I might meet eventually. After the calls to discuss my day and your pretending to listen and care, it's just a matter of time before we hook up so you can tell your buddies over beers how you 'fucked Jason's sister' and that she 'likes to swallow'."

"I didn't know that you did," he blurted out, as it was the only thing he could think of.

"It was just to paint the picture. For the record, and your own peace of mind, all women in love swallow. And some who aren't, but that's a whole other story."

"So, basically you're saying there's a chance that you would fall in love with me."

"Of course. But you already know that, right? You know that as long as you do and say the right things, I am a sure catch. Problem is, how to determine what the right things are…"

"I guess. See you around. Later."

"Later."

James walked away, confused with her reaction and a bit irritated with himself for assuming her to be a textbook case. *What in hell went wrong? I did everything by the book – played it cool, fun. How did she get the impression I was a player? OK, so she's as smart as she is beautiful, and to make matters worse, intuitive as hell. Is it possible she was just bluffing? Whatever. I guess it was pretty obvious that the friendly tour around town offer was an ill-disguised move. Damage control. That's what I need now. Every goal is obtainable. As they say, one day at a time; one day at a time…"*

He spent the rest of the night staying as far away from Karen as possible. He needed to make her see their conversation hadn't made that big of an impression on him. At the club James was usually reserved, somewhat cold even. But that night he was talkative and charming after they finished playing. He walked around, socialised and even stayed several hours after Jason left with his sister. Usually it was James who was the first to storm out of the bar. Tonight, however, he needed to obtain as much inside information on her as possible from the other members of the band. Later, while helping Darren sort out the cables and put away the equipment, he decided to casually check what Darren might have learnt. Darren was unnecessarily thorough when it came to sharing inappropriate details about people he had just met.

"Nice set tonight, huh?"

"It was all right."

"Any plans for Tuesday? Poker night, my place. Couple of friends, beer. Nine-ish?" James suggested.

"I don't know, man. Those the friends who are professional poker players?"

"That's Sean. Lyle doesn't play professionally anymore."

"Being robbed blind is *not* my idea of a good time. Hey, speaking of a good time, what about Jason's sister, huh? Did you see the body on her?! I could rock that shit all night long."

"I don't know, Darren. She seemed pretty unattainable to me."

"It's the ones that play hard to get who give it all up front."

"You're probably right. What's her deal anyway?"

"Textbook bullshit: a big brother, watching over his little sister, who looks up to him. They're from Seattle, born and raised; their parents have a house in Bellevue I think. Brother heads to the East Coast in pursuit of independence and his aspirations as a professional musician and ends up gigging at one of the many bars to make ends meet, like the rest of us, you know how it is. I heard Karen's been accepted into Dartmouth. She couldn't wait to get the fuck out of Seattle. She recently broke up with her boyfriend."

"Did she love him?"

"First love, I think. Major drama."

"Do you know why they broke up?"

"Apparently he fucked anything that crossed his path. I feel for the guy. If I was with a woman this hot, I'd feel pressured to cheat. How can you hold your shit together if you feel inadequate next to your girl? It's fucking insane."

"Good point. Listen. Think about the game. I'll head out. Talk to you Wednesday."

"See ya."

Darren meant well, even with his slightly demeaning remarks about women, relationships and love. He was the perfect example of a good guy gone cynical after one too many heartbreaks. In reality that was pretty much everyone's problem. He never stuck his nose in other peoples' business and as far as work went he was as professional as could be. All of the musicians looked for his sound and mixing services and overall he was an enjoyable company for a guy's night of poker or sports. His friends could always count on him to pass along any information he had obtained, not knowing what to hold back even if it wasn't in his interest to share. Darren was that open-hearted and simple.

James enjoyed driving home at that time when night and day blended in a hazy dawn and no one could be seen hurrying down the streets just yet. He liked to think of it as the physical expression of the solitude in this town, which was otherwise always subtly present. He turned up the volume of the stereo in an attempt to suppress his obsessive thoughts. *Buckethead's The Elephant Man's Alarm Clock* made for the perfect background to his overwhelming emotions. "So many years wasted," he muttered. *And for what? A career? Fame and fortune? It wasn't worth it, missing out on everything important.. I can't do this alone anymore. I need someone. Someone like Karen. She's a keeper, you can tell; tough on the outside, soft and kind on the inside; easy to bend and shape as you like. Maintenance fees are low. Maybe it's time to settle down. She's someone I could really fall for.*

CHAPTER FOUR

Her week was going great both professionally and personally. One day before her dinner with George he called just to let her know he had made reservations at the Pomodoro Rosso – a tiny, almost-impossible-to-get-into Italian restaurant on the West Side, and to ask if she had any objections to the time or place. Sylvia didn't know what she was more impressed with; his manners, the fact that he had managed to make reservations on such short notice at one of the tightest places in town, or his flexibility. If she was looking forward to their date before, she was even more excited about it now. With every fiber of her body she knew this was the guy she had been looking for ever since she moved to New York. This was why she had attended all those irksome work-related dinners and brunches; why she had gone to university and graduated with honors all just so she could bag herself the ultimate husband-material. She was smart enough to know marriage and love had very little to do with one another. As a woman she had done her fair share of daydreaming about and crying for the wrong guy, watching her sand castles crumble down on top of her former self to make way for a new, improved version. In a way, Sylvia had evolved from a vulnerable, passive and naïve girl into a strong-willed, adaptable and calculating woman who had paid her dues and didn't settle any longer. Most women found it ugly to compare an intimate relationship to a business transaction, but Sylvia didn't suffer from unnecessary prudence and had learnt the hard way that love – regardless of its kind –

existed only on the basis of well-defined arrangements. Unsettled accounts between lovers inevitably led to the dying out of any positive feelings between them, which was the reason she kept clean records with all of her exes. She never gave anything she didn't receive in return and always retained just enough to keep the other party interested and motivated to keep coming back for more.

On Thursday she returned home earlier than usual, having left before her work day was over since her boss always disappeared around noon to start off his long weekends. He had assigned her next week's workload the previous evening, and as she was preparing for her date with George, somewhere in a cramped Brooklyn studio Stephen was working overtime on the reports Sylvia was supposed to hand in to Mr. Foster on Monday. She was walking around in her lingerie, drinking champagne and trying to pick an outfit for the night. As much as she was aware of the importance of this date it struck her as unusual that she wasn't even remotely excited about it. The mirror reflected her calm, collected movements, and Sylvia stopped and looked for any sign of emotion in her pale blue eyes. The woman in front of her was staring back with a cold and rather snobbish demeanor – courtesy of all the years she was cradled, looked-after, and had every need and whim satisfied at the drop of a hat. There was still a note of playfulness in her eyes, although it had gotten more perverse with time. She was aware of this and used it well to her advantage, as it served her much more than the painful shyness that accompanied her throughout high school. Men were much more responsive to the image of sex, raw, uncensored, unpretentious sex. A while after she stopped perceiving her partners as responsible for her happiness, Sylvia had gained the necessary distance to be able to amuse herself with men's endless antics, lies and charades. She found it entertaining, how everything they did revolved around or was because of a woman. Women, on the other hand, acted mostly driven by their own urges and occasionally in an attempt to impress one another. She saw some universal irony in this. Men's biggest mistake was their assumption that women couldn't differentiate between love and sex, considering this their biggest advantage over the fairer sex. What they didn't know, however, was that the attachment that formed in the course of a relationship based primarily on sex was a one-way street down which women rarely walked.

A woman's best friend and a man's worst enemy was time. It was time that gave women the ability to distance themselves, adapt and outgrow their infatuations while leading men into a loop of obsessive thoughts, uncertain feelings and growing attachment. It was exactly what had happened with her and James. She knew that for years he had considered her to be his back-up plan, anything other than girlfriend-material, but instead of hurting her, this knowledge brought her only relief and freedom. What would normally have been just another broken-hearted-girl story turned into the driving force behind Sylvia's realization of what she needed and wanted, and gave her the motivation to pursue it. James never found out that she stopped loving him before she had even started, but for years their unspoken understanding worked for him. Or so he thought, utterly oblivious to the fact he was becoming hooked on her permeating presence in his life through her constant availability. Where he saw comfort, she saw opportunity and took it. Somewhere in the middle their roles had shifted, unnoticed, and the inexperienced girl stopped looking for anything other than a good time with the unavailable guy, who started contemplating their relationship for more than it was or could ever be.

In the end, Sylvia had become a powerful amalgam of both male and female traits that made her so good at reading and predicting what both sexes wanted and expected. She possessed all of James' strong qualities, such as being fully self-sufficient and able to masturbate with her partner instead of giving herself away as most women did. She didn't suffer from James' inferiority complex because of their background, and she wasn't nearly as sensitive as he was. Her female intuition balanced out the coldness she had picked up and helped her simulate an intensely real sense of vulnerability and desire to please her partner, which men found irresistible. Her biggest asset, however, was her ability to let go of the past, which was the main reason she didn't hold any grudges against the man who had taught her all of this. The way she saw it, James had set her free by showing her the way to make the most out of a world where people were nothing more than their physical appearance, and relationships were built and based solely on fiction.

Sylvia intentionally led him on, as she did with all the others. She knew perfectly well that her biggest ally was the male ego – the most fragile element in nature. She made sure everyone felt as good, safe, desired and needed in her company as they could. This covered all the basic requirements for men to start letting their guard down and viewing her as something more than just "a good time". She didn't share or inquire, she never demanded explanations, and she always laughed at their jokes, even when she was hearing them for the hundredth time. She projected an image of an easy-going air-headed girl, who was into living her life and didn't delve into things that didn't concern her, which was only partially true. Her B.A. from Stanford University, albeit obtained with the help of daddy's connections, wasn't all for show; she was intelligent, but smart enough to know guys didn't need to know it. In her relationships with men like James she was submissive, generous in bed and reserved in conversations – the ideal combination for sustaining the established routine of nothing too serious, but stable enough to provide frequent means for getting off and getting stuff done. With George, however, she was planning on being something entirely different. Luckily, she had all the necessary background and experience to pull it off.

Walking around barely dressed, she was thanking James in her mind for teaching her to let go of all inhibitions and the necessity to be tied down, which most women inherently possessed. His detachment and unwillingness to commit had led her through a long and fulfilling journey of becoming a self-sufficient, zealous woman, perfectly aware of her power over men. His insatiable desire for her, which he couldn't hide or deny as much as he wanted to, had made her extremely confident. Because in spite of all the women he had dated or continued dating – as skinny, pretty, slender and sexy as they were, sooner or later he always ended up at her door in the middle of the night, swearing she was "the best sex he's ever had". Her relationship with him had taught her that being the most attractive rarely meant being the most beautiful.

At eight o'clock sharp there was a ring. Dressed to impress, Sylvia hurried towards the door. As she reached for her purse she took one last look in the mirror and nodded contentedly before stepping out. Her curls were immaculate and her make-up barely noticeable, which was her specialty. If clothes made a statement, she was coming across as just as the right amount of pretentious and high-maintenance.

The moment she stepped outside the building she noticed the luxurious car parked out front and the man standing next to the back door. She immediately recognized the brand new Bentley thanks to her subscription to several car catalogues. George smiled warmly at her and opened the door invitingly.

"Good evening."

"Good evening," Sylvia smiled charmingly. "It's good to see you, Mr. Huntington."

"George, please," he corrected her softy, glancing at her with delight. Sylvia was satisfied with the positive response she was getting. Everything about her this night was meant to impress – from her simple but flattering dress to her inviting body language.

He helped her in, closed the door and walked around to get in next to her, nodding, on his way, to the driver, who immediately started the car. Sylvia liked powerful cars. She liked their leather seats, the extra space and the social statement they made. The way she saw it, desperate women learned to read Tarot cards; a woman who wanted to be in control of her life and carve her own destiny, had to learn to read real estate and cars. *I could certainly get used to be driven around in this,* she thought, sliding her hand against the leather seat.

The drive was quick and enjoyable, even though they were silent for most of the time. When they arrived the restaurant was full, although its quiet and intimate ambiance remained undisrupted, and as soon as they walked through the door they were escorted to their table by an unusually attentive hostess. Before they sat down, George took her coat and pulled her chair, barely touching her shoulders. Sylvia felt strangely excited.

Not nearly a minute into their conversation, a waiter approached the table with a bottle of Barolo. After receiving a nod from Mr. Huntington he opened it, pouring a small amount in his glass. Mr. Huntington sipped carefully, tasting the wine, and only then nodded in approval.

"In an optimistic gesture, I picked the wine. I can assure you, you're in good hands. My grandfather owned a vineyard in California and I spent several summers learning all there was to it. Personally, I prefer Italian wines. They are considerably stronger, with a fuller palette."

Sylvia smiled in response as they clicked their glasses. It wasn't the taste, but the label of the wine that she was interested in.

"Do you think you trust me enough now to allow me to order dinner?" he asked.

"Given the excellent quality of the wine, I have no reservations whatsoever," she assured him. He smiled back and glanced at the menu. "You must've spent most of your summers in California when you were growing up then?" she shot out, unable to think of any other way to keep the conversation going.

"Not most of them. My family owns an estate in Napa Valley, which a quick getaway throughout my teenage years, I'll admit. Naturally, when father was elected governor, focus shifted from the wine business to something more tangible." While talking George had called over the waiter with a discreet gesture and dictated their order concisely and quickly.

"Naturally. Although as frugal as politics can be, having a back-up business plan is smart thinking."

"I don't think my family ever looked at it as more than a one-time investment done out of curiosity and desire to experiment rather than a pension fund guarantee," he observed amused.

"Oh, I am sorry! I didn't mean to imply that you would give up the solid name you've built up for your family just to venture into something as risky as the wine business. Obviously you know better than that," she stuttered.

"I know. You don't have to apologise. What about you, Sylvia? I can call you that, can't I? Or maybe you prefer Vassilena?"

"Sylvia. Vassilena is my Gam Gam. She's always had a sweet spot for me; I was her favourite when I was born and my father insisted I carried her name too."

"If you were as beautiful then as you are now I can see why."

"Thank you. Truth is she's very much into tradition and, you know, naming a child after a grandparent as a classic sign of respect."

"Tradition is good. It's what's left when everything else fades away."

"That's well put."

"Excuse my asking, but is your family originally from here? Your grandmother's name is somewhat exotic."

"I get that a lot, but I'm afraid I'll have to disappoint you. I'm just your typical Midwest girl, coming from a long line of cattle breeders and ranchers- turned-servicemen. The most exotic thing about anyone in my family is their name," she laughingly admitted. "Someone might say we're compensating for something."

"That's understandable, I suppose. I, myself, come from a rather boring line of several generations of men who've made a living from politics. My family would be nothing less than shocked should I even dare to dream about a different line of career."

"Doesn't that bother you?"

"Which part?"

"Living up to someone else's expectation all the time?"

"No, Sylvia. Other people's expectations, hopes and dreams of us are what makes us better people; what keeps us in line. You take that away from a man and he will, without a doubt, fall victim to his most primal and destructive urges."

They had unknowingly moved closer to each other, leaning over the table with the subtle intimacy that only occurred when two people connected on a personal level. Sylvia was gazing into his eyes and George was discreetly admiring the gentle curve of her collar bone, covered by an unruly curl. Both of them had their hands on the table, only inches away from touching. Just then their food arrived. Quickly and discreetly the waiter placed the beautifully-arranged appetizers in front of them, refilled their glasses and walked away. Sylvia looked at what she had just been served.

"*Mozzarella Pomodoro Basilico* – mozzarella with basil – and *Carciofi Alla Romana* – steamed artichoke in white wine lemon sauce. They'll bring the main course later," George explained as he invited her with a gesture.

"What are we having?"

"*Ravioli Alla Aragosta* –ravioli with lobster meat in cream sauce."

"Everything sounds exquisite. You seem to know your food."

"I'm a regular here. You'll see. Once you taste it you'll want to come back."

"I don't know if I'll be able to. This place is harder to get into than The White House."

"If you like it I think we can arrange something."

"Are you hinting at the possibility of a second date?"

"Not hinting. I'd very much like to see you again, Sylvia. May I?"

"Yes, George. I'd like that."

They continued eating, smiling at each other and occasionally interrupting the silence with the kind of small talk people used when it didn't need to be broken, but rather emphasised because it didn't feel awkward. The two *Cafe Pomodoros* with complimentary biscotti and *Coppa Stracciatellas* were a perfect finish to a special evening several hours later.

As soon as they finished the waiter brought over the bill. Pretending to stir her coffee, Sylvia managed to catch a glimpse of the 50% tip, which really impressed her. George signed the receipt, stood up and pulled out her chair. She thought he would try to hold her hand or touch her accidentally as most men did, but the only physical contact he attempted was holding her coat for her to put on. George was nothing less than the perfect gentleman and as they walked outside, she was coming to realise he was one of those old-fashioned guys, who believed in romance and didn't mind waiting for some things. He hailed a cab for her and just before she got in he reached for her hand and lightly held it between his palms. Sylvia took the opportunity, leaned in and gave him a peck on the left check. She then quickly stepped back, wished him good night, and disappeared inside the car.

The last thing she saw before the cab turned right on W 69th Street was George's tall figure standing in front of his car, looking in her direction. She leaned back, sinking in the seat and shrugged. *The Bentley was much more comfortable,* she thought.

CHAPTER FIVE

James was feeling more restless than usual. In moments like this, when he needed to chase away his loneliness and paranoia and the booze wasn't strong enough, he turned to his good friend Lyle Heimowitz. Lyle was his closest, only friend even, and, despite their difference in backgrounds, the two had a remarkably strong friendship. Born and raised in Rochester, New York, Lyle was a 3-time World Series of Poker winner and by far one of the most intelligent, collected and sharp people James knew. They had met at a Texas Holdem live tournament years ago where Lyle was sponsored to attend and they instantly hit it off – both bringing into the friendship what the other person lacked. Lyle enjoyed James's ability to let go of all reservations and inhibitions and James tried to learn the secret behind Lyle's composure and quick wit. For a while Lyle tried teaching him to play poker professionally, but after a couple of years it became obvious that James' utter incapability to control himself as well as his love for taking unjustifiable risks were cold stone signs that gambling wasn't his cup of tea. Lyle was the only person whose criticism and advice James accepted and listened to without feeling threatened or offended. "You're a dreamer, James," his friend often pointed out with sadness in his voice. "And a hopelessly disappointed one, I might add. You haven't given up on fixing the world just yet, but what you don't realise is the world is fine. There's nothing wrong with it. It's exactly as it's always been and it doesn't need fixing. You have to find more practical uses for your time. It's not your job to fix anything; it's your job to live well. That's your birth right. Everyone knows it, but far too few people actually take to implementing it."

Lyle lived in a 2-bedroom apartment he had bought for himself years ago in the neighborhood James rented in. With the money he made he could easily afford a place in Tribeca or Soho, but he liked to keep a low profile. He didn't feel the need to show off, and didn't mind the fact that the neighborhood was run-down and not the safest at night. Unlike James, Lyle had chosen this location for the very reasons that made it so unpopular and made the best of them by purchasing several apartments on the cheap, renovating and renting them out. For him Hell's Kitchen combined the best of two worlds – all the venues, restaurants and bars for his personal enjoyment as he was quite a social guy, as well as regular access to and easy management of his real estate network. Lyle often came down to the bar to hear James play and, most importantly, to study the dynamics of owning and running this type of venue as it was an investment idea he had been considering for a while.

Fifteen minutes after calling him, James was buzzing Lyle into the building. "I met someone," was the first thing he blurted out as his friend was closing the door behind him.

"You meet someone all the time, James. What else is new?"

"I'm serious."

"K, and what's so special about…?"

"Karen."

"Karen, right."

"She's not like other women."

Lyle laughed sincerely at the bold statement. "No, I'm sure she's not. All women are special and unique. Before they catch a glimpse of your bank statement at least."

"I'm telling you. There's something about her I can't put my finger on, but she's different. Tried hitting on her, went by the book and she didn't go for it."

"Brother or sister?"

"Brother. Older."

"There's your answer. Women with brothers are often ahead in the game because they've been given inside information, which comes quite handy when talking to random guys at bars."

"For picking up guys, maybe; but she wasn't *trying* to be attractive or anything. She was trying to blow me off from the beginning."

"No wonder. Poor girl smelled the desperate on you," Lyle burst out laughing and so did James.

"What would you make of a woman who stands alone at a bar, turns down every man who comes near her and dismisses all compliments she receives?"

"*That* I gotta see. Sister probably set the bar too high and no one can make the cut."

"Or?"

"Or…" Lyle opened the fridge, picked up a beer and paused for a moment. "Let me guess. Painful break-up, resulting in tons of emotional baggage and a subsequent penis-embargo."

"Yep."

"Good luck to you." He raised his can. He then went over to the couch, sat down and started flipping through the guitar catalogues scattered around on the floor. "This one looks good. What do you think?" he asked, pointing at a black Parker.

"It looks good, because it *is* good. You know I'm a Parker fan."

"It looks like the one you taught me on years ago. What happened to that thing?"

"In the case behind you."

"How many guitars do you have?"

"Thirteen since last week. I bought that red Ibanez on *eBay*."

"How many guitars does a guy need? I've only seen you play two of them."

"It's not about necessity. You know my family struggled financially when I was growing up. There was never enough money for anything. Let alone a guitar. Now I can afford as many as I want."

"I'm telling you, James, you should think about something more tangible as an investment. Why not buy your place?"

"This craphole?! Not my idea of an investment!"

"You could fix it up; rent it out for double the price you're paying."

"You know me. Sounds like a lot of work and I just can't be bothered."

"You're thirty-two, it's about time you started thinking about your future instead of hoarding guitars and living by the day."

"What future, Lyle? I'm a 30-something college drop-out, I have no social skills, no savings and the only thing I know is how to play the guitar."

"Exactly, what have I been saying. You need multiple streams of income. Right now you're living from paycheck to paycheck. That's not smart at all."

"Not everyone can be a talented poker player like you and save up the money for a successful venture on the side."

"Talent has nothing to do with it, James. It's self-control and determination. Everything else is pure bullshit."

"Whatever you say. Anyhow, I gotta find a way to ask Karen out without giving her the option to turn me down."

"You're putting way too much time and thought into this. That alone should be a red flag. Last time you got so worked-up over a woman nothing good came out of it, remember?"

"True. We'll see how it goes this time."

"Ever the optimistic one. Gotta run. It's nice to sit back and chill, but I'm taking Rose to the new musical, *American Idiot*. She's been raving about it for weeks. With her thesis due next month and everything else we've got going on we could barely find the time."

"Yeah, Rose. How are things with her?"

"Never better."

"Glad to hear it. No limit Texas Holdem, Tuesday, nine o'clock."

"I'll be there. Wouldn't it be easier if you just gave me your money?" Lyle grinned, throwing his empty can in the trash.

"Fuck off. Don't you have a musical to go to?"

"Right. Hope things work out with...."

"Karen. Between you and me, I really hope they do."

"Are you telling me you're in love?"

James smirked. "To be in love at my age would mean not to have learnt anything at all."

"Good to see you still have some sense left in your sorry ass. See ya."

As Lyle let himself out James lay back on the couch and reached for his guitar. He didn't have to leave for the club for another hour and he caught himself wishing Karen wouldn't be there tonight. *That's odd. If I liked her so much wouldn't I want to see her again right away?* He thought, fingers gently pulling the strings. *I just need some time to shape up before I can face her again. I need something to take the pressure off. Or someone...* Still holding the guitar, he picked up his phone and speed-dialed three.

"It's me."

"Hey, you."

"I get off work at two. It's about an hour to your place. I want you naked when you open the door."

"You've got it."

Suddenly he felt reassured and confident. He closed his eyes and started playing. Anything seemed obtainable now. Even Karen.

Especially Karen...

It was just as any other night at the bar – noisy and crowded – but it didn't bother him this time. He played as absent-mindedly as he could and didn't even notice all the things that usually bugged him enough to hinder his performance. A couple of drinks, three sets and it was time to head out.

Driving down Madison Ave., James rolled down the window and took a deep breath. Just the thought of seeing her tonight made him hard. *How is it that the people you care for the least have the most effect on you?* He wondered. *Not to mention are the best sex you've ever had,* he thought, amused. The city seemed deep asleep. It was nearing four in the morning, but it was still dark. His fingers were tapping on the wheel to the tune of some radio station he had pumped up. With Sylvia he never had to worry about anything, which was what he liked the most about their 'so-called relationship. *It's so liberating being around someone you're at ease with. You can go with the flow, never worry about what you say because she doesn't care what you meant or didn't mean. A guy can't swing a dick without picking up another demanding, overanalyzing, insecure psycho bitch these days.* It came as a surprise to him, but for a brief moment he felt lucky for having Sylvia in his life. He remembered there was always booze at her place, lots and lots of it. That was just an added bonus.

Twenty-five minutes later he was rushing up the stairs. When he reached the fifth floor, the door on the left opened invitingly, revealing her naked curvy figure with nothing but a silky scarf around her neck. *Perfect timing! As always. How the fuck does she do it*!? he wondered as he headed towards her. They had done this more than enough for either of them to hesitate – it was like a dance practiced many times before, where the partners had grown immensely familiar with each other. He reached for her tanned skin and eagerly locked lips with her, pulling her hair and pressing her against the wall. Sylvia was stepping back, leading him into the bedroom and undressing him eagerly on the way. Clothes were falling or being thrown to the floor and glasses knocked over, but they were oblivious to their surroundings. As quick as the sex was, it wasn't hard to notice the intimacy behind every playful slap; behind every dirty word spoken, yelled or moaned. Those were all things which, if done with the wrong person, exposed the pornographic nature of the relationship, but if done with the right one, accentuated an intimacy only obtainable when two souls connected on a much deeper level. They were like two lovers on a honeymoon, when a desire to explore and knowledge of the flesh met up to blend in the ultimate cocktail of lust and love. Both had sufficient tricks up their sleeve to make the other cum in less than five minutes; both knew where and how to touch; and both enjoyed taking their time to explore new means of satisfaction every now and then.

Ten minutes later, struggling to catch their breath, they were lying, satisfied, in the king-sized bed. Sylvia stood up and disappeared towards the living room. There was something incredibly sensual about her naked curves and the way she walked around without displaying the slightest sign of shyness. *Few things are as off-putting in a woman as insecurity and low self-esteem. If only more women knew,* James pondered, watching her walk away. A second later she returned with a gin and tonic in a tall glass that she graciously put next to him on the nightstand. *She knows what I like outside the bedroom too. Is there anything about her that's not great?* He thought, as he reached for his drink. He was in the mood for cuddling, but she turned away and disappeared towards the bathroom. A minute later he heard the shower running. Perhaps it was a habit slowly built up over years of him jumping out of bed the moment he came, trying to find excuses for leaving, or throwing her out. Whatever it was, she had picked it up as well. The problem was that this time it was James who suddenly found himself wanting more.

"Screw it. I must be mellowing out with age," he said out loud, and downed the rest of the glass before he followed her into the shower for a second round.

Twenty minutes later, he was sober enough to leave and tired enough not to want to. But James knew Sylvia well enough to know that asking her if he could spend the night would be an irreversible mistake. Everything between them existed on a pre-set system of regulations, carefully detailing their roles in the relationship, and he knew she wasn't the type of woman who would tolerate a mid-game change of rules. Just like any other woman, Sylvia's interest in him was only proportional to her uncertainty about his feelings for her. James couldn't bring himself to risk revealing that somewhere in the process of having someone easy and convenient that he had genuinely started to care about her. For now he would have to perpetuate the image of the emotionally-detached, unavailable guy, who came and went as he pleased and she would continue to be vulnerable, passive and eager to please.

Or they would, at least, keep pretending for the sake of the *status quo*.

The last thing he saw before the door closed behind him was her soft and candid smile, which left him thinking there was at least one person in the world that genuinely cared. She was the closest to a family he had had for years, even if he continued fooling himself that he only saw her as a reliable *fuck buddy* and nothing more. One thing he couldn't deny, though, and it was that he had gotten used to having her in his life. Even if only as a back-up.

CHAPTER SIX

Men are adorably weak.

Sylvia grinned at the thought of James' expression as she shut the door behind him. Suddenly she realized she was starving and went into the kitchen to grab a bite. She opened the fridge and carefully studied the scarce remains of take-outs, but nothing seemed appetizing. She finally decided to fix herself a smoothie and go out for brunch to Le Monde, which was just a couple of blocks away. Eating alone was something she avoided religiously. *Who is available at 7AM on a Saturday?* She picked up her phone and speed-dialed two, preparing her most charming voice.

"Stephen, hey! I think I'm ready to take you up on that offer. Do you want to join me for brunch? Le Monde. Yes. How soon can you get here? Working?!" the disappointment and chill in her voice were notable. "Of course I understand if you *can't*. I am looking at several very busy weeks myself. I'll be virtually grounded at the office…maybe another time. Oh, you *can*! Great. Please hurry, though, I'm starving. K, see you in a bit."

She hung up, content. He had a good 45-minute drive to her place, which gave her plenty of time to lie down for a bit since she hadn't slept at all last night. Returning to the bedroom, she lay on the side where James had been just half an hour ago, burying her nose in the pillow. She found a man's natural scent intoxicating.

Sylvia liked everything about being a woman, enjoying what came with it – the attention, protection, games, devotion and constant power-struggle with the opposite sex. Men always let her have her way because she knew how to make them feel on top even when they were getting royally screwed. *The trick is to let him think he's winning while you're robbing him blind,* she giggled. The male ego was her biggest ally and she knew how to milk it. Two things she never allowed herself with a man: to criticize and to demand. And did it pay off! *Funny how men mistake a complete lack of interest for a casual fling. Of course I would give any guy I sleep with all the space he cold possible want – I never wanted to be part of his life anyway. Besides, it's not like we share anything in common besides his dick.* Unlike most women, who felt offended by the perpetuated stereotype that portrayed the fairer sex as unable to distinguish between love and sex, Sylvia immensely enjoyed and used it to her benefit. She was greatly amused by the fact that most men continued to mistake lust for infatuation in women. *Even James, poor deluded James. He thinks I love him because I agree to everything he wants in bed; because I ask nothing about his work, his goals, his life. He perceives my complete lack of interest as a sign I don't want to pressure or bother him. How cute is that! It's much better this way. In the female world the male black is white; try explaining to a guy that the fewer boundaries you agree to in bed and the more in life, the more certain it is you don't, never did and never will love him. It's sad how many men try to build a relationship on top of something they mistake for solid ground.*

She closed her eyes and covered her head with the duvet. *And where there isn't the need to make a strictly sexual relationship into something it's not, there's the other type of "filler guys" like Stephen. Honestly, I can write a bestselling book, comprised of just two sentences. How to get and keep men interested in you (A Guide for the Modern Woman): Put them in the "friend" or "fuck" zone. Leave them there. I'll make millions,* she concluded happily and buried herself deeper between the nine Eiderdown pillows. The silky touch of the sheets felt soothing and cool against her naked skin and she blissfully started dozing off.

Nearly forty-five minutes later she woke up at the sound of the doorbell. "It fucking better be Stephen," she muttered as she draped the sheet around herself and went to buzz him in, leaving the door slightly open. When he walked in she was in the bedroom, still in her lingerie, throwing out clothes one after another into a pile on the bed. Stephen didn't seem surprised. He was used to Sylvia walking around barely dressed in front of him. Even though they slept together less and less frequently than before, she hadn't changed her behavior, and some level of intimacy still existed. Aside from routinely helping her with work-related stuff he was always the one she came to for a relaxing massage or a quick shopping trip to Downtown Manhattan. Stephen was also the guy Sylvia brought back to Fargo for every family gathering, birthday celebration, Thanksgiving, and Christmas, in order to avoid the ever so painful, *"When* will you get a boyfriend?" He gladly posed as hers, clinging to the slight hope that if he was good enough for her family, who adored him, eventually he would be good enough for her. Sylvia was extremely careful in encouraging him to believe that. The truth was that with George coming into the picture her almost nonexistent interest in Stephen had plummeted to the point of absolute zero, and if there was a way to keep him in her life only for the benefit of the favors he performed, without so much as an effort on her part, she would've instantly taken it. But she didn't kid herself, fully aware that her entire life was built on the always effective model of "tit for that". *If only he wasn't as dull in bed as he is in life,* she sighed. *He's a good guy. Poor schmuck. He doesn't stand a chance. He'll die before he asks a woman to "bend over and take it", and right there was the end of anything he might have had going on with her. I don't know anyone who wants to be treated the same in bed as they are in front of their grandma,"* she winced.

"You can go make yourself coffee if you want to," she told him, aware he always waited for permission to do anything around her. It had gotten to a point where it was actually bugging her.

"Thanks. I need a strong one. It was a long drive and I worked till late last night."

"Busy couple of months?"

"Yes, I have several projects due at the same time."

"Good for you. Five more minutes, ok? I am just gonna do my hair and we'll go."

"Sure." Stephen sat on the couch the moment he heard that, knowing there was a good 20-minute wait before they left. He was used to it and saw no point in complaining, even though he was starving. There was a pile of Cosmopolitans on the end table, so he reached for the top one and started reading Ten Tips to Help You Please Your Guy. "How's your mother, by the way?" he said, looking up.

"Fine. Everyone's fine. Gamy's asking about you," she shouted from the bathroom.

"Tell her I look forward to seeing them this Thanksgiving," he said.

"Yeah, well, we'll see. We might not be going this year."

"Why not?" He suddenly lost interest in the article and threw the magazine back on the pile.

"I've got a lot going on at work," she tried weaseling out. "Look, it's too early to know for sure. We'll talk about it another time, ok? I am really hungry, just let me get ready." Sylvia opened the door and smiled apologetically, hairdryer in one arm and brush in the other.

"Yes, of course. But just for my own peace of mind – there isn't a problem, is there?"

"No, everything's great!" She went back into the bathroom, shutting the door behind her.

He sat there, listening to the sound of the hairdryer, pondering. Having gotten so used to spending all holidays with Sylvia and her family, it came to him as a shock to realize he had been neglecting his own. Now, faced with the possibility of their long-term arrangement falling through, he felt frightened and lonely. *After all this time she still doesn't know how I feel about her. What am I supposed to do? Double my efforts. That's the only thing left. Maybe then she'll finally realize how much she means to me and that we belong together. Her family sees I'm the perfect guy for her. Why can't she?"*

When Sylvia came out of the bathroom, the disheveled, puffy-eyed mess that had answered the door had disappeared. Her unruly curls were sleek and shiny, and she was dolled up from head to toe. Stephen was the only guy she ever allowed to see her without make-up because she knew it wouldn't make a difference. She loved the sight of her own reflection in his pale grey eyes; few things made her feel as beautiful as his honest admiration. Even with her interest level in him well below zero it was still a reliable source of self-validation that was worth keeping.

Between the getting ready and the 2-block walk to the bistro, they got to Le Monde just as the waiters were taking the last of the brunch orders and putting out the sign with the lunch offers. They were both relieved at the sight of the few available tables left. Sylvia, who was never one to hold back on anything she craved, felt at ease with Stephen since she didn't have to act all ladylike in front of him and could splurge on whatever she wanted. Knowing her tastes all too well, he called over the waiter and ordered without so much as looking at the menu.

"Two burgers, one Le Monde and one Turkey Provençal, both with extra French fries on the side, one orange juice and one sparkling water, please."

The waiter walked away, but quickly returned with the drinks. Sylvia leaned back on the chair, looking at the bubbles in her glass. She was glowing in the bright light of the late spring sun. *She's so radiant.* Stephen gazed at her, enchanted.

"I'm glad you finally found time for a quick bite out with me."

"Come on, Stephen," she said, strategically resting her hand lightly on his on the table "You're the closest thing to a family I have this far from home. What would I do without you here, all alone…"

"I'm sure my place will be immediately filled by another hopeless romantic who has fallen victim to your charm," he joked.

"Naturally, but it wouldn't be you. After all, we grew up together. We went to the same high school. We've been friends since…" she paused with hesitation. "Forever. And," she leaned in, gazing into his eyes, "I was your first. This is something truly special."

"*It's now or never,*" he thought, encouraged by her sudden public display of intimacy. "Sylvie. It's not that I don't care you were my first, but I... I simply want you to be my last." Her hand moved away from his as quickly as it had appeared there.

"Stephen, please. Not again. We've been over this."

"I don't want you to feel pressured. I am just telling you what I want."

"I've said it to you hundreds of times. You can't be with one person your entire life. You have to go out there, play the field for a while. It's something you owe to yourself."

"People do that when they aren't sure what they want, but I *am*."

"Of course you think that. You've only been with one woman!"

"That's more than enough for me."

"Listen, I am telling you as a friend. You need to sleep around for a while before you're able to settle down. You owe this to the both of us if you're even remotely serious about ending up with me for the rest of your life."

"But that's ridiculous!"

"Listen to me! There is no conceivable way to know what you want before having tried several things off the menu. Otherwise, you're setting up yourself to fail."

"Sounds to me like a lot of fancy talk just so you can get me off your back, hoping I will get infatuated with another woman in the process of false soul-searching."

"You never know," She winked, and chuckled.

The waiter arrived with their burgers and they started eating in silence. She went straight for the fries and as soon as she downed hers, she moved on to the ones on his place. He moved the plate to the middle of the table, so she could reach them more easily, and continued eating pensively. Sylvia smiled. She was used to always getting what she wanted.

"I know just where you need to start. Go to a bar, any bar. They're all full of fun, promiscuous women on the prowl for cute guys like you."

"So funny I forgot to laugh," he frowned.

"Come on, you're adorable! And not being aware of it is what makes you even cuter." She reached over and wiped his bottom lip with a napkin. For a brief moment their eyes met and he could swear there was something more in hers than the cold blueness of the sky, but she looked away too quickly for him to be certain.

"Well, if you think that's what I need to do, by all means, I will do my best. And since you're so informed about my needs, how about you take me out and coach me in some cool hip club downtown tonight?" He tried tricking her.

"No self-respecting adult uses the word 'hip', Stephen. Seriously!" She looked away "I can't tonight. I have plans."

"What plans?"

"A date."

"Really? Do tell."

"Nothing much. Just this guy I've been seeing for a while now. A couple of months, so nothing serious."

"All right. How about tomorrow then?"

"I am seeing Josh."

"Still on that guy, huh?"

"On that guy is very accurately put," she giggled.

"I thought it wasn't long-term the…whatever it is you've got going on."

"We have nothing going on. It's just friendly sex. Something you should get much more of." she pointed out.

"I thought sleeping around was a male trait."

"Wake up, Stephen! Hasn't been for the past twenty plus years. And thank God, I might add. A girl's got needs too, you know. Good thing we were finally granted the freedom to stop apologizing for ours."

"You know I didn't mean it like that. Of course you have needs and shouldn't apologize for them. All I meant was that maybe, just maybe, the focus has been shifted way too much from settling down and pursuing those needs with one person to passing through life no strings attached."

"To each his own, I always say. Anyhow, thanks for lunch, but I gotta run, love. I didn't get any sleep last night and I have to look my most fabulous tonight."

"Why? Did you, by any chance, work on that report you're supposed to give on Monday?" he teased.

"Why would I? You've already finished it for me, haven't you?" she asked, and he nodded. "You're a real sweetheart. James spent the night."

"What?! Sylvie, no! He's a jerk. You know he's always treated you like shit. Why do you keep going back to him after everything he's done to you?!"

"First of all, I am not going *back* to anyone. I am a free girl. Second, it wasn't all bad. He made it perfectly clear he was unavailable from the start. I was the one that imagined a relationship into existence at some point, but that's long gone. Now we're on the same page. Just sex, no strings attached."

"I strongly disapprove of this. So would your father, by the way. You know he hates that guy."

"Yes, and as far as daddy is concerned, I haven't spoken to James since high school. Let's keep it that way, O.K.?"

"I don't know, Sylvie."

"Oh, come on, Stephen! You're not gonna go all big-brotherly and rat me out to daddy, are you? Is that what friends do?"

"No, friends sit back and watch their friends make the same stupid mistake over and over again," he said with sadness in his voice.

"Pleeease, pretty please with cherries on top!" She fluttered her eyelashes, curling a lock of hair with her fingers, which she always did when she wanted to get her way.

"You know you have nothing to worry about. I would never put you in such a position. I am just worried about you. Sometimes you're acting like a teenager," he said, displeased, as he paid the bill.

"I'm a big girl now, Stephen. I know how to take care of myself."

They walked the two blocks back in silence. In front of the building she watched as he got into his car and rolled down the window. She gazed into his eyes for a brief moment, then leaned in and pressed her lips against his. It lasted for a second, but it was sweet and gentle. Then she turned around and walked inside the building without looking back.

She spent the rest of the afternoon trying on one outfit after another for her dinner with George later that night. When she had asked him where they were going, he told her it was a surprise.

"How can I dress appropriately if I don't know where we're going?" Sylvia objected.

"A gorgeous woman like you can walk into a room, wearing something off the rack and still pull it off. But let's just say I'd put on something fancier for where we're going tonight," was all she could get out of him.

She went through a dozen outfits before deciding on a vintage high-wasted skirt and a scalloped lace Prada blouse, topping it off with her favorite nude Jimmy Choo pumps. Satisfied, she stood in front of the mirror, marveling the effect of simple yet feminine class. She liked George's impeccable style, which was evident in everything from his mannerisms to his tailor-made suits and she had unconsciously been mimicking it ever since they started going out. It had just been several dates, but he always pleasantly surprised her by taking her to quiet, intimate, always trendy and high-profile places. They were always seated upon walking in – without waiting or reservations – a polite, reserved nod from George to the hostess and the VIP treatment was guaranteed. Just as any other woman in pursuit of a potential provider, Sylvia had doubled her weekly visits to the hair and spa salon, skyrocketing her maintenance expenses. She wasn't too worried about it, however, as it was a smart investment. She knew she needed to be at her most fabulous every time they were together. After a quick trip to the spa studio followed by a mani-pedi, it was already nearing nine when the doorbell rang.

"Who is it?" she asked through the intercom system.

"George. If you're ready you can come down. I know I'm twenty minutes early, but I finished work sooner."

"Just five more minutes. Do you want to come up instead of waiting downstairs?"

"All right. Be up in a minute."

He looks even better than before. was the first thing that went through her mind as he walked through the door. Putting on her earrings, Sylvia tilted her head to the right and smiled at him.

"I am so happy to see you, George."

"As am I. You look..." He paused for a moment, checking her out from head to toe with moderate excitement. "Simply beautiful."

"Thank you. I am afraid I'm a bit overdressed, but you wouldn't tell me where we're going."

"Guilty as charged. But for your own peace of mind, you're not overdressed. What is it with women and knowing just what to put on for every occasion, even when you don't have all the details?"

"I believe it's the infamous female intuition you're referring to."

"Ahhh, right. I had forgotten about *that.*" He smiled with a boyish grin. "By the way, I like your apartment very much. Small but spacious; very stylish and original. Very effective. Very you."

"Thank you. My father bought it for me as a graduation present. I hired a decorator to help with the basics, but generally I just went with what I liked and what felt right."

"You have excellent taste."

"You should know. Why else did I agree to go out with you?" she said as innocently as possible, smiling at him.

George laughed candidly. "And thank you for the compliment. Shall we?"

He gently put the coat on her shoulders and walked her out the door. The car was waiting for them at the entrance of the building. This time of night W 111th Street was unusually quiet. There were only a few people walking their dogs. It was warm and the only thing reminiscent of the passing spring was the brisk wind. Sylvia wrapped the coat around herself as she slid in the car next to George, waiting to hear the instructions for the driver as she was curious about where they were going. But George just nodded at the man, who barely touched his hat in response and drove slowly down Broadway. They sat next to each other, her hand in his, both looking out separate windows without the silence feeling awkward. Sylvia looked at the people passing by who were struggling with the sudden gushes of wind and seeking shelter in their jackets, and snuggled into George. He gently rested his chin on her hair and breathed in her sweet fruity scent, closing his eyes.

A short while later, but what seemed much longer to them, the car pulled out and stopped in front of The Four Seasons Restaurant. Sylvia couldn't hide her delight. She looked up at George, impressed, and smiled contentedly. They walked in and were immediately sat at a small cozy table for two in the infamous Pool Room. The restaurant was bursting at the seams, but they didn't notice anything except each other. A waiter was quick to come over, handing them menus. With a quick and polite "May I?" George pulled hers from Sylvia's hands and ordered for both of them.

"A toast," George raised his glass after the waiter brought over the champagne. "To what, I sincerely hope, is one of many nights to come."

"I don't see any reason it wouldn't be," Sylvia replied, eyes sparkling.

"I am surprised you haven't mentioned my astounding wit and creativity yet," George teased her.

"I'm sorry?" she asked confused.

"Well, we are in the Four Seasons and we are in the room with the infamous trees. Need I say more?"

"I'm really sorry," she blushed. "I was never good at these things. I am afraid you'll have to spell it out for me."

"God, I guess I'm not as original as I thought I was. There go hours of trying to be romantic and creative. How can I impress you if you don't even notice my laughable efforts!"

"You don't have to impress me, George," Sylvia smiled at him reassuringly, caressing his hand with her fingers. *You've been at the top of the game from the day we met,* she thought. "Please, tell me about the significance of this room."

"I suppose you know they change the trees according to the season, hence the name of the restaurant?" She nodded so he continued "Tonight is the last night the trees remain in spring, and since we met in Spring I found it only appropriate to take you here, marking the end of the first part of our…acquaintance, if you will. And the next step in our, well, what will hopefully turn into a summer."

She sat there perfectly still, looking at him, studying every word and every gesture under the warmth of his eyes. She could feel his sincerity with every molecule of her body; although years of disappointments had made it virtually impossible to trust or to even truly open up to another person. Sure, these were all the right words a woman longed to hear, said in the sweetest possible way at the perfect place and time, but her ego was getting the best of her. George was a large prey and Sylvia knew anything else would probably be aiming too high even for her. So she was more than willing to settle for a man of his caliber. However, deep down in her ever-calculating and reasoning mind, she was hoping for something more at the end of the night. A thrill, a sense of restlessness, the ever so seductive game of dominance. She thought of James as she raised her glass.

"I would very much like that, George. To summer," she said, quietly.

The first of their seven-course meal arrived, and she studied the exquisitely-arranged appetizer. "White truffles," George said as he picked one up and invited her to try it. She took a small bite and licked her bottom lip. Her move was so deliberately sensual yet innocent that George put his fork down, wiped her lip with his finger, leaned in and kissed her. It was a brief, but loving display of affection and for a mere moment they were the only two people in the restaurant. As he moved away from her Sylvia gazed in his eyes and all she could see was her own reflection magnified a hundred times. She found it intoxicating. It was the first moment she felt disconnected from her past and from James; able to contemplate a present and a future with George. Deep down in her heart she knew he was the best that she could ever do.

Four and a half hours later he was dropping her off in front of her apartment at 504 W 111th Street. The weather had shifted from pleasantly cool to chilly in the last few hours and she was quick to walk in the building. In the car they had already agreed on seeing each other towards the middle of the week with George telling her to pick the restaurant and send him a message, so he could make the reservations. Just before she walked out, he had held her in his arms and kissed her again – this time it was a deep, passionate and demanding kiss – something she found particularly arousing as she loved any display of power in a man. Her tender four-foot eight-inch frame was lost in the strong embrace of his arms. She passively succumbed to his every move and when they parted lips she wished him good night, turned around and stepped out of the car.

She walked into her apartment, tossing her keys in the tray on the cupboard and threw her coat on the couch. The light on the answering machine was blinking; there were two new messages. Sylvia pushed the play button, drumming with her fingers on the kitchen counter as she listened.

"Hey, girl. I don't know what to think; either things are exceptionally good or extremely bad and I'm hoping it's the first, because nothing else can explain this graveyard silence on your end for the past month and a half. Last time I saw you, you were heading home with that blonde hunk. Give me a call to let me know how things are. Love you."

Sweet and caring Tanya. Genuinely interested as always, Sylvia thought. They hadn't seen each other since the night they went out clubbing after her first date with George. She didn't remember much of it, though, because of the extreme amount of tequila shots they had had. But she distinctly remembered the blonde guy she went home with. The second message was from him.

"Hey, gorgeous. Wanted to let you know I had an awesome time. Hit me up whenever you feel like it. It's Alex."

Alex was an investment banker on Wall Street, as easy-going and superficial as Sylvia, so they had instantly hit it off. Later, back at her place, it turned out they shared the same love for a rough fuck. It became obvious that was the beginning of a beautiful friendship with many benefits, since so much of their personalities, work, acquaintances and lives in general intercepted. She quickly texted Tanya with the date and time to meet up next week and turned off her phone for the night, having the feeling James could call with his never-ending demands. They had become particularly frequent lately and she didn't want to deal with him right now. Switching the phone off, Sylvia realized it was a first for her, which gave her a new-found sense of confidence.

CHAPTER SEVEN

It had started off as a way to fill in what was missing in his life, but soon afterwards James had discovered the benefits of using the Internet as a substitute for the real world. Night after night he would browse through countless sites, blogs and forums in search of everything he didn't otherwise have the time or the energy for, enjoying the added bonus of how much easier it was to get women to fall for him online. He had never been too fond of socializing, but just as anybody else James craved sympathy, understanding and intimacy. Online he could get all of that with minimal effort, all the while keeping things neat and simple. He would exchange a few messages followed by photos, and if he liked what he saw, meet up for a casual fuck. His network of acquaintances that he could call for a late night workout was remarkable. While each and every one of his new achievements started out promising, his interest quickly disappeared a few months down the road. Women came and went from his life so fast he no longer kept track.

Maybe it was his notorious lack of empathy that made it impossible to maintain relationships that required regular face-to-face interaction, or maybe it was just his proficiency at alienating people. Whatever the reason, the result was as predictable and obvious as was his desperate need to hold onto someone, anyone. Soon, his remarkable collection of *just-in-case* women was reduced to one, the one he had never expected to stay but, in spite of everything, did – Sylvia. Unknown even to himself, in time James started to feel grateful and connected to her more than he had ever expected. Still unwilling to accept her as his only option, even though he had started to warm up to the idea, he found himself reluctantly relying on her more than he used to. To make matters worse, Lyle was constantly hinting at the idea and never missed the chance to encourage him to take things further with her.

"I don't see why you won't even consider her an option. She's smart. Maybe not book-smart, but still. She's decent-looking, nice and her family is loaded. You have a lot in common. You went to the same high school. You know you were her first love and she adores you. I'll be damned if I know what she saw in you. A shiksa-goddess like her falling for a schmuck like you! Why are you kicking away your luck? Man up and do something about it before someone takes her off the market!" he often told him.

But the truth was that James was satisfied with the *status quo*, and feared change. He had gone out of his way to make it perfectly clear that he was unavailable, and that was how it was going to remain. That was the foundation of everything between he and Sylvia, and he wasn't willing to risk ruining it. Maybe he had fallen too much into the pattern of looking for a permanent solution to his loneliness online. Or maybe he just valued her friendship too much to risk trying to convert it into a full-on relationship. Or perhaps he was too certain in the possibility of being able to go from that friendship to something more serious at any given time that he just felt compelled to explore all other options before settling on that one. Whatever the reason, he religiously stuck to the pattern of dating sites, Craigslist ads, and chat rooms.

There was a personal blog by a young girl he had been following for some time. He felt drawn to her candid emotional posts as her words resonated with him. Night after night he would return to her blog, and it wasn't long before he noticed she updated it around the same time he was online. *Funny thing,* he thought. *She writes to fill the void that I read to fill.* He liked the way she bared her soul behind the convenience of Internet anonymity, although he found it alarming at times.

"Emotional exhibitionism is one block away from whoring for attention," Lyle often said, and James agreed with him.

"The Internet allowed us to lay it all out there. Everyone's got a story and everyone thinks theirs is worth telling and worth listening to. But in reality it's mostly pure garbage," his friend would add.

"You know what I find amusing?" James said. "The way every chick with a camera thinks she's a professional photographer. Nine out of ten women have it in their profile description. I've got news for you, love; taking a crappy picture of your duck face or your ass in yoga pants in the bathroom mirror doesn't make you a fucking photographer. It makes you plain annoying as fuck!"

"Or an artsy picture of your lunch," Lyle added.

But even though he laughed at people being too honest online, James spent a lot of his time on her blog. He liked everything about it – from her morbid obsession with depressive topics to the sad and moving articles, as well as the fact that she replied to every comment. There was something in her ability to open up to complete strangers that he found appealing. *Together with her inclination to be unnecessarily dramatic, this should make for an easy catch,* he told himself.

She had foolishly left her email on the contact form, which was all the encouragement James needed. *She must receive a lot of these.* He stared at the message screen. *I need something to stand out.* After several writings and re-writings, a brief, "Are you happy?" went out from his inbox into hers. Ten minutes later he received a response.

"Happiness is overrated. But I am looking for something if that's what you're asking. Aren't we all?"

The frequent e-mails had turned into texts, the messages had turned into phone conversations, and it wasn't long before they had started contemplating meeting each other in person. She had already sent James a picture of herself and he was pleased to discover her looks exceeded her mind, which he hadn't thought was possible. She hadn't asked for his picture yet, so he saw no reason to suggest sending one himself. Even though he had always felt comfortable in his skin, he knew a great deal of the internet glow of all relationships was attributed to the fact that so much was left to the woman's imagination. She had already created, polished and sculpted every aspect of his image. "Who am I to disappoint her?" he grinned. One of James' strengths was going along with other people's perception of him in a way that worked to his advantage – something eased incredibly by online communication.

He didn't mislead her out of spite; he honestly saw nothing wrong in pretending to be someone else just to maintain the real friendship that had come to be between them. In just a short period of time the flashing light next to her name in the messenger had turned into the high point of his nights, and he had genuinely started to care about a person he had never met – more than he could say about any of the women who had passed without leaving a trace through his life. And the more James came to know her kind and unpretentious heart, the more it seemed necessary to live up to her idea of him and to never let her down. Until now he had always gone through life indifferent to people's needs and wants, but for the first time he was as close to putting someone's wellbeing before his own as he could get. Or so he would like to believe. He had caught the scent of her passion, sincerity and childishly naïve belief in people just like a carnivore picked up the scent of its prey. Without knowing it, he was attracted to this girl for all the wrong reasons. She was his way out; the light he hoped would lead him away from an apathetic existence and back into a life that didn't just pass him by. And while he was so collected and reasonable in so many areas of his life, James didn't even realise how big of a failure he was setting himself for. Perhaps if he had stopped to think about how all of his past relationships had inevitably gone down the drain, he would have spotted his pattern of making his lovers shoulder an unbearable amount of responsibility. He always expected them to do the impossible and save him from himself. Naturally, they all failed miserably and he hated them for it. Years later he was still filled with resentment and anger towards all the women he had ever loved and chased away. James was never the type of person to look for the reasons for a failed relationship in himself, or to go as far as to even think it could have been his mistake to begin with. But the many disappointments had made him doubt his ability to sustain a relationship at all. He continued blaming it on woman's ephemeral nature and transient emotions, but at least he had started acknowledging his part in all of it. He no longer saw the need to hide his boredom and indifference, having learned that women found them strangely challenging, albeit the effect was short-lived, like most of his relationships.

James didn't consider himself to be exceptional with women, but whatever tricks he had picked up had always worked for him. Until he met her. Sitting in front of the screen, he felt like he was learning to read all over again, having known the wrong alphabet his entire life. None of the things he knew about women worked with this one. Where others were motivated by challenge, she found it obsolete and disrespectful; where the ever so effective *push and pull* worked wonders, she found it unnerving and immature; where his silent and distant demeanor was a vital part of his personality, she was driven away by his pose, which she saw as a waste of time over the Internet. He tried impressing her with what he did, but she pointed out she wasn't a groupie; he tried coming off as sensitive and considerate, but it didn't add up with the rest of his behaviour. For months he banged his head against the wall, trying to figure out what could get her attention, what could make her like him even more.

"You don't have to try so hard. In fact, you don't have to try at all. I'm here, aren't I? At four in the morning, talking to you. I think it's pretty obvious that I like you," she reminded him again one night.

"Just like?"

"Don't push it."

"I tend to do that."

"Do you really want to know what I want?"

"Yes."

"This. No games, no pretending, no false advertising. Am I asking for too much?"

"No. That's what I want too." *Funny thing how people are. We'll lie like hell to get the real deal,* he thought, looking away from the screen.

There were other reasons behind James' solitary existence apart from the fact that all his relationships went up in smoke. One of the things he detested the most was the beginning of every romance, that inevitable play on wits, charm and role establishment he found mentally exhausting. It was like a perpetual job interview, and for a person who always looked for the easy way out, any relationship quickly lost its appeal, regardless of his initial interest level. One night close to his thirtieth birthday he had reluctantly realized that the only lasting relationship he had ever had was based primarily on sex and mutual indifference. He looked around and was surprised by all the steady, happy, loving families all his friends and past lovers had created, while he had persisted in his wild goose chase. It was a wake-up call. His competitiveness didn't allow him to settle for less than everyone else, whom he thought didn't deserve as much as they were getting. "If they can do it, so can I," became his motto. James never even stopped to think whether it was what he genuinely wanted, or whether it was the fact that everyone was in serious, monogamous relationships that made it appealing enough for him to pursue one relentlessly himself. And while his new potential online partner met every criterion of a desirable candidate, he was still thrown off by his regular routine and continued to screw things up on occasion. At first he did the only thing that seemed logical to him. He put her in the spotlight to try and find a reason to run for the hills. But after not receiving any alarming responses, he gradually learnt to be at ease and just enjoy her company. Time passed and he became more and more infatuated with this stranger, who was bringing out a side in him he had effortlessly chased for years. In just a short while, James had seen enough to believe that she was his ticket to the good life. Or at least to a life he thought was good, judging by the apparent happiness of everyone living it. He studied his friends' and past lovers' Facebook albums and video footage for weeks until he was certain of one thing. *They all have one thing in common, being in a stable, long-term relationship; being settled down with that someone special. That must be what's missing from my life. That's what I need for everything else to fall into place.*

Autumn turned into winter, winter into spring and spring into summer, but they were too engulfed in the online delusion to even notice. And as the first signs of summer started to appear outside their windows they felt confident enough to contemplate meeting in person. Distance was the only inconvenience at the moment as James lived on the East Coast and she – on the West, until one cool April morning he woke up to a message in his inbox that made him as excited as he hadn't been in years:

"I am moving to New York."

For the first time in his life things were actually working out for him. He was close to trying on a different type of relationship without risking anything. Fidelity wasn't even an issue as, even though she had made it perfectly clear how much loyalty mattered to her, it was his principal rule that anything, she doesn't know about, never happened. James didn't even try to cut any of his female friends out of his life or try and alter existing agreements. He knew it would only drive him away from the woman he was interested in. He wanted this to work too badly to mess it up by stressing himself over something he was incapable of doing – staying faithful. He was well aware he would need a quick way to relieve the stress from maintaining the act that had won her over, and it was not the time to start burning bridges. *Try explaining to a potential girlfriend she needs to be thankful for, and not intimidated by, your exes. She'll bite your head off! If only women could understand and appreciate that sleeping with other people brings the two of you closer.* He laughed at the thought. *She can't get hurt if she doesn't know, right?* He sincerely believed he wasn't doing anything wrong if there wasn't any possibility of him getting carried away with someone else. Keeping it to the bare minimum – which, in his opinion, was meeting up for sex – meant things couldn't get messy, and James was confident in his abilities to control himself.

Then one night at the bar, several weeks later, he had met Karen.

Poker was one of the few remaining social activities James still looked forward to, despite the fact that with the passing years, the once regular gatherings had changed from weekly to monthly, at best. It seemed that all of his friends had stopped making time just for themselves. But every now and then they took time off their jobs, relationships and hobbies to show up for a game for old time's sake. The game itself was more of a decoy for these gatherings, which were a brief escape from the seriousness of adulthood and the harshness of a life these guys hadn't chosen for themselves, but were, nevertheless, trying to sustain.

Lyle and Sean were the first to show up. They frequently hung out together, as a few years back they had collectively invested in a 3-floor residential building they had been jointly managing ever since. Sean was the first to go into poker and to start playing professionally, and he was the one who had tried teaching James after Lyle had been unsuccessful. Lyle had quickly picked up on all the tricks and was able to make a living off of it in his mid-twenties, but James hadn't been as lucky. He struggled with the psychological aspects of the game, and was unable to hide either his giveaways or his anxiety. The initial enthusiasm he put into everything made up for his lack of skills and his inability to learn from his mistakes, making him successful for a short while. Always too full of himself and unable to look realistically at things, he attributed this fleeting success to his innate talent for the game rather than what it actually was – plain beginner's luck. He and Sean had been close friends since high school, but as they grew older, they had grown in different directions. As touchy as he was, James couldn't help but take it personally that Sean and Lyle had distanced themselves from him after he had introduced them to each other. He believed the reason to be that he was the only one of the three who continued to pursue his musical ambitions. Both Sean and Lyle had given up their teenage curiosity in jazz for far more practical interests, with Sean studying Economics in the New York University after having postponed his education for his poker career for a long time; and Lyle holding a BA in Mathematics from Columbia. The friendship, which had revolved around a bold, boyish dream of making it big, had suffered fundamental changes with the two more realistically-driven friends condescendingly accepting James' musical ambitions, which had cost him everything. To James, they had committed the cardinal sin of giving up on their dreams and joining the rat race, and to them he was just another college dropout with ambitious plans and no money. Despite the mutual feelings of contempt, however, they had managed to maintain a civil relationship, centered on the occasional poker game or discussion about the purpose of meaning; the latter, of course, only after sufficient booze.

Darren was late as always, which normally annoyed the hell out of James, but this time it conveniently gave the three an opportunity to catch up. An hour into the conversation, James was surprised to find out he was enjoying Sean's company. *It's probably because I haven't seen him in a while*, he thought. It almost felt like they were back in high school, without the worries, the serious conversations about the future and the disagreements, back when they just played and played to kill time. Having given up the guitar long ago, his friend had lost his touch with it and James complacently jumped at the chance to flaunt the latest techniques he had mastered. He naively thought this would impress the hell out of him, but Sean and Lyle just sat there, drinking their beers and discussing real estate, investments and stock market fluctuations, indifferent to his efforts. Every passing minute made it all the more apparent just how much distance time had put between the once-close friends. *I could just as well be playing in front of a bunch of gorillas*, James noted, annoyed *Why bother? It's like the time Van Gogh's paintings were first shown to the public. They wouldn't know what's good if it hit them in the fucking faces!* He stood there silent while the two went on and on about numbers and statistics until he reluctantly realized he had to force himself into the conversation.

"What else have you been up to lately besides the boring crap you're talking about?" he said to Sean.

"Really funny, Jimmy. If I have to guess, I bet you're asking me what I've done to culturally enrich myself such as art or music or pottery."

"You used to be one heck of a bass wiz. I'm just wondering where all that talent and hard work went."

"You know darn well where it went. It went into building my life with tangible, physical assets."

"Life isn't just about the material, Sean."

"You're becoming very predictable. That's so typical for a 30-something musician, who doesn't even own his place, to say. Wake up and face reality."

"A bit hostile, aren't we? I am perfectly content with my life."

"Are you? I'm not so sure."

"Well, you *are* the expert at everything," James frowned. "And I suppose it's up to you to show us the way, oh Enlightened One."

"Jesus, again with the poker thing? It's not my fault you were a crappy student, dude. I showed you everything I knew; same as Lyle did. Can't blame the teacher for the student's shortcomings."

"Yes, of course you would teach me every trick up your sleeve to be successful, because that's one thing professional poker needs, *more* competition."

"You can believe whatever you want to make yourself feel better, but you darn well know this isn't the only thing your temper has ruined for you, Jimmy."

"No!? Illuminate me," James snarled.

"Enough, you two! Do you have to do it *every* time?" Lyle asked. He was always the arbitrator in their ongoing quarrels.

There was a brief pause while Sean and James locked eyes. The story of their friendship could be read in that single moment, with the two friends always trying to outdo one another, while Lyle acted as a buffer to keep the peace. The silence was filled with years' worth of unspoken things.

"What was the last long-term relationship you had?" Sean asked slowly, with satisfaction. "Oh, wait! I forgot. You *can't* hold onto a woman, isn't that right, Jimmy? They all leave eventually. You drive them away with that wild temper of yours. It's what you're known for."

"Get your facts straight. Not *everyone* has left me."

"Ah, yes, your infamous back-up plan. Sylvia doesn't count, dude. Have you actually tried *being* with her? Like *in* a relationship? Exclusively?"

"So what if I haven't? She's begged me countless times. It's been over ten years and I can tap that ass anytime I like. That's the agreement and she's pretty committed."

"You're so delusional, it's not even amusing. It never occurred to you that maybe, just maybe, she still comes to you because, apart from getting her ass tapped, you perform all these additional services? If I recall correctly, she passed most of her exams in university mainly due to your writing skills applied in her term papers. And don't even get me started on her self-esteem issues, which have been at the core of your so-called relationship."

"Whatever, dude. My love life is actually one of the few areas, where everything is exactly as it should be. And FYI, I met this gorgeous chick, who's totally into me."

"Gorgeous? Are you sure it's not Beth all over again? Like I said, you have a consistent tendency to delude yourself that most of the women you pick up are above average looking."

"Wanna see a picture, smart ass?"

"By all means."

James turned around and quickly browsed through the folders. He found the picture he was looking for, opened it and gloated at Sean. Lyle pulled his chair to catch a better glimpse.

"Not bad at all," he noted. "Where did you meet her?"

James paused nervously, since he knew they would bust his balls when he told them.

"We sort of met online."

"Dude!" Just as he had anticipated, Lyle wasn't even trying to hide his disappointment. "Online dating is… How do you know she's not a 200-pound hog, who sent you a picture of some random hot chick?"

"I know for a fact she's not, all right? Just back off. She's really great. She makes me feel good about myself."

"I'm not surprised. Everyone can seem charming over the internet, even my 94-year-old grandma. You have time to properly market yourself, safely hidden behind the glow of your monitor, carefully choosing your words and pacing your witty remarks. But Mona Lisa from up close is totally different than her picture."

"It's not that easy to conceal yourself. There are signs that give away your true nature."

"Really?" Sean jumped at the opportunity "So have you shown her your true, charming self yet?"

"You mean have I lost my temper with her? No, I guess she doesn't rub me the wrong way."

"*Everyone* rubs you the wrong way, James. No exceptions."

"How do you know *for a fact* that she's not a dog?" Lyle insisted.

"I saw her. Last week. Turns out she's the little sister of one of the guys I play with. Joshua. You've met him."

"The two of you go out?" James shook his head "Talked to her at least?" Lyle continued.

"We did; just for a bit though. I knew she was coming to New York, but I didn't expect to see her in the bar. I didn't get a chance to tell her who I was."

"Didn't she recognize you?"

"I use a fake name online."

"How mature. Play-pretend in Neverland. What a great start to what you're hoping will turn into a serious relationship," Sean remarked, putting the empty beer can back on the table.

"Are you gonna tell her?" Lyle asked.

"Eventually. I just gotta find the right time and way."

"Good luck with that." Sean opened another can.

"Better be careful, dude. Sounds to me like the first impression wasn't a good one. Whatever you do from now you'll always be the guy who intentionally deceived her at some point. Women can be very fixated on these things," Lyle remarked.

"I know. I'll figure something out."

"She the girl you've been yapping about how different and special she is?" Sean grinned.

"You told him?" James snarled at Lyle. "You two are like an old married couple. Are your periods synched too?"

"Easy. Yes, I told him. I didn't think it was *that* big a deal. And you did talk about her a lot. I didn't know it was an online thing though. That changes things."

"How so?"

"Well, first you should ask yourself, what is wrong with her that she needs to pick up guys online?"

"She wasn't trying to pick up anyone. She was quite reluctant to start talking actually. She's very introverted and withdrawn, a bit morbid too."

"Even worse. I am sure it's cool and rock'n'roll to sit at home in the dark and slit your wrists. It's harder and a lot more life-affirming to actually enjoy yourself."

"I wouldn't expect you to understand, Lyle. You've always had it easy. You never had to…"

"What? Struggle?" he interrupted James, amused. "Are you fricking kidding me?! I guess you think you're special in some way because you're the only one who has to work for his survival in this country? We've all been there. The crappy apartment, the even crappier jobs. And don't tell me you're still struggling. People who have it rough don't buy a new guitar every month," Lyle pointed out, visibly irritated.

"Yeah, it's time to give up that whole martyr thing," Sean added.

"Fucking great. Gang up on the least successful guy in the room and kick him while he's down," James frowned.

"Oh, whatever, dude. You want sympathy and compassion? You're looking in the wrong place. You're just like everyone else, trying to make a living, and *don't* expect me to feel sorry for you for doing what's expected of a grown man," Lyle stressed.

"Of course you would say that. You don't have to work for a living."

"Really? This comes as a surprise to me. What am I doing then?"

"Renting out doesn't count. Nor does contemplating your next investment. You go to bed and wake up with more money in your bank account while I *have* to get up, get dressed, drive all the way across town, play in front of a bunch of people and drive back every day of every week to make just enough to get through another month."

"And whose choice is that?"

"Oh, yeah, it's *my* choice, Lyle. I choose to live from paycheck to paycheck like a fucking rat in a wheel."

"Actually it *is* your choice, Jimmy," Sean interrupted. "We started out in pretty much the same social circumstances. Our lives followed similar patterns in the order of things we had to deal with and overcome to get to where we are."

"The only difference is that both of you made a living and your fortune from playing poker while I am still swimming neck deep in shit. How is that fair?"

"How is that *not fair*?! We started learning about poker at the same time, James, remember? We used to play all the time to try and advance quickly and learn from each other. I, personally, have showed you and Lyle so many subtleties to the game, which is more than anyone has ever done for me. But you don't hear me bitch and moan how I had to learn the hard way."

"So you're saying it's my fault I am a failure at poker and everything else in life?"

"Whose fault do you want it to be? Your parents'? For the emotional trauma they've inflicted on you? Give me e break. Every family is dysfunctional in its own sick little way, with plenty of baggage to pass on to the kids. Like I've told you before – if you can channel all the energy you use to feel sorry for yourself and trying to get others to feel sorry for you into something useful you'll make more money than Lyle and me combined. You're way too emotional, Jimmy. And way too incapable of self-control."

"Thank you for the analysis. I wasn't aware you did some volunteer psychotherapy on the side of your successful poker career. Or do I owe you for these insightful observations?"

"You're an idiot, James. But your head is too far up your ass to realize your ego is what's holding you back."

"And you're a stuck-up self-righteous know-it-all, who thinks he's better than everyone just because he excelled at one single thing."

"No, that's still you," Sean disagreed.

"Let me know when you're both tired of your bullshit and want to play." Bored, Lyle got up and walked towards the window, glancing outside. "When is Darren getting here anyway?"

"He's always late."

"Call him. If he's not here in fifteen minutes, I'm leaving. I have better things to do than listen to this."

Lyle turned away and looked down at the street as James called Darren. Sean was sitting pensively on the couch, drinking beer and flipping through the guitar catalogue on the table. Everyone felt awkward. It was typical for James and Sean to jump at each other's throats every time they hung out; the years of growing up together and sharing interests weren't sufficient to eliminate the almost vicious competition between them. They were constantly trying to shine with the one thing they were exceptional at, thankful it was also a field where the other one was far from successful.

"Is he coming or not?" Lyle turned to James as he put down the phone.

"Five minutes. He's parking the car."

"Good. By the way. While we're still on the topic. I don't understand why you're wasting your time with some chick you don't really know and you won't even consider Sylvia, who's always been there for you. Despite the fact you've treated her horribly for years. That's gotta tell you something, but you don't know your own best interest."

"Sylvia is not a woman I see myself with. She's too high-maintenance. I can't really trust her after that stunt she pulled when we lived in Schaumburg, remember?"

"And you're not? Stop kidding yourself. As far as the 'stunt' goes, it takes a liar to know one. You're not exactly the faithful type either. You two are made for each other."

"It's not really your place to tell me what I should or should not put up with. If I say she's not right for me, then she sure as hell ain't," James replied. Agitated. He went to the door to let Darren in.

"Whatever helps you sleep at night. And you," Lyle remarked, turning to Darren as he was taking off his jacket. "Did you walk here? Next time we're not waiting for you."

"Sorry, man, got held up at the store. Some of us have two jobs in this economy. What are we playing?"

Sean pulled his chair and cut the cards. "We're playing the same as always. Five-card draw. Small blind is a buck and big is two. Buy-in is two hundred bucks .I'll deal. Questions?"

Everyone sat at the table as he dealt the cards. James pulled his pile of chips towards himself and started playing around with one of them, spinning it off the table. Darren eagerly reached for his cards and intently stared at the rest of the guys as they were checking theirs. He licked his bottom lip and threw two chips.

"I'm in."

"Me too."

"I'll raise you four." Lyle threw four more chips on top of the pile.

James looked at the King of Hearts and Ace of Diamonds in his hand. "I call."

"Call," Sean said.

Darren looked at everyone and gazed at his hand. "Fold." He sat back and opened a can as they dealt the flop. James could barely believe his luck when the King of Cups, King of Diamonds and the Ace of Spades lined up neatly on the table.

Lyle glanced indifferently. "Check."

"Check," James followed.

"I bet two-thirds of the pot." Sean threw in several chips.

"Call," Lyle responded.

"Call," James added.

Sean turned the next card and James barely held back a sigh at the sight of the Jack of Spades, but was quick to reassure himself it was still looking good for him. He knocked twice on the edge of the table after Lyle.

"Check."

"Check."

"Check."

He stared intently as Sean reached and turned over the last card, revealing the unbelievably fortunate Queen of Spades. Lyle checked and two sets of eyes were now on James, waiting for his move. Slowly and indifferently, he took some more chips and placed them on the table.

"I bet two-thirds of the pot."

"Call." Sean was as calm and collected as always. It was impossible to tell if he was bluffing or sitting on a flush. His refined arrogance was uncanny.

"Fold." Lyle put his cards on the table.

"All in." *Not this time you fucker,* James thought confidently. *This time you're in for a rude awakening.*

"Call." Sean pushed his chips to the middle of the table.

"Full house." James laid his cards on the table with a smirk.

"Straight flush," Sean replied, putting down his cards.

"Nice one, man." Lyle nodded approvingly to Sean.

As Sean reached and pulled all the chips James struggled to take a breath. A heat wave rushed through his body and dimmed his eyes for a fraction of a second. He was so sure he would win this game. *The story of my life.* He swallowed his disappointment. *No matter how good my hand is; no matter how well I play it; someone else is always dealt a better one.* Lyle was talking to Darren, but there was a ringing in James' ears, and he had to make an effort to physically get a hold of himself.

He re-bought, and the game went on without much chit-chat. Sean lost two mid-sized pots and folded about a dozen times when James re-raised him preflop, but his expression stayed the same regardless of the outcome. It was almost as if he didn't care. *I bet I'd be calm and collected too if I knew I was sitting on several millions in the bank,* James observed bitterly, although deep down he knew that had little to do with Sean's calm demeanor. The truth was he had been that way as long as James had known him. For some reason he managed to remain calm in any situation. James could barely recall one or two instances when he had seen him showing any emotion, although there was no way to know with certainty. Sean was quite good at bluffing in life too, so there was no way of knowing if he hadn't faked it. Lyle, on the other hand, was a bit more emotional, albeit just as capable of self-control, and rarely got excited enough about something to feel the need to express his emotions in a visible way. For the first time in his life, James contemplated the possibility that maybe, just maybe, his friends were so good at the game because of traits they had always possessed, rather than because of any qualities they had acquired.

As the hours passed, James lost focus. He made mistakes even a newbie could've avoided, which only made him nervous and jumpy. The angrier he got, the more mistakes he made. It was a vicious circle, and as it progressed, his pile of chips started decreasing at a quicker pace. But while Darren was dealing with his defeat in a nonchalant manner, laughing his way through the game, James felt his resentment building up towards the two guys, sitting across the table and robbing him blind. *Look at that smug grin on his fucking face. It must be a nice feeling to take money from people who have to work twice as hard to earn it. What's he going to do with my three hundred dollars? Buy another apartment building? Fucker.* He sat there, drinking beer after beer to keep his calm, but alcohol had long ago stopped having that effect on him. The years of abuse had rendered James immune to the numbness it could bring to those who used it with moderation, so he only became more agitated and started glaring at Sean in a threatening manner. Granted, he knew he stood no chance of punching him hard enough in the face to forever wipe off his smug grin, since his friend was in much better shape than he ever was, mainly due to his Black Belt in taekwondo. James had never been the fighting type, and all his life he had been exceedingly careful to avoid physical confrontation. In front of friends he preferred to come off as reasonable and even-tempered, but the truth was he was afraid. This shined in the way he treated women. Sooner or later in a relationship his inability to cope with his shortcomings and with reality manifested itself through emotional and verbal abuse. James had never admitted that to himself, but he enjoyed hurting those weaker than him. There was something endearing in the sight of a crying woman, upset by words spoken out to hurt her. It made her so wonderfully vulnerable, so small and insignificant that he felt compelled to swoop in like a savior, offering understanding, comfort and a strong embrace. But they left, they all left. All but one; the one he didn't want: Sylvia.

She stayed by his side through the most awful times in his life. She was always there, always picking up the pieces, and she didn't mind the drunken outbursts, the sober depression, the regular *push and pull* routines, the detachment, the indifference, the emotional unavailability and the violent sex. When he finally saw himself through her eyes and realized what she was putting up with, it horrified him how far he had gotten from Her in such a short while. He opened up the folder with the only picture he kept to remind himself of what She looked like because as much as he loved Her, time had started to ruthlessly erase those features he adored so much and he dreaded the day he would no longer be able to recall Her face. It was already painful enough for him to be slumming it with Sylvia and other women who didn't even come close to Her immaculate and gentle beauty, but he could not bear the thought of having to lower his standards in the emotional department as well just to make it through the rest of his life. It was then and there that James made the conscious decision to pull himself out of the gutter and trade the string of self-abusive relationships for something long-term, stable and healthy. He would try creating something for a change. He would make an effort to be the guy every woman wanted to be with. What he didn't realize, however, was that having spent so many years destroying, it had become all he was capable of.

The game came to its end around two in the morning and everyone was quick to leave. James wasn't particularly fun to hang out with under normal circumstance, but in an agitated state he was downright unbearable. He shrugged indifferently at the sight of the empty beer cans around the table, the pile of dirty clothes next to the bed, and the half-eaten pizza in a cardboard box on the kitchen counter. He turned around and gazed at the guitar, trying to figure out if he felt like playing. It usually calmed him down, but tonight he felt exhausted. Pulling the chair and sitting down, he kicked a couple of cans away. He turned on the computer and waited for the screen to load.

She was online as usual. James sighed with relief and changed his status to *away*, so no one else would bother him. He opened up a chat window. He never initiated the conversation, as he didn't want to appear too available. But he never had to anyway, since she always wrote to him a minute or two after he logged in. This flattered him, as it was his habit to make women work for his attention. James had stopped trying since he discovered that detachment and distance were like a female brand of heroin. "Women are funny creatures," he used to say. "Treat them like shit and they'll keep coming back for more. But show the slightest sign of interest or affection and you'll immediately see their backs." He was careful with Karen, though, as she was unresponsive to his usual tricks. Just as he was looking through his extensive collection of porn, deciding on which one to play in the background, a message popped up on the screen.

"Hey. You there?"

"Yes."

"Trouble sleeping?"

"As usual."

"Same here. Haven't heard from you in a bit. Everything all right?"

"Been busy. Had a couple of friends over for poker."

"Sounds fun. You should teach me how to play sometime. Maybe we can play online."

"It's too much work teaching someone from scratch. Educate yourself. There's plenty of information online."

"K."

While the conversation usually flowed well without so much as an effort on both sides, tonight it started off on the wrong foot. James was too irritated to watch out what he was saying, feeling bored and edgy from the game. Sex was the only thing able to bring him out of these moods, but since Sylvia wasn't picking up her phone, he was forced to look for alternatives. For a moment he was overcome with rage. *Great! Another whore with a sudden unjustified sense of self-worth,* and threw his phone aside. Despite spending a lot of time in the last couple of years building up a stable safety net of contacts precisely for such occurrences, there was no one he could call at four in the morning. These casual encounters were his only source of validation, which was the reason he put so many efforts into maintaining them. So it really came as a surprise when one by one they all started being unavailable. *Look what I've been reduced to, jerking off to porn like the rest of the losers out there.* He was relieved when he noticed Danny coming online. *Have to play this one right,* he thought, as he brought up the window next to his chat session with Karen.

"Listen, I'm gonna fix myself something to eat. Can you wait ten minutes?"

"Sure. No problem. I'll be here."

He changed his status to *invisible* and opened a window for Danny.

"Hey love. Why are you up this late?"

"Hey you," she instantly replied. "What? I'm not allowed one night away from the old ball and chain? I think I had way too many tequila shots though…"

"Haha, sounds like someone had too much fun, huh? Feeling horny?"

"You have to ask?"

"Let's do something about it."

"What do you have in mind?"

"One of those video chats we haven't done in a while."

"I had forgotten about those. Sure, what the hell! Any requests?"

"Yeah. Take off your panties and turn around. I want to look at your ass."

"You got it, love."

Their video session was quick and to the point as always. James had a habit of talking to women online, so he knew exactly how to get them wet in less than a minute. These chats were his personal brand of porn; often he even recorded them. In his experience, if a woman agreed to a mutual masturbation session online she didn't say no to much else either. Ironically, most of them objected to being filmed performing. He found it weird how women were more than willing to do virtually anything (on and offline), but objected to any material evidence of it. "Pretend principles," he liked to call it, finding it mildly annoying. "Women and their fucked up logic, or lack thereof. It doesn't matter if you're a whore; it's important not to have taped proof of it."

Danny was one of the many casual encounters he had had in his early twenties, back when he was trying to prove to himself that he was likeable by building up his credibility as a good lover. Apart from being from the same town and having gone to the same high school, they had nothing in common and, naturally, time did with their relationship the same thing it did to those purely based on sex. They drifted apart, keeping scarce feelings of friendship and intimacy. She moved away, finished college and started a family, so they could only occasionally continue to fool around on Skype. It actually worked for James as he had gotten out of this one just in time. He had always found women's inclination to imagine an entire relationship, based only on the fact that the sex was good, utterly frightening. Even Sylvia had done it at one point, but luckily she grew out of that phase pretty quickly, although not without his help.

As soon as he came, he reached for the towel he kept under the desk, trying to come up with a polite way to end the conversation. It turned out he didn't have to bother.

"I had forgotten how much fun this was. Thanks! We have to wrap it up though. I can hear the baby acting up in the other room. She wakes up if I'm gone for too long."

"I keep forgetting you're a respectable mother and wife now. How old is…?"

"Audrey. Nine months. Anyway gotta go. We'll talk some other time."

"Sure, love. You were great."

"Thanks. Goodnight."

"See ya."

Satisfied, he went over to the kitchen, grabbed a slice of the leftover pizza, and returned to the computer. He leaned back and brought up his chat with Karen.

"Hey, love. U still there?"

"Yes, watching a movie."

"Well, turn it off. I want your undivided attention."

"Wow, you turn into a different person once you've had something to eat."

"Men are simple creatures. It doesn't take much to make us happy."

"Good to know."

"How did the moving go? All settled in?"

"You can say so."

"How are you liking New York so far? Fitting in?"

"People like us never fit in."

"Haha, so true. Wonder why that is?"

"Because we move from place to place trying to escape. Problem is, if you don't know what you're running away from, chances are you'll bring it along anywhere you go."

"Well put." James lingered over her last sentence, moved by her ability to capture so accurately everything he felt. "I love your mind, love. You're amazing."

"You've already told me that."

"Haha, getting tired of me already?"

"You know that's impossible. It's just that I don't understand why you keep saying it."

"Because it's the truth."

"Never looked at it that way."

"When do I get to take you out on a real date?"

"Are you asking me out?"

"More like asking you in. I'd like to show you my apartment. There's something in the bedroom I think you'll like."

"Are you always this subtle?"

"Yes."

"Don't tell me it works."

"You'd be surprised."

"Not to be a buzzkill, but using the same highly efficient techniques you apply on every woman is not exactly the way to get me all warm and fuzzy inside."

"No? What is the way then?"

"Try the no-bullshit approach. You might actually get used to it."

"I doubt it, but I'm just kidding anyway. My joke was distasteful. I know this isn't the right approach to you. That's why I am so crazy about you."

"I bet you say that to all the girls."

"There are no other women. Just you."

"You're too sweet."

"I'm glad you think so."

James found her sincere naivety both adorably touching and highly entertaining. As far as he knew all women past twenty had learnt their lesson and were aware male-female relationships were based on anything but honesty. Yet, there he was with a girl who still believed in the Santa Claus of dating, a no-bullshit, tell-me-everything-exactly-as-it-is approach. "Jackpot!" he said to himself. Perhaps he could have appreciated her openness and lack of prejudice if he was a few years younger, not so cynical and adrift in life's harrowing lessons. But he had slept with way too many women; broken too many hearts and cheated on every single person he had been with to be able to appreciate a fair game in love. As far as he was concerned James saw anyone who served their heart on a platter as begging to be taught a rather harsh but necessary lesson. After all, he was handed a golden opportunity and it was his moral imperative to take advantage of it. That was about as far as his principles went. Of course, he couldn't overlook the charming innocence of Karen's unbroken belief in the good in people, which made her rather cute, despite the fact it was a disaster waiting to happen. *I gotta make her get rid of that cutesy bullshit if I am to make her my girlfriend. The risk is way too high. If I can trick her, so can any other asshole with an Internet connection. Other than that she's top-quality girlfriend-material,* James observed.

"Listen, love, as much as I love talking to you I'm gonna call it a night. It was a long day."

"Sure. I don't want to keep you up if you're tired."

"I'll call you tomorrow to set a place and date. Did you change your number?"

"Yes, I sent you the new one."

"K. And Karen?"

"Yes?"

"I can't wait to see you."

"Are you sure it's a good idea? After all, this, here; it isn't real."

"It's more real than anything else in my entire life."

"You honestly mean that?"

"Of course."

"Thank you. You're really special. I'm glad I met you."

"Me too. Talk to you soon, love."

"Goodnight."

"Goodnight."

Grinning, he logged off. *God, I can't believe how easy this is. She's almost taking all the fun out of it,* he thought, as he searched for a movie to fall asleep to. He finally decided on an old sitcom he often watched as it reminded him of simpler times, back when he was a different person and some things still mattered. He opened up one of the pictures Karen had sent him and critically examined her. She was gorgeous. This made him feel a bit uncomfortable as he had never enjoyed the ruthless competition that always came along with dating beautiful women. Partly for that exact reason and largely due to low self-esteem, James had always stuck to average-looking women slightly on the unattractive side. This enchantingly different girl, who was as serious, intelligent, sweet and insecure as she was attractive, was the highest he had aimed for. Years of dating had built up his confidence enough to know that his manipulative tricks would surely work on her. *The only potential problem is keeping her away from the other pricks out there, who know how to talk their way into a woman's mind, and bed,* he concluded pensively.

James slipped into his king-size bed and lay on his back, crossing his arms under his head. Staring at the ceiling, he started to drift away. *I wonder what she tastes like,* was the last thought that went through his mind before he fell asleep.

CHAPTER EIGHT

The last couple of weeks were a blur of candle-lit dinners in fancy restaurants, where the waiters were particularly attentive to the attractive couple, midday walks in Central Park, and a couple of Broadway shows, where they were seated in private booths. Sylvia was quickly getting used to the attention and first class treatment she received when she was with George. She was infatuated with the sense of power he emanated and the way people responded to it. They were dating, that much was clear; but neither of them had yet initiated a conversation to clarify their status, although this did not worry her at all. There was a certain old-fashioned charm to his gallant approach and his desire to take things slowly in a manner that was as unusual as it was thrilling and new to her. She liked the way George always took her places where they were spotted by friends and coworkers: women eyeing her with undisguised envy and men with reserved respect. Sylvia couldn't keep herself from comparing things to James and the way he never risked being seen with her in public. She had only been introduced to Lyle and Sean because James was renting with them in Schaumberg the same summer she stayed with him between semesters. And here she was personally being introduced to most of George's friends, colleagues and fellow Harvard students only weeks after they had started going out.

Evidently I've made the right choice, she concluded, sitting across from George one night at a charming little French bistro downtown. They were openly intimate, but were yet to sleep together. As moved as she was by his respect and care for her, Sylvia couldn't help but miss being just thrown on the bed and fucked unceremoniously. *Too bad you can't have both*, she sighed with regret, thankful she had James on the side to satisfy those needs. Sex had become a vital part of her life and if she didn't keep a reliable safety net of guys for a quick fix, the dry spell she would otherwise be going through would have been a nightmare. "You can't possibly get everything you want from a single guy. The key to having everything" she often told Tanya, "is convincing every one of the men in your life *he is* your everything without expecting wonders from him. It's *that* simple."

A few days ahead of her seventh date with George, Sylvia found herself with no plans and no dinner reservations one Tuesday night. She was finishing up updating Mr. Foster's itinerary, making sure all the meetings had been confirmed for his upcoming trip to Washington when she realized she didn't feel like going home after work. *What's Tanya up to these days?* She wondered. A brief phone conversation later they had agreed to meet up at the Wall Street Plaza and go for sushi at Ichiro. She stopped double-checking all the dates and smiled at the thought of her upcoming days off, as there was no need for her to come to the office in her boss's absence. It was agreed that she'd remain on call if something came up, but Sylvia was sure she would be able to enjoy two days of an uninterrupted shopping spree. *Something I'm in desperate need of,* she frowned, looking at a scratch on her favorite pair of Jimmy Choo's. She pulled up her pad from the top drawer and quickly went through all the treatments she had booked. *Mani-pedi, tanning, hair appointment, waxing; anti-cellulite massage and a facial - check. It's shaping up to be one hell of a weekend!* She felt as excited as when she was a little girl at the sight of her father dressed up as Santa, sneaking in their living room with a bag full of presents. Only this time the presents were much more worthwhile.

As she was putting away the pad in her purse something on the itinerary caught her attention.

"Shit, fuck, shit, shit!" Even though her desk was far away from everyone else's, Sylvia turned and looked around to see if anyone had overheard her outburst, but her colleagues all seemed preoccupied with their own business.

There it was, in bright red towards the end of her to-do list for her boss's trip, the thing she had overlooked, since, reluctant to deal with James, she had been putting if off for weeks. The presentation Stephen had prepared had to be translated into Russian, as Tim was meeting with some potential investors from St. Petersburg. Sylvia was in charge of all translations from and to Russian, French and German since she was fluent in all three languages. Or at least that was her résumé said. In reality it was stacked with every skill the men she slept with possessed since in her opinion it was, "virtually the same thing". In addition to that, she was an avid believer in the online databases of hundreds of desperate freelancers from all around the world, racing to the bottom and underbidding for scraps, who were able to get any job done within a matter of hours to a remarkably high standard. These sites had saved her more than once, although she tried to avoid them as much as possible because of the trail and the prominent level of incompetence among the applicants. Having someone trusted and familiar do the job made her confident no one would ever bother checking if she actually knew what she claimed she did. Fortunately, Mr. Foster was just like any regular boss, more concerned with the result rather than the means to achieve it. It was always just about quarterly figures. Anyone who claimed otherwise was a liar. or an idealist, or both.

She quickly speed-dialed five and as he picked up, put her cutest, most enticing voice to work.

"Hey, watcha doing? Because I thought of you and wanted to hear your voice… I know… Don't be mad, you know I would never screen your calls, I've just been up to my ears in work…Well, I guess I'll have to think of a way to make it up to you…Yes, I can think of few… How about this Thur… oh, shoot! My reminder just popped up; I can't. I have to find someone to translate this presentation to Russian by Wednesday... eighteen pages... Really?... And why would you do that for me? Ahhh, I see. I just *love* how your mind works. Well, since you'll be doing me such a huuuge favor, I guess I have to give you a little something in advance, won't I? Will you be online tonight? Sure. What time? Ok, I'll be waiting. Yes, just the way you like it. Talk to you later."

That was easy, Sylvia thought as she hung up. Sure, it had taken her years to learn how to press James' buttons to get the response she wanted, but as of late he was becoming far too predictable. She used to enjoy the game of screwing him over without him realizing it, although, surprising even to herself, she had grown out of that phase. Now it was just about a simple exchange of services plus a little rough fun on the side. *If George fucks the way he talks, I'm going to have to keep James. Besides, no reason throwing something away just because it's gotten old. You never know.*

She looked through the presentation, as she hadn't done so since Stephen had sent it over. It contained page after page about investment options, benefit packages and superlatives about Riverdale Bank's steady growth over the past decade and, more specifically, in the last quarter. Although she had briefly studied Russian in high school, Sylvia couldn't translate it even if she wanted to. Luckily, she had never had aspirations to do things she could get others to do for her. *God bless Russian dating sites and webcams,* she thought amused, pulling out her mirror and applying her lipstick. She knew James was fluent in the language mainly due to a crush he had developed for an Eastern European chick he had met on the Russian version of Facebook years ago. He had a thing about women from the former Soviet bloc; Ukraine, Poland, Lithuania. They were all so desperate and determined to get out and explore the options capitalism provided that any Western guy seemed like a good catch. She had learnt from James that they gave it all upfront without hesitation or any inhibitions through the wonderful channels of virtual communication. For the brief time they lived together in Schaumberg she had stumbled across his very personal and detailed collection of image and video files, neatly classified in folders. Then and there, browsing through pictures of women she never knew, she came to admire the openness of their sexuality; the way they used their femininity in the most efficient way with all of this helping her realize it wasn't subtlety that got and kept a guy. Of course, the desperation that was shining through every single thing they had agreed to, was beneath her. In a time when people paid for professional consulting to learn how to flirt and explore their sexuality, Sylvia had encountered a few particularly good personal trainers of her own. She picked up most of her tricks from Ukraine-born Masha, Lusia and Maria from Russia and Justyna from Poland. These women knew more about what drove a man crazy than all those self-proclaimed gurus of dating with backgrounds in psychology who vomited out book after book combining useless advice and comforting reassurance. Years ago, while she was still in college, a friend had dragged her to a seminar on *Relationship Basics* and sat there impressed with the level of confidence the hostess demonstrated, regurgitating the same old shit they had fed women for ages. Sylvia had looked around stunned at the way women were eating everything up. Had she never run into James and, subsequently, his private collection, she would never have owned up to the realization that it wasn't about how the guy acted, but about how the woman reacted. Years later she continued thanking these Eastern European women for showing her the key to getting what she wanted had been in her own hands all along. It was then that Sylvia stopped waiting for men. And that was the moment men had started lining up, waiting for her.

Fifteen minutes later she was approaching Tanya, who looked unusually somber as she stood at the corner of the Wall Street Plaza.

"Hey, love. Why the long face?" Sylvia asked as she gave her friend a peck on the cheek.

"Remember that promotion for a Senior Editor I was up for? I didn't get it. It went straight to my boss's nephew, fresh out of college," Tanya explained hastily, unable to hide her disappointment.

"I'm really sorry. But it's not the only publishing house in Manhattan. Maybe now's a good time to consider changing employers."

"I can't quit now. I've put too much time and efforts into this job, Silvie. If I left it would've been all for nothing. I'll just have to stick it out."

"You're a tough cookie," Sylvia winked at her. "Anyway, I know just the thing that'll get your mind off this subject?"

"Don't say a date," Tanya wrinkled her nose and shook her head.

"Yes, a date! How do you expect to have some fun if you've buried yourself in work? Live a little!"

"I get the sense you're living it up for the both of us."

"George is working on the election team for the mayor's campaign and next week I am meeting him for a benefit they're throwing for their sponsors and supporters. Most of George's friends are straight, single and serious white-collar types – just the way you like them."

"I don't know."

"I do. You're going."

"Only if I can wear my $32.99 dress from The Gap."

"That's not an acceptable outfit to a black-tie benefit, or anywhere else for that matter!" Sylvia said.

"I'm sorry, but my ball gown is still at the tailor's," Tanya said mockingly.

"Come by my apartment Sunday afternoon. We'll figure something out."

"Why are you so nice to me?" Tanya asked with gratitude.

"Because you're the best and I'll be damned if you don't start believing it yourself." Sylvia grabbed her friend by the hand and they hurried down the street.

Ten minutes later they were sat at a small corner table at Ichiro.

"So…" Tanya leaned in, lowering her voice. "How are things going with the exemplary boyfriend?"

"That's very accurately put, thank you very much," Sylvia smiled and tucked a lock of hair behind her ear. "He's perfect, from looks to manners."

"Come on. There's always something."

"He's everything I am looking for in a man."

"Really? There isn't a single thing that's bugging you? You can tell me."

"This is sooo sad to observe. And in you, of all people."

"What is?"

"The mark of the narrow-minded person," Sylvia shrugged. "Years of middle-class suburban oppression breaking down any aspiration for more, resulting in mediocrity. And what's even worse, in putting up with it for the rest of your life. Disappointments piling on top of disappointments, all of which you were prepared for by being told that you don't always get what you want."

"But that's the truth, Sylvie."

"That's *your* truth, *not* mine." She shook her drink and the ice cubes clattered against the glass. "I used to find it mind-boggling that women start relationships based on the notion of changing what they dislike in the guy. Such a waste of time," Sylvia shrugged. "But people are often raised up to believe life is built upon making exceptions and compromises. No one tells you that you should never settle for anything less than what you want."

"Sometimes the price for happiness is a compromise or two," Tanya argued.

"Where? Show me."

"Well, it's like with me and Daniel. There were a lot of boundaries that had to be respected. He was an up-and-coming author and I was just an intern editing his novel. You can see why it was a bad moment for him to start a relationship. Even his publishing agent said so! So we fooled around for…"

"Four years."

"Four, right. As far as others were concerned, we were not a couple. And I was fine to hide our relationship because what we had was special and meaningful and that's all that mattered."

"Were you happy?"

"What? When?"

"When you were with him."

"Sometimes I was. And then there were times I wasn't."

"Why do you think that was?"

"Because we wanted different things. I wanted him, but he wasn't ready to commit."

"What would you have done if he was ready to commit?"

"I don't know. What's with the questions, Sylvie? I honestly don't know. It was like million years ago, I don't remember. There was too much at stake. His name, my job… Maybe it turned out for the best."

"But it would've made you happy, right? To be with him in the open, fully committed to each other?"

"Of course," Tanya admitted with sadness.

"This is exactly what I am talking about. Everyone says they want to be happy and yet they kick their happiness away every single chance they get. People don't know how to be happy; they wouldn't know what to do with their lives if they woke up one morning and discovered they had everything they ever dreamt of. It would drive them insane. So they go around, missing all their chances, consciously enslaving themselves with dead-end careers and relationships that need *working on*."

Tanya stood there, silently poking at her salad. "So you're saying there are two types of people: those who're afraid of happiness and those who aren't?"

"That would be a little too convenient," Sylvia shrugged. "As far as I'm concerned, there are three types of people: the ones that don't know what they want, the ones afraid to go after it and the ones that pursue their goals." she paused. "You figure out what makes you happy, you go after it and you make it a reality. It's really *that* simple, which is why people think it's so damn hard."

"So George really has it all then?"

"He certainly does."

"Then what are all the other guys for?" Tanya asked, confused.

"You might want to ask what they *aren't* for," Sylvia giggled. "Old habits die hard, you know, and a girl's gotta eat."

"Well, you've got quite the appetite."

"Let's toast to that." She raised her glass.

"Cheers," Tanya said, peeking at her watch. "Let's eat, because I have to hurry home, ok? Mrs. Vallow dumped this enormous manuscript on my desk just before I left the office. She wants it proofread for Friday."

"There are people, I mean men, that can do that for you, you know."

"No, Sylvie. No. I appreciate Stephen writing that report for me, but it was one time, crisis-type of thing. I still feel awful about it. It just isn't right."

"Well, maybe if you had your own little web of meticulous helpers…"

"Unfortunately my libido isn't strong enough to sustain a web of the necessary proportions to meet the workload of my job," Tanya winked at her friend and they chuckled.

"To each his own I guess. Let me know whenever and if ever you decide to quit martyring yourself. There aren't going to be plaques handed out at the end of our lives to those who've worked their souls off. And even if there were – what a waste that would be!"

"Damn, why did you have to go and say that? What is there now to look forward to?" Tanya sighed, and the two women burst out laughing.

"Look, don't overcomplicate things," Sylvia pointed out "Bottom line is, life is like a penis. It doesn't matter how long it is as long as you're satisfied with it."

"But I bet a few extra inches can't hurt, right?" Tanya asked jokingly.

"*Exactly*! *Now* you seem to get it," her friend nodded with approval.

Thirty-five minutes later they were saying goodbye and getting in two separate cabs in front of the restaurant.

"I'll call you to remind you of the benefit," Sylvia said to her friend as they hugged. Then she disappeared into the cab.

She walked up to the door of her apartment, juggling her phone, handbag and pumps as she dug for her keys when the sound of a text startled her. *How predictable,* Sylvia winced. It was James with a brief and straight-to-the-point "I am online" message.

She unlocked the door, threw her handbag in front of the mirror, her shoes to the floor and dropped down on the couch. Her feet were swollen and she moaned with pain as she rubbed them. The Jimmy Choo's she had worn all day were killing her one toe at a time. *Maybe it doesn't help I'm wearing one size smaller than I should.* She frowned, but the idea of coming to terms with her size eleven feet was more than she could bear. Besides, fashion was all about altering oneself to fit a particular image and Sylvia had learnt how to use that to her advantage. It wasn't about what she had in terms of physical assets, but rather what she thought she should and wanted everyone else to think she did. She was amused by women's morbid obsession with the glamour and style of celebrities, but above all she was sincerely entertained by the blind belief that famous people were born with it. "We're a generation of stars, Sylvia liked to tell Tanya. "It's never been easier to buy and emanate class and elegance."

She reached across the table and pulled the laptop in front of her. Her Skype account was always open with her status on *away.* It was one of the simplest and most effective ways to fool men she was unavailable, therefore making her more desirable. The funny thing was, James used to pull the same stunt long ago, when he was the first to move away from their home town and they could only stay in touch through email and messengers. Sylvia frowned, remembering how she used to beg for his attention, but smiled contented at the thought that she owed all her tricks and schooling to his carelessness. Over the years James had given her what no other man had; the opportunity to observe and study him thoroughly without him suspecting it. He introduced her to the game, taught her the rules and showed her the way to a clean and easy victory without so much as realizing it. Sylvia was particularly thankful for his arrogance, as it made him blind to everything else, especially to the fact that at some point their roles had subtly shifted and he was no longer in control. At first she was careful in trying his own tricks on him, but when several of them went unnoticed in a row, yielding even better results than expected, she became more confident and daring.

She pulled a pearl lip gloss from the make-up purse and dabbed it on her lips; then she ran her fingers through her curls, disheveling them. She studied herself in the laptop screen, pleased with the result. The screen flashed with a message.

"Warming up to your pictures. I love your cunt."

Pulling down her tight-fitting top to reveal the purple lace of her bra, she made herself comfortable, snuggling up to the giant soft pillow. "I hope you mean the real thing," she teased.

"Finally. Where the fuck have you been? I'm about to burst."

"Sorry, love, got held up at work. Let me make it up to you."

"You'd better. I want you naked on the table with the dildo up your ass when I dial you. Got it? Just jam it up in there, no lube. That'll be your punishment."

His raw and primal ruthlessness turned her on immediately. A smirk hovered over her lips while reading his message. Her left arm wandered down her chest, pinching one of her nipples, then continued down, disappearing under her panties. She was wet. Under normal circumstance she would've followed through with his instructions without hesitation, but his visible agitation put her in a mood to experiment, giving her the courage to play around with his boundaries a bit. *It's what he's been doing with mine since we've known each other. It's only fair that I return the favor,* Sylvia moaned as her fingers slid inside her.

"You know what? I am not really in the mood for that tonight. I'd like something different."

"What??!!!"

"Tell you what. I'll make you a deal."

"What kind of deal?"

"For everything I do, you have to do the exact same thing."

"What the fuck? I'm not putting a dildo up my ass!"

"Fair enough. Neither am I. But you do want some anal play right? What would you be comfortable with? I know you just love a good rim job. Sooo… Wanna take it up a notch?" she was getting even more turned on by her audacity. *Power is intoxicating*, she thought.

"Not sure. What do you have in mind?"

"Call me with video and put the camera under your cock. I want to see you sliding a finger in your rectum while you massage your balls and rub your dick."

"You're seriously fucked up, you know that?"

"It's you that made me this way, love."

"What do I get in return?"

"Same thing? You can watch me rub and smear my pussy as I ram my ass at the same time. But for every finger you want me to add you'll have to do the same. That's the deal. Take it or leave it."

"Fine, I'll take it. You know just how to make me crazy, you twisted slut."

"That's because we're the same, you and me."

The video chat was quick and intense. Any other time Sylvia would have enjoyed it even more as she wasn't one of those women unable to disconnect during sex, but now she was too focused on James' reactions. The years they'd been sleeping together had taught her to embrace her natural lack of inhibition and make the most of it. Sure, there was a brief period when her inexperience dictated she act shy and insecure, but Sylvia was a passionate student, making up for everything with eagerness to learn and experiment. The biggest irony was that during the time James used to push her limits Sylvia had discovered that she didn't have any. Or perhaps she had just reached the limits of the young girl schooled by the older bored guy, who had decided to milk her first infatuation, teaching her to put up with anything and to eventually embrace everything they tried. That was the thing about human sexuality, once pushed over its limit it quickly became deviant and corrupted. Now, years later, the tables had turned and it was Sylvia who was putting James's boundaries to the test. Unlike him, she wasn't doing it just because she could or out of spite to settle the score. Her motives were far more simple and pragmatic. She just wanted to see if, with the right stimulus, everyone was reduced to their most primal and depraved urges. The whole process was entertaining to observe. Years of social conditioning and education, moral beliefs and taught norms peeling off like an excessive layer of skin to give way to a new breed of people, lovers that didn't get attached or overly emotional; that knew how to turn pain into pleasure; that could go well over the physical threshold of their bodies to experience the full spectrum of human emotions.

She stood there, watching James intently and mirroring his every move. He wouldn't go over a finger, but even so Sylvia considered this a substantial milestone in their relationship as well as a very personal and sweet victory. He came quicker than usual and she could tell his orgasm had been an intense one as he stood there, breathing heavily without even bothering to wipe the cum off of himself. With his clean hand he reached and started typing.

"I gotta admit, this was kind of nice."

"I knew you'd like it." She barely held in a smirk. *It's always the ones that act all tough and macho, who like to take it up the ass*, she observed indifferently.

"What is it about you? You always know exactly what I like and need."

"I just know you better than you know yourself, love."

"I'm starting to think you may be right. Thank you."

"For what?"

"Everything. For being here with me now."

"Anytime," she paused. *Wow. Going soft on me now. This is new. And quite off-putting*, Sylvia winced.

"We gotta try this next time we hang out."

"Definitely. Not sure when that'll be, though, as I'm swamped with work."

"You don't pick up your phone; you make me wait for you online and now you're telling me you can't make time for us to meet? If I didn't know you better I'd say you were blowing me off." James was really disappointed.

"Of course not. How can you even think that? You know how much you mean to me."

"I thought I did. Are you just playing hard to get then?"

"No, love. I would never play around with you. I've just been really busy. That's all."

"Too busy to send me some new pictures and a video or two to keep me hard and entertained?"

"Haha, let me see what I can do. Do you have something particular in mind?"

"Some close-ups of that juicy cunt of yours would be nice. And try and make the video more anal, but I want your face to be visible throughout."

"Sure, anything for you, love."

"Great. Will be waiting."

"Thanks for the workout. Talk to you soon."

"Anytime, love. Later."

"Goodnight."

Usually James was the first to hang up and log out, but this time Sylvia didn't even bother waiting for the program to close. She shut down the computer and pulled her panties up. As she reached for her phone she was surprised to see it was well after midnight. *We always lose track of time when we're together. Even virtually,* she noticed, browsing through the messages George had sent her. He had been quite busy with the PR campaign for the mayoral elections and for the past week they had only seen each other over a quick coffee. She had grown so accustomed to his presence in her life in just a short while that it was only now she was realizing how much she missed his calm, mature demeanor. This made her twice as delighted to read his candid message.

"Hello princess, have you started missing me yet? I'm sure missing you. Are you free for a late romantic dinner after the benefit? I want to make it up to you."

Sylvia read the message a second, then a third time; a smile hovering over her lips as she snuggled to the pillow. She could feel herself physically aching for George's presence. "Something tells me this is going to be the night," she whispered. "I'll make sure of it."

CHAPTER NINE

It was an early night at the bar. There was something about Saturdays that made people party like it was their last night on Earth, largely because they got to deal with their hangover in the safety of their own bathrooms the following day. They had called him in three hours earlier and when he got there James could barely make his way through the crowd. He was in an exceptionally good mood throughout the sound check, as the last week had flown by with him and Karen talking every night for hours. He had reached a real milestone with her having started confiding more and letting him in on many personal details about her life. Even though Darren had already spilled the beans, she elaborated on the relationship she had just ended with James content to learn there was still a significant amount of emotional damage. Like his father always told him: "The first thing you ask a woman is what her last relationship was like. If she has anything nice to say, move along." As he grew older James came to see through experience that women who had been hurt required fewer efforts to impress and keep, a thing that worked on many levels for him. The problem with confident women was that they expected the same level of self-sufficiency from their partner. But James was damaged goods and he was well aware of it, so he had excelled at picking out women with a painful history. It was a common topic of discussion with his friend Matt.

"I just sit there and pretend to listen, browsing through submityourflicks.com as she goes on and on about her betrayed trust, hurt feelings and whatnot; all she wants to hear is 'That's awful' and 'I am sorry this happened to you' every once in a while, because apparently women call that *bonding*. How about *them* apples?!" he often told him.

Like most guys James hated talking about his feeling, albeit for different reasons. Rather than out of fear that he would seem weak and emotional, he had spent so many years burying them deep in the back that, as far as he was concerned, he didn't have any left. The sad truth was James was like any other single guy, sucked into the alluring life of casual encounters mainly due to its easy sustainability. The only real feelings still haunting him came in the rare moments he thought of Her and could swear he could almost pick up Her scent of late summer. She had made him a survivor. He never got too close, too attached, or too hurt. He got in and out of women and relationships in a quick and clean way. Sylvia was the only woman he had told about the immense disappointment upon his first encounter with love, but this was only because she was the first woman he ran into afterwards and he needed some sort of justification for the horrible way he treated her. In time she learnt not to take it personally and James learnt to feel comfortable enough around her to talk about his fears, demons and goals, allowing both of them to move forward, in a way. Still, their relationship remained chaotic and violent, the way his life had always been.

That night, as he was cheering his progress with Karen, he caught himself marveling at her ability to open up to a complete stranger. For the first time he didn't try to ridicule her naivety, but was actually moved by her serenity. *That dude didn't get the best of her, even though she thinks he did*, he noted. There was bitterness in her; that much was clear. But this attracted him even more. Through experience, James had learnt to pick up all of the unmistakable signs of vulnerability in a woman, everything that pointed to her being an easy prey. True to his reasoning and cynical nature, he immediately tried to find an explanation for her behavior. It was difficult for him to accept her honesty at face value, although he sensed he was wrong this time. She had opened up to him – free of prejudice and fear – just out of the goodness of her heart, believing there was no need to withhold anything from him.

Struggling with his hectic thoughts and overwhelming emotions, he actually felt happy and excited when he saw her making her way towards the stage at the end of the first session. Jason was behind him on stage and it almost seemed as though she was looking and smiling at James, rather than her brother. For a brief moment he was deaf and blind to any other sound or image, watching as she walked towards him. *I have to make it work. She's the one. She must be,* he thought as he played mechanically. He barely made it through the end of the song.

As soon as the first set ended he jumped off the stage and walked over to her. She looked at him as he came near.

"I think we started off on the wrong foot," James began carefully. "Can I have a second go?"

"Sure, go right ahead," she said. Her smile was warm and reassuring.

"Listen, I am sorry if I came off as a womanizer, looking for his fix for the night. I can certainly understand why it would've seemed that way. I respect your brother. He's a great musician, great guy too. Offering my help to his little sister, well, I should be so lucky. It was a friendly suggestion. Nothing more."

"Fair enough."

"Can I get you a drink?"

"Beer is fine."

"Classy," James winked at her.

"Don't judge. I grew up with an older brother. What do you expect?"

"You should be grateful. That's a gift."

"What is?"

"The unfair advantage you have over men given that you have so much inside information about their behaviour," he explained, nodding to the bartender. Mike immediately opened and handed him two bottles.

"Good one. I'll have to remember it."

"Here." He handed her one. "Cheers."

"Cheers. Thank you. James is it?"

"My friends call me Marshall."

"I'll call you James then, being that I'm not one of them."

"We can change that."

"Again with that. Seriously?"

"What?" He shrugged.

"Look. I'm sure you're a great guy and everything, but before we continue with the whole you-pretending-you're-not hitting-on-me-and-me-pretending-I-don't-notice thing, you should know I am involved with someone."

"Boyfriend?"

"Not exactly."

"Husband?"

"No."

"Lover?"

"What's this? Relationship trivia? It's none of your business."

"So lover then," James concluded with disappointment.

"If you must know he's not a lover." She regretted saying that the moment it slipped out.

"You lost me. How is that then? Are you stalking the most popular boy in school at soccer practice?" *Provocation always does the trick.* James was amused by her discomfort, although

Karen laughed in an attempt to cover it.

"It's a bit more complicated than that."

"Illuminate me."

"Well, it's sort of an online thing."

"Oh, no, no, no, hell no! You look like a smart girl and your brother is one of the sharpest guys I know. You should know better than that!"

"He doesn't know and I'd appreciate it if you kept this to yourself. And if you must know one in three relationships start online these days."

"And the divorce rate in this country has risen to unprecedented levels, but I am sure it's completely unrelated. How can you fall for some loser, who dazzles and bullshits you from behind the comfortable anonymity of his monitor?"

"He's nothing like that."

"I bet."

"Go on, make fun, but we talk about a lot of personal things. You might even find it interesting to know he's a musician just like you."

"A fellow musician? Run! Let me tell you something about musicians. They're scum, horrible people. Will say virtually anything just to get a woman into bed."

"My brother is a musician."

"Except him, of course. He's a neat guy," he pointed out jokingly.

"I don't care what you think. You just don't know this guy like I do."

"I have no doubt about that," he ridiculed her, but quickly realized he had taken it too far, so was quick to add, "I'm just teasing. Don't mind me," James smiled apologetically. "People always judge what they don't understand. Who knows? Maybe I am a bit jealous of this guy, who's so great he managed to take you off the market. Lucky bastard."

Karen looked at him and tucked in a lock of hair behind her ear. *She's even more stunning when she's nervous,* he thought.

"Anyhow, thanks for the talk. Let me know how things turn out."

"Yeah, sure. Thanks for the beer."

"My pleasure. Later."

He turned around and walked back to the stage, savoring her palpable hesitation after he had worked his magic. *This time it went significantly better than before: just enough to mess with her head and make sure she doesn't hate me for deceiving her when we finally meet up,* he thought, as he picked up the guitar and put the strap around his shoulder.

As they played, James could see Karen looking at him from time to time, studying him as if she was trying to figure something out. James knew that look. It meant he had played his cards well and it was time to up the ante. *One day at a time,* he thought. *One day at a time.*

It was nearing four in the morning when he returned to the quiet comfort of his apartment. The first thing James did after walking through the door was head towards the shelf where he kept his liquor and pour himself a tall glass of gin and tonic. He then turned around and walked over to the hibernating computer. He pushed the button and logged on. She was online. He always had a sixth sense about these things.

"Late night out?" he typed.

"How did you know?"

"Just a feeling. Same here."

"What are the odds, huh?"

"I'm telling you, love. This is meant to be."

"You're extra soft tonight. To what do I owe the pleasure?"

"To your being here."

"I met a guy tonight."

"Oh? Do you like him?" James leaned back, sipping his drink.

"No, it's not like that. We just talked, but when I told him I was attracted to someone I met online he thought it was stupid. He was quite mean."

"The bastard's got a point," he typed laughing. The buzz from the liquor had started to kick in.

"What are you saying?"

"What we're both thinking, but are afraid to admit."

"?"

"There's no need to dramatize. It's fairly wild and quite ridiculous of us to think something serious can ever come of this."

"I didn't know you felt that way."

"I am a practical guy, love. It's time to face reality."

"Why don't you fill me in?"

"I am not your prince and you are not a princess. This was never a fairy-tale."

"Never said it was. I still don't get what this has to do with believing there can be something real and meaningful between two people who've never met in person?"

"Because it's downright ridiculous, that's why. Straight from a fairy tale of the digital age."

"Maybe you're right."

"You know I am."

"So what now?

"This conversation turned too serious. How about a quick poker game to take our minds off it?"

"I am afraid I am not very good at it."

"No way! You cannot be bad at poker. It's like saying you're bad at life."

"Which I kind of am."

"Don't say that. We make our own reality. If you think negatively you'll attract negativity into your life. It's a vicious circle."

"I resent that. It's a dangerous philosophy."

"Meaning?"

"Meaning you're basically advocating that people consciously infantilize themselves by eliminating their capacity to think critically. It's inhumane to think positively all the time. And people who manage to do so don't achieve the ultimate bliss and experience only happiness, surrounding themselves with bushy-tailed rainbow-pooping ponies. No, they're just as insecure, lost and miserable as the rest of us. Just more deluded maybe."

"All right. Relax. I didn't know you were PMSing."

"I'm not. I'm just expressing an opinion. You can't go to your happy place every time you need to, simply because that's not a sensible approach to dealing with things."

"You're over-thinking this. It's not a good thing for a woman to think so much."

"Excuse me?!"

"Women are emotional creatures. One gesture or lack thereof triggers an elaborate schematic of predetermined what-did-he-mean-by-that questions and before you know it you're starring in your own version of *Leaving Las Vegas*. You know, 'you think you can get away with this, but I'll top it by showing you what hurt really is' just to end up being gang-raped in the ass by a bunch of drunken college guys."

"You're obsessed with that movie."

"It's the ultimate real-life love story."

"How is it the ultimate love story?"

"Come on, two people utterly beyond salvation, who cling onto one another in a last vain attempt to save themselves, promising and hoping they'll change, only to realize they're only accelerating the process of self-destruction. It doesn't get any more real-life than that. A match made in heaven while it's a match made in hell."

"I thought the only sure thing in life was change."

"That's what they teach you in preschool. But do you honestly believe that the hopeless alcoholic or the inveterate whore are capable of changing?"

"I guess not. Is this what you think you and I are?"

"Are you a whore?"

"Don't see a reason to believe that I am."

"Then no."

"What are we then?"

"Two people looking for the same thing in all the wrong places."

"And what might that be?"

"The purpose of meaning. LOL. That's from an old Dexter's Laboratory episode. I used to love it as a kid."

"I know where it's from. Seriously though?"

"I don't know, love. What do you expect me to say? Not sure what *you're* looking for. Come to think of it, not sure what I am either. How to 'get out of that sea of pain that we all need to get out of' as Adrien Brody so eloquently puts it in *Detachment*? What life is about maybe?"

"I can tell you the answer to that."

"Please do," James grinned at her impudence. *This is going to be good,* he thought.

"I have two friends. One is madly in love and the other one thinks he's in love. They're both utterly miserable. That's what life is about."

His fingers froze over the keyboard as he went back and re-read her message. Suddenly he realized his buzz had worn off. He felt emotionally drained, confused and sad. Hovering over what he had written, he knew he had taken things too far and instinctively leaned on the desk, holding his head between his hands. *No, James, no. Fucking moron. Months of hard work just to blow all your efforts in one drunken chat. You should've just kept your mouth shut. Fucking shit.*

He stood there numb, wondering how to move the conversation forward as if nothing had happened. "Women like it when you play it cool. I'll pretend it's not a big deal and she'll get on board with that. She'll have to." He didn't realize he was mumbling out loud. Apologizing seemed unnatural and out-of-place at the moment. His best bet was to write it off. But before he could begin to put together barely enough thoughts to come up with something comforting and witty to write, Karen's status changed to *offline*.

James felt his body going stiff. His first impulse was to call her on her mobile, but some faint glimmer of sanity in his drunken condition helped him get a hold of himself long enough to overcome the urge. He stood up and wobbled to his bed in a drunken haze. He lay on his back and stared at the ceiling, wishing for the room to stop spinning. Rambling thoughts were racing though his head, making him feel even more disoriented and drained. He turned around and covered his head with the duvet. *I'm sorry, Karen. I'm a fucking bastard* was the last thing that went through his mind before he lost consciousness.

He woke up late in the afternoon with an uneasy feeling. It took him ten minutes to get the room to stop spinning and to slowly start to focus everything around him. The sun rays were shoving their way through the blinds, making his eyes hurt. With an effort he reached and picked up the bottle of water he always kept next to his bed. He poured half a gallon down his throat before managing to quench his hangover thirst but the headache was killing him. James looked towards the kitchen, trying to figure out if the pain was stronger than his unwillingness to get up, then he grunted, turned around and covered his head with the sleeping bag.

Twenty minutes later, still tossing and turning, he kicked away the sheets and went over to the kitchen for a Hexadrine, turning on the computer on his way. Going into the bathroom something caught his attention. There was more dried up blood in the sink. James stared at the little drops intently, but there was no doubt as to their origin. *Fuck it. It's not like I'm planning on living to be a grandpa anyway,* he thought as he drank his beer, washing the blood away with his warm piss. He looked with interest at his swollen eyes and the dark circles underneath, shrugging with indifference. *What do you expect? Years are flying by and you're not getting any younger. Now you're a middle-aged guy with a drinking problem. Congratulations. You've turned into a raving cliché.* James walked back to the computer and logged into Skype. No one was online. Agitated, he scrolled through his entire contact list. He wasn't used to such a permeating absence. He liked to think all his friends and acquaintances were using Skype as a surrogate to real life like him and he hated to be proven wrong. Normally, he would start his day with a quick jerk off, although lately alcohol had started to take its toll and he no longer woke up with a boner as often as he used to. And in the rare moments he did he was frequently not in the mood to do anything about it. *God, I miss the mornings all I had to do was grab Sylvia by the hair and shove my dick down her throat,* he sighed, scratching his balls. Bored out of his mind, he opened last night's chat with Karen and browsed through it, trying to numb the vague feeling of something gone wrong. As he read on, he could feel a sense of panic building up. *Don't tell me I've done it again! Fuck me, I thought I had stopped with these drunken mishaps.* He angrily tossed the beer can aside as he continued reading. In a vain attempt to distract himself from the gloomy thoughts that ran frantically through his mind, James turned up the volume to the max and tried drowning his angst in some Limp Bizkit. He sat there, staring blankly at the screen when Sylvia came online. A smile unknowingly plastered on his lips as he jumped at the opportunity to distract himself and have some fun. He opened up a chat window.

"Hey, love. This is a nice surprise."

"Hey you."

"Two days in a row. How lucky am I?"

"I am trying to buy this cute bracelet and I logged on to talk to the store's support department."

"Of course you are. How about a quickie?"

"I can't, I'm sorry."

"What?! Are you serious? When have you ever said no before?"

"I know. I guess this is a first … Get used to hearing it more often, though, as I am with somebody now."

"You don't say. When did that happen?"

"Well, we've been going out for a while now, but it just got serious."

"How come it wasn't serious yesterday?"

"Because I just decided it was."

"Haha, of course. It's always the woman who decides."

"*Naturally*, we're ladies after all."

"Sometimes I wonder. So, who's the unlucky guy that gets to go out of his way to cater to your pretentious ass day and night?"

"It's scary just how well you know me!"

"No shit, Sherlock."

"His name is George."

"George sounds like a douche."

"And he's exceptionally stable, well-mannered and kind, things you know nothing of."

"Guilty as charged; although I thought that's what you liked about me."

"It does give you a certain boyish charm, but it grounds you in the fuck buddy zone. You're not exactly boyfriend-material."

"Amen to that!"

"Seems to me this attitude will eventually turn into something you are going to regret."

"No worries. Should this happen, I have several willing and readily available Russian hotties, working their way towards earning an invitation to the Land of the Free on my account as mail order brides. And we all know Russian women are adaptable, easy and low-maintenance."

"During the trial run, perhaps. But you can't handle a Russian woman, love. Nor any other woman for that matter."

"I've handled you plenty of times."

"Fucked and handled are two different things."

"Then I'm screwed."

"You are."

"I can't believe you're going to leave me blue-balled, having to resort to our old video footage to take care of myself."

"Shit happens."

"Don't tell me you've decided to turn into a Stepford girlfriend; putting an end to our decade-long history filled with amazing fuck-a-thons?"

"You know me better than that. A girl's gotta have options. Plus, you know what I always say."

"?"

"If it's worn-out but it ain't broke, don't throw it away just yet."

"Agreed. Hit me up then when you get sick of the Upper Side theatrics and want an actual dick to fill you up nice and hard the way you're used to."

"I marvel at how delicate you can be."

"You know me, love, it's not my style."

"That's why I like you so much."

"And I like that I don't have to impress you."

"We're a good match. I'll call you later this week, k?"

"Sure, you'll have to make up for today."

"I will. Bye."

"See ya."

Although he went out of his way to try and pretend he was fine with Sylvia blowing him off like that, James was furious. At least now he knew the real reason behind her growing unavailability the past month. *So, there's a guy in the picture.* He had known about this for a while now – having a sixth sense for these things – but was irritated at how long it had taken her to come clean about it. They both knew they weren't exclusive; they weren't even dating. But there had always been an unspoken rule that boyfriends and girlfriends came and went, but their arrangement continued indefinitely. It was the first time she was giving someone preference over him and James felt offended. He knew he treated Sylvia disrespectfully and was sometimes downright abusive, but she had never objected to his behavior. She simply went along with it as it had always been the case. It was only recently that she had started to distance herself, making him realize he had no control or power over the woman who had stayed in his life the longest. This filled James with fear. Fear brought along anger and anger made him bitter and even more unpleasant towards the rest of the women in his life. Someone had to pay for Sylvia's betrayal. Before, he could regularly count on her to fight off his demons and drag him out of his destructive patterns of self-abuse, but after she started disappearing off the map James was thrown back into his usual circle of random hook-ups, online chat sessions and alcohol - lots of alcohol. And just as any self-respectable person on the verge of drowning, his instinct for self-preservation kicked in just in time to make him realize he needed a more permanent substitute for Sylvia's presence in his life. That was the moment he turned to Karen. Ironically, it was the denial of his feelings for the woman he had spent most of his life with that became the catalyst for the relationship he was pursuing with Karen. The only problem was that James couldn't stop punishing her for everyone else's mistakes; including his own. His only smart move was to try justifying his illogical and hurtful behavior from the previous night.

He tapped the keyboard, wondering how to explain last night's fluke. It wasn't the first time it had happened and he was pretty sure it wouldn't be the last, which meant he had to be even more careful. If there was one thing he knew with certainty about women it was that the easiest way to blow his chance with them was with the overuse of excuses. Sadly, it was a rule James violated quite frequently, and he always suffered the consequences. Then again, he was in the bad habit of over-sharing everything with everyone, from excuses to plans and opinions; something that even Lyle had pointed out as detrimental to him. James thought for a moment before typing in the chat window.

"I have a horrible headache. You probably don't want to talk. I just wanted to say it wasn't fair of me."

He looked at his message, content with its ambiguity He was never one to openly apologize. The message remained undelivered for quite some time, which bugged him so he deleted it. He re-typed it on his phone and sent it as a text. He felt relaxed and confident that he would manage to weasel out of the situation without a lot of fuss. If there was anything James was sure of it was his ability to get away with almost anything when it came to women. At least until they got to know him well enough to emotionally disconnect and move on. Karen, however, was far from reaching that point. Aware of that, he wanted to capitalize on it for as long as he could.

About half an hour after he had sent the text and his paranoia was beginning to spiral out of control, she came online and a message popped on to his computer screen.

"I got your text. Sorry I didn't reply. I was on my way home."

"No worries."

"It's true. It wasn't fair. But it's all fine."

"I think you misunderstood what I meant."

"Sorry?"

"I meant that it wasn't fair of me to change my mind like that. First I told you what seemed logical and then the alcohol got the best of me and I said what I actually wanted to say."

"I see."

"That doesn't change the way I feel about you, Karen. I really want to be with you."

"Seems to me like you're trying to find excuses not to be with me."

"I'm sorry, but I won't apologize for speaking my mind. You have the right to know how I feel and I was just being honest, even if I seemed rude."

"Seemed? Anyway, I still don't understand what you want from me."

"I want you."

"Why don't you just tell me that?"

"Because it's the last thing a man should say to a woman he has hopes of winning over. The minute she picks up his interest in her she runs for the hills. Indifference and arrogance are what keeps a woman coming back for more."

"I'm not interested in arguing over the specifics of what appeals to women in general, but I can assure you what you just described is the quickest way to make *me* run for the hills. I don't have time for games. What's, more, I don't have the energy."

"I know, that's why I like you so much. Force of habit I guess. I'm sure you've noticed by now that the *push and pull* routine is quite frequent with me."

"That's not a valid excuse."

"I know it's not. But with you around I feel it's starting to fade away. I guess I have more emotional baggage than I thought."

"Don't we all?"

"Haha, right? You're truly a remarkable person and I want to be with you. I'm just a very unstable guy. Not that it's breaking news for anyone, but still."

"What happens now? We can continue doing whatever the hell *this* is."

"I want more, Karen."

"But you said it yourself. It doesn't seem realistic. People usually fall victim to their own limitations."

"Meaning?"

"Meaning, when we're convinced of something we fabricate reasons to justify it and we end up believing them. It's not that we can't actually do it; we've just crippled ourselves mentally before even having tried."

"I don't know what to say, but I have the feeling something changed on your part."

"Would it matter if it did?"

"Yes. I wouldn't ask otherwise."

"I don't think that it has. At least not to my knowledge."

"I just feel awful. With these self-destructive mishaps I hurt the people I care for the most."

"Blame it on the alcohol."

"Maybe I should stop blaming it on anything or anyone else but myself. That sort of thinking got me to where I am now."

"Fair enough."

"Can I call you? I want to hear your voice."

"Sure. What do you want to talk about?"

"There's something I've been meaning to tell you."

"Yes?"

"I love you."

"Are you serious?"

"Yes."

"I don't know what to say."

"You don't have to say anything. I just want you to know it."

"…"

"Do you want to meet up?"

"For real?"

"I really want to see you. I want to feel your skin and get lost in the soft baseline of your neck."

"Wow, that was corny, and sweet."

"Where do you want to meet up?"

"You can pick me up and we'll see afterwards."

"Inviting me straight to your place? Not a particularly smart move. What if I am a total psycho?"

"I know you are. But so am I."

"Haha, touché."

"It's 52nd St,, Woodside, 1137. Say Tuesday, 9-ish?"

"Sounds good."

"Great."

"Should I wear anything particular so you know it's me?"

"I think that the restraining shirt they gave you at the asylum will suffice. Not to mention the unmistakable sign of ringing my door bell, so I think I'm good."

"Got it. I'll just bring my usual charming self then."

"Be sure to do that."

"Listen, love. I gotta run. I'd much more prefer to stay and keep talking to you, but I have to go. I am really glad you're not mad at me."

"Sure. All is fine."

"Looking forward to Tuesday."

"Me too."

"See you soon then (this time for real)."

"Bye."

James logged off and leaned back in the chair, stretching his arms. The conversation had gone better than he had expected. There were times when Karen was a straight textbook case, which worked to his advantage. Ordinarily, he wouldn't push for a face-to-face meet-up just yet because he always wanted to ensure the woman was as hooked as she could possibly be beforehand. However, he sensed he couldn't postpone things with this one any longer. *She's wonderfully weird in so many ways,* James thought, pleasantly surprised his headache had disappeared while they were chatting. The connection they both felt was undeniable and he saw no reason not to act on it while the initial flame of attraction was still kindling. *The worse thing about women is the brevity of their emotions. Not to mention that every guy out there gets one shot per woman in a lifetime, and since I have the tendency to use up mine rather quickly, it's probably a good idea to move things forward while her interest level in me is still high,* he thought as he made a note of the date in his calendar, knowing he would forget it.

CHAPTER TEN

It was nearing two o'clock when Sylvia walked into her apartment and dumped her bags next to the sofa. Her entire Sunday morning had passed by in a frantic shopping spree in search of the perfect outfit for the benefit. She had gone through all of her favorite stores, but none of the clothes she tried fit the idea she had of herself walking hand in hand with George in front of all his colleagues and friends. "Our first official outing as a couple." she noted with excitement. He had already invited her to spend the night at his place afterwards, and Sylvia knew exactly what that meant. She spent hours scouting round for a dress that would accentuate her best features without being too vulgar and revealing in the light of what promised to be a very long and sensual night.

All her favorite stores that would otherwise have everything she needed to put together a glamorous and stylish look for any occasion seemed to offer clothes that would be out of place at the event. *It's George's fault,* Sylvia wrinkled her nose playfully. *Next to him everything seems out of style and not nearly as classy.* She didn't normally go for vintage clothes, but, passing by a small boutique in the lower part of the Upper West Side, a simple dress caught her attention with its unostentatious cut. She was so impressed with it she swerved into the shop and immediately requested to try it out, forgetting to even ask what the label was, which was new for her. Ten minutes later at the cash register Sylvia was delighted to learn the label fit the cut and she had purchased a Prada cotton wool and silk sleeveless knee-high dress. Everything about it mirrored Jacky Kennedy's prim and sophisticated style, which Sylvia knew would be just the way to look next to George. She dedicated the rest of the morning to the search for the perfect accessories to complement the dress and after hours of running up and down Broadway finally fixed her eyes on a pair of Manolo Blahnik Sedaraby's, exquisite pear-shaped Bulgari emerald earrings and a large white gold and pavé diamond bracelet. The earrings were the only ones to contrast with the otherwise conservative look she had chosen for the night, but Sylvia used every chance to draw attention to her crystal blue eyes, which she recognized as one of her best features.

There was a message on her answering machine from George, informing her he would pick her up at eight sharp, which gave her plenty of time to get ready. She smiled and started undressing on the way to the bathroom for a quick shower. *Looks like by now he knows his audience,* she thought, aware just how much he disliked waiting for her to get dressed whenever they had plans. However, he never expressed any discontent over her taking forever to get ready. Just as with everything else, an unspoken understanding had started to form between them. They complemented each other as if they had been together for years. Sylvia was extremely careful about the personality traits she allowed George to see, and only showed what she thought he would value in the woman next to him. In turn, he treated her like a queen, showering her with gifts and attention. "Overall, this is shaping up to be a good investment for both parties," she confided to Tanya while treating herself and her friend to a deep conditioning treatment and styling at her favorite salon on Columbus Avenue.

Scott J Salons was impossible to get in, especially on short notice, but Sylvia was a regular and always received a highly personal and preferential treatment. Normally, Tanya would have waited for months for an appointment at one of the top award-winning salons, not to mention the fact that she was unable to afford it, but Sylvia knew Scott personally and gladly treated her friend to an hour and a half of ultimate bliss.

After the shower she unpacked the bag the doorman had delivered earlier in the day, carefully pulling out the dry-cleaned dress. She put it on and studied herself in the mirror. Tanya was supposed to come around six so Sylvia could do her make-up, which gave her just enough time to do her own and then strut around the apartment in her new shoes to break them before the big event. She twirled around with a childlike excitement at the sight of her own reflection, delighted with the way the dress wrapped around her curves. Her hair coiled loosely around her face, glossy and soft thanks to the Saturday visit to the salon, and Sylvia carefully tucked several curls away.

She went to her bedroom and started applying her make-up, standing in front of the dressing table the way she always did it when she was too excited to sit down. She was a real pro at applying everything from an eye-liner and mascara with a steady hand to mixing just the right shades of foundation and blush thanks to a 2-month long, ridiculously expensive make-up course from a celebrity artist guru. Sylvia smiled, remembering how she had nagged her father for weeks to pay for it until he finally caved in the summer after she had just turned fourteen. *Not that he was ever able to say no to me. Not that any man ever could*, she concluded, as she studied herself critically in the mirror.

She was dabbing some gloss on top of her lipstick when the doorbell rang. *Tanya's here*, Sylvia thought, glancing at the clock on the wall. It was ten minutes past six. She walked over to the door, buzzed her friend in and, leaving it barely open, returned to the bedroom. Tanya walked in just as Sylvia was putting on her earrings.

"You're late." she remarked without turning away from the mirror.

"I'm sorry. Traffic downtown is horrible. I should have left earlier."

"No worries. George won't be here before eight."

"Then why did you make me come so early?"

"We have a lot of work to do." Sylvia walked over to Tanya and gently sleeked down her hair "At least you haven't ruined

Lisa's work. The highlights she gave you are terrific; they really flatter your skin tone."

"I have you to thank for it all, Silvie. It was really nice of you to pay for it. How much did everything cost: therapy, conditioning, haircut and all?"

"I told you not to talk to me about money." Sylvia pursed her lips.

"I feel really uncomfortable. Everyone knows you shouldn't mix friendship and money."

"Who's everyone? Are you honestly telling me you still follow what other people are telling you to believe?"

"No, but…"

"But nothing. Just say thank you and we're even."

"Thank you."

"Moving on. What are you planning on wearing tonight?"

"Umm... This." Tanya untied her trench coat, revealing a rather plain knee-high black dress with the same color Mary Janes."

"Wait! You mean you *weren't* able to find anything more boring?!" Sylvia found other people's limitations very amusing "Have they finally opened a Mediocre department at Bloomingdales?"

"It's easy for you to say. Not everyone can afford your lifestyle choices. What's wrong with it? It's simple, neat and classy," Tanya tried explaining.

"An ideal choice for jury duty. But you're going to a benefit gala at The Pierre. Some might say there's a slight difference," her friend pointed out sarcastically.

"It's the best I can do on my budget."

"I had a feeling this might happen. Let's go in the bedroom; there might be something in there for you," Sylvia said as she ushered her towards the door.

"No more charity, Silvie!" Tanya cried out.

"It's not charity if the clothes don't fit me anymore. You're actually doing *me* a favor, taking them off my hands."

"This would be more convincing if everything you gave me wasn't my size *and* brand new."

"Sizes vary sometimes, you know. Besides, why return something I got a great deal on if I know you'll love it?"

"It's just too much, Silvie," Tanya said, shaking her head.

"We're friends, aren't we? These kinds of things shouldn't matter."

"I know, but I just can't shake off the feeling I am taking advantage of you."

"Please! If someone is taking advantage of anyone it's me," Sylvia grinned, knowing her friend wouldn't understand the irony.

They walked in the bedroom, where a tight lacey dress was hung on the wardrobe door. A cashmere and mink cape was wrapped around it and underneath was a brand new pair of Manolo Blahnik's Embellished Satin Point Toe Pumps. Tanya stood in awe for several minutes before she actually summoned the courage to pick up one of the shoes and slide her palm over the flower-like adornment on the side of the silky pump.

"I take it that you like it." Sylvia was delighted with her friend's reaction.

"*Like*?! That would be an understatement," Tanya muttered in shock.

"Try it on. Then we can do your make-up."

As Tanya slid into the sleek dress, Sylvia couldn't help but notice her slender physique and feel resentful. *It's Murphy's Law, I guess* she thought with pity. *Good figures are often wasted on women with no sense of style or fashion.* She got up and helped her friend zip up the dress, fixed the lace on the sleeves and stepped back, examining her critically.

"Looks good. You're gonna turn a couple of heads tonight."

"It's amazing, and the fabric is like nothing I've tried before. But I have a feeling the neckline is a bit deep for me. Are you sure it's not tacky?"

"You're wearing Dior. Tacky is not a word I would use to describe any of their creations."

"You know what I mean. I'm just not used to being on display."

"It's not like you've got a lot to show in that department, so you're safe either way. But for your own peace of mind, the neckline is just right. The cut makes it work."

"You're right about that," Tanya giggled, holding up her breasts. "I just don't want to be perceived as a walking set of breasts and an ass. The bimbo thing is so not me."

"That's such a Sylvia Plath thing to say. Relax, there are no feminists around to applaud your inspirational statement. We can cut the crap."

"What do you mean?"

"You've picked up the corporate fever," Sylvia observed.

"The what?!"

"Women who've been on the corporate scene for too long wrongly assume male qualities and virtues, believing it will make their lives easier. And since we are chameleons by nature they quickly adapt to convince themselves they're fine with the new order of things. But the bottom line is all women want to be objectified," she explained indifferently.

"That's a rather bold statement."

"Nevertheless, it's true. Every hot vixen strutting her stuff on the catwalk and every zit-covered Krispy Kréme-stuffing Jane, Mary or Amber builds their sense of self-worth based on other people's perception of them. We always look at ourselves through the eyes of the people we surround ourselves with. There's no way to convince me that there's anyone out there who's fine with being disliked or made an outcast because of their looks."

"Naturally, but what does that have to do with women wanting to be objectified?"

"Being objectified means men find you sexy, desirable and irresistible. There's nothing more powerful than a woman's sexuality. Unfortunately, society constantly tries to make us repress it for all the wrong reasons until we're completely dissociated from our sexual life and start experiencing it as observers."

"Not sure I am following you."

"Do you enjoy sex? "

"Yes, of course, everyone does."

"Right. But do you fully lose yourself in the physical act of having sex? Do you manage to turn off your thoughts and become one giant string of emotions, playing a different tune under the touch of your partner's fingers?"

"That'd be a bit too easy, don't you think? Like anyone can do *that*!" Tanya gasped.

"What do you usually think about during? "

"I worry how my body looks in daylight, or nightlight for that matter; if he saw those few hairs I forgot to pluck; and you know that large mole I have on the side of my stomach. I hate how big it is!"

"Exactly. If you were objectified, meaning if you knew the man you were going to bed with was madly attracted to you and had to have you right away, wouldn't that give you that extra dose of reassurance to build enough confidence to *actually* enjoy yourself rather than dissect every second of the experience?"

"I suppose so. Still, it sounds ugly when you blurt it out like that."

"The truth is rarely pleasant to hear, but it does wonders for your other senses," Sylvia winked at her friend. "It's nearing seven and we've still to do your make-up. Put the shoes on and sit over there. I'll go get my stuff. I just bought this new concealer. It'll go great with your skin tone!"

She had just finished filling in Tanya's lips with a soft pink nuance and was applying a touch of glitter to her pale cheekbones when the bell rang. The two had chatted away the time and George, punctual as always, was waiting downstairs with the driver. Sylvia handed her friend a matching cashmere cape with a real fur straight trim and, noticing her grimace, shook her head with disapproval.

"We're going to a place where first impressions are everything. It's really not the time to be prudish."

"I know. It's just, does it have to be *real* fur?"

"Imitations are for people with no money or taste."

"I do fall in the first category."

"If you move in the right circles and act the part I'm hoping we can change that. Don't tell me you want to spend your entire life groveling before someone 9-to-5, living from paycheck to paycheck."

"No. But I have high hopes for the next Senior Editor position that'll open in mid-June. I've been working my ass off on this manuscript and I think it's being noticed."

"You've *got* to stop deluding yourself. The only way to make it to the top is to sleep your way to it. The sooner you make your peace with it the better."

"Sylvie! Ewww! Mr. Lam is eighty-one. I doubt sleeping with him is the way to go. Besides, I'm sure he's got more important things on his mind."

"He's got a dick, which effectively means that he doesn't. And I didn't mean the sleeping had to happen at the office per se. You find yourself a nice fellow and play the part of the educated, philanthropic Stepford wife."

"Being submissive and docile may be your thing, but I'd much rather live modestly and make my own choices."

"You're confusing the two. Leaving a man to think he's in charge has nothing to do with you not making your own choices. You know what I say. What he doesn't know, doesn't count," Sylvia laughed as she locked the door behind her.

"And how do you let him think that?"

"Getting what you want from a man is the easiest thing in the world. All you have to do is convince him he's the best you can do and you're aware of that. Men need to feel appreciated even more than women. The easiest way to drive a man away is to show disapproval or dissatisfaction. Gaze at him adoringly, praise every single bullshit thing he does and let him think he's the centre of your universe. Women can do anything they want, but it's so much more fun when a man's paying for it. And if the price is to bat your eyelashes and constantly tell him how great he is in return? I'd say we got a pretty good deal."

Robert, George's personal driver, was standing next to the limousine as they stepped out of the building and opened the rear car door when they approached. Sylvia turned to him, displeased.

"Mr. Huntington isn't here?"

"Sincere apologies, Ms. Watson, but Mr. Huntington is already at the benefit. Unexpected events required his presence there. He personally instructed me to pick you up and drop you off at The Pierre, where he will be waiting for you."

"Thank you, Robert."

"Please Miss, allow me." He helped them into the car.

The drive was quick and enjoyable. This time of the night the city entered into a new phase of its vibrant cycle, one of dazzling lights, rushing cabs and dressed up people in search of new sensations. Sylvia enjoyed observing the New York rhythm of life around her – it was a whirlwind sensation that made her feel like she belonged.

The car stopped in front of the hotel entrance on 61st St and the porter rushed to open the door, escorting the two ladies inside. Apparently, Robert had contacted George at some point during the drive because there he was, standing in the lobby, all smiles, looking his usual elegant self. He greeted both of them with gentle pecks on their hands, something Tanya found old-fashioned and pretentious, but Sylvia loved because she had come to understand he sincerely enjoyed these small gestures and used them without ulterior motives.

"Good evening, ladies. May I say you look awe-inspiringly breath-taking?"

"Thank you. George, I finally have the pleasure to introduce you to my very close friend Tanya Stonick."

"The pleasure is all mine, Miss Stonick. As I plan on being a large part of Sylvia's life I sincerely hope you will take a liking to me."

"Give it a minute or two and you'll love him, trust me," Sylvia smiled.

"I've got to admit you're a very charismatic man, Mr. Huntington. Especially after the many, many wonderful things Sylvie has told me about you."

"I'm sure she's exaggerating. She is biased, after all," he laughed. "Call me George, please. Mr. Huntington is my father. This way if you please, ladies."

He led them into the Garden Foyer, at the entrance of which another hotel employee took attendance of the guests crowding around him. George skillfully guided them through the mass of people with just a nod of his head to the attendant. They made their way towards the Grand Ballroom, where the benefit was held.

Tanya had fallen slightly behind as George had wrapped his arm around Sylvia upon entering the Garden Foyer, but she tried keeping up while looking around in disbelief and awe. Although Sylvia had done a great job to dress her up for the occasion, she still felt like she didn't belong anywhere within a 100-mile radius of this place and the people present. The people… They were even more enchanting than the hand-painted mural and lavish decorations. She saw women with jewelry that could make the Queen of England scowl with envy and the men were the epitome of timeless class and elegance. Even more striking, however, was their effortless demeanor as if though gliding through a ball room in a 5-star hotel, filled with their exquisitely-dressed peers while sipping Moet and snacking on hors d'oeuvres with beluga caviar and Jamón Ibérico, was just another Sunday night. As she skipped behind her friend, trying not to get lost in the sea of disorienting sights and sounds, she caught the approving smile of a tall handsome man, who raised his glass in a polite greeting. Tanya barely smiled in response and turned away, blushing. *He wouldn't be so interested if he knew I spend all of my days and most of my weekends buried under piles of manuscripts just to make it to the next sale at Macy's,* she thought. She marveled at the way Sylvia fit so naturally in this snobbish surrounding of people who thought, no, who were certain they were better than everyone else, and she wished some of her friend's confidence would rub off on her, even if only for a night. *Sylvie's right. I have every day of the rest of my life to be my usual boring self; this night I can be someone else for a change, someone who can appreciate the finer things in life,* she reassured herself.

Walking next to George, Sylvia noticed the interest people took in her as they made their way through the room. For the first time in her life she felt like she was receiving the level of attention she deserved and she enjoyed every second of it. Her simple and polished outfit contrasted with the dramatic ball gowns the majority of the women wore, but that served to her advantage as it made her seem all the more right for George. Everything about them – from the effortless elegance of their wardrobe to the subtle body language – made it evident they were an item. She could feel women scanning her from head to toe with the ill-disguised what-does-she-have-that-I-don't stare, and men sliding their eyes down her curves with a perverse and approving smirk. It came as a surprise to her that everything about this event felt so natural. *I've arrived,* she thought, as she looked around triumphantly. George guided her towards the middle of the room to a group of people around the mayor. Sylvia had never been interested in politics, other than viewing men involved in it as some of the most reliable providers; this was the reason behind glancing at newspapers every now and then just to be able to put names to the faces of people in the circles she was hoping of getting into. She immediately recognized the Governor of New York Matt Peterson, Democratic Congressman Roe Vallone, his son Democratic Council Speaker Vallone, Jr. and former New York State Attorney General John Talcott. *All those months of cramming politicians' names and positions finally pay off,* she noted as they approached the group. The men stopped talking and turned to George.

"Former, current and, hopefully, future mayor of New York David Hellman, this is Sylvia Vassilena Watson, daughter of Frank Elmore Watson, mayor of Fargo."

"Pleased to meet you. You've landed yourself quite a catch, young lady," The mayor smiled warmly as he briefly held her hand.

"Thank you, sir. I happen to agree," Sylvia said candidly.

"And this lovely lady is her close friend Tanya Stonick, editor at Norton Publishing. "

"Pleasure."

"This fine gentleman is Governor Matt Peterson, one of our most active supporters. Next to him, father and son Roe Vallone, they're our voice in the Senate. And last, but not least, Attorney General John Talcott," George continued.

Everyone nodded at each other upon introduction without excessive courtesies, with Roe Vallone, Jr. remarking, "Daughter of the mayor of Fargo you say? Do you ever settle for anything less than the offspring of a politician?"

"Settling is for losers, Roe. And an inappropriate topic given that promising campaign results and upcoming elections are the reason for this gathering," George replied, prompting the rest of the men to laugh and nod in agreement.

"You look familiar. Didn't I see you at the Emerging Markets Investment summit hosted by Riverdale Bank?" he asked, indifferent to George's remark.

"Sylvia is Tim's personal assistant," George replied.

"No kidding," he studied her with interest. "Well, if Tim picked you for his personal assistant you must have *some* qualities. Is your father a Democrat or a Republican, *Miss* Watson?" Roe continued with a clear emphasis on the miss.

"Last time I checked, he was an outspoken Democrat."

"One of ours, then. All right, she's good." Roe's tone was considerably softer. He raised his glass in her direction, turned around and started chatting with the Attorney General.

"Don't pay attention to Roe. He's a bit direct, but once he gets to know you, you'll be charmed by his wit and intelligence," Hellman said, signaling to a waiter passing by with a tray of champagne. George took three and handed her and Tanya one each.

"So, tell me, beautiful young lady, what are your intentions with our George? He's one of my finest contributors; sometimes it seems he's single-handedly running this whole circus. You're not going to go and break his heart now, are you?" he asked, his question sounding more fatherly than rude and inappropriate.

"Wouldn't even think of it, sir." Sylvia gazed lovingly in George's eyes. "As for my intentions, I can only hope his are as serious as mine."

"I am sure they are. He's a man of fine caliber: just like his father."

"That's really good to hear."

"What about you, then. Can I count on your vote?" he asked jokingly.

"Of course, sir. Although I have to admit it will be the first time I will be voting since I moved to New York almost nine years ago."

"I see. Moving with the right crowd made you change your mind, did it?" The men laughed.

"Let's just say I've never been particularly interested in politics; it has always seemed a rather..." she paused, unsure. "Male field to meddle in."

"Smart girl," Hellman nodded approvingly, looking at George. "And what about your charming friend?" he turned to Tanya.

"I apologize, but I hardly have time to be interested in anything other than my job, sir."

"Well that's a shame. Especially for a young lady. You should spend this time of your life enjoying yourself, not slaving away. See?" he said, turning to the two men next to him. "This is a prime example of the screaming necessity for the policy of tax reduction and a viable social safety net we're trying to push. Anything so the life flow of this nation doesn't have to suffer the consequences of our overloaded financial system. Unfortunately, at this point all we can do is resolve as many issues as we can locally before there can even be talks about changes on a national level."

As Hellman went on about projections and campaign targets, with Vallone and Peterson listening intently and nodding along, George embraced Sylvia and led her and Tanya away to a group of Wall Street types, chatting on the other side of the room. She wasn't too surprised to spot Alex amongst them; nor did she feel uncomfortable that one of her most reliable fuck buddies was moving in the same social circles as her boyfriend. She had learnt these types of things had a way of sorting themselves out by not surfacing, since maintaining the *status quo* was beneficial for all parties involved. After all, Alex was accompanied by what seemed to be his girlfriend; an attractive, slender blonde who was all over him. *How typical*, she noted. *They always go for the opposite of what they have at home.*

Tanya, on the other hand, became visibly embarrassed when she recognized her friend's rendezvous, and tried appearing as nonchalant as possible. Noticing it, Sylvia smiled reassuringly at her. Alex had seen George making his way with his companions through the crowd and had already given Sylvia a slight conspiratorial nod. As they approached the group the men turned and greeted George with warm handshakes and pats on the back.

"Awesome turnout, man. How you manage to do it is beyond me!"

"Told you our boy could do it."

"Guess who I ran into? Mark! He's in town for a month or so. He's staying in East Hampton. He invited us over for the weekend. Me, Jeff and Alex are thinking of going. You in?"

George made an effort to break away from their circle and gently pulled Sylvia near him, shifting the focus towards his companions.

"Sylvia Watson, Tanya Stonick, can I introduce you to this very loud and overbearing group of hyenas, former classmates from Harvard and current colleagues of mine: Alex Renske, Kenneth Kaufenberg and Benjamin Levine, honorary Harvard alumni currently working for Paulson & Co., and their lovely better halves Jennifer Stano, Alessandra Ciarro and Eleana Margolies."

The men acknowledged the newcomers with a nod, but the women critically examined them from head to toe, and smiled benevolently only after spotting the designer clothing and staggering Bulgari jewelry. Alessandra stepped forward, and noticing the undisguised intimacy between Sylvia and George, gently embraced her arm, speaking with a charming Italian accent.

"I'm guessing this is the woman responsible for your frequent absences from the social scene, darling, no? She's marvelous. Muy bellissima!" Sylvia smiled at the remark.

"She's the one, Alessandra." George pulled his girlfriend back, holding her tightly. "Get used to seeing a lot of her, as she'll be my plus one from now on."

"How come you kept her hidden for so long, darling?" Jennifer raised her brow "Are you ashamed of her or something? Not that I see any reason you should be," she added in a low voice, turning to Eleana. "At first sight, that is."

"You're a tough crowd, my dear, and God knows I didn't want someone important to me subjected to your ruthless scrutiny. At least not before I made sure she had fallen head over heels for me and would gladly put up with your snotty selves." Everyone laughed at his comment and he continued, turning to Sylvia. "I can only hope my timing was right."

"It was. Perfect as always." She held his hand.

"And these two upstanding fellows helped me put the gathering together, my colleagues Paul Ronson and Jeremy Connor."

"Paul Ronson? You're the..." Tanya stuttered.

"Son of Chief Justice John Ronson. Yes." the man confirmed, pleased with her recognizing him. "And you are?"

"Tanya Stonick. It's a real pleasure to meet you. My thesis was on the impeachment trial against Andrew Johnson and Rehnquist over which your father presided."

"What field did you specialize in, Miss Stonick?"

"I have a Masters in Journalism and a Bachelors in Social Studies."

"Interesting combination. How did you convince your parents to fund it?" Everyone laughed at Jeremy's question.

"I... They didn't. I mean, they couldn't, so I had to work through college. I did win a couple of scholarships that covered a large part of my educational expenses though," Tanya explained, embarrassed.

"How awful!" Jennifer squealed "College is supposed to be a fun time. And don't tell us you *work* for a living too!" Everyone turned in anticipation towards her.

"Well, yes. I'm a Junior Editor at Norton Publishing."

"You're not one of those journalists that nose around particular social circles in search of some spicy story and then make one up when you fail to find one, are you?" Eleana asked, unnerved.

"That's not what an Editor does, I'm afraid. I just sit around, reviewing and revising manuscripts before they're handed in for publication."

"Norton Publishing, you say," Paul said, thoughtfully. "Donald is an old family friend. Any friend of George is a friend of ours, and we look after our own. Perhaps I'll be able to put in a good word for you and a promotion may be in line given your commitment to your job."

"Donald? You call Mr. Lam, Donald?" Tanya stammered in disbelief. Everyone laughed at her ignorance and simplicity.

"People usually call their friends by their first names, don't they?" Paul remarked, indifferently.

"Right. Thank you. I don't know what to say, Mr. Ronson. How can I ever repay you?"

"You can let me take you out to dinner. That should even things out," he said looking at his watch. Sylvia glanced at him. She knew his type. He was the one that was always after all new additions to the group, because he had already fucked everything in sight. However, she didn't feel compelled to warn her friend. *Tanya can use a good fucking. She's become way too uptight, and a dick is just the thing to unwind her,* she thought.

"Of course, that's the least I can do. Shall I give you my number? "

"Leave it with George. Now, if you'll excuse me Governor Koch just came. I must go over and say hello."

"It was really nice meeting you, Mr. Ronson."

"Enjoy your evening," he told them before walking away.

Tanya turned to Sylvia, glowing with excitement. *She's so bad at reading signals,* her friend observed with pity. *But she'll have to learn. We all do eventually. Those who don't perish in the world of dating. Darwin should've come up with a law for that.* She smiled warmly at her, overhearing Jennifer as she whispered loud enough to Eleana for Sylvia to hear, "Paul always goes for the mediocre ones". Sylvia wasn't surprised at Jennifer's reaction to their introduction to the group. It was a textbook example of a woman aware of her fiancé's infidelity, thus viewing everyone new as a potential threat. *In a way she has a point,* Sylvia thought. *But you have nothing to worry about, love. You can keep your precious investment banker. He's nothing more than an occasional time-filler,* and she pressed against George.

More people started pouring into the ballroom as the mayor prepared for his speech and George gently led Sylvia to the front of the crowd. As Hellman started with the typical pre-election promises, projections, milestones and figures, she looked around, scanning her new social circle. A tall, unattractive, but lavishly dressed woman caught her attention. Leaning over to George, she nodded in her direction.

"Is that…?"

"Anastasia Chapligina, yes. She's a close family friend. Do you want me to introduce you later?"

"Of course! She's made quite a name for herself. Who is she with?"

"Alina Zielinska. The daughter of the CEO of PNO, one of Poland's biggest oil concerns. They're close friends. Anastasia's voice is divine, but she has an even lovelier personality," he explained, directing his attention to the speech.

Sylvia gazed again at the blonde woman. *Naturally. She has to have a lovely personality. All ugly women do. Not that any man would jump at the chance to fuck a lovely personality. If given the choice, of course he'll pick the hot piece of ass.* She turned away and continued listening to Hellman's speech, vacantly. Upon its end the room broke into applause. Everyone seemed overly excited, so Sylvia tried to appear more interested. Politics bored the hell out of her, but it was a necessary evil she had to tolerate for a life in the spotlight of power. People were crowding around the mayor. George, excusing himself to her and Tanya, walked over to take part in accepting congratulations and encouragements. As everyone's attention was directed towards the understandable stars of the event, they could take their time to look more carefully at the people present. Tanya was over-the-top with excitement, turning her head in all directions like a child at Disneyland.

"I have to say, Silvie, at first I didn't think it was a good idea for me to come, but I'm glad you made me!"

"I'm happy to hear that."

"Can you believe someone like Paul is interested in me? Isn't he wonderful?"

"You might want to not get your hopes too high with that one, Tanya."

"Why?"

"He's the first guy to show interest in you and already you're picking out china patterns? Such a dumb female thing to do. Please don't be *that* girl."

"What girl?"

"The obsessive, cutting-her-wrists-when-he-doesn't-call type. It's a step down from where you're at now."

"I distinctly recall a certain someone doodling a Mrs. Sylvia Marshall on her notebooks in biology class."

"Right. In class. We're all allowed that awkward phase when we act against our better judgment. The point is to grow out of it, which you still haven't, apparently," Sylvia snarled at her friend. "By the way, there was no need to spoil a perfectly good evening by mentioning that guy."

"*That* guy?! That's a first for you," Tanya looked at her, amazed. "The closest you've come to expressing any dissatisfaction with James is an ambivalent disapproval of his *push and pull* technique."

"Things change."

"So I see. And for the better."

"We all choose what direction to move on in. The fact that some people mistake cycling for a direction is a whole other story."

She noticed Jennifer, Eleana and Alessandra approaching, so she said nothing more and slapped on her most charming smile. Even though it was dislike at first sight, Sylvia was excellent at sensing who the alpha female was, and she knew it was one of the driving forces in the female world not to be fought against. Her best bet was to try and make Jennifer aware that she wasn't a threat to her or anyone else's *status quo*, as she had an agenda of own. *Most women are aware the female friends of a man are either a deal-breaker or a deal-sealer, but few know there is virtually no way you can get on their good side. The only thing you can do is try not to rub them the wrong way and lay low, so you don't attract unnecessary attention,* she reminded herself as she observed Jennifer's snobbish and exceedingly confident demeanor.

"Having fun?" the charming blonde tweeted. "This is probably quite an event for you."

"This is quite an event for anybody." Sylvia replied indifferently.

"Yes, brilliant turnout. Still, your friend must not be used to moving in such crowds. Isn't this true?" she turned to Tanya.

"Yes, Miss Stano. I…"

"Jennifer, please. Since *our* George seems to be so smitten with your friend, this can only mean we're bound to see more of you, so we should get to know each other."

"How nice of you!" Tanya cried out, delighted. Sylvia observed with the corner of her eye as Jennifer smirked. *Thank God for Tanya's naivety to balance out the conversation. If she didn't have her head up her ass she could actually notice these women are like a pack of vultures, praying on the weak and helpless. But I guess she lacks the experience."*

"I must say," Jennifer continued, looking at Sylvia. "I love your outfit. Simple, yet classy. I could never get away with something like *that!* People always expect me to dress up to my stature. Being the daughter of a business magnate has its drawbacks." she added, sighing dramatically.

"Thank you for the compliment."

"Honest and concise without suffering from unnecessary modesty. I think we'll get along just fine." Jennifer looked at Eleana and Alessandra, pleased, and they nodded along. Then she turned again to Sylvia. "If you don't mind my asking, how long have you and George been going out?"

"A little over two months now."

"So I assume you've already slept together. He's great in bed, isn't he?" Jennifer teased, as Alessandra and Eleana giggled.

Sylvia stared at her with the stillness of a laboratory researcher, dissecting a rather peculiar subject. There was mild amusement mixed with curiosity in her eyes, but that was as close she got to showing any interest in the person in front of her. This was an obvious provocation and a moderately good one, one most women would never let slide. *Most stupid women that is,* Sylvia thought. People rarely got to her, at least not any more. One of the few things she was particularly grateful for picking up from James was learning to perceive other people as objects; as simple means to an end: hers. He was born that way and she came to learn how to do it, which gave her the benefit of being able to fake a connection with people. Because of the way he had dehumanized Sylvia in his obsessive need to drain everything from her for years, James had unintentionally let her in on the ultimate secret of thriving in life. As commonly happened, the student surpassed the teacher, as she achieved much better results that stemmed from her ability to fake genuine care about what others wanted and needed, while James' misanthropy got the better of him. So she stood there, face to face, with the pretty blonde, who was going out of her way to annoy her. But what Jennifer didn't and couldn't know was that to get to someone they had to first consider her their equal. As far as Sylvia was concerned, the two of them were light years apart. To her, Jennifer was the girl Sylvia used to be before she evolved. Sylvia didn't hate or pity her. Her existence was simply irrelevant.

"He's great at everything he does," was all she said in a calm and collected voice.

"I hope you're not offended," Jennifer continued picking at the topic, unsatisfied with the reaction she got. "There are no secrets in this group, and since you're going to be a part of it, we're just giving you a friendly head's up. We girlfriends should stick together, don't you agree?"

"Is there a reason I should be offended?"

"No. I…" she was getting more and more baffled. "Anyway, I'm glad we're on the same page. We couldn't be happier for you and George. You suit each other."

"Thank you."

Sylvia felt someone caressing her neck and, upon recognizing George's strong touch, she pressed her cheek against his palm lovingly. He moved to her side and smiled at the women.

"Ladies, I hope you won't mind if I whisk away my better half."

"Not at all, darling," Jennifer replied. "I was just telling her what a beautiful couple the two of you make."

"Thank you. I happen to think so too." He smiled, and gently led Sylvia away. Tanya looked around helplessly, and skipped after her friend like a puppy.

"Jennifer wasn't too rude, was she?" he asked suddenly. "We used to date briefly before she and Alex got together. Then again, a lot of the men I know have dated her, but she does maintain a certain sense of ownership, if you will, over everyone she's gone out with."

"There's no need to explain," Sylvia reassured him softly. "And no, she wasn't rude. A bit envious perhaps, but that's about the extent of it."

"That's a perfectly understandable reaction." He gave her hand a slight peck, and looked around, nodding to a waiter carrying a tray of champagne-filled glasses. He exchanged the empty ones she and Tanya were still holding. He picked one for himself as well, but Sylvia noticed he had barely touched the one he put back on the tray.

As he guided them through the vast assortment of hors d'oeuvres, two men approached and he directed his attention towards them.

"My father mentioned you'd be in town this week," he remarked to a tall, dark-haired man with sharp features. "I was wondering if you would come tonight."

"I wouldn't have missed it. I must say you're not wasting your time at all. Look at you in the company of *two* beautiful ladies. Will you introduce us?"

"Of course. Sylvia Watson, daughter of the Mayor of Fargo, Frank Elmore Watson and her friend Tanya Stonick; please meet Sarkis Abramovich and Ciril Prokofiev, old family friends, investors and philanthropists from Russia, currently splitting their lives between New York and Saint Petersburg."

"Daughter of the Mayor of Fargo? Not too shabby, even for you," Ciril remarked. "What about her friend?

"I am an Editor at Norton Publishing, Mr. Prokofiev." Tanya replied.

"Running the rat race? Cute." He turned away, uninterested. "Did you see who's here? The full set."

"Anastasia and Alina. Yes, I promised Sylvia I'd introduce her later."

"You'll have plenty of time to do it. Guess whose plane they flew in on," Sarkis pointed out.

"Both of them? You're working hard or hardly working?" George turned to Ciril and he smirked.

"You know Ciril, always after the next big thing on the entertainment scene, at least till the tabloids have gathered sufficient evidence of him with his new toy. Sadly, Alina is proving more than he can handle," Sarkis remarked. "Even for someone used to chasing after these spoiled prodigies."

"Take it from me, my friend. Never go out with a woman who's used to having everything handed to her on a diamond platter. Nothing you ever do is good enough. But on the upside, they're insanely depraved and perverse," Ciril added.

"Why am I not surprised? You can't really expect anything other than wham-bam-thank-you-ma'am from this one. You know what they say about Polish women. They can't stay faithful even in a convent," Sarkis pointed out.

"Thank you for the advice, but personally I won't be trying it out. I've found a woman I'm perfectly happy with, and I plan on keeping it that way," George said, pulling Sylvia near him.

"Yeah, well, good luck with that. Because with women you never know," Ciril noted, indifferently.

"Enjoy your dinner and we'll see you next weekend. I promised your father we'd stop by to discuss the deal," Sarkis added.

"Great. I'll see you then."

"Ladies," Sarkis nodded politely. Ciril was scanning the room for Alina. He saw her getting too intimate with a business associate of his, so he pulled Sarkis and hurried in their direction. As the two men walked away Sylvia turned to George.

ALICE WALSH

"Who were those men? Investors and philanthropists is too generic."

"Sarkis is in the oil and gas industry. He recently purchased the majority stake in Russneft and Base Petroleum's joint venture; right now he's pushing for a joint exploration deal with Exxelon."

"Your family are shareholders, am I right?"

"Yes."

"And Ciril?"

"Textbook example of the offspring of a Russian oligarch. His grandfather sits on the board, and his father is CEO of Yuzhny Nickel. Ciril was put in charge of the company they spun off after purchasing gold mining assets, Poly Gold."

"You have very powerful friends."

"You should always surround yourself with people of your own caliber. People higher than you in the social chain will never treat you with the respect you deserve because they'll deem you unworthy of it. Ironically, people lower than you will do the exact same thing for the exact same reason."

"That's an interesting way of putting things. You are talking about friends, right?"

"Friends, acquaintances."

"Does the same go for the partners we choose?"

"It depends. Men should always aim for women who are, ideally, higher in the social chain because women like to be conquered, earned if you will. Women, on the other hand, should go for men who are lower, or, at least, equal to them because the last thing a woman wants is for the man to feel too comfortable around her. Your partner should feel safe enough with you to want to build a life together and just restless enough to know a better suitor can come along at any moment, thus motivating him to win you over again and again."

"'So, you're basically saying that women need to work men every chance they get."

"In a way, yes."

"Doesn't that bother you?"

"No, I am comfortable enough with my masculinity to know what I'm worth as a provider and a partner to be able to deal with the female manipulations. Besides," George smiled. "They bring color into our lives."

"Can I ask you something?"

"Anything, princess."

"I noticed you put back several glasses that were barely touched, yet you keep accepting refills. If you don't want to drink why don't you just walk around with a half-full glass and decline the offers?"

"Good question. I don't mind drinking, but I do it in the comfort of my own house. Social occasions are not the place you want to wobble around, which is bound to happen if you accept 'every refill in keeping with the social etiquette. Having said that, it's not something I want people to know, for two reasons. First, it's rude to decline offers for a refill, and second, you want people to trust you. Ironically, walking around with a glass of alcohol creates an instant invisible bond since they're drinking as well. Makes them lower their defenses and loosen up. It's when people loosen up and start talking that you make money."

"That's very smart."

"Thank you. I like that you make me feel comfortable enough to share these things with you. Personally, I think a solid, honest foundation makes for the strongest relationships."

"I couldn't agree more."

Great. Another defender of the way of the truth, Sylvia winced. *Such a cliché. Men always lie their ass off to build a relationship, but demand truth afterwards. It's time they adopted our approach to things. Lie throughout the relationship, and disregard truth always. What good does it do? Does it buy me the new Chopard? A trip to Saint Bart's? What use to do I have for it then? At least with the honest ones you don't have to worry about protection as much, or unknown thrushes and emergency gynecological trips.* She smiled at him.

"Are you finished? If you're still hungry we can arrange for something more substantial before we head home."

"No, everything was wonderful, George, but I think I am ready to go now." she said slowly and deliberately, pressing against him with her most enticing smile.

"Perfect. If you'll excuse me I have to say quick goodbyes to a couple of people. I don't think they have much use of me here for the rest of the evening." He turned to Tanya. "When you're ready to leave, my driver will be waiting downstairs to drop you off at your place, Miss Stonick. Just let him know the address."

"That's incredibly nice of you, Mr. Huntington! I hope it's not too much trouble. I can take a cab," Tanya stuttered.

"Please. This is not an option. I came to the hotel in my personal car, so Sylvia and I will be driving home in it. I'd be more than happy if you take the other one."

"Thank you so much. If you and Silvia are leaving now I prefer to go as well," she said, gratefully.

"I will let Robert know then. Thank you for your company tonight. I hope you enjoyed yourself. I know some of the people from my circle can be a bit difficult to deal with."

"Not at all, Mr. Huntington! It was a real delight. And I have you and Silvie to thank for it. I never would have had the opportunity to be part of such an exquisite event if it weren't for you."

"Glad to hear it. Have a lovely evening."

"Thank you. You too."

He walked away and Sylvia turned to her excited friend.

"Someone looks happy," she observed.

"Are you kidding? Maybe you're used to all of this, but for me it was like going to the premiere *and* getting into the after party!"

"That's a nice way of putting it," Sylvia laughed. "By the way, you can keep the clothes."

"Are you serious?"

"You know what I like about you, Tanya?"

"I don't think that you've told me."

"There are no lies about you. You let your emotions shine through so much. It's endearing in an almost childlike manner.

It reminds me of what I used to be like, what we all used to be like at some point in time, before…"

"Before?"

"Before life happened."

"So basically I haven't learnt my lessons yet?" Tanya chuckled.

"I'm afraid not, but I hope to God you never do. If it happens the world will have gained one more recruit to the endless line of disappointed, pragmatic cynics."

George approached Sylvia from behind and gently touched her arm to let her know he was ready. As the three made their way across the room towards the exit he nodded to a lot of people and exchanged brief goodbyes with several of them. Robert was waiting in the lobby and hurried ahead to open the door for them. Sylvia hugged her friend and Tanya got in the car with the driver closing the door after her.

Sylvia looked around, curious.

"What are we leaving in?"

"This," George said, unlocking the silver Rolls-Royce Phantom parked next to them. "Allow me." He reached and opened the door for her.

"Thank you. I'm impressed," she remarked, getting in.

"Nothing but the best, princess. Get used to it."

"You know what? I already have," Sylvia said out loud, looking at him in the mirror as he was going round the car to get in the driver's seat.

They slowly drove down 5th Avenue.

"What did you think?" he suddenly asked.

"Impressive turnout. Tanya was over the top when she spotted several Pulitzer winners and the owner of one of the biggest publishing houses in New York."

"That's good to hear, but I am not really interested in your friend's impression of the event. I understand the complicated relationship you have, but I was asking about your opinion."

"What do you mean by complicated relationship?" Sylvia stopped staring vacantly through the window and looked at him with interest.

ALICE WALSH

"You know. Do I need to spell it out for you?" He briefly gazed over at her and laughed. "She's your obvious personal charity case. We've all been there. These friendships are quite typical for our social circles actually. Someone with the resources and opportunities with a less fortunate friend, tries their best to make up for things they're not responsible for by taking it upon themselves to help out said person. I am not saying it's not commendable, but in time you'll realise it's unnecessary and pointless. All you're doing with your gifts and pampering is reminding her of what you have and what she'll never be able to afford."

"I don't think she's like that," Sylvia objected. "Tanya's very loyal, and very grateful. She's happy with everything that's thrown to her."

"I noticed. Like Paul's marked indifference at getting her into bed."

"She's bad at reading signals, that's all."

"And it's neither your fault nor your responsibility to guide her through life."

"It's my way of thanking her for having always been there; for never criticizing. Sometimes I feel I'm the one using her. She's my last point of contact with the real world. I feel I need to keep holding onto it before I surround myself with stuck-up snobs and their snooty girlfriends."

"It's ironic you should say this, considering you want to be part of that world," George remarked without looking at her. "And no matter how much you're clutching onto your friend, she'll never be able to give you what you're looking for, since it's all just a pose. You're not looking for an actual contact with the real world. If you were, you'd be out in it, living like all 9-to-5 middle-class underachievers. But you're not. All your life you've consciously moved towards this very moment, towards a sort of initiation, if you will, into the social circle you've longed for, one that being born into a life of luxury and politics made possible for you to get into. "

"Your point being?"

"My point being that regardless of how many needs you think this friendship fulfills, it fails to meet a lot more. You're from different worlds, and that's never going to change. You wouldn't want it to change. People may not tell you how they feel about you, but they always show you. Pay attention."

"That doesn't mean we can't be friends."

"Of course it does." He looked at her, surprised. "Friendship presupposes you're of equal stature. Intellectually, socially, financially even."

"So what is this *thing* then?" Her interest in the conversation was growing by the minute.

"If you don't mind me saying, socially successful women having underachieving girlfriends who look up to them. It's the female equivalent of a man going to a hooker. You pay for something you should be getting for free, from someone of similar, if not equal, stature. You're not keen on your normal circle of friends finding out, and you do it to satisfy urges whose satisfaction you can go perfectly well without."

"I see."

"Don't get me wrong. I am not advocating you shouldn't see your *friend*. All I am saying is that soon you'll outgrow that *need* you're talking about," he reassured her.

"Because I have you?" Sylvia turned to him.

"Yes," he confirmed in a serious tone of voice. "Because you have me. And all loose ends must be tied. It's going to be you and me against the world from now on, and I need you as a co-pilot, not as part of the cargo. Being overly nice and compassionate towards childhood friends is cute when you're on your own and have too much time on your hands. But when you decide to join together with another person it becomes a liability."

Sylvia had her eyes fixed on him as he explained. *Funny, this sounds like something James would say,* she thought.

"I understand, George. The last thing I want is for you to think of me as a liability."

"I don't. I consider you an asset. Just don't prove me wrong."

The car turned down East 91st Street and stopped in front of a tall building on the corner of Madison Avenue. A

ALICE WALSH

doorman immediately approached them as George turned off the car.

"The conversation became way too somber for what I had hoped this night would be," he looked at her. "But I prefer to get some things out of the way early on, so you know what to expect, so you can decide if you're interested or not."

"That seems fair."

"I think you're special, Sylvia. I want you to know this before we go any further."

"I am happy you feel that way, George. I think you're wonderful too." She reached out and laid her hand on top of his.

"Let's go upstairs."

The doorman was standing next to the car, and as George made a gesture, he opened the passenger door and helped Sylvia out of the vehicle. George walked around it and handed him the keys. Then he walked over to Sylvia and escorted her inside the building.

The 11th-floor, corner apartment was spacious, decorated with exceptional taste in a minimalistic approach. Wood and leather mixed in a natural and effective way to blend into a modern interior with a timeless class. An original brick wall in the living room and a fireplace gave it a warm feel. Several large windows uncovered a staggering view over the Reservoir. Sylvia looked around, amazed, as George locked the door and adjusted the lights to a much softer glow.

"Do you like it?"

"Is it yours?"

"Yes. My family owns three apartments in Manhattan; one on the Upper West Side, one in the Flatiron district and this one, which I turned into my bachelor pad."

"Not too shabby for a bachelor pad," she remarked, not hiding her excitement. "Did you decorate it yourself?"

"No. I have a friend who's an interior designer. She did most of the work, but I oversaw the process. I think it's important to proactively participate in every aspect of the construction of your life, both physically and mentally."

"You have excellent taste!"

"I know. I picked you, didn't I?" George glanced at her. "Shall I play some music?"

"Please. I'm curious to hear what you listen to."

"I'd be surprised if you recognized it," he smiled. "It's a bit unorthodox, to say the least. Not a lot of people have heard it."

"Let's see if it was meant to be," she teased him.

He pushed a couple of buttons on the panel of the sound system and the smooth blend of melodic jazz filled the apartment. Sylvia looked around.

"Where are the stereo speakers?"

"They're built in. Would you like a drink?"

"Sure. What are you having?"

"Macallan. Neat."

"Make it two."

"Well? Sound familiar?"

She looked at him with a smirk. *Finally, some other use for James' tiresome presence in my life. Who knew all those years of listening to his boring rants about genres, artists and what not would pay off?*" He walked over to the cabinet, opened the built-in bar with the push of a button and started pouring the drinks.

"I have to say," she began, as he handed her the glass, "your excellent taste in everything continues to surprise me. I don't know anyone else who listens to that album by Frank Sinatra and Carlos Jobim. Unorthodox, yes, but I have to agree with you that his voice is beautifully complemented by Jobim's harmonic playing."

"You're the first woman to recognize the artists." He stopped and stared at her with interest. "Not that I have played it to that many women," he added quickly. *Smart move,* she noted. "I hope you don't mind my asking, but this isn't normally something women are familiar with. How do you know it?"

"My father has a close friend who's a jazz musician. Guitar players are a strange breed. They spend their entire lives obsessing over different techniques and what not, convinced everyone else is just as passionate about that stuff. So I spent most of my adolescence being force-fed the genres, sub-genres, artists, playing techniques, guitar models and so on," Sylvia explained without so much as batting an eyelash.

"Was this friend anyone famous?"

"Not really. He was just your typical mediocre musician convinced in his excellent and never-before-seen talent and technique, always anticipating the big break just around the corner."

"Did it ever come?"

"Of course not. I'm describing a real-life story, not the ending to a Disney movie. Funny thing though; last time I heard of him he was still sure that fame and fortune awaited."

"Delusion and denial are the most powerful catalysts in people's lives," George remarked.

She walked over and stood next to him as he looked outside the window. He had finished his drink, but she had barely touched hers. Surprising even to herself, Sylvia sensed she was nervous. As safe as George made her feel there was the added pressure of the stakes being too high. *Dating someone you don't care about is much easier,* she thought, discreetly observing his handsome profile. *You can't be bothered whether they come or go; if they find you good in bed…it's always about you. Why does it always have to get messy when feelings are involved? Fuck! Did I just use the word "feelings"? Great job, Sylvia. You're in deep shit now.* The sudden realization startled her, and she looked around helplessly. George noticed her confusion and gently embraced her, taking the full glass from her hand. He put both glasses on the counter and gazed into her eyes for what seemed like an awful long time. An almost undistinguishable smile lit up his face as he caressed her cheek.

"Let's go to the bedroom," he finally said. Sylvia nodded passively. It was the first time he was bossy with her, which caught her completely off guard since she had become accustomed to him asking rather than telling her what to do.

As he led her through the narrow corridor she held tightly onto his hand, fearing she would lose her way if she let go.

Closing her eyes, she wished some of his sense of confidence would rub off on her. The bedroom was unusually homey for a bachelor's apartment, with the same brick wall as an accent and a low king size bed, which took up most of it. There was nothing more than the bare necessities to make this room as useful as it should be and the same minimalistic approach throughout the whole place shined through in the clever utilization of the available space. With a sense of relief she felt like she belonged.

George stopped at the bottom of the bed, turned around and faced her. His gentle caress of her face ended with a firm grasp of her chin as he locked her lips in a deep and permeating kiss. Sylvia responded passively, carefully simulating inexperience and shyness. *Tonight I have to give the performance of a lifetime if I am to stay in the game*, she thought, concentrating on her body language as he pulled her closer. Stepping out of her six-inch heels, she was embarrassed to discover her head could barely reach his shoulders, but George found her minute size endearing and embraced her protectively. His smile was contagious and they both burst out in laughter, which immediately lightened the mood. Sylvia tiptoed and nuzzled in his neck as he unzipped her dress and pulled it down. Normally she would have undressed him completely by now, but she had a sense he was one of those men who preferred to do it at their own pace as it made them feel in control. So she stood in front of him, watching as he untied his tie and unbuttoned his shirt.

He sat on the edge of the bed and pulled her towards him, kissing her stomach while his hand firmly pressed the lower part of her back. He slowly worked his way up and undid the bra, slipping it off her shoulders; then started caressing and kissing her breasts. Sylvia tried to pay attention and be present as much as possible, but it felt too surreal. She caught herself staring at her own reflection in the glassy wardrobe door, examining her figure and concentrating on the imperfections, which looked magnified at the subtle light. *I guess this is what Tanya meant*, she sighed. *Why do we have to complicate our lives?* As if sensing her nervousness, George stopped sliding his hands up and down her body and looked her in the eyes. Slipping off her panties, he didn't take his eyes off her face. He pulled back and lay on the bed, drawing her on top of him. As he kissed her neck, holding her head with his right hand, he started rubbing her clit with the other one. Sylvia let out a restrained, but sensual moan and pressed her palm against his stomach. Rolling over to the side, he covered her with his body and pinned her down to the bed. She was pleasantly surprised by his clear demonstration of desire to dominate in a way that didn't hurt or overwhelm her. She couldn't help but compare his technique to James'. *So there is a way to dominate without humiliating your partner,* she thought bitterly *I'm sure James would be just as surprised to find out. Although I guess it requires a pretty high level of confidence in one's masculinity and sense of self-worth - two concepts lost on him,* she concluded.

Slowly she began focusing on the present moment and disconnected from her mind. George's presence made her feel safe, and Sylvia started giving in to his influence. Her submissive nature responded in the most natural way, by looking for ways to please him. Being particularly orally fixated, Sylvia would have otherwise expected her partner to go down on her as part of the foreplay, but she sensed it was too forward for something this intimate on their first night together. However, she did take note of the fact that he wasn't quick to shove his penis down her throat as most men were so fond of. *Courtesy of the fact we're a generation raised by porn,* she thought. George was either capable of respecting the boundaries of normal sexual conduct or was incredibly adept at controlling his urges. Knowing the male nature, Sylvia was more inclined to believe it was the latter. *It's always something with them. Especially the strong silent types. Well, we'll just have to wait for it to surface. Let's just hope to God it's not some sick shit due to unresolved mommy issues.* If there was one thing she detested in men it was how much they were susceptible to outside influences. That was particularly noticeable in James. *He just has to try every single fucking thing he's seen in porn. What does he care that women in those movies do that kind of stuff for a living and it's unreasonable to expect your partner to live up to such downright outrageous standards? If it's a hole, force it in; it's bound to get in eventually. That's his philosophy on everything. Life included.*

Interestingly enough, reminiscing unconsciously about her sex life with James had made her unbelievably wet, which George noticed with delight. He made no attempt to stop for a condom, but she didn't object. Getting pregnant was something she had started contemplating since turning twenty seven a few years ago and having inadvertently learnt most of her high school classmates were married with children. Sylvia was never one to fight against her biological clock, but she had tried her best to postpone all life-altering decisions until absolutely sure she had found the best provider of financial and social comfort as well as genetic material. In George she saw all of that and much more. His disregard for protection didn't bother her for another reason as well. Being a passionate advocate for experiencing the full spectrum of sexual sensations, Sylvia was never one to insist on using a condom. Contraceptive pills made her weight fluctuate and diaphragms were uncomfortable to insert. She preferred practicing safe selection of partners instead.

George penetrated her in a brusque and deep manner, which made her let out a moan as she clenched his back. Pulling her hair, he exposed her neck and started fucking her far rougher than she had anticipated. Every now and then he kissed her briefly. It was the perfect amount of dominance with just a hint of tenderness and no humiliation whatsoever; her submissive nature was thriving. She wrapped her hands around his waist, guiding his thrusts to increase the frequency and lifted herself on her elbows. Sylvia was one of those women who had grown into their sexuality from the exposure to too many things over a short period of time, but this had actually made her comfortable enough with her own body. Sex without an orgasm was something she never tolerated, especially since she knew how to get hers.

Noticing she was getting closer, George pressed his lips to her ear and whispered "You're gorgeous," as he picked up the pace so they could finish together. Sylvia tilted her head back, her eyes dim with delight. Normally, she was a big fan of dirty words and loud vocal effects in the bedroom, but in the given situation the well-timed compliment also hit the spot. Even in the haze of the pre-orgasmic bliss she couldn't help but think of James' talent to talk dirty, which drove her crazy. *Too bad lately he started overdoing it, like everything else,* she noted with regret. *It's like he's borrowing lines from a bad porno.* Seconds before she came, one last conscious thought entered her mind. *How fucking great is this? We're a perfect match in the bedroom too!* She felt George climaxing inside her and she held him even tighter with her legs, so he wouldn't pull away. She loved the sense of power that knowing she was fully in control at his most vulnerable moment gave her. "It's fun to keep him guessing." she liked to say, enjoying the way she could wind men around her finger later on, once the guilt and fear from the cold realization of the severity of the possible repercussions from a night of fun would start to dawn on them. Most of the men she slept with demanded pregnancy tests be taken, some like James even went to the extent of doing it on a regular basis and she always assured them she had done so. She never did though. Sylvia was one of those women who knew their body well enough to be able to tell with 100% accuracy if she was pregnant or not. In the rare occurrences when she was late she didn't freak out as she just knew it was not yet her time to have a baby. And while most doctors would find her reasoning downright laughable and ridiculous, her intuition had never failed her since she had started having sex thirteen years ago.

George pulled away from her and rolled on his back, but his silence wasn't awkward or cold. He turned to the night table, pulled out an ashtray and lit a cigarette. She scowled as he put back the lighter and let out a puff of smoke. *One thing I'll have to re-educate him on. Disgusting habit!* she thought, as she smiled at him.

"If it bothers you I can put it out," he said.

"Not at all," she replied encouragingly. *Don't jump on the criticism train just yet!* she reminded herself.

They lay there, holding hands in silence. Both seemed comfortable and happy with each other's presence and the way the night had gone. He put out his cigarette and stood up.

"I'll take a shower. Do you want to join me?"

"I don't have a towel."

"Will a robe do?"

"Do you have a spare one I could borrow?"

"Not a spare one. Your very own," he corrected her, walked over to the built-in closet and came back with a brand new crimson Versace robe. "A little gift to welcome you to my place."

"It's beautiful. Thank you. Was I supposed to get you something?"

"Next time. When we spend the night at your place," he smiled at her. "Shall we?"

He opened another door that led to a spacious bathroom with a bathtub and a separate shower. Sylvia hung the robe on the rack without even putting it on and, walking by the wall mirror, pausing briefly to look at herself. She was delighted to realise her confidence had returned and she didn't feel self-conscious as she had just minutes ago. George observed her lack of inhibition with approval as he was adjusting the water.

"I love how comfortable you are around me."

"So you don't think I'm too full of myself?"

"Why would I think that?"

"I've been told so before."

"By people with particularly low self-esteem I would imagine. Even if you are, and you are within completely reasonably amounts if you ask me, it's a positive thing. No one is going to build up your confidence for you."

She turned towards him and he caressed her hair. "So I take it you find me attractive then?"

"You have no idea, princess. And part of your charm is the strong sense of self-worth you exhibit. It's sexy," George replied as he reached and pulled her under the stream. He pushed her against the wall and began kissing her insatiably. The second time around was, surprisingly, not a quickie as she expected. Most men she had been with, despite their desire and best of intentions, couldn't make it past a couple of minutes after having just finished round one, but George took his time to get her going. He slid his hand between her legs and started rubbing and fingering her intensely since he had noticed she liked it when he got straight to the point. She leaned back on the cold wall, arching her back at the touch of the cold tiles to her skin. Reaching out, she pulled him closer, showing she was ready for him to start using more than just his fingers. He held her hands above her head with his right hand as he used his left one to lift one of her legs and pin it to the wall as he entered her. The water ran down their faces, leaving them out of breath as he didn't stop kissing her even for a moment. She came first and briefly afterwards he followed, resting his head on her hair.

When they finished showering George stepped out first, took the robe off the rack and wrapped it lovingly around her. Sylvia huddled up in it and gave him a peck on the lips as she walked past him on the way to the bedroom. The doorman had already brought up her bag and George left her to get dressed as he slipped out on the balcony for a smoke. She stared intently at the three nighties she had packed, but neither seemed sexy enough for a first night stay, so she decided on sleeping in her lingerie instead. Peeking behind the curtain, she strategically waited for him to finish his cigarette and started dressing after he came back into the room, taking her time. With the corner of her eye she could see him following her every move and was careful to stand, making the best out of the lighting. When she was ready she shook her head, running a hand through her curls and nuzzled against him in the giant bed. George wrapped his arm around her.

"I still can't believe how many days off Mr Foster has been letting me get away with lately. I don't have to go in until the middle of the week," she remarked.

"Tim can be quite lenient," George replied. "Let's just say you'll be looking at many more to come. Now that you have more critical duties to attend to."

"Such as?" Sylvia looked at him expectantly.

"Such as being the significant other of a very powerful man," George replied briefly. He then kissed her gently on the forehead, turned off the light and wished her good night.

Sylvia lay in the dark for a while, still deeply impressed by all the events of the night, until she had to calm herself to be able to fall asleep. *Tanya's childish enthusiasm is contagious*, she thought. *It was just another night – one of many to come – in a place and amongst people to whom I belong. Good girls get what they want, don't they? And I've been good... enough.*

She was quickly getting used to the pace of the new lifestyle she had adopted; lunches with George's business associates, late night drinks with his Harvard school mates, romantic dinners at expensive restaurants and sex. Lots of sex. As George had promised her, Tim found fewer and fewer reasons to call her into the office, going as far as hiring a second assistant to fill in for her working obligations. Sylvia was formally in charge of training the new girl, but had so much going on she couldn't be bothered with any of it. Surprisingly, even to her, none of her actions, or lack thereof, resulted in the disruption of the regular flow of a salary to her bank account. She had all the time on her hands to truly start living it up; although with George's constant attendance of events in connection to the mayoral campaign as well as the maintenance of his high-class friendships and acquaintances, Sylvia found herself working twice as hard on her appearance. Her days were filled with hair-salon appointments, spa treatments and shopping. She had never felt more fulfilled in her life.

One by one her old lovers started falling out of her life, partly due to lack of time, but largely because George was meeting all of her needs, inside and outside of the bedroom. However, every now and then, when she found herself with time to idle, Sylvia continued to entertain her old habits. She stopped picking up new men, but maintained several of her most reliable fuck buddies including James and Stephen. Her sexuality had gotten used to a rhythm of its own and juggling several guys at the same time had been the norm for years. The ego boost this offered was another thing she wasn't willing to give up just yet. *Men are so predictable.* She grinned in the mirror while getting ready for a late night visit to James' apartment. *They always sense when you start slipping away from their league and it's right then that their desire for you morphs into a sick craving.* She knew he was trying to nail some twenty-something college chick and she was sincerely amused by his rants about how cute and special he found her to be. The last couple of years he had consecutively lowered the age of the women he chased after. Despite his efforts to convince himself and others it was due to his "high standards", this was a sign of utter desperation to try and entice girls while they were still naive and inexperienced enough for all his blatant lies to work. *It's as if he believes this time he'll get it right,* Sylvia chuckled. She enjoyed lying naked in his bed, watching him play the guitar and occasionally talk about this new crush of his, vulnerable, trusting and oblivious to the truth. *That's the thing about men like James,* she concluded. *The only reason they make it through life relatively sane is due to their convenient short-term memory loss... and self-delusion.* Unlike him, though, she kept a thorough track of every relationship that had gone down the drain in his life; every woman he had rejected, hurt, deceived and lied to; every broken promise and every broken heart, including hers. *Such a shame he'll never know the only reason I stopped holding a grudge against him is because it's much more entertaining to watch him self-destruct than it is to assist him with it.* She shrugged.

James knew she had been seeing someone for the past few months, but apart from the occasional question out of curiosity, he didn't care. As long as their agreement was valid both showed little, if any, interest in what was going on in their lives besides each other. All his questions regarding her new boyfriend were only meant as a means for him to assert his position as the best fuck she had ever had, a delusion Sylvia was particularly careful to perpetuate. She enjoyed the fact that, the less she divulged, the more James was convinced of his superiority. It had become the norm for him to sink down on his pillow next to her after sex and smirk.

"Bet you can't get a fucking like this on the Upper West side."

Sylvia smiled and started putting her clothes on as he observed her carefully.

"Come on, admit it," he insisted. "Why else would you keep showing up at my door, begging for a good ramming, if Mr. Picture Perfect knew how to fuck you senseless?"

"George manages just fine," she replied.

"There's a word you don't ever want to hear when it comes to your bedroom capabilities. Fine. What does that even mean? That he's trying and it's the thought that counts?"

"That's not what I meant. And I keep coming back to you because you're the best, love!"

"You mean the best you've ever had?"

"Sure."

"So how is Mr. Perfect in bed anyway?" James asked, scratching his balls.

"Just like he is everywhere else in life. Respectful, competent, charismatic."

He burst out laughing. "Respectful, huh? Poor guy. That's like shooting yourself in the foot. Looks like some things cannot be learnt in Harvard; like the fact that it takes a strong hand and an even stronger dick to keep your women happy and in line."

"Right. He's less dominating than you; that much I can tell you for sure."

"Do you swallow when he blows his load in your throat?"

"I don't give him blow jobs."

"Letting him fuck you in the ass is out of the question then?" he grinned.

"You know you're the only one I've ever done that with," Sylvia glanced at him.

"Poor schmuck. No blow jobs, no anal sex; I feel sorry for him." He puffed contentedly and got up to go to the bathroom. On his way, he slapped Sylvia's ass, squeezing it for a bit as he liked how round and plump it was. As far as he was concerned, all the stuff women were constantly obsessing about, labelling "excessive" and "ugly" in the lower department made sex all the more enjoyable and fulfilling. *It's one of those things in life, where the more is definitely the better,* he concluded, observing her with satisfaction. Watching her from behind through the open door made him hard again.

Several hours later, George was picking her up from her place for a night out on the town. They had already exchanged keys for each other's apartments and when he let himself in Sylvia was in the shower, washing away all evidence of what she had done earlier that day. He called her name as soon as he walked in; she heard him, but took her time in the bathroom. Nearly twenty minutes later she came out wrapped with a towel and gave him a kiss.

"What have you been up to, princess?" he asked, sipping the drink he had poured himself while waiting.

"Not much. I was out shopping, looking for a cocktail dress. I need something less formal."

"Find anything you liked?"

"No," she sighed dramatically. "And to think I lost several hours, going from store to store. My feet are killing me!"

"Come here. Let me take care of that," he offered, putting down his drink on the side table.

Sylvia smiled gratefully as she sat next to him on the couch. "You're too nice to me, George. What would I do without you?"

"Let's hope you never have to find out," he teased her.

They stood there for a while with him caressing her feet more so than massaging them. Her skin was warm and soft from the shower and George liked sliding his hand up and down her smooth legs.

"Do you feel like going to East Hampton for the weekend?" he asked suddenly.

"You mean like a romantic getaway?"

"Unfortunately it will be anything but romantic," he shrugged. "Remember my mates from Harvard, Alex, Kenneth, Mark and Benjamin, you met them all at the benefit? Sarkis and Ciril have rented a house in East Hampton and invited us all for the weekend," George explained.

"The Russian philanthropists?" Sylvia laughed. "So I'm assuming the opera diva will be there."

"Of course. Everyone's going to bring their significant other or, in his case, the person they're trying to get in bed."

"So Jennifer, Alessandra and Eleana will also be there?" she asked indifferently.

"Yes, it will give you a perfect chance to get to know them better. Who knows, it might even be the beginning of a beautiful friendship," he remarked, and both of them laughed.

"Sure, that sounds like it would be... interesting. I can use a weekend away from the city. When do you want to leave?"

"We can spend the night at my place on Wednesday and leave Thursday morning to avoid traffic."

"Sounds great, but I'll have to see if Mr. Foster will let me take a long weekend, *yet again*."

"Don't worry about that. In fact, last time I saw Tim we had a little chat and agreed that at this point it makes more sense for you to be employed as an External Consultant for the company rather than a full-time employee."

"What exactly will this change mean for me?" Sylvia asked unsure.

"Technically, it means you will only get called in when they need you to complete a task no one else is competent to do."

"Will it happen often?"

George smiled at her ignorance. "It almost never does."

"What about my salary? Will that be affected it in any way?" she persisted.

"It will get doubled, although you'll work as a contractor. Consultants are paid more than regular employees. Plus you'll save so much more on taxes. I'll have my accountant file your return for you. I told you I'd take care of everything, princess," he explained.

She stretched gracefully and snuggled up to him. "You know, a trip to East Hampton sounds wonderful."

They left a little past noon on Thursday. Although George wanted to avoid traffic, the original plan fell through since they overslept after a long and exhausting night of sex all at his apartment. They finally decided to take a bath to cool down, but their wet, sleek bodies touching had the opposite effect, so instead they opened up another bottle of Veuve Clicquot and gave in to the overwhelming passion. Both were sufficiently experienced to know the initial period of infatuation would soon start to wear off, so they took every opportunity to take full advantage of it while it lasted.

Unlike Sylvia, George was a morning person, so regardless that they had gone to bed in the early hours of the night he still managed to get up before nine o'clock, leaving her to sleep in as he had to run some errands before they left. He woke her up with a kiss and strong black coffee in bed at eleven sharp and half an hour later they were stepping outside the building. Sylvia came downstairs and looked around for the Rolls-Royce they came home in from the benefit when her gaze fell upon a metallic Maybach Xenatec the attendant was parking. She turned to George, who was carrying their bags.

"Is that…?"

"It most certainly is," he smiled.

"Impressive!"

"Thank you, princess. Shall we?"

She slipped into the front passenger seat and slid her hand on the leather. *An impeccable combination of style and class,* she observed, content. As George was adjusting the mirrors and setting up the coordinates in the GPS system, she gazed at him lovingly. His mere presence made her feel secure as never before in her life. Even though Sylvia was quickly getting used to the feeling of luxury being driven around in a limousine with a personal chauffeur brought into her life, she was even more comfortable when she realized George would be driving. He was the same behind the wheel as he was everywhere else, calm, collected and highly attentive. She couldn't help but recall James's frantic, nervous and incoherent driving, which always made her hold onto the seat for dear life. *It's so nice to be with a man who has his shit together,* she concluded, making herself comfortable in the seat.

Three hours later, he was parking the car in front of a big, albeit mediocre-looking waterfront house with several lavish rides lined up in the driveway. As they walked up to the front porch she looked inquisitively at George.

"A bit shabby for a rental by a Russian investor slash billionaire."

George smirked. "Sarkis values his privacy. To him it's not a matter of other people knowing how much he makes. Besides, in our circles he's known well enough not to have to demonstrate wealth and stature. Although I can assure you that the rent of this place is probably no less than several grand a night," he explained, as he opened the front door.

They walked into a spacious and illuminated living room with a fireplace, ceiling-high windows revealed a sensational view of the ocean. He put the bags at the bottom of the staircase and directed her to the garden door upon hearing laughter and voices coming from the back.

Everyone was gathered near the pool with the women lying on the sun beds and the men tossing a ball around in the water. Sarkis was standing near the bar, observing with moderate amusement Ciril's desperate attempts to impress Alina. As soon as they saw George and Sylvia walk through the door, the guys shouted out a greeting with Benjamin and Kenneth jumping out of the water and running towards him. He nodded at them, but refrained from shaking the extended hands, knowing they were just looking for a way to pull him into the pool as they had since college. Walking to the nearest lounge, George stripped down to his swim trunks he had underneath his trousers. Sylvia looked around and saw Alessandra waving at her to join them, but she hesitated. George gently gave her a nudge as he leaned in and whispered, "Go on, princess. I'll be right here if you need me." He gave her a long and loving kiss and went in for a dip. As she walked over to the tanning women, Alessandra jumped and gave her loud pecks on both cheeks, hugging her rather intrusively. *Her whole demeanor has that well-meant, but annoying Italian thing,* Sylvia thought, squashed in her arms. She smiled with reservation at Jennifer and Eleana and undressed, revealing a one-piece emerald La Perla jeweled swimsuit. The rest of the women were wearing two-piece bikinis that were flattering to their features, but in terms of figure none could even come close to Jennifer's svelte physique. She was practically flawless. However, Sylvia was undeniably the most comfortable in her own skin. There was a certain reticence about her gestures and an almost cat-like grace in her walk that put her classes above the rest of the women. This was something they could all sense. As she slipped out of her shoes and lay on the sun bed Jennifer lifted her sunglasses. "Are those the new Lanvin snakeskin sandals?" she chirped.

"Yes."

"They're gorgeous. I was thinking of getting a pair," Jennifer continued.

"Thank you." Sylvia gazed at the overload of bracelets on her wrist. She could count at least five. "That is quite a collection you have dangling there."

"Isn't it?" The blonde was radiant with joy at the fact they were being mentioned. "These three are my favorites, of course; Dannijo, Cartier and YSL."

"I can see why," Sylvia remarked. *Blonds always appreciate something shiny and massive. Then again don't we all,* she thought. She noticed George had gotten out of the pool and was talking to Sarkis near the bar away from the rest of the guys, who continued to make excessive noise while pretending to play water volleyball. She caught Alex's gaze briefly, but didn't make much of it. "Can you tell me which of the rooms is ours?" she asked, turning to the sunbathing women.

"Oh, are you leaving already?" Alessandra asked. "But you just got here, darling! Stay awhile longer. The sun feels wonderful!"

"I want to have our bags sent up," Sylvia explained.

"They've already been," Jennifer remarked.

"All right." Sylvia put her feet back on the sun bed, making herself comfortable.

A waiter quietly approached and placed four cocktails on the tables between the sun beds. Sylvia reached for hers without looking and asked, "What are we drinking?"

"Daiquiris! A summer classic," Alessandra said. The conversation continued with brief remarks about summer plans, parties and events attended until it eventually dropped to nothing and everyone just lay there, enjoying the warm rays.

Sylvia was just beginning to doze away when the loud and sharp sound of shattered glass startled her. She lifted her glasses and looked in the direction it came from. The game of volleyball had ended abruptly with the ball bouncing out of the pool and onto the table with the Daiquiris. Jennifer and Eleana jumped as if stung and were furiously wiping the drinks off of themselves. Eleana was shaking with outrage as she alternated between screaming and crying. *Funny. That's the first time she's expressed anything other than polite boredom. So she is capable of other emotions from the human spectrum,* Sylvia observed, putting her glasses back on. The men started climbing out of the pool, ignoring the women's hysterics. They huddled around the bar, joining in on George and Sarkis's conversation. As Sylvia sipped her drink and flipped through the Vogue she found lying next to the lounge she felt someone touching her shoulder. It was George.

"They're all going down to the ocean. The guys want to try the jets they've rented. Do you want to take a stroll down to the private beach?"

"There's a private beach?" she lifted her glasses. He nodded.

They walked down a narrow path surrounded with luxuriant plants and ended up on a small strip of sand. Several jets were tied together near the water and the guys walked towards them. Sylvia turned to George. "Are you getting on one of those?"

He shook his head. "You've got to be a bit of a daredevil to pull stunts like this, and God knows I've grown out of the wild carefree years of adolescence. But you know, boys will be boys."

"I'll say," Jennifer agreed grimly. "Sometimes I feel Alex will never grow up, at least not with all his buddies from college still tagging along everywhere we go."

George lightly touched her arm in a compassionate gesture, excused himself and hurried forward to catch up with the rest of the men. Jennifer held Sylvia by the shoulder so they would wait for Eleana and Alessandra, who had fallen behind. As they approached Eleana wrapped herself with a silver fishnet pareo and looked at Jennifer.

"Did you ask her?"

"Not yet," Jennifer replied, turning to Sylvia. "Darling, do you have any plans for September?"

"Isn't it a bit early to plan that far ahead?" Sylvia remarked.

"Not for what we have in mind. You simply *must* come with us to the New York Fashion Week!" Jennifer exclaimed.

"I'll have to check with George if we're doing something then. But it sounds like it might be fun," Sylvia said indifferently.

"*Fun*?! Darling, you still have some learning to do. This is a social function that someone like you *has* to attend," Eleana stressed.

"Oh? I wasn't aware it was *that* important."

"Not an issue. Now that you're part of our group you'll catch up with all the dos and don'ts. You'll have to if you want to *stay* part of it that is," Jennifer dropped the hint casually.

"I'll keep it in mind," Sylvia noted.

"Has anyone made dinner reservations yet?" Alessandra joined in.

"I think Ciril arranged for the cooks to come to the villa tonight. We're eating in," Eleana replied.

"Too bad. I packed way too many outfits waiting to be given a walk around town." Alessandra sighed with disappointment. "Oh, well."

They had reached a small and narrow quay, but the wooden planks had too many holes for the heels the women were all in. They lingered around it for a bit, looking over to the raving men on the jets. As the conversation became focused solely on the upcoming New York Fashion Show Sylvia lost interest, excused herself, and went over to George, who was standing with the Russians not too far from her. As he saw her approaching, he nodded to his friends and, holding her hand, walked back to the villa.

They came down late in the afternoon to find everyone gathered around the long dining table littered with platters of fresh salads, caviar and exotic fruits. Several waiters were scurrying about the table, pouring drinks. As they sat down Sylvia took an interest in a tray filled with several types of raw meat – steaks, fillets, fish and other seafood servings. She was starving after their afternoon workout. It was like a honeymoon preview, she thought, happily. George noticed her interest and confusion with the raw meat on the tray next to the table, so he leaned in and explained in a low tone of voice, "You pick out what you want and the chef will cook it for you right here." As they filled their plates Sylvia lent an ear to the conversation between the men.

"That's a nice piece of hardware you're sporting," Benjamin said, pointing to Mark's wrist.

"Hublot's new King model. Had to book it in advance." He proudly showed it off to the rest of the group.

"Not bad. The new Rolex Sky-Dweller," Benjamin replied with a smirk, showing his.

"Impressive. But Ciril's got you both beat. The Patek Philippe Nautilus Chronograph," Alex noted.

"It's impossible to outdo that guy!" Mark sighed. "What it is with Russians and their manic obsession with style and class; always one step ahead of fellow Americans?"

"You mean to say that's the best watch, no?" Alina suddenly joined in intrigued.

"It damn well better be," Alex remarked. "It cost twenty grand."

"Maybe more," Kenneth remarked.

"But it looks, how do you say, so simple." She scowled at its plain design.

"That's the trick, my dear," Sarkis pointed out. "*That* is the luxury we're paying the extra ten or twenty grand for."

Ciril remained silent, sipping his Blood and Sand, pleased with the sudden interest Alina had taken in him after spending most of the day demonstrating mild absent-mindedness, which at times passed into blatant indifference. Sylvia made a gesture to one of the waiters to refill her glass. *Fascinating,* she observed. *The only difference between rich and poor men is in their toys. I guess Fitzgerald was wrong.* She directed her attention to the meat platter, wondering what she felt like having next. As she struggled with the unimaginable number of options, George, who had spent the entire night chatting with Sarkis, leaned in. "Tomorrow you'll be on your own for about an hour or so, princess. I have some business to attend to with Sarkis. We shouldn't take longer than an hour or two, but I'm sure you'll find a way to entertain yourself. You can go with the girls to the beach if you want," he suggested with a playful smile.

"I'll think of something," she replied. "When are you leaving?"

"We have to leave before eight, but will probably return around noon."

"All right."

As soon as everyone was done with their main course the waiters took away the platters and brought a wide variety of beautifully-arranged desserts. Sylvia waited for George to finish his conversation with the Russians and as soon as she caught him in between sentences she gently placed her hand on his arm, letting him know she was ready to leave. He nodded assent, wished everyone good night, and left the table.

She woke up to find George had already left, so she took a shower and went through all the clothes she had brought to kill some time. When she finally came downstairs it was well past twelve; Eleana and Alessandra were at the door, discussing something with the driver and several of the guys were leaving the house with surfing equipment.

"Good morning, Sleeping Beauty. Must've been one hell of a night for you to be so exhausted," Eleana rolled her eyes.

"We're going shopping. Do you want to come?" Alessandra suggested.

"Where?" Sylvia asked.

"Main Street. There's a local shop with a wonderful selection of cashmeres," Alessandra said.

"Thank you, but I'll pass. I think I'll go for a stroll down by the ocean."

"Are you sure?"

"Yes, besides George will come back any minute now. We were supposed to have lunch together."

"Your call. Have fun, darling!" Alessandra gave her a peck on the cheek and followed Eleana into the car.

As she turned around and looked around the house, Sylvia noticed the only person left was Alex, who was browsing through a New York Times on the couch. She walked over to the bar and looked at the ridiculous variety of liquor.

"What are you drinking?" she asked.

"Vodka Tonic," he replied without looking up.

"Vodka Tonic it is," she muttered to herself, pouring the drink and walking back to the couch. As she sat down he put the paper away and glanced at her.

"Where is Jennifer?"

"Upstairs with a migraine," Alex said with blithe indifference.

"Something she ate or the weather perhaps?" She tried to appear interested.

"No. Incidents like the one at the pool yesterday are typically followed by several days of pouting accompanied with inexplicable health issues."

"I see."

"Look, we don't have to do this. It's you and me. After all, we've exchanged practically every bodily fluid there is, so we can cut the crap. I know exactly what you see when you look at Jennifer because I see the same things."

"If you're referring to her stunning beauty, yes, that is what I see when I look at her," Sylvia remarked casually.

"That too. Just for the record, I *am* aware her looks are only surpassed by her wickedness and spite. She is a horrible person. It's a real ordeal being with someone so self-absorbed and shallow."

"Then why are you with her?"

"Because I'm no different."

"Still, seems like a waste to spend your lifetime with a person that repulses you to such an extent," Sylvia pointed out.

"You mean to tell me you've never been with anyone you've secretly despised?"

"Of course I have. Makes for the best sex ever. That being said, I would go with someone who evokes slightly less negative feelings for a long-term relationship."

"True, but things are not that simple, doll. There's too much at stake and you just can't cut someone from your life on a whim. The best thing you can learn is to make do."

"I will remember that," she smiled reassuringly at him, peeking at her telephone. There was an unread message. She opened it and frowned as she read it.

"What does the soul mate write?" Alex asked.

"They're running late. Will be back for dinner."

"Perfect. With *my* significant other's migraine I'd say that leaves us with just enough time for a quickie. What do you say?"

She looked at him and downed the remainder of her drink. "Where do you suggest we do it?"

"The laundry room behind the kitchen. We'll hear anyone coming in or walking down the stairs. You go in first. I'll follow in a minute."

She stood up, looked around and went down the corridor, opening the first door on the right and sliding in. The room was large and bright with several laundry machines and dryers lined up against the wall. The only window overlooked a part of the garden no one walked through. She heard the door behind her closing, turned around and faced Alex. A second after he had walked in they were all over each other, pulling off and throwing clothes to the floor. They kissed eagerly, fully aware of the brief amount of time they had at their disposal and determined to make the most of it. Alex picked her up and put her on top of one of the dryers, pulling his pants off as he fingered her. Sylvia moaned loudly, pulling him towards her. Within ten minutes they were lying exhausted on the washed and sorted towels the housekeeper had neatly arranged in a pile. As they struggled to catch their breath Alex embraced her tightly for a moment.

"You realize this is probably one of the last times we will be able to do this. Now that we move in the same circles and all."

"I know. We had a good run, though. And all good things must come to an end," she smiled at him.

"Such a waste," he shrugged and started putting his clothes on. "I think I hear Eleana and Alessandra in the driveway. I'll go out. Don't be too long. No woman from your circle will be caught dead near this room," He grinned.

"Got it. Can you stall them for a while, so I can run upstairs and freshen up?"

"No problem, doll."

He gave her one last kiss and slid through the door, closing it behind him. She paced back and forth for a minute before she followed out after him. Halfway through the living room on the way to the stairs she realized she could hear George's voice, coming from outside. Sylvia ran up the stairs and slipped in the shower. She was just finishing when he came into the room and opened the door to the bathroom.

"I'm sorry I'm late, beautiful. I know we had an arrangement for lunch."

"That's all right. I can think of one way you can make it up to me." She reached out for him. He smiled and began to undress, joining her under the shower.

Fifteen minutes later they came down for dinner, happy and content. Sylvia noticed Jennifer's migraine fit had passed and she had put on a figure-hugging dress as she cheerfully chatted with Benjamin and Kenneth with Alex's hand around her waist. As they approached the group he made no acknowledgment of Sylvia's presence, but turned straight to George and started a conversation about equity investments. She breathed with a sign of relief. *There's only a problem with these types of flings when you run into the possessive type; God forbid he starts believing he's got some rights over you just because he's had his dick in you. Good thing Alex is nothing like that. Which reminds me,* she pondered. *It's time to start weaning James off.*

CHAPTER ELEVEN

He spent the time before they were supposed to meet thinking of Karen as little as possible. Although he hadn't planned it that way, James was pleasantly surprised with the level of self-control and ease he felt in the light of the otherwise unnerving event. He usually sought comfort in his guitar in an effort to block out any paranoia and anxiety. On Sunday night he spotted Karen at the bar, but she seemed busy talking to her brother in between sets, so he didn't even bother going up to her. He felt a bit offended by what he misconstrued as a blatant demonstration of indifference, but was quick to remember he had never relied too much on one woman's attention and approval. What started out as a slow and disappointing night turned out quite well in the end, considering he even got to meet a blonde he had picked up on Craigslist a while back. After exchanging e-mails for some time she had agreed to come down to the club.

Jesse was blonde, outgoing and well preserved for her age. She was older than James, which was a first for him, but he had grown tired of the constant game of courtship all young women expected and the attention they demanded. Besides, he wanted to try out for himself Matt's words: "Older women are the best! They know time is ticking, so they're quick to get on the last train," he would often say. His friend was a real pro; he only went after the ones who were divorced with kids and James had no intention of copying his dating pattern, but he had always wondered if there was any validity to his words.

Coming across this 31-year old blonde presented a good opportunity to find out. They both knew what they were in for. There was no pretence and no unnecessary flirting; just the constant struggle for power typical of any relationship. With Sylvia becoming more and more unavailable, he was in desperate need of a good workout. Still, packing up his guitar and leaving at the end of the night, James was particularly careful no one saw Jesse getting in his car. She wasn't exactly his type and James couldn't chase away a vague feeling of having sunken too low in going out with her. They chatted at the bar and he did his best to make sure he seemed just as aloof as usual. Things were unnecessarily complicated with Darren sniffing around like a bloodhound and James was certain anything he did was going to be passed on to the other guys and from them to Karen. That was something he couldn't afford to let happen. With women, he knew, misunderstandings were the beginning of the end. "The moment you start explaining yourself to a woman the relationship is doomed," he liked to say.

They went back to her place, where the first thing James did was to pour himself a large water glass of gin and tonic. He sat back on the couch and let her suck him for a good twenty minutes as he drank the alcohol. He couldn't erase the look of boredom off his face as he flipped through the channels. After draining his glass he lifted her legs on the couch. The sex was quick and mechanical, but they both got what they wanted out of it with Jesse screaming loudly, "Oh my God!" until she came. As selfish and emotionally withdrawn as he was, James had a thing about the women he slept with cumming first; it was something necessary for his own sexual fulfilment. Or so he'd like to believe. Having failed in making a woman happy everywhere else in life, the only place he still felt remotely in control was the bedroom. In a way his obsession with his partners' orgasms was an expression of that same selfishness and fear of rejection that haunted him. As soon as she finished he pulled away and turned her around, preparing to enter her from behind. She didn't expect it, but didn't object either, staying still while he penetrated her. After a good ten minutes of rough fucking James came, got up and went straight to the bathroom. Jesse followed him and looked over his shoulder as he pulled off the bloodied condom.

"Just toss it in the toilet," he heard her voice. "I've never had anal sex before," she added with an apologetic smile.

James threw it in, indifferent to her remark. *A bit too loose to be your first time there, but whatever. It's not like I care,* he thought, as he washed in the sink.

They went back into the living room, where he poured himself another glass and leaned back, closing his eyes. Suddenly he felt exhausted and annoyed and didn't sense Jesse trying to nuzzle against him. He turned his head and saw she had cuddled in his arm, so he jumped, screaming, "Don't fucking touch me!" The woman pulled away in shock, her bottom lip wobbling, stood up and disappeared towards the balcony. Realising what had just happened, James pulled his boxers in a hurry and followed her outside. She was smoking with tears in her eyes.

"I'm sorry if I scared you," he tried sounding remorseful.

"It's all right," Jesse replied, unable to stop shacking. But there was nothing that was all right in her voice.

"I'd better go," James said, completely sobered.

"That's probably for the best."

He turned around and walked through the room, picking up his clothes from the floor. He put them on quicker than he had taken them off and left.

On the drive home he received a tearful message, but the truth was he didn't really care about what she had to say. "It'd be good if women came without any of the drama," he muttered, as he switched radio stations.

Several days later, as he was going up the stairs to the fourth-floor Woodside apartment, James felt a brush of excitement, the same one he remembered from his teenage years. This was surprising even to himself because he had always considered he lacked the romantic streak; he had even considered showing up with a flower at her doorstep, but had promptly dismissed the idea as "too corny". He rang the bell and tried reassuring himself. *Karen's not into these sorts of things. That's one of the reasons I like her so much.* He heard steps and a second later she was standing face to face with him. She was wearing plain jeans and a loose sweater with a freckled shoulder coming out, her long hair draping down her shoulders.

They stood there, staring at each other for a while, and he could feel the nervousness overwhelming him at the sight of, what he thought to be, disappointment and reproach in her eyes. But she just looked at him in a calm and somewhat distant manner with an almost undistinguishable smile on her pale lips. James was unable to make out if it was a good or bad sign. He felt uncomfortable under her piercing look; it was as if she was dissecting and studying him like a lab subject. Strangely enough, at the same time she felt familiar and her presence made him feel at home. Suddenly, just as she was staring intently, Karen burst out into an honest and contagious laughter and threw herself in his arms. James embraced her tightly, fearing he would break her. *She's even smaller than she seems,* he thought as he held her. She buried her nose in his neck and sniffed him – something he found endearing. Several long minutes passed before Karen pulled away and led him in, holding his hand.

"You could've said something at the bar," she smiled. "We talked like five times."

"I thought this would make it more effective," James shrugged.

"Don't know about that. Rather sneaky, I have to say."

"When you deal with women you have to be."

"Whatever you say. You're the expert."

They walked into a cosy living room with several patchwork cushions on the sofas and a shelf stacked with books. There was a homey feeling in everything, from the way the drapes were tied with an old-fashioned bow to the smell of ginger cookies coming from the kitchen. Two Siamese cats were sitting in front of the window, staring at the guest in an inhospitable manner. James flinched. *Crazy cat lady alert!* He hated animals in general and detested cats in particular. There was something about their outspoken independence and unwillingness to obey that really pissed him off. *A dog would've been fine. Dogs are predictable. You feed them and they repay you with loyalty and genuine happiness. But cats... you feed the useless sack of shit and when you wanna pet it, it just walks away. Where's the point in that?* He strained every nerve to turn to Karen and smile. Noticing he was looking at the cats, she nodded in their direction.

"That's Cappuccino and Mocha. I brought them with me from Seattle; couldn't stand to leave them behind."

"You never mentioned you had cats. I knew you loved animals, but I don't think you said anything about owning any," James remarked, sitting as far away from them as possible.

"I think I did. Just goes on to show you don't pay attention to what I say." she laughed.

"In my defence, you're so gorgeous it can be distracting."

"What a line. Has it ever worked?"

"You tell me."

"Not with me. Can I get you something to drink?"

"Got beer?"

"Sure. Bottle or can?"

"Either."

"K," she said, disappearing towards the kitchen.

James sat on the edge of the couch, unnerved. Turning around, he noticed one of the cats had jumped off the window sill and was now lying on the other side of the couch. He moved closer and tried to shoo it away, but it just hissed back and continued licking its paw. *Feisty little fucker, aren't you?* James thought, annoyed. *Picked the wrong person to hiss at, you useless bag of shit.* He turned around and made sure nothing could be seen from the kitchen, stood up and kicked it off the couch. The cat immediately ran and hid behind the drapes and he sat down, contented, although he could feel its piercing blue eyes following his every move. Karen showed up with two cans and handed him one as she sat next to him.

"Where's your brother?" James asked as he looked around.

"Really? I thought I was more your type," she teased.

"Hilarious. I don't want him showing up in the middle."

"Middle of what? Are you under the impression something is going to happen?" she tried sounding playful, but it just came out naive.

"I'm never under any impressions. I make things happen."

"A bit cocky, aren't we?"

"I thought that's what you liked about me."

"Actually, that's one of the things I dislike about you, but it's too soon to be having *that* conversation."

"Fair enough. Criticism should come later on in the relationship."

"This is a relationship?"

"It has every chance of turning into one," he grinned, putting the can back on the table. "You didn't answer my question – is he coming or not?"

"He's spending the night at his girlfriend's."

"Well ain't this a happy coincidence!"

"Coincidence? Know your audience..." Karen rolled her eyes.

"Good girl. Looks like you've done your homework. You deserve a reward," he said, pulling her over and kissing her before she could say anything. It was a deep demanding kiss, although he tried for it to appear as gentle as possible. He didn't want to come off too strong. They lay on the couch kissing with her body on top of his and his arms tightly around her waist. It almost felt surreal. *God, she's so light I can barely feel her weight on me. And that scent... that intoxicating scent,* James thought. He couldn't remember how long it had been since he had kissed with his eyes open, but he was afraid to close them. He wanted to memorise every single detail of this moment – the way her long eyelashes trembled; her milky shoulder peeking from the sweater and those luscious locks falling on her soft skin. He pulled away and held her face in his palms, studying it intently. His lips opened in a candid smile and Karen smiled back. James leaned in and kissed the dimple on her neck, nuzzling into her shoulder. He couldn't get enough of her scent. It was almost ethereal. They lay on the couch for a while with his hand caressing her back, watching as the sun started to set behind the building across the street. In the warm light the room looked even homier and for the first time in years James felt like he belonged.

"I could get used to this," he said after a long silence.

"I would hope so." Karen looked up in his eyes. For a moment her honesty frightened him.

"So. Cats. Why exactly cats?"

"A relationship with a cat is pretty much the same as with a person. Emotionally I mean. You can do everything right and still not earn their respect or love. If you fuck up they'll remember it till the end of time, making sure you never forget your mistake. You're equal in every sense, even if you think they depend on you for their physical survival."

"Why would I want to earn the love or respect of a sack of crap that has nothing better to do than walk around, drop hair everywhere and wait for me to pick up its shit?"

Karen laughed at what she thought was his attempt at a joke. "You don't get it. That's too oversimplified."

"Life is not supposed to be complicated. Neither is love."

She rolled her eyes. "I love such awe-inspiring pearls of wisdom that sound deep, but are practically meaningless."

"I heard it from a friend and thought it sounded nice. Anyway, I don't want to argue," James said vacantly.

"Me neither. Forget I said anything." She glanced at him. *Why is the slightest difference of opinion with him always an argument?* she wondered.

"Look, I'm turning thirty-three this year and I've had plenty of time to do the sleeping around, the talking and the clarifying of things and let me tell you, it never ends well. I'm at a place in my life where I want to settle down with someone, who I don't have to discuss every single fucking thing with and just enjoy some peace and quiet," James explained, noticing her reaction.

"Of course. It's just, I wouldn't necessarily perceive some clarification as a discussion."

"You have your opinion and I have my own. We can spend the entire afternoon laying out arguments and we still won't reach an agreement. Everyone believes what they want to.

There's no point in digging in the obvious. Trust me, we'll only end up drifting apart."

"If that's how you feel I can understand. Although I was left with the impression you wanted someone you could talk to in your life, as opposed to a fuck buddy."

"Between a woman I have to clarify things with constantly and one I'll just fuck, I prefer the latter."

"Good to know."

"That doesn't apply to you, of course. I'd *love* to sit around and analyse to bits everything *after* we've fucked," he said, convinced the best way around the excessive chatter was sarcasm. It always worked for him.

"Smooth move, Counsellor," Karen laughed, but held his hand in hers to keep him from lifting her sweater. "I think it's too soon for that though."

"Are you a virgin?" he asked sympathetically.

"No."

"Then you can't be saving yourself for marriage either," he grinned.

"What does that have to do with sleeping together on the first date being too soon?"

"Technically this isn't a date. I didn't take you out, I didn't bring you flowers and you're not in a skanky outfit, highlighting your best features."

"Touché," she said, allowing James to pull her towards him and shut her up with a kiss.

He had waited so long to hold her in his arms that he was impatient to get as much of her as possible, but tried his best to pace himself. His habit of fucking had hardened into character and he had to make an effort to recall a time he considered foreplay to be something more than mutual exchange of oral sex. Instinctively, he had placed her on the sofa and leaned over her as he was pulling down her jeans, but he had to lay out all his strength to pay attention to other parts of her body other than the obvious ones. He undressed himself with one hand while caressing her face with the other before he moved down. After what seemed like an awfully long time James decided the foreplay he had lasted through was enough, so he pinned her down on the couch, positioning himself. He leaned in to kiss her, but stopped himself and pulled away.

"Are you on the pill?"

"Yes. I started taking it like you told me."

"Good girl."

He entered her eagerly and moaned with delight at how tight she was. Noticing an expression of pain on her face, he stopped with the thrusts and held her head with concern.

"Are you OK?"

"Yeah, it's fine."

"Am I hurting you?"

"Just a little. Don't worry. It happens. It's been a while"

"I'll go slow. K?"

She nodded and he started moving again all the while covering her face with kisses. *This is weird,* he pondered for a moment. *I guess making love is just like swimming, there's no unlearning it.* As she wrapped her arms around his shoulders and buried her face in his neck James felt his excitement growing. Karen's genuine vulnerability shined through in every single move; even her moans sounded more like sighs. He was used to the loud encouragements the women he fucked had picked up from porn; the back scratching, which for some reason they thought was unbelievably hot and the lack of all the usual elements startled him at first. He wasn't prepared for her laying out in front of him so much of herself the first time they were together; in a way she was naked emotionally as well as physically. The cynic in him picked up the scent of the inexperienced woman almost instinctively, sensing the great potential before he could find her uninhibited honesty endearing and appreciate it. He wrapped a lock of hair around his fist and pulled it tighter to expose her neck and stick his tongue in her ear as he was biting it. His whispered name was the last thing he heard before he came.

Normally, James pulled away immediately afterwards, but for some reason he wanted to stay connected with Karen for as long as possible. They lay naked with him inside her as he caressed her pale skin, shocked at how natural and non-sexual the whole experience could be. What startled him even more was how much he seemed to enjoy the tenderness and intimacy. *The rule of not having gotten some in a while. Everything starts to feel nice,* he concluded. Karen reached behind her head and turned on a floor lamp next to the couch. The soft light spilled down her body and he followed it unconsciously. It struck him how petite and delicate she was, *like a fragile figurine,* he observed, noticing with disapproval the small size of her breasts. Being used to a handful of something other than ass to grab, hers were barely filling half of his palm. James often joked the only woman hot enough to pull off a small cup size was Keira Knightly, but in Karen's fine frame he saw it as a notable defect. Looking further down, he stopped and examined her hip bones, which were visible underneath her fair skin, almost anorexic for his taste. He sighed and thought with pity about Sylvia's curves. *If only more women embraced their God-given charms and stopped torturing themselves and us with diets! Still, she somehow makes it work. Lovely little thing.* Looking up to her face, James noticed two freckles on her top lip and it made him smile. *That's a first! On the lip itself. Everything about her is so wonderfully weird and enchantingly different.* He leaned in and kissed them.

"I hope you don't think this was a bad idea," he broke the silence.

"I don't know. It feels right."

"That's all that matters."

"Are you hungry?"

"You read my mind," he laughed. "Do you wanna order a pizza?"

"Actually, I've already fixed something up. Do you like chicken parmesan?"

"I love Italian food," he looked at her, surprised.

"Great, you stay here and I'll be back in a bit. Another beer?"

"Can you be any more perfect?"

"I can try," she chuckled, disappearing towards the kitchen.

James lay naked on the couch for a bit when one of the cats jumped next to him. He looked at it and smiled, reaching to pet it. The cat lowered its back and he ran his hand down its soft fur. Afterwards he got up and went to the bathroom. When he returned Karen had brought a plate with a rather generous portion and was setting it down on the table.

"That looks delicious," he noted, pulling up his jeans.

"Thanks. Cooking is sort of a hobby. A way to unwind. Although I don't get to do it often."

"Why not?"

"It's always better to have someone to share it with and my brother has unofficially moved over to his girlfriend's. I don't really see a point in cooking just for myself. Besides, often I'm so worn out after classes and work all I want is to crawl under the covers and pass out."

"I know exactly what you mean."

"Eat up. I'll go to the balcony for a smoke."

"Thanks. I fucking hate the smell."

"You do? See, this relationship is doomed from the beginning," she laughed, pulling out a pack of Marlboro Lights.

"Not necessarily. You can always quit," he winked at her with a smirk.

"Don't count on it. I enjoy smoking."

"Why?"

"For the same reason you enjoy being an asshole. It comes natural to me."

"You do know your audience. Fine, I guess you're allowed one bad habit." He laughed.

"Why thank you for bestowing your divine approval on me." Although she meant it as a joke, it came out harsher than intended. *He's pushing it with all the rewards and permissions remarks,* she justified herself. James picked up the irony and it annoyed him, but he quickly judged the pros and cons of a home-made meal, something he hadn't had in a long time, and ruled in favour of overlooking it. The closest someone had come to cooking for him was Sylvia's meagre attempt at the stove, when they were living together in Chicago years ago, and he could still taste the god-awful thing she had prepared after hours in the kitchen. Watching her struggle with measuring units and basic cooking principles, James had decided then and there he would go for someone more domesticated for the long-term thing. *I'll let this one slide,* he thought. *But if it happens again, we'll have a lesson on proper partner behaviour.*

As he ate in silence Karen brought her laptop from the bedroom, putting on a movie for some background noise. James couldn't be bothered with anything or anyone else when he ate, but he made an effort to look up occasionally; he didn't want to give her the impression he was rude and inconsiderate. *She'll have plenty of time to discover that on her own later on,* he thought. He cleaned his plate and looked around as she picked it up, taking it away to the kitchen. Several canvasses with unfinished sketches were piled up on the ground behind one of the couches.

"Are these yours?" he asked when she returned.

"What?" Karen looked in the direction he was pointing. "Oh, these. Yeah. They're really old. I haven't painted in years."

"Why not?"

"Honestly?"

"Yeah, you can tell me." He leaned back on the couch, interested.

"I find it hard to finish a painting. I don't think I've ever finished one. I get bored and move on to the next, again and again. After a while it gets pointless to even start a new one if I know I'm not going to finish it. Come to think of it, that's a pattern I'm quite fond of in life as well," Karen explained slowly.

"ADD?" James jokingly suggested.

"I wish. More of a chronic failure to see things through to the end."

"Any idea why that might be?"

"Well, Mr Freud, as is with most of our neuroses and behavioural patterns, the roots of the same are buried deep in our childhood," she replied, with sadness in her voice.

"Sorry, didn't mean to sound like I was analysing you. I was just curious."

"No worries. Are you spending the night?"

"I thought it was too soon for that?" he teased.

"Hasn't been for the past twenty minutes."

"In that case, I'll take you up on that offer," he replied, reaching out and pulling her next to him on the couch. They snuggled in the blanket she had brought. James was used to falling asleep while watching a movie and the sound of the voices on the screen in combination with the warmth of another body quickly took its toll. The last thing he remembered before dozing off was the weight of a purring cat on his feet. It brought him a recollection of a long-forgotten feeling of comfort from his childhood.

The days rolled into one another and James found himself getting used to Karen's presence in his life quicker than he had expected. She would often come to the bar after classes and wait for him to finish work, so they could go back to her place afterwards. With her brother practically having moved in with his girlfriend of four years James saw fewer and fewer reasons to return to his own apartment. He enjoyed coming home to a cooked meal; washed and sorted clothes; no piles of dirty glasses or empty pizza boxes and guaranteed sex. But above all, he got used to Karen's gentle and loyal nature and her genuine joy in taking care of him. Against his better judgment, James found one of his favorite things at the end of the day to be talking to her as they lay in bed. They chatted about everything; his past, the present and the future, and he continued to surprise himself by revealing more than he intended or expected. It had been years since someone had taken an interest in the driving force behind his life or any of his goals. His ambitions for fame and fortune slowly started subsiding to make room for a more attainable and palpable reality as James realized the calm pace of the domestic life really appealed to him.

If someone had told me I'd be just another victim of the female domestication agenda I would've punched him in the face. Funny thing, what you run from the most always catches up with you, he concluded one Sunday afternoon, examining the newly added weight around his stomach in the bathroom mirror. Karen liked to cook and spoil him and James liked to indulge; the disastrous effects of the combination were laid in front of them from the beginning, but both were too busy sinking in the illusion to notice any of the red flags. And there were many...

Jason was the only one capable of impartially assessing the situation and seeing it for what it really was, two people who hardly knew each other going out of their way to simulate a relationship just for the sake of being in one. Sadly, in all his advice Karen only saw big brother jealousy and overprotection. He knew his little sister well enough to be certain she was setting herself up to fail yet again, looking for the things she needed in the wrong type of guy; and he knew James well enough to be sure his habits of womanising were far too ingrained to be broken for anyone. The problem was that Jason had never approved of any of the men that had come within a one mile radius of his sister, so she had learnt to overlook his disapproval, dismissing it as something unimportant and unreliable.

"Be careful with James, Karen," he insisted one day as he was packing the rest of his stuff. "I know men like him have a certain way of charming women, but it's all a pose."

"I appreciate you're still trying to protect me, but you're wrong about him. There's a side to him no one else has seen; he's different when he's with me. You just don't know him the way I do."

"I wish it were true. Just promise me this. If there's ever anything you need you'll call me straight away. All right?"

"Of course. But I don't think it'll be necessary. I am really happy for you and Elle, by the way. And a bit surprised you got engaged in such a hurry, but if it's something you both want..."

"Yeah, well, often things have a way of happening at their own pace and you just have to go along with it."

"You don't sound too enthusiastic for someone who just got engaged. Isn't this something you want?"

"I think you know the answer to that question," he replied, letting out a puff of smoke pensively.

"I hate seeing you like this," Karen said, saddened. "I wish there was something I could do."

"There is. Take care of yourself." Jason briefly gazed at her, gave her a quick peck on the cheek and left in a hurry. Brother and sister were extremely alike; both sparing on kind words and tenderness, but what was left unspoken they made up for in presence and support through every hardship in their lives.

With Jason officially moved out of the apartment James found no more excuses for making the unnecessary trips every couple of days to his old place for new loads of clothes, so he decided to cut right to the chase.

"Let's move in together," he suggested one morning after sex, as Karen was getting ready for classes. *It seems more logical than trying to come up with excuses not to get up and go home,* he thought.

"Isn't it a bit too soon?" she asked, startled.

"It's common sense. Moving in is the next logical step and a point of falling apart for many couples. Why postpone the inevitable? Wouldn't you rather find out if we're compatible before you've invested too much in this relationship?"

"I guess that makes sense." Karen didn't seem convinced. "And I *do* enjoy spending time with you. Sure, why not. Let's give it a shot."

"Great! I'll start moving my stuff in immediately. Just a few ground rules before we make it official," he remarked casually. "No one touches my guitars. And I mean *no one.*"

"K," she replied, indifferently.

"And another thing, I like my personal space. When I come back from a long day at work I need time to unwind. I know women can find it offensive if you don't give a restatement of every single bullshit thing you've done throughout the day, but it's nothing personal. I need to be left the-f-alone."

"No worries. I think it's pretty evident by now that I'm not big on talking either."

"Also, I know we haven't discussed exclusivity, but for me it's kind of self-evident that being in a relationship excludes sleeping around."

"I absolutely agree."

"And just for the record, infidelity isn't necessarily a physical thing. The emotional kind can, at times, be far more detrimental to a relationship. I know it from experience."

"Know what exactly?"

"Let's just say the moment a third person gets involved, physically or emotionally, it's a sure sign things are in the gutter."

"I consider loyalty to be extremely important as well."

"Glad we're on the same page."

"We are."

James observed her reaction of pleased reassurance with reserved satisfaction. *Women...They all want to be exclusive. A couple of sweet words buy you the ideal cover to do whatever the fuck you wish*, he thought with satisfaction.

After only a couple of weeks of dating their unexpected decision to move in together was met with suspicion and shock by all their friends and family. Some even tried to talk them out of it, but James and Karen would stubbornly lay out their reasons to anyone willing to listen. Lyle was the first to laugh out loud when James told him of his plans over a beer one afternoon, when he asked for help with moving his stuff.

"I've known you for years and you've done a lot of stupid things, but I gotta say – you've really outdone yourself this time!"

"You're allowed to think whatever you want. Your approval isn't something I need," James snarled as he packed one of his favorite guitars.

"Hey, you asked about my opinion. I'm just saying, what do you really know about this girl?"

"More than enough to know this *is* a smart move."

"I think it's a recipe for a shit-filled cake."

"You're a smart guy, Lyle, and I value your opinion on everything except women. Look at you and Rose. You've been going out for ages and presumably know each other perfectly well, but still you're not even close to moving forward any time soon. Your constant on and off relationship-kind-of-thing is unnerving to say the least. We all thought you'd be the first to tie the knot. What the hell happened?"

"Emotionally we're on the same page, but you know Rose. She's painfully ambitious. She doesn't want to settle down before she's sure she's gotten the most out of her career. Her clock is ticking, though, and she's aware of it. Sometimes I feel she's not sure what she wants herself."

"You just described virtually every woman out there."

"I wonder, has Karen had the delight of witnessing your charming misogynistic self yet?"

"Nah. All in due time, my friend, all in due time, "James replied, with both men laughing. As hard as he tried to dismiss Lyle's grim predictions, he couldn't quite get rid of the gut feeling that preceded all his life-altering decisions. All exes he told of the situation found it unbelievable and James ended up spending more time convincing them it was going to happen than receiving any advice whatsoever. Danny and Ana found it downright laughable and, to add insult to injury, even started betting how long the trial period would last. In between packaging guitars and moving stuff he got a call from Sylvia and a sense of relief overwhelmed him. She didn't show the least sign of surprise at the boxes or the emptied apartment. The bed was still there, and they made sure to take full advantage of it. Lying naked afterwards, he sparingly filled her in on the latest developments in his life. She listened in silence, vacantly twirling a curl around her finger.

"I can't recall a time you talked about moving in with a woman you've dated. Ever," she noted with interest. "I've never thought of you as the settling down type."

"People change."

"Some, perhaps. But not you."

"What makes you so sure?"

"Remember when we lived together in Schaumburg? All your mindless efforts to try and force yourself into the type of life you thought you should be leading? It was painful to watch."

"I think we were far too young back then. We were still completely lost in trying to determine what we wanted out of life."

"I think you're one of those people who deal perfectly well with the routine of sleeping around all the while mourning your one great love, but function dreadfully in a monogamous relationship."

"Why am I trying so hard to be in one if I hate it so much?"

"Honestly?" He nodded, so she continued "You're awfully competitive. Everyone's in one, so you can't possibly fall behind. Seems to me like you're just trying on this girl to see if she fits," Sylvia observed, indifferently.

"She's a little tight, not gonna lie," James grinned. "Maybe you're right, love. You know me oh-so-well, but few things are irreversible, and no one has made a commitment of till death do us part, so there's no harm in, what did you say? Trying her on."

"Of course. The problem is that I highly doubt you're on the same page. Something on an entirely trial basis for you may very well be a lifelong commitment for her."

"And that's *my* problem because?"

"It's *your* problem because *you're* the one pretending and potentially messing up someone's life. If you're playing the part you have to rise to the occasion. It's not just about you anymore," Sylvia explained, realizing the absurdity of the statement the moment she said it.

"I'm sorry, have we just met?" James lifted his brow in a boyish manner.

"Forget I said anything," she sighed impatiently.

"What's the worst that can happen? Fall in the sexless pattern that all women in a relationship do eventually? Big deal, I have you to count on for a quality fuck." He pulled her near him, squeezing her ass.

"Things are a bit more complicated now. We're both with someone we're trying to make it work with. We can't fool around like we used to. The stakes are way too high. For me at least."

"I have to say, love, you've come a long way since that gold-digging girl who thought the best thing about cities like London were the sales."

"I wish I could say the same about you. But you haven't changed a bit."

"Consistency is good, I hear. Women look for it in a man."

"There's a difference between consistency and stagnation," Sylvia pointed out as she got dressed.

"Not sure I'm following you."

"Never mind."

"I remember telling you that was one of my favorite Nirvana albums."

"Do you ever take anything seriously?"

"Yes, my guitar."

"I meant more along the lines of other people and your relationship with them."

"It's easier to live when you stop caring about others," James pointed out apathetically. "So what am I to understand from your mindless chatter - that based on your loving boyfriend standards I fail miserably?"

"Do you really want to know what I think?" she paused, unsure.

"I'm asking, aren't I?" James said, irritated.

"I think if you were so sure in your decision you wouldn't be running to everyone for reassurance."

"Excuse me for asking my friends what they think. It's something that's important to me, so I assumed it would be important to them too. My mistake," James scowled.

"Didn't mean it like that. Don't be mad. Want to hear my opinion? Here it is. If you feel like moving in then go for it. Few things in life are irreversible, like you said. Besides, if things fall through and you need a place to crash you can always stay in my apartment. I'm not using it."

"Thanks. That means a lot. You're a real friend. It's nice to have someone in your life you can always count on," he said, touched.

"Not a problem. It's the least I can do after everything you've done for me." She smiled warmly. James walked her to the door and hugged her goodbye. "Stay in touch, beautiful," he told her, before she disappeared down the stairs, remaining at the door until the clacking of her heels trailed off.

Unlike James, Karen had a significantly smaller circle of friends since she was quite introverted. The only person, besides her brother, she allowed herself to brief in on the situation was the only one she ever referred to as her "friend", a girl she grew up with in Seattle. Their friendship had withstood the test of time and distance. As different as the two were, both women shared an understanding about everything they considered important in life – from values and opinions to relationship can't-go-withouts. Mia listened carefully to her friend's intentions and, after a brief moment of silence, sighed with regret.

"Do you know those people that fell in love, moved in and lived happily-ever-after?"

"No."

"Me neither."

Their communication was always vague and unnecessarily complicated. It was something that came natural to them, courtesy of years spent with their noses buried in books. James found it mind-numbingly irritating. In combination with Karen's reticence he could barely remain calm whenever she went into some long, seemingly unrelated explanation whenever she was asked a simple question, only to come to the answer in the most roundabout way possible. In those moments he acutely missed Sylvia's simplicity of thought, speech and life in general. *She's a nice girl; though still far too young and lacking in life experience...* He would try to justify her proneness to melancholy, introversion, and what he generally perceived as weird behavior. In truth James did little to try and understand what drove or motivated Karen and had no real interest whatsoever in doing so. He had arranged his life around certain principles and beliefs and was very careful to dismiss anything that conflicted with them or anything that required extra thought. He recognized Karen as intelligent and well-read and valued her opinion greatly, but sometimes he found it difficult to take someone so disparate seriously. James had spent most of his adolescent years intentionally simplifying his life, to the point where it started to consist merely of satisfying certain urges with no thought as to the consequences. According to him, consequences were non-existent. He saw no point in anything he didn't perceive as practical or logical, laughing off people who delved too much in the non-material side of things. He was convinced that "the only things that remain in life are the ones you eat, shit out and fuck", as he often said. With Karen, however, James was careful not to show his cynicism, as he knew time would take care of her adolescent idealism. *Sooner or later, she'll let go of all this unnecessary bullshit. We all do eventually,* he concluded patiently. As much as he was amused by her naivety at times – a laughing topic with some of his friends – he still felt drawn to the goodness and openness of her nature. *It's been a long time since I've seen a woman more interested in my personality than my bank account,* he thought. In a wildly optimistic belief, James clung to the hope that Karen could wake up the part of him that used to care. However, with his intuition telling him otherwise, he couldn't overlook the feeling that this relationship was doomed from the beginning. What was most unfortunate for both of them was that he had spent most of his life deluding himself and gotten quite good at it.

The paradox was that he was attracted to her kindness and integrity as much as he was repulsed by them. He had had far too many partners to know that neither of those streaks guaranteed a good time in the bedroom, and since Sylvia had entered his life, James had gotten used to having all of his whims satisfied. The constant need to pace himself with Karen – both in words and actions – was exhausting, and left him feeling more irritable than when going through a dry spell. Still, he continued to convince himself he was in this relationship because he wanted to be, and not because he had reached a point in his life where he had run out of things to try out. *The only thing this goody-goody shit is useful for is knowing she won't screw me over. Which is something, I gotta admit. It's no fun lying awake at night at the thought of all the guys she's potentially contracting STDs from,* he noted with satisfaction. *If only she wasn't so darn boring in the bedroom. No matter. There's time to teach her all the things she needs to know.* James had lived without affection for a long time; now that it was being given to him on a daily basis he felt divided between the longing for intimacy and the craving for depravity. Delving into those thoughts, he realized just how dangerous Sylvia and all his other exes were to what he was desperately trying to simulate. One by one, he started cutting them out of his life by being a simple no show online. However, Sylvia's presence in his life was far too fixed to remove it altogether. Not that he tried to that hard either. He felt connected to her in a way he did to no one else, and the sense of security she gave him was something James valued dearly. Years of convincing himself Sylvia was but another casual fuck had made him oblivious to the fact that he had started to genuinely care about her. For the first time in his life he was faced with the inability to let go of a woman that he had never made any efforts to keep. Faced with this realization, James concluded that in the light of the life he was trying to have, staying as far away from her as possible would be the best he could do for the moment. She possessed an immense power to draw him in, particularly when he was at his most vulnerable. Making a conscious decision to fully commit to the relationship with Karen, he threw himself in it, fulfilling everything he thought was expected of a loving boyfriend. Desperately trying to strengthen what he so devotedly relied on, he even went as far as proposing to her one late night as they snuggled on the couch. He knew the loyalty, kindness and love of this woman wouldn't suffice to keep him there. He needed something more, something official and final.

"This is very unexpected, James." She hesitated, studying his face. "I'm not sure what to say."

"Then just say yes," he pressured her.

"Can I think about it?"

"That's a polite no as far as I'm concerned." He frowned.

"But we've barely started living together. And frankly I don't even think you're *that* happy with me. Are you sure it's the right way to go?"

"Look, I'm thirty-three and I've done my fair share of living it up, if you know what I mean. I know everything there is to know about you, I think. And you know everything about me. What else is there?"

"You can never know everything about the person you're with," she objected softly, but stopped at his expression of disapproval. "Fine. If this is what you want, all right. Marriage has never been on my to-do-list, but if it means that much to you..."

"Yes. It does. And if it's not important to you, what's the big deal, right? Sign a piece of paper and you're done."

"I guess."

He sat back, relieved. *There, old friend. Now you can't back down. You're in this for the long run,* he reassured himself.

As different as they were, Karen and James shared the same painful addiction to caring about other people's opinion of them. For her it translated into a constant need to please others, while for James it was nothing more than the sub-product of his ego that craved attention at any cost. In a twisted way, their perceptions and needs intertwined long enough to fuel a necessity-driven relationship that had little to do with reality and everything to do with make-believe. The transition was undoubtedly easier for Karen. Being naturally the homey type, she genuinely enjoyed having someone to take care of. *The role of someone's girlfriend was made for her,* James thought, as he watched her go about all the dull tasks that would have driven a slightly neurotic person crazy, without even complaining. Unknowingly, he was comparing her to Sylvia, remembering how impossible it was for his ex to be caught dead doing something she could pay someone else to do instead. Not to mention that cooking was something she had done incidentally when they lived together only because both had forgotten to order in. Karen, on the other hand, was always on top of products they were running out of, the best time to go to the grocery market, and the way he liked his eggs for breakfast. *This is what having a live-in maid must be like,* he concluded with satisfaction. James got used to being pampered quite fast. For the first time in his life he was exclusively on the receiving end of a relationship, and he saw it as some sort of retribution for all the years of chasing after self-centered broads he had to do the impossible to impress. With Karen he felt a wonderful sense of comfort and security, mainly because she was so unpretentious. She never expected or wanted anything in return for her efforts, and pretty soon he stopped trying altogether, justifying his lack of consideration and his indifference with the all so convenient, "that's the way I am".

In just a short while, James found himself at ease in Karen's presence; he started looking forward to the feeling of tranquility that overwhelmed him as he walked through the door of her apartment. But above all, he liked that he could open up and talk about things from the past that still dictated his present. She seemed to understand and – what was even more important to him – to withhold judgment. He wasn't telling her everything, of course, but elective permeability of information was something he religiously believed in and always applied in his communication with the opposite sex. For some reason, James felt compelled to talk to Karen about Her; the one that got away. He couldn't remember the last time anyone had sat and listened to his painful rants about their history. There was a time when he talked about Her so much that people stopped pretending to even listen after a while. But Karen didn't seem to mind. She satisfied his obsessive need to re-live all those moments from a past he had spent years idealizing to the point of completely rebuilding it to better fit his idea of how it should have been. She never questioned the validity of any of it, offering her usual compassion and attention in an effort to soothe his disturbed mind. They regularly stayed up all night, both battling insomnia in their own way: Karen with work and James with his guitar.

"Is there something I could've done differently?" he asked out loud as he was staring blankly at the monitor one of those nights.

"No," she answered instinctively. Karen always knew what he meant; she was very intuitive.

"How can you be so sure?" he demanded.

"Let me set you at rest. You will meet someone who makes you happy without having so much as a clue as to how She does it. Every minute spent with that person will be pure bliss. Her very presence will soothe and move you at the same time. She will evoke a smile in you without a single effort and you will have the feeling She knows you better than yourself. You will talk or be quiet together. Often you will be amazed at how alike and different you are at the same time. There will be trust, respect, tenderness, passion and everything else that makes you certain you are meant for each other and that you will never part ways. And when all of that is in the past and it's been a long, long time since you've seen or heard from Her, you will ask yourself if there's something you could have done differently. The answer is no. People you love simply have to leave your life when the time comes. And they will. That's the way it goes. There's nothing you can do about it."

"So years pass and people fall out of love just as they've fallen in? If it happens with everyone it will most certainly happen with us too," James concluded mockingly. He tried to make it seem like he was just teasing, but he was actually hoping she would argue him wrong.

"We won't fall out. It's different for us," Karen said firmly, without looking at him. *We were never in love to begin with,* she thought, but couldn't bring herself to say out loud. He seemed pleased with her answer.

"Good. I don't think I could lose another person I've loved."

She looked up at him. "You never really lose anyone you've loved," she said.

"I beg to differ," James objected. "Is She falling asleep next to me every night? No. That seems like losing to me."

"Physically, perhaps. But things are a lot more complicated in reality. You can't tell me you don't still feel Her presence in your life; if not all the time at least half of it. In places you visit, music you hear, and people you meet; even a mid-summer scent of overripe fruit can trigger a memory or a feeling you experienced when you were still together; an emotion only She could bring out in you. You'll grow up and change, at least you'll convince yourself you have; you'll find a job and become responsible; meet a woman and propose. And She'll be there for all of it. The day you get married you'll look over to the strange woman next to you and picture Her standing next you instead. She was *supposed* to be there, wasn't She? After all, it was Her you first said the words always and forever to, wasn't it? You never quite meant them as much afterwards. The day you hold your newborn child, you'll gaze at the little face and wonder what your children would have looked like with Her. And as you watch them grow you'll keep wondering if they would've been any different if She had mothered them. So, in a way, She'll be with you till the day you die, when Her name will be the only thing you remember clearly right before you let go of a life you never chose for yourself," Karen said all of this slowly, with unusual sadness in her voice. Her warm hazel eyes were somewhat cold and distant as she gazed at him.

"I guess you're right," James muttered, just to put a stop to the conversation. He hated long and philosophical monologues.

"As usual," she replied, returning to her work.

They went about their business without so much as an indication that anything from the conversation had made any impression on either one of them. James was too engulfed in his chat with a couple of people on the messenger to notice that Karen looked away from her screen, studying him for a few minutes, like she was verifying something.

In the months that followed, Karen and James quickly got used to routines, especially in their love life. They looked and behaved like two people in a committed relationship, although neither of them viewed themselves as being in one. James continued fooling around with exes as well as flirting with random women at the bar, and the only thing stopping Karen from doing the same, was her rigid belief in monogamy. Meeting somewhere in between the comfort of having someone somewhat reliable in their lives and not waking up alone in the middle of the night, both genuinely believed theirs was nothing short of a real relationship. In spite of their continuous efforts to simulate one, though, they were even more careful to respect each other's boundaries. Neither took too much interest in the other's field of work, circle of friends, or general outlook on life, and they rarely discussed anything other than domestic tasks and daily routines. The issue of privacy and personal space was non-existent as every laptop, tablet and other electronic device was password-protected, with both of them taking extra care not to leave any accounts open or unlocked. While sometimes both Karen and James saw this secrecy and caution as a sign of insincerity and potential danger, they were quick to dismiss any worries as they had a rather strange way of understanding normal human interaction. They were firm believers in the fact that people anticipated from others what they were capable of themselves, which in James' case translated to his conviction that all women were prone to infidelity as it was programmed in their DNA. As for Karen, with her high regard of monogamy and honesty, she was certain people only started relationships with the clear desire to stand still with someone. She wasn't against promiscuity; she just didn't see the point in cheating. In a way each of them found a comfort zone that worked well enough to feel secure in this relationship – mainly through self-deception.

As time passed they became more comfortable with the roles they had taken upon themselves. Unfortunately, to James, getting comfortable equalled becoming sloppy and, since he hadn't broken with his old habits, he became increasingly careless in covering his tracks. Still thinking of himself as single and eager to have the best of both worlds, he didn't so much as stop to think about the possible effect of his actions. As far as he was concerned – as long as things were fine as they were, there was no need to change anything. Besides, what Karen didn't know couldn't hurt her in any way.

It was just another Wednesday night when James came home in the small hours of the morning, threw his guitar case in the middle of the living room, and headed to the bathroom for a shower. It was the first thing he did after coming home. He needed the feeling of comfort it brought, with water washing away all the tension and stress of the day. As much as he loved playing he found it emotionally draining to stay on stage for hours, giving himself away to total strangers. "It's just not worth it," he often complained to Lyle. Earlier that day he had phoned Sylvia in a moment of sentimental nostalgia coupled with desire to catch up with an old friend. Her no-answer agitated him, but by the time he came home he had completely forgotten about it. The manager had announced a new schedule for the sets and James was unhappy about the change in his routine, which distracted him. As attentive and cautious as he usually was, he left his phone on the coffee table in front of Karen before he slipped in the shower.

She was working late as usual, but noticed his absent-mindedness. The sound of the bathroom door closing prompted her, albeit for a moment, to entertain the idea of digging around in his phone, but she quickly dismissed it. *Never dig where you're sure to find something,* she reminded herself, making an effort to focus on her work. Building her relationships and life on denial and self-deception had turned into a habit of hers and she religiously continued to stick to the pattern of dysfunction. James had given her many red flags and showed many signs that she had every reason to be wary of him, but Karen continuously ignored her better judgment as well as the uneasy feeling in her stomach that made her restless around him. It was nearing three when the phone rang.

"Can you get that?" James's voice sounded from the bathroom. She reached for it, weirded out by his request. *This is a first,* she thought.

"Sorry I've missed your call, love." The female voice on the other end was sexy and confident.

"James is in the shower. What should I say this is in regard to?" Karen asked, making an effort to pace her racing heart.

"Tell him he can swing by later if he wants to," the other woman chirped before hanging up.

Karen put the phone back onto the table and stared blankly in front of her for what seemed like an eternity. Blood was gushing through her ears and it was the only thing she could clearly hear; everything else was a blur of thoughts, sounds and a strange numbness that was quickly overwhelming her body and mind. Even in this condition, however, she was able to pull herself together to realize with crystal clarity what the call meant. It allowed her to piece together James' emotional detachment, occasional unavailability and blatant demonstration of an obsessive need for privacy. On some level she had always known, but it was in that particular moment that Karen faced what she had been denying for a while now and that sole realization made her feel foolish and embarrassed. What made it even worse was the calm and collected demeanor of the other woman, a sign she clearly knew who Karen was, but didn't perceive her relationship with James as any obstacle or even a nuisance to what they had going on. *Clearly, something with a lot of history behind it.* Karen was particularly good at sensing these things, albeit too late.

James came out of the bathroom, spilling water all over the carpet. She had to make an effort to look up at him.

"Sylvia called."

"Sylvia... K. What did she say?"

"That she's available and you can stop by later tonight if you feel like it," Karen said slowly, without a note of reprove in her voice, although her eyes were piercing him. The silence that followed was awkward, heavy and cold. He had picked up the phone and was going through his call log and messages, casual and uninterested. But deep down he knew the damage was irreparable.

"She's just an old friend. Been out of the dating game for a while; she's probably feeling depressed and lonely and wants someone to talk to."

"You don't owe me any explanations," Karen responded, more sharply than she'd intended to.

"I can see that you're upset. I'm just trying to explain before you start coming up with all sorts of scenarios in your head and leave them to fester enough until the whole thing blows out of proportion. Women can find drama everywhere."

"Don't do that."

"Do what?"

"Whisk it under the table like it's not a big deal because it's a *big* fucking deal." She lowered her voice, which alarmed James. Her reaction was nothing like he was used to. Clearly she was upset, but the angrier she got the calmer and quieter she became. *Hell, if I took a booty call for her at this hour I'd be screaming my head off, banging my fists against the walls,* he thought, confused. *I wonder if anything at all can get to her.*

"We both know what this call stands for," Karen continued. "The question is, can we be civil and deal with the whole thing quickly and painlessly?"

"And by that you mean?"

"Splitting up."

"Is that what you want?"

"It doesn't matter what I want, James. It's what needs to be done."

"That's the stupidest thing I've heard. Why wouldn't it matter? When did it stop?"

"The moment you started sneaking behind my back, doing the one thing you know is unacceptable to me, and lying to my face about being committed and faithful."

"Do you have proof I've done anything? No! All you have is one phone call from a friend, suggesting I stop by her place *if* I feel like it. That's all! I cannot be held responsible for other people's words and actions. Do you see me getting dressed and heading out? You're creating a problem out of nothing."

"Seriously? That's your argument? Are you kidding me?"

"Look, it's been a long day. I'm tired and don't need this right now. You can stay up and obsess as much as you want. I know women *love* that. I'm going to bed." He gazed at her, agitated. "I expected more of an intelligent woman like you, Karen. You're really disappointing me."

"I'm disappointing *you*? You *must* be joking!" She was looking at him in disbelief, unable to hold back her smile at the absurdity of the situation.

"What the fuck are you grinning about?" he snarled.

"The nerve you have."

"Yeah, so? Let's look at the facts: an irrelevant phone call by a friend you know nothing of. I'm not a virgin – you knew that when we started dating. I've had other girlfriends before you, so what? When did it become a crime to stay friends with an ex?"

"A few moments ago she was just an old friend, and now she's an ex. The story is unfolding in an interesting manner," Karen noted, amused.

"Stop picking at every word."

"I'm not picking. I'm just pointing out that truth always has a way of surfacing. You were 'explaining why this whole thing wasn't an issue,'" she reminded him softly.

"Right. As you can see *clearly* I'm more interested in standing here, putting your mind at ease. I could've just put on my pants and taken advantage of the offer."

"And I am supposed to be grateful for the gracious and thoughtful favor you're doing me?"

"I didn't say grateful, but it wouldn't hurt if you piped down and shut the fuck up. Most women will tone it down if they just learnt the guy they're with has other options; start thinking of ways to make him stay instead of questioning him like he's on trial. I don't owe you any explanations."

"That is true. Neither of us owes the other anything," she somberly agreed.

"What is *that* supposed to mean?"

"We're both in this relationship because we've chosen to and nothing keeps us in it besides our good will and determination. The moment one of us decides otherwise, it's over."

"Are you saying you want out?"

"I have no other choice."

"How convenient!"

"How is it convenient?"

ALICE WALSH

"The moment things get rocky, it's always the woman who abandons the relationship to save 'herself. You never give a fuck if the man still cares, especially since you've managed to already emotionally distance yourself. You're all a bunch of cold, heartless cunts."

"Generalizations always win an argument by default. Let me ask you this then – do you still have feelings for me?"

"Of course."

"How exactly does lying and cheating fit in with the image of a loving and caring partner you are trying to convey?"

"Love has nothing to do with sex. So what if I sleep with other women once in a while? It's even safer to do it with an ex as you can rest assured that since it didn't work out with that person, *clearly* I have no intention in going back to them."

"You are right! I do feel reassured in your commitment to our relationship now. This is by far the biggest proof of undying love for me anyone has ever given me."

"Sarcasm is unnecessary and uncalled for."

"So is your bullshit. In fact, sitting here listening to all this shit is even more hurtful than your infidelity and dishonesty."

"How is my trying to explain hurtful?"

"Because it shows your complete lack of respect for me, for us, if you're able to stand here, trying to convince me there is no problem when I'm telling you this is something I can't and won't tolerate. Who are you to belittle what I feel?"

"I'm not saying there is no problem. I'm saying you're blowing it out of proportion."

"So if I maintained casual relationships with my exes or other male acquaintances you would be OK with that?"

"Of course not. But it's different for men and women."

"Really?! Illuminate me."

"You're being sarcastic again."

"No, I'm *genuinely* interested in hearing this," Karen said leaning forward.

"Look, it's just plain biology, all right? A man fucks; a woman gets fucked – it's that simple. A man takes and a woman gives. When I go and stick it in some random broad it doesn't mean anything – it's just sex. But a woman always has to bring in all sorts of emotional crap into the bedroom. It's never *just sex* for you. That makes it potentially dangerous," James explained, agitated.

"Some women exhibit the same behaviour as men in sex and love."

"You can kid yourself all you want. I'm telling you how things are; it's your decision if you're going to believe the obvious truth."

"And you're so sure *this* is the truth because…"

"I have a little more life experience than you, girly. I've fucked so many women, who've thought they have it together and can pull off a one-nighter only to burst into tears the moment you pull out of them even with a condom, 'just to be sure'. And you know what? Even the toughest ones tear up when you're half way through the door on your way out, and start begging you to stick it up their ass just so they don't have to spend another night alone."

"Wow. This was insightful beyond my wildest dreams. I think you went a bit overboard with the visuals, but I do appreciate your honesty. However, it doesn't change my opinion or the way I feel."

"You know what?" James stared at her angrily. "No."

"Excuse me?"

"No," he repeated in a calmer tone. "I will not have another failed relationship, where the woman gets to walk away scar-free, all bushy-tailed, merry-fucking-happy-go-round and move on while I'm left picking up the pieces after her snobby ass, yet again."

Karen stared at him with interest. "So you'll stay in this relationship just to spite me?"

"No! What's so hard to understand? I'll stay in it because I have feelings for you and because I'm a grown man, who makes his own decisions!"

"Those decisions being fooling around behind my back and lying to me."

"Look, this is getting way out of hand. I'm not saying you don't have the right to be offended or hurt because of what happened, but like I said before, you're making too big a deal of a back-up plan, which, let's be honest, is the smart thing for a person in this situation."

"Right. The situation being that they're unsure whether they can rely on or trust their partner."

"It takes quite a bit of time to figure that out, and we've been together for how long, four, five months? I'm sure you can appreciate my situation. I move in with a woman I don't know so well; the smart thing is not to put all my eggs in one basket, so to speak."

"I see. And I suppose letting a guy I know just as well move in with me is considerably less risky?"

"I know you're being ironic, but it is. If all goes down the crapper tell me, what changes for you exactly? You still get to live where you've lived until now – no moving out, no starting from scratch, which are just some of the added bonuses on top of the piled heartache. Not to mention it's easier for a pretty young woman to get back on the dating scene."

"So I guess that's why you've never left it, to stay in shape," Karen pointed out, pensively.

"Now you're just making stuff up. There's a difference between keeping an ex on call and dating. Fine, guilty as charged on the first. But based on *my* standards, I've been nothing but faithful to you," James said, unnerved.

"I'm impressed. And a bit scared, I'll have to admit. I'd hate to imagine how being unfaithful translates in your language."

"Believe it or not, you're the first woman in my life I've been faithful to because I've made the conscious decision to be in a committed relationship. Let's just leave it at that."

"Flattered. But your fidelity is not the kind I'm looking for, or need from the person I'm with."

"Then you'll just have to give me time to live up to your high moral standards and accept that not everyone is fucking flawless as you are."

"I never said I was."

"You sure seem like you're thinking it, all high and mighty on your fucking horse! Isn't it possible that I've just made a mistake, that I've learned just how important loyalty is to you in *every* aspect possible, and that we can move on from all of this?"

She studied him for a bit, and her hesitation was the sign James was desperately looking for to sweep things under the carpet. He carefully moved closer, sat on the other end of the sofa and extended his hand apologetically towards her. Karen looked at him, confused, then stared at his hand. *She's never seemed more vulnerable,* James observed with delight. She hesitated for another moment, and then placed her hand in his open palm. He squeezed it without looking at her.

"Look, I'm sorry. The last thing I wanted to do was hurt you. Old habits die hard, I guess. I just needed a while to get used to the idea of being in a committed relationship. When you've lived alone for as long as I have you forget to take into account other people's feelings. All I know is I don't want to lose you, and I'm willing to do whatever it takes to make this work. I need you to help me," he said, gazing into her eyes. It was his experience that nine out of ten women would fall for the *savior* routine. *What is it with women and their constant need to save men from their own daemons? I swear to God, this Wendy dilemma thing is as amusing as it is predictable. It sure works wonders though*, he concluded with satisfaction.

He pulled her closer and just as he expected, she made no effort to resist. Her head rested on his shoulder; James could feel her confusion and exhaustion penetrating through her whole being, imploding her better judgement and self-preservation mechanisms. Her body felt weak and soft in his arms. He could faultlessly recognise the signs of victory. *Time to seal the deal,* he smiled to himself, *which in female lingo, of course, means keep them guessing and throw 'em off some more.* He embraced Karen tightly, picked her up, and carried her to the bedroom.

That night he was the most passionate he had ever been with her, if a bit ruthless. The feeling of dominance was a major turn on for him. James was right in presuming it would confuse her even more after their conversation and his reaction earlier. If Karen had had sufficient life experience, she would have seen right through his manipulative patterns and realised he wasn't so passionate because he loved or wanted her, but because he was intoxicated with the feeling of superiority. She fell right into the trap he set for her and, just like so many women before her, received the reassurance she needed to lie awake, coming up with excuses to justify him having hurt her. *Perhaps he's right. Perhaps I made a bigger deal than it actually is*, she tried convincing herself persistently, ignoring the fact that, in spite of all the reasoning and simulated intimacy, she had never felt lonelier or more miserable in her life. *Maybe we both just need time*, Karen concluded, gazing at him in the dark. His undisturbed sleep gave her that additional reassurance she needed to snuggle up against him and force herself to let it go.

CHAPTER TWELVE

Sylvia hung up with a smirk. *I couldn't have timed it better if I had tried,* she thought, as she ran her fingers through her hair. Although James had been extremely careful not to reveal too much about the woman he was living with, he had mentioned enough for her to know the call would be irreversible. After years of rejection, unfulfilled promises and jerking her around, Sylvia felt things were finally falling into their rightful places and she was close to getting even. Despite the fact that she had buried her feelings of hurt and disappointment deep in the back of her mind years ago, she had never stopped entertaining the idea of some sort of retribution. The problem was she was neither vengeful nor determined enough to get back at James directly. This made hearing the female voice on the other end of the line all the more enjoyable. *Years later, same mistake. Arrogance and short-sightedness, God's greatest gift to women,* she giggled, fully aware of the damage the brief call had caused.

In a fraction of a second, things over which she had lost sleep over for years, fell into place. For the first time, she felt superior to James. Sylvia knew he wasn't the type of man she needed or wanted next to her, but the veil of him being her first love continued to make him appealing to this day. Strangely enough, it was this moment that brought her the long-awaited closure.

She looked around. All the vases in the apartment were filled with Calla Lilies, her favourite flowers. George had had fresh ones delivered every three days since they had started dating. Breathing in the subtle sweet aroma, Sylvia glanced with a smile at his latest gift around her wrist – a discreetly lavish and delicate Patek watch. She loved the way he matched her style to his own. He had truly introduced her to a whole new world of style and class, where subtlety was the manifestation of worth and wealth. *A world of truly powerful people*, she thought, studying her reflection in the mirror. *Standing out is a sign of ignorance.* Sylvia loved everything about her new lifestyle. Although she had never been one to deny herself the small luxuries all women needed and enjoyed, it wasn't until she met George that she experienced the full extent of the benefits the privileged and wealthy enjoyed. Her life turned into a blur of dinners at five-star restaurants, brunches in secluded and exclusive country clubs, exquisite spa procedures – all with the added benefit of a 24/7 royal treatment by the personnel of every venue she attended. It seemed that everywhere she went people were already expecting her, ready to cater to her every whim. Still, she accepted all of this as something natural and long overdue and was far from being overly excited about the spoils George surrounded her with. As always, Sylvia reacted to this change in the calm, collected manner with which she faced every single thing in her life.

The sound of her phone ringing startled her. A smile lit up her face upon seeing George's name on the screen. Sylvia loved that he was still able to make her feel excited – something she hadn't felt for a man since high school.

"Hey you … Nothing much… You're back already? Are you coming over tonight? Driving? Right now? That's great. Are we going out for dinner? Oh, all right. See you in a bit. I've missed you too. I'm really happy you're back early… Me too."

Sylvia hung up and ran to the mirror to fix her hair and make-up. She was one of those women born with the effortless ability to apply eyeliner so evenly that even a professional make-up artist couldn't tell where her fake eye lashes ended and her real ones began. She used all female tricks so proficiently and subtly that with the slightest of expressions she could flit between girlishly wholesome and full-on-sex – a combination men found irresistible. The pressure of looking her best since she started going out with George had been piling up as of late, so she took a real pleasure in the few days he was out of town, in not having to get dolled up all the time.

Fifteen minutes later she was her usual spectacular self with that ethereal feminine finesse all men loved about her. She sat on the couch and started flipping through a magazine, so it wouldn't seem like she was counting the minutes to George's arrival. It wasn't long before his steps echoed in the hall. Sylvia looked up and smiled breezily at him when he entered. As happy as she was to see him it took a significant effort on her part to retain that smile when she saw what he was holding – a small bassinette with a brown and white Papillon pup. She forced herself to breathe out slowly before standing up and walking across the room to give him a kiss.

"What is this?" Sylvia asked softly.

"*This* is a present for you, princess. Her name is Missy Mae – a true pedigreed beauty. Her father is Argyll Centurion, three times state champion, and her mother is Daisy Mae, direct descendent of the royal line of pets belonging to king Louis XIV. You know animals are very favoured in my family, so I think it's time you joined the tradition of having one."

"I didn't know you were such an animal lover."

"How could you have missed it?" he laughed.

"You went hunting for God's sake! And from what I understand, it's a family tradition. I think it's understandable if I'm a little confused," she explained, anxiously.

"That has nothing to do with how much of an animal lover I am. I told you about my hounds at my parents' estate. My brothers and I were always surrounded by pets growing up. It's something I miss in the city."

"No, I know. I'm sorry, I'm being rude. Mine is the reaction of a person who's never owned anything bigger than a goldfish and that was years ago. I'm not even sure what happened to the poor thing," Sylvia blushed.

"That's exactly why I want you to have her," George said as he handed her the basket, stroking the puppy's head. She whimpered, and pressed her tiny body against his palm.

"Having a pet is one of the greatest joys in life. It is difficult to explain the type of love a person can receive from an animal."

Sylvia tried looking as enthusiastic as possible when she picked up the puppy. Fortunately for her, the years of acting her ass off in front of everyone had turned her into a real pro. There was no visible sign of the excruciating disappointment and disgust she felt at the sight of the small dog. *What the fuck am I supposed to do with this giant gerbil?* she cried out in her mind. *Wanna bring me a present? There are tons of things that don't require maintenance or pampering and won't turn all my clothes in a flea-infested lair. Why anyone would willingly commit to a life of servitude to something as useless as an animal is beyond me.* George laughed at her awkward attempt at holding the puppy like an oversized ball.

"Clearly you're new at this. Never mind. Think of it as practice for our future kids."

She looked at him, startled. "Are you serious?"

"I think it was clear I was from the very beginning," he replied, walking over to the bar. He poured himself a neat Dalmore and returned to her.

"Yes, but we've never talked about these things," she stuttered.

"We hadn't because it wasn't yet the time."

"And now it is?"

"We've been going out long enough to know sufficiently about one another. You've met my friends and colleagues and I've met yours. All that's left is to introduce each other to our families," George said, studying her face. Sylvia couldn't hide the nervous excitement that overwhelmed her the moment he said "family", but she managed to compose herself and smile charmingly.

"I am so happy you feel that way, because I can really see a future with you."

"'I love you, princess – plain and simple as that. And I'm a firm believer that if you've already found what you were looking for you should hold tightly onto it."

"So how, when would you like me to introduce you to my family?"

"Knowing your background, I assume there will be a big gathering for Thanksgiving," George said.

"Of course. They're very much into having all the family together for the holidays."

"Sounds familiar. I think it would be best if I accompany you to Fargo this Thanksgiving."

"Won't your parents mind that you're not spending it with them?"

"I think they can spare me for a weekend."

"All right, I'll call and let my mom know. Everyone's dying to meet you. They've already learned everything they can about you through friends and the Internet, so all that's left is to match the stories to the face," she laughed.

"We shouldn't keep them waiting too long then. But why all the hassle?"

"They, my dad particularly, have always worried I'd end up with someone who's not right for me."

"I guess they must have a good reason for that."

"We've all dated wildly inappropriate people at some point in our lives."

"Granted. I'm sure it's tougher for the parents of a gorgeous, charming and smart girl like yourself. You don't raise a pearl just to throw it to the swine."

"I am certain they are going to love you as much as I do. Frankly, I am more concerned about meeting your parents."

"You needn't worry. They already adore you, princess." George smiled candidly.

"How is that possible?"

"Ever since you met my brothers they've been satisfying my mother's blazing curiosity by providing her with all the details. Or to put it simply, they've both been raving about your qualities for months now."

"That's good to hear. I'm glad your family thinks so highly of me."

"It would be impossible for them not to. You're clearly a refined lady with excellent taste in men," George teased.

"True," Sylvia giggled.

ALICE WALSH

"It's getting late, princess, and I'll be taking off," he excused himself as he stood up.

"You're not staying over?" she cried, unable to hide her disappointment.

"Actually, I am so tired I wasn't planning on coming at all tonight, but I wanted to give you your present, so the two of you could start bonding. Glad I did. Look, Missy has really warmed up to you," he said, nodding with approval at the dog napping in Sylvia's lap.

"Why can't you stay?"

"Early meeting tomorrow. I have a few things I need to attend to, but I will be done by noon and will come straight here. Sounds good?"

"Perfect. We'll be waiting for you," she said hugging the puppy. George gave her a kiss and rubbed Missy behind the ears. "Goodnight, princess. I'll call you tomorrow to let you know when I'm done."

"Goodnight."

She could barely wait for him to leave the apartment. The second the door closed behind his back Sylvia dropped the dog on the floor with disgust and started removing the hairs from her clothes. The puppy woke up, startled, and started whimpering, but she just looked at it, annoyed. *There's gotta be a way to take care of this useless bag of shit. Think!* The puppy tried rubbing against her foot, but Sylvia quickly lifted her legs on the couch, observing its feeble attempts to reach her. As she was watching it with indifference a smile lit up her face. She picked up her phone and speed-dialed Stephen.

"Sorry to wake you up, love. Are you free for coffee? Friday? That's in three whole days! No way you can make it sooner? Deadline? Fine. Friday it is. Bye."

She stood up and went into the bedroom, avoiding the puppy's attempts at making contact. It wobbled around her feet, looking up expectantly, but Sylvia shut the door behind her, ignoring its whimpering. She slid underneath the cool sheets and listened to the weak animal cries and the tiny paws patting on the floor. *First lesson in life, hon, No one gives a fuck about your wants or needs,* she thought, burying her head in the

210

pillow and covering with the duvet. That night she fell asleep quicker than usual.

Stephen had reserved her favorite table at Flat Top. Her call earlier that week had completely taken him by surprise, but what struck him even more was her unusually gentle and seductive demeanor. *Naturally, this means she'll want something,* he thought grimly. He knew her too well to ignore the pattern of being an on-call service person in her life, but deep down Stephen was unable to escape the pit fall of every man in love – he continuously expected and hoped for a magical turnaround in their relationship. Sylvia was running late as usual, which only added to his anticipation, and made him perceive the meeting as something special and particularly important. He had done this many times throughout his life – leaving it up to his imagination and hopes to fill in the missing pieces of reality to make his life complete and bearable.

He finally saw her making her way through the room with determination. A smile lit up his face as he followed her every movement. There wasn't a single thing Stephen didn't love or admire about Sylvia. She never failed to surprise him with sides to her that continued to enchant him and today was no exception. As soon as he saw the little hairy head of a puppy hanging from her designer bag he could barely keep his jaw from dropping. She noticed his reaction and rolled her eyes as she approached the table, dumping the bag with the dog next to her on the floor.

"I never thought I'd live to see the day."

"Don't! Just don't!" she interrupted him, agitated.

"Why? What's wrong?" Stephen asked with concern, leaning sideway to take a look at the dog. It was trying to climb out of the bag and sniff his shoe.

"George came home from his parents' this week and brought back this… *thing* with him as a gift." Sylvia explained, glancing at the animal with disgust.

"Maybe he's trying to tell you he's ready to get serious with you. You know, settle down, start a family, buy a nice home in the suburbs, have 2.4 kids," he joked.

"Ugh. What is it with men constantly drawing comparisons between pets and children? What's having a fucking dog got to do with having kids? Seriously?"

"Animals have *everything* to do with raising children, Sylvie. It's practically the same thing. With the slight difference that children eventually grow up and learn how to take care of themselves, whereas an animal is forever dependent on his owner as his sole provider just to have a chance at survival."

"That sounds like a pretty sweet deal, for the mutt. What's in it for me?"

"A type of unconditional love and loyalty you will never receive from a person. Ever."

"Thanks, but no thanks. People seem to overlook the simple fact that love is valuable precisely because it *is* conditional. Why would an intelligent being settle for an unbalanced dead-end – for a lack of a better word – relationship, where he's forced to pick up shit, literally, after someone incapable of taking care of themselves?"

"You just don't get it. You're putting too much emphasis on the material side of things. You don't always have to get something out of a relationship for it to have value."

"Of course you do. Everything else is just being plain stupid."

"Let's agree to disagree. Clearly, you're not an animal person; let's just leave it at that," Stephen said, patting the puppy on the head.

"Exactly. And this is where you come in," she said with her sweetest voice possible. He looked up and met her asking gaze.

"You don't expect me to... No, Sylvie, I can't. I work 24/7. Taking care of a dog is a huge responsibility. If you hate it so much why don't you just have Prince Charming take it back to wherever it is he got it from?"

"Brilliant. That's *exactly* what I'm going to do, ask him to take back a present; you couldn't think of something quicker to drive him away? You wanna be with someone, you shut the fuck up and accept everything they offer you; even if it's a genital itch! The basic ABC of relationships, Stephen, you should've learnt *at least* that by now!" Sylvia raised her brow.

"I don't need a lecture on relationships. I'm not the one stuck with an unwanted display of affection from my better half," he scolded her.

"Obviously. In order for that to happen first you must *have* another half," she said with a smirk, enjoying it as his face turned red. *You keep forgetting I can read you like a clothing label, love, you and the rest of your kind. You believe you have your shit together, but no one buys how cool and collected you think you are*, Sylvia thought with satisfaction. All I'm saying is that years are passing by, Stephen, and your last serious relationship was when, three, four years ago? Do you think you're increasing your chances of meeting someone sitting at home, working *all* day, every day? A dog is a real pussy magnet, I can tell you that much."

"Not for you, obviously."

"True. But I'm high maintenance, let's not forget that. You need a nice, simple, loyal girl who will love you unconditionally, the type of crap you spewed when selling me on pets. What's a better way to meet such a freak than walking your bag of shit in the park? It's like a romance straight out of a Jennifer Aniston movie!"

Stephen looked thoughtfully at the puppy. It had curled up in a ball against his foot. She clearly adores you, Sylvia buttered him up.

"What's her name?" he asked.

"Missy Mae. I wasn't paying much attention, but apparently her lineage is kind of a big deal. Her parents were show dogs or something."

"That doesn't matter," he interrupted her, and extended his hand for Missy to sniff. The puppy instinctively pressed against his palm and wagged her tail. "Maybe you're right. It would be nice to have someone to come home to, even if it's just a dog." He picked up Missy and put her in his lap, where she curled up in a ball and started dozing off.

"I knew you'd come to your senses!" Sylvia sighed with relief.

"What are you going to tell George? Won't he ask where the dog's gone?"

"Don't worry. I've got this all covered," she winked at him.

"You know you can come and see her whenever you like, right?"

"Thanks, I'll keep that in mind," Sylvia rolled her eyes "Let's order. You know I'd kill for their cheesecake!"

She returned to her apartment in the late afternoon. Sylvia never hurried for anything, but this time she made sure she climbed the few sets of stairs in a rush, so by the time she reached her floor she could barely catch her breath. As soon as she walked through the door she pulled her phone and speed-dialed George.

"Love, I'm, something bad happened! How soon can you get here?" she started out with a trembling voice, which quickly escalated to a cry. "I am fine, but Missy, she ran away! In the park. I took the leash off for just a second and she just ran! I've been wandering up and down the boulevard for the past hour! I'm worried sick!" she sobbed. "All right, I'll wait for you... I'll try."

Hanging up, Sylvia wiped away the tears that were running down her cheeks. She took pride in the fact that, just like any self-respecting woman, she could cry on cue. *Few things are more effective than a woman's tears*, she concluded with satisfaction as she examined herself critically in the mirror. Crying had made her cheeks blush, which gave her skin a wonderful natural shimmer. She knew she looked amazing – something crucial if she was to make sure George would buy the story she was trying to sell him.

Twenty minutes later he walked through the door and she sobbingly threw herself in his arms. He held her tightly and helped her to the couch.

"It's all right, princess. We'll find her. Calm down and tell me exactly what happened."

"It's my fault! She was behaving so well the last few days I thought I could let her off the leash for a bit. I took her to the

214

same park we've been going to all week and halfway through the walk I took it off," Sylvia explained, as she struggled to compose herself.

"Where were you exactly?"

"Near the pond. I took it off and she went over. I thought she was curious about the water, but next thing she just turned and ran! I don't know if something scared her," she explained hastily.

"That's probably what happened," George sighed. "Did you see the direction she ran in?"

"Towards St. Luke's I think. I'm not sure. That's why I walked all the way up and down the street, asking everyone I passed if they have seen her."

"Don't worry. I'm sure Missy's fine. Someone probably took her in. I promise you we'll find her. I'll take care of it. You just need to calm down and get some rest," he said, kissing her on the forehead as he cradled her for a bit. Sylvia remained still and quiet for a moment, swallowing a cry or two, but as she looked in his eyes more tears started rolling down her cheeks.

"I'm so sorry, George. I hope you can forgive me. I know I'm new to owning a pet, but this doesn't excuse what I did."

He gazed at her and held her chin with two fingers. You have nothing to apologise for, princess. It's all fine. These things happen. It's an animal for God's sake. They're known for being unpredictable."

"So you're not angry with me?" she asked timidly.

"God no! How can anyone be angry at you! Look at you, poor little thing. You're so upset over Missy's disappearance it's safe to assume this whole ordeal is a lot harder on you than it is on her. She's probably somewhere warm and cosy, getting pampered as we speak," George assured her with a smile.

"I hope you're right. I will never forgive myself if something happened to her!" She sighed dramatically, although deep down she was cheering. What took other women years to understand, Sylvia had guessed intuitively back in high school, that men determined the validity of what they were told based on the amount of tears shed over it, and the more the better.

In an effort to console her, George took her out to Pisticci, where they had a quick dinner since, despite his best efforts, she was still quite emotional. Walking back to her apartment, she was quieter than usual and stared sombrely in front of her. He wrapped his arm around her and she shivered.

"Do you want me to stay over tonight?"

"I'd love for you to, but I don't think I'm too good of a company right now. Maybe I should just be alone, at least till I can pull myself together," Sylvia sobbed weakly.

"All right. You just get as much rest as you can and try not to worry. You have to look after yourself."

"I'll try."

"I'll call you tomorrow. I'm free on Sunday, so I can stay over. How does that sound?"

"Sounds great," she said, tired.

"I'll take you out. We'll have dinner some place nice. It'll take your mind off the whole thing, I promise. And by the time you're done with dessert, Missy will be back home safe and sound!" George tried cheering her up.

She gazed at him with hope. *I wouldn't bet my money on it!* she thought, relieved. "I hope you're right. Thank you for being here." She nestled in his arms.

"Of course, princess. I'm always here for you." He held her tightly. "Call me if you need anything?"

"I will. Goodnight."

"Goodnight."

They parted and she walked inside the lobby. He stood in front of the door until she disappeared in the elevator. Upon entering her apartment she was greeted by blissful silence and a feeling of complete freedom. *How do you cope with someone constantly expecting stuff from you? It's fucking exhausting and irritating is what it is. Good luck, Stephen!* Sylvia cheered as she poured herself a drink.

She slipped into her nightie and slid under the thousand-count cotton sheets. Just as any good performer, she had gone a little overboard with the acting earlier and her eyes were killing her. "Now *this* is something to lose sleep over – waking up with puffy eyes." She got up and went to the bathroom, taking out of the cabinet two herbal pads. She returned to bed, placed them on her swollen eyes and laid her head on the soft pillow.

Falling asleep, she wondered what made her happier, the undisturbed silence, or the fact that she had managed yet again to transfer her responsibilities to someone else.

Over the next month George did the impossible to track down the missing dog as well as keep comforting Sylvia, who was putting all her efforts into not getting over her lost pet too quickly. For her this whole ordeal served a dual purpose: not only had she successfully removed a major irritant from her life, but it also provided new means for bonding with George. She made sure she used the latter to her full advantage. Sylvia knew the surest way to cement her position in a man's heart and life was through the definition of his role as sole provider. Or as she explained it to Tanya later, "Most women simply don't get it. They fight for equality and try to show men they are capable of providing for themselves, taking care of themselves, comforting themselves, pleasuring themselves, deciding for themselves, fighting for themselves, thinking they will earn respect and admiration that way. But the only thing they'll earn is fear, and possibly a fair amount of disgust. Then they spend their nights complaining to other frustrated women about how unfair it is that men don't appreciate their hard work. But what have they really accomplished? I'll tell you what. They have blatantly demonstrated to a guy just how unnecessary they consider him to be, or in other words, how *worthless* they find him. Congratulations!"

Sylvia was very careful to acknowledge George's attempts at making her feel better after the alleged incident with Missy, all the while remaining relatively distressed. It wasn't difficult to keep up with the act, but the night he made it clear it seemed less and less likely that they would find her pet, Sylvia felt genuinely relieved, and had to make an effort to appear saddened by the news. She sat quietly and listened sombrely as he delicately explained it to her.

"You think someone liked her so much they decided to keep her?" she asked.

"It seems the most logical thing. No dog vanishes without a trace on the Upper West Side. If something had happened to her, say she was run over, we would've heard of it. I have friends in several veterinary clinics across town as well as on the board of Animal Care and Control. No one has seen or heard anything about a dog that fits Missy's description. This can only mean that whoever found her was well aware she's an expensive, pure breed and to prevent her owner from tracking her down has probably taken her away from where she was lost."

"I guess that makes sense," she sighed. "I just hope she's well."

"Trust me, she's more than well. It just pains me seeing you this upset. I've grown up with animals and I know how painful it is to have them leave your life, but the best thing you can do is accept she's not coming back and move on."

"I see."

"I was going to get you another dog to take your mind off Missy, but I wanted to ask you first. My parents did the same thing when my first dog passed away and, even though they meant well, it was too soon. You can't rush these things."

Sylvia felt a chill down her spine at the thought of going through the whole ordeal again, immediately jumping at the opportunity to shoot it down. "Thank you for being so understanding, but you are right, I don't think I am ready for another pet. It'll take some time to get used to the fact that Missy isn't coming back," she muttered with sadness.

"You never know. Hopefully she might turn up when you least expect it. But for the time being, I think it's best that you don't entertain the idea too much. No new pets then," George agreed. Sylvia smiled, relieved, turning away to hide her face. "Is there anything else you can fill you time with? I think it's important not to sit at home and delve into what happened," he said.

"Jennifer and the girls invited me to attend Fashion Week with them."

"Great. Do that! When does it start?"

"Next week."

"Go, have fun; Jennifer and Eleana know all the designers. I'm sure you'll even get to go to the after parties, they never miss those."

"Don't you want to go?"

"I don't know how to put this delicately. Fashion is not my field of interest," George laughed. "You go, mingle with the cream of the crop and enjoy yourself. Afterwards I'll treat you to a nice quiet weekend upstate. It'll be nice to have some time for just the two of us before spending Thanksgiving with your family."

"Sounds wonderful! Why do you keep spoiling me like that?!" she asked, unable to hide her excitement.

"I'm just treating you like every bit of the refined lady that you are. And I feel I have to make it up to you for this whole Missy fluke. I only wanted to give you something that would bring joy into your life. Instead I have to stand here and watch you be sad and upset over it. I guess the road to hell *is* paved with good intentions," George said, caressing her cheek.

"It's not like you intended for any of this to happen. And I do appreciate your bringing Missy into my life, even if it was for such a short time. You were right – the love of an animal enriches you in so many ways."

"It does, doesn't it? It makes me really happy you've felt that!" he said enthusiastically "Never mind, in time we'll have it all – the house, the secluded getaway, the big family with several dogs and a spoilt fattening cat, and you'll love them just as much as you loved Missy, you'll see."

Sylvia gazed lovingly into his eyes. *I'm not so sure, but the rest sounds like a good bargain, so I'll take it.* She leaned in and kissed him, resting her head on his shoulder. *If his ridiculous attachment to animals is the only thing I need to put up with I guess I can consider myself lucky.* The thought of James crawled into her mind as she remembered how they shared the same contempt and disgust for everything and everyone else, including each other. For a brief moment she longed for his hate for animals, one of the many things they had in common.

It was nearing midnight. Somewhere in Brooklyn, Missy was skipping cheerfully alongside Stephen during her sixth walk of the day. He stopped and looked up at the few lit windows in the buildings around him, then down at the small joyful creature in his feet. *I should've done this a long time ago,* he thought, as he picked her up, held her gently, and hurried home.

Stepping off George's private jet on the runway at Hector Airport, the first thing they saw was the tall figure of Dan Rennie – the butler of Sylvia's parents. She smiled warmly at him and he gave her a hug. Having worked for her family since she was a baby, he was unofficially more like an uncle than anything else. He was one of her closest people largely because of their difference of stature and the safety barrier that he provided. Sylvia turned to the tall handsome man behind her.

"Dan, I'd like you to meet someone very special. This is George William Huntington the Third. He's the son of the governor of New Hampshire."

"Pleasure, sir," he nodded respectfully.

"The pleasure is all mine. Sylvia has spoken quite fondly of you," George replied, shaking his hand.

"This can only make me happy, sir. She is like a dear daughter to me."

"So I've heard."

"This way if you please," he pointed them to two grey Lexus limos parked aside on the runway.

Sylvia shook her head with a smile. "Father hasn't changed a bit," she noted. "He still goes with the things that draw the least bit of attention."

"That's always good," George remarked as they got into the second one. The driver immediately started the car and followed the one in front.

Her parents' estate was on the other side of the town on Rose Creek Boulevard. As they passed through the centre of Fargo, Sylvia was amazed at the palpable provinciality. There was a time when she used to enjoy coming home for a brief stay in between semesters, to immerse herself in the atmosphere of inertness, typical for a Midwestern town. For the first time she was somewhat ashamed of her origin. *I've outgrown this place,* she concluded, glancing at George to study his reaction. His face, however, didn't show the slightest sign of disappointment or disapproval as he looked through the window with his usual expression of reservation and indifference. It was impossible to read his thoughts, as he rarely showed an emotion of any kind. *Ever the calm and collected one,* she smiled. *Just like daddy.*

In a little while, the cars entered the patio and pulled up in front of a spacious residence. Several house servants were lined up on the stairway and started unloading the luggage as soon as the cars parked. Her father appeared at the door just as Sylvia and George were getting out. She immediately threw herself in his arms and he embraced her affectionately.

"I'm so happy you're home, princess. Is it just me or are you getting prettier with each visit?"

"You're just saying that because you're biased," she laughed.

"Guilty as charged! And who is this fine young gentleman?" He turned to George.

"George William Huntington the Third, sir." George extended his hand. "It's an honour to finally meet the father of the woman I love."

"Frank Elmore Watson. You sure cut right to the chase, Mr. Huntington. I like that."

"George, please."

"George then. I like that," he repeated, nodding with approval at his daughter and her companion. "This way, please. We're happy to welcome you into our humble home." He led them inside. "Everyone's in the living room. Tanya's here too," he added, turning to Sylvia.

"She is? When did she fly in?"

"Last week. You know her father is my most trusted bridge partner. They'll be joining us for Thanksgiving. I understand you've already met Mrs. Stonick," he turned to George, "and you've passed the initial stage of the trial process otherwise known as the *girlfriend review*. And God knows that's one of the milestones in the life of a young man, am I right?" he laughed, patting him on the back.

"I couldn't have said it better myself, sir," he grinned.

"Well, my dear boy, you can almost relax. And I say *almost* because all that's left now is the collective family review."

"I'm not worried, sir. It's what I'm good at."

"With a background such as yours, it's understandable. I know your father. Well, not personally, but through mutual friends and from what I've heard, he's a man who stands firm for principles and traditions."

"He does run a tight ship."

"Yes, exactly. A man of value."

"Thank you, sir. I'll be sure to tell him that."

"Please do. This way." Mr. Watson led them through a sun-lit corridor into an even brighter room filled with people. All talk ceased the minute they walked through the door, and Sylvia felt a bit uncomfortable, noticing the scrutiny on the faces of all her relatives. *Great. Any minute now he'll turn and run in the other direction, saying, "This provincial girl is soo not worth any of this shit!"* She glanced at George, alarmed, but nothing in his expression indicated discomfort or even mild annoyance.

Upon entering, Sylvia's mother, a tall, radiant brunette, got up and greeted them with a smile. "It's so wonderful to meet you." She held George's hand, then turned to her daughter. "Well done, sweetie! We're so proud of you."

"Thank you for welcoming me to your home, Mrs. Watson," George said respectfully. "I must say, your house is spectacular."

"Isn't it?!" She was delighted at his compliment. "Later I'll give you a tour. It was built in 1907 and together with the land comes to about 7,204 acres. But first, please, come and meet the rest of the family." Holding his arm, she led him inside the room. "This is our beloved Gam Gam; Sylvie's named after her." She nodded to a fragile, white-haired woman with surprisingly piercing and lively eyes. "My brother Todd, his wife Joanna, and their children: Michael, Hannah and David; my sister Catherine, her husband Patrick and their daughter Alexis. Tanya you've already met. She's like a daughter to us."

All eyes were on Sylvia's handsome companion, and it was clear he was being scrutinized to the smallest detail. Still, he retained his calm as he was led from person to person, giving everyone the same polite, albeit reserved, greeting.

"That wasn't so painful, was it?" Mr. Watson's voice sounded from behind his back. He put his hand on George's shoulder. "If it's any consolation, Patrick had to go through the exact same thing, am I right?" He smiled at his brother-in-law, and the tall man nodded. "And you don't even want to imagine what the boys that Alexis brings over must endure," Frank added, prompting everyone to burst out in laughter. "She's quite the heartbreaker our little Alexis. It's the Watson women family curse I suppose," he concluded breezily, looking approvingly at his niece. She pouted coquettishly, enjoying the attention.

"I can see why, sir. Your family has certainly been blessed with a whole lot of beauty," George gave him the pleasure.

"I'm glad we see eye to eye on this one, my boy," Sylvia's father replied, delighted.

"You must be tired. Let me show you where you're staying," her mother interrupted.

"I was actually thinking we could stay at my apartment," Sylvia began hesitantly.

"Nonsense, my dear! Now that you've finally decided to visit for a whole week and bring this wonderful man along, do you honestly think we'll let you out of our sight even for a moment?" her mother exclaimed.

"Your mother is right, princess. What's the whole point of Thanksgiving if you can't be with your loved ones for as long as you can? Before you know it, everyone will have left and it'll be just your mother and me again. After a certain age the holidays are all we have to look forward to," her father pointed out, sombrely.

"My parents say the exact same thing, sir. Of course we'll stay here with you," George reassured him.

"It was just a suggestion. The house seems a bit overcrowded," Sylvia tried explaining.

"What good are nine bedrooms if you don't get to put them to use every once in a while?" her mother asked. "Come, we've put you in Sylvia's old room; it's the same as when you left for college, dear – your father wouldn't let me change a thing. You can rest today and starting tomorrow we have something planned for each day till you leave on Tuesday– we want to make the most of your stay."

"Did you, by any chance, put some time for doing nothing in the itinerary?" Sylvia asked, irritated.

"That's one thing you've always had plenty of, dear. But first you and I are going shopping tomorrow."

"That actually does sound good."

Mrs Watson took them upstairs and opened the door to a bright bedroom with pale blue walls. Posters hung on the wardrobe doors, and teddy bears adorned every chair and window sill. *Time's frozen here*, Sylvia thought, as she looked around. When the door closed behind her mother's back, George picked up one of her stuffed animals and smiled.

"I never imagined you as the type of girl to have these, let alone to be keeping them after all these years."

"It's not me. It's my father. He's turned this place into a shrine to me," she explained defensively. "These are all gifts from him. He continued giving me stuffed animals till I was fifteen! I never managed to convince him that at some point I grew up."

"I've heard fathers have this problem with their daughters," George grinned. "It's endearing."

"It all depends on which side of the fence you're on," she shrugged. "My biggest victory was getting him to buy me an apartment downtown to stay at every other night in my last year in high school."

"Quite a bold move for a young lady," he raised his eyebrow.

"A girl needs to affirm her independence. How am I supposed to ever do that with my mother snooping around, trying to steer my life in the direction she sees fit?"

"I sensed a bit of tension there. Anything you want to talk about?"

"Nothing worth mentioning. Just your typical mother-daughter drama, where she's unwilling to accept the fact that she's getting older and it's time to sit back and hand over the torch to her younger, better version," Sylvia explained, as she began undressing.

"*That* you are, princess. *That* you are," he agreed and wrapped his arms around her from behind as he began kissing her neck and shoulders, moving down.

The next morning Frank insisted on taking George to the Country Club, which was his way of being diplomatic about introducing his potential son-in-law to friends and colleagues. At the club the two men enjoyed an early brunch followed by a game of golf. Meanwhile Sylvia's mother dragged her to West Acres Mall for a last-minute holiday stroll around the shops. In front of Helzberg, Sylvia spotted James walking around gloomily with his mother. He nodded at her and slowed down, waiting for a greeting or any reaction from her, but she stared right through him. She had always been over-the-top when they ran into each other every time she came home for the summer, but seeing him just felt exhausting now. *He'll wanna meet later*, she frowned, *and I won't be able to say no, as usual.* Sylvia walked away, leaving him behind in disbelief. James had become so used to receiving her undivided attention, convinced he was entitled to it, that he had failed to notice the gradual shift in attitude as well as the subsequent shift of power that had occurred in their relationship. Sylvia followed her mother into the next store. They didn't head home until Dan started having difficulty carrying all of the bags.

She had barely gotten out of the shower after they returned when her phone went off with the sound of a text message. *Right on cue*, she smirked, as she picked it up.

"Happy Thanksgiving. I'm free if you wanna meet up later."

Rarely surprised with anything, Sylvia couldn't help but raise an eyebrow at the fact that James had switched from demanding to suggesting. She looked at the wall clock and ran the possible scenarios in her head. George was still conveniently occupied with her father and the rest of her family was idling away time till dinner in mindless chit-chat downstairs.

"I'm free now. Meet me at our usual place," she texted back, and started dressing.

Fifteen minutes later, she was getting out of the car on the corner of 14th Ave. and South University Drive. James was already there, although he lived further. *He must've left straight away,* she thought, as she approached him. They hugged each other and walked down the street. It felt just like old times when she would skip classes just so they could hang out.

"I wasn't sure if you were coming home for the holidays," he broke the silence after a block or two.

"Yeah, well. It was sort of a last-minute decision."

"Did you come alone?"

"No, George is tagging along."

"Ah, right. Mr. Perfect."

"What about you?"

"Just me, thank God!" James bit his lip the moment he said that, although he seemed relieved.

"Things not working out with the significant other?" Sylvia asked, a little surprised that for the first time in her life she wasn't at all interested in the answer.

"Not so much," he replied, sombrely.

"Last time we spoke you were head-over-heels in love. What could've possibly gone wrong in such a short while?"

"The change of coat oh-so-typical for the female population. You know the routine."

"I'm familiar with it. And more specifically?"

"Specifically, she went berserk at that phone call, you know which one. One thing led to another and let's just say she has a problem with me staying in touch with ex-girlfriends. She thinks it's damaging to our relationship."

"She has a point. You know yourself. Have you ever stayed faithful to anyone?"

"Even so, who the fuck does she think she is to tell *me* what I can or cannot do?!"

Sylvia laughed. "Did she *actually* tell you *not* to see your exes? She really doesn't know her audience that well."

"Not exactly," James admitted reluctantly. "She just said she won't be in a relationship where the partners disrespect each other."

"That sounds fair."

"Sounds like an ultimatum to me."

"You haven't changed a bit," she winked at him, knowing he wouldn't sense the irony. She was amused by his tendency to destroy everything potentially long-term in his life out of sheer contempt for others people's needs and wants.

"Thank you. It's good to know at least one person appreciates me for who I am. You're a real friend," he said, relieved. Sylvia smiled, but didn't say a word. *His lack of touch with reality is scary,* she thought.

"What about you. How are things going with that guy?"

"Good. Average-ish..."

"Average-ish," he repeated pensively. "Not that well, huh? Is he giving you a hard time outside of the bedroom?" He laughed at his joke.

"No, he's fine in every department. But he's not nearly as good as you are there." She glanced at him suggestively. James immediately swaggered.

"It takes experience and skill for that."

"I know."

"Maybe you need to try and point the poor guy, so he can give it to you good and hard like you're used to. A nice blowjob usually does the trick."

"I told you I don't do that with him."

"You have a relationship with this guy and you won't suck his dick? No wonder he's not performing well," James pointed out.

"It takes a certain level of intimacy for that. I haven't done it with anyone since you," Sylvia remarked, observing his reaction.

James was flattered. "Still, I think you need to suck his dick. You'd be surprised how everything will fall into place after that."

"I'll make a mental note of that." Ordinarily she was amused how easily he fell for her lies, but now she just found it sad and disheartening. *This is effortless. I'm not even trying anymore and he's still buying it. At least before there was the thrill of the push and pull routine,* Sylvia noted with boredom.

"What are your plans for tonight?"

"Big family dinner."

"Same here. Don't you just *love* those?"

"It's a necessary evil," she sighed.

"Do you wanna go to your apartment? I've got a couple of hours…" He stopped and looked at her. Sylvia squeezed the key chain in her pocket and wondered for a brief moment. Ordinarily they would've been half way through undressing at this point, but now she was hesitant. She was still attracted to him, albeit through the force of habit and convenience; they had been fucking for such a long time that the comfort of knowing each other perfectly well made it sure getting off was on the menu every time she ordered from it.

"I'd love to, but I left the keys at home. Plus George is supposed to get back from a day out with my father any minute, so I'd better head back."

James grinned. "Ah, bonding with daddy-in-law. Good luck to him. Thank God I'll never have to go through any of that shit!"

"Lucky you," Sylvia agreed. "Anyhow, I'll call you when I'm back in the city. Or if you prefer I won't stir up trouble in your love life," she added snidely.

"You can call anytime you want, love. Karen's just gonna have to deal with it. I don't give a fuck what she thinks is appropriate or acceptable in a relationship. I'm thirty-three for fuck's sake, and I've lived like this my entire life. I'm not about to start changing just because some dumb broad has problems with insecurity and low self-esteem. There's a big difference between someone you've been dating for the past couple of months and someone who's been in your life for more than ten years. If she keeps pissing me off she's in for a rude awakening."

"Well said. A person should know what's important and what's not worth losing sleep over."

"I know, right? There are some people you can't throw out of your life just because your current boyfriend or girlfriend feels like you should. And I know you'd agree if your picture-perfect boyfriend pressured you to do the same."

"Of course. You're far too important for me to lose you," Sylvia acknowledged, pressing against him. They stopped and hugged for a brief moment and she breathed in his familiar scent.

"Call me when you get back, K?"

"I will. Happy Thanksgiving."

"Happy Thanksgiving."

She walked away and hailed a cab. James stood and watched as the car drove away. Normally, he was the first to hurry off. *I guess some things do change,* Sylvia concluded, indifferently, looking at his figure in the rear-view mirror. She tried recalling what she used to find so irresistible about that man, but was unable to. He seemed sad and obsolete to her now...

Upon returning home, she rushed upstairs, walked into her room and quickly started undressing. In the dim light of dusk, she didn't see George sitting in the corner armchair. Turning around, the sight of him startled her.

"My apologies, I didn't mean to scare you," he said, softly.

"That's all right. I didn't realize you were back," Sylvia stammered. "I didn't see father anywhere, so I assumed you were still out."

"We came back right after you left."

"I'm just going to go freshen up and we should probably join my family downstairs. They've already lined up around the table. Stuffing your face, isn't that what Thanksgiving is all about?" she joked to chase away the awkwardness.

"We will. As to your question, as far as I'm concerned it's about spending time with loved ones. You know, people you consider *close,*" George pointed out.

"That too. I am being silly," she excused her remark, confused by his brisk reaction.

"While we're on the subject, what exactly do you want to get out of this?"

"I'm sorry, out of what?" Sylvia asked, alarmed.

"Our relationship," he clarified in a low voice.

"What kind of question is that? I think I've made it perfectly clear how important you are to me and how committed I am to a future with you," she explained hastily, and somewhat outraged. Appearing offended was a tactic Sylvia used often in her communication with men since she had found it usually put them on the defensive, and made them start apologizing to her.

"Right, you have," he agreed, thoughtfully. "However, when you meet behind my back with your exes on numerous occasions you send a rather… what's the term? Ambiguous message."

Sylvia froze, half-naked, in the middle of the room. She felt blood rushing to her head and her cheeks blushing in the dark, knowing he could sense her embarrassment and discomfort even though he was unable to see them. *How could he know?! I was so careful.* Frantic thoughts ran through her mind.

"You're probably wondering how I know? Allow me to point out a very major miss on your part, a rookie mistake, if you will, one that everyone with a small town background makes upon moving to New York. You think the city is big enough to hide all your indiscretions. You believe in anonymity. That's where you're wrong. No such thing exists. At least not in the here and now, where all your steps – virtual and real – can be traced to the smallest detail. People see and people talk."

"George, I…"

"Let me save you the embarrassment of trying to deny something, which might put you in the awkward situation of having to lie to my face. I'm no saint myself and God knows a man needs variety. We have said the L word to each other, but we've never discussed exclusivity… until now," he added, staring at her. "The bottom line is this. I've had my fair share of sleeping around, but there are things I'm required to do from now on. My family expects a lot from me; I expect a lot from me. While I can appreciate that my girlfriend straying is not the end of the world, it is something I will not tolerate."

"Why the sudden change of heart?" was the only thing that came to her mind.

"We know sufficiently about each other now, and you are aware of the line of work I want to get involved in. I believe you are future governor's wife-material, and with the right amount of strict but gentle handling you can excel at it. Of course, this brings us to the logical question; is this the type of life you want?"

"You know it is. I already told you."

"Then you'll have to give up your habit of re-living past thrills every once in a while, as it is not about you and your needs anymore. I need to project a certain image at all times and I can only associate with people who reinforce that image. That goes particularly for my family and friends."

"I understand."

"And to clarify all possible future misunderstandings and clear any doubts, don't – really, just *don't* – think there is any, even the slightest possibility, of getting away with anything of this sort. Don't feel limited, though. Think of it this way. You're free to do as you please, but be confident that I will find out one way or another. Does this sound like a fair deal to you?"

"Yes," she answered, without hesitation.

"I'm glad we're on the same page. It's time you started acting according to your stature, Sylvia. Meeting up with dead-end musicians is below you," he winced. She could physically feel his disapproval. *Funny,* she thought. *He's offended by James' social status rather than the act of infidelity.*

"That's why I met with him today, to end things," she muttered.

"Wise decision. One more thing. Due to the fact that we move in the same social circles, it would be impossible to cut them out of our lives, but I strongly advise you to be cautious around our dear friends Jennifer and her fiancé slash your ex-lover Alex. It's foolish of you to think anything could go unnoticed there."

"I... I'm sorry... it was just that one time..." she began explaining.

"Please, I *don't* need you to be sorry; I *need* you to not let it happen again," he interrupted her.

"I won't."

"Good girl. Now come over here and kneel."

Sylvia obediently approached him in the dark as he unzipped his pants. This new, firm, and somewhat menacing side to his character was an incredible turn-on for her.

An hour and a half later, they came downstairs smiling. The rest of the family was sitting around the dinner table, but everyone stopped talking when Sylvia and George walked in.

"George, my dear boy, come sit next to me," Frank patted the chair on his left side. "Sylvie, you sit right here, on my other side. I want to enjoy my children's company as much as I can during your short stay." As soon as they sat down, dinner was served. Mr. Watson looked at his family and everyone joined hands as he began saying grace. Sylvia enjoyed these festive moments the most. She was amused by the irony of her non-believing family clasping hands in a collective prayer. She knew her father did it purely out of respect and love for tradition and family values, but it still seemed fake, even though over the years everyone had started taking the ritual more seriously. *The universal rule,* she concluded as she took advantage of the fact everyone had their eyes closed and looked around at their concentrated faces, *everything becomes more serious when you put a ritualistic feel to it – even things that are not that important.* George didn't have his eyes closed either. They glanced at each other and smiled.

"You're a man of a different time, George. You probably find these traditions outdated and unnecessary, am I right?" her father asked, as he finished.

"Not at all, sir. Everything serves a purpose if it brings even the slightest sense of relief or reassurance to a person."

"Yes, well, you get older and you start re-examining your life, and I mean everything – your stance on good and bad, right and wrong; you rethink the values you have lived by; what's important and what you've missed in the mindless chase of fortune and success… but by the time you start figuring things out, the birds have already flown far away from the nest, mainly because you've chased them away with your chronic ambitions and perpetual lack of time." Frank sighed.

"You're getting emotional again, darling. We've been through this; there is no need to be so dramatic," his wife heckled him.

"I understand you perfectly, sir. The moment of re-evaluation of the worth of a man's life is staring us all in the face and it's the time quite a few mistakes make themselves known; only a strong man can face his with the courage to correct them while he still can, rather than spend his remaining days regretting and lecturing others on not making any themselves," George acknowledged softly.

"Well said, my boy. Well said." Sylvia's father seemed pleased. He finished cutting the turkey and turned to the young man. "Now, you'll have to excuse my bluntness, but I must ask the question that's been on all our minds since the moment you started going out with our beloved Sylvie. What are your intentions with her?"

"None other than serious and strictly honorable, sir."

"I don't expect anything else from a man of fine caliber such as yourself, but would you care to elaborate?" Frank urged him.

"Certainly. The reason I insisted on accompanying Sylvia on this Thanksgiving is because I'd like to ask for your daughter's hand in marriage," George explained, pulling out and opening a small box with a delicate ring inside. There was a wave of silence around the table as all female eyes froze on the spectacular piece of jewelry. Mr. Watson looked at his daughter, and upon seeing her reaction of sincere shock and awe cleared his throat, pleased with the fact that it was him that George was asking first.

"Obviously, you know that this is her decision to make, but I can say, without a sign of doubt, that I would be honored to have you as a son-in-law, my dear boy." He turned to Sylvia. "What is your answer, princess?"

She looked at him and back at George, unable to answer right away. The realization of the prey she had bagged seemed too good to be true. The whole experience was somewhat surreal; it was as if she had dissociated and was having an out-of-body experience. Slowly she regained control of her senses and a smile lit up her face.

"Yes!" she cried out, ecstatic. Her mother started sobbing on cue. George stood up, walked over to Sylvia and placed the ring on her finger. She threw herself in his arms and kissed him eagerly, but he pulled away sooner than she would like. Even in the most emotional of moments he still maintained social decorum. The rest of the family started congratulating them hectically.

She was glowing. Looking down at the timelessly classic piece of jewellery on her finger, she felt truly happy. The vintage 2.7 carat ring sparkled in the light of the chandelier. But it wasn't its physical qualities that made it so valuable to her – it was the look of jealousy in the eyes of all her female relatives. Sylvia smiled. *The only one way to determine the worth of something is to see how much other women want it*, she reminded herself with satisfaction.

Months flew by in a blur of frantic wedding preparations, giving Sylvia the reassurance she needed to realize she was a signature away from officially leading the life she had always wanted. No one was surprised at the announcement of the engagement of Fargo's mayor's only daughter to the eldest son of the governor of New Hampshire, and well wishes poured in from everywhere in the form of gifts to the houses of both families. Classmates Sylvia and George hadn't heard from in years went out of their way to get invited to the highly anticipated event. Ordinarily, she would've weighed the pros and cons of such "renewed" acquaintances, but now she couldn't be bothered. Between meeting her in-laws and making sure her wedding would be every bit as spectacular as she had pictured it, Sylvia couldn't make time for any ghosts from the past. Faithful to his nature and pattern of social conduct, George had insisted they keep it small, inviting only family and close friends.

Looking at her reflection in the mirror at the Monique Lhuillier boutique and marveling at the custom-made, embroidered, strapless lace gown, Sylvia frowned. *What's the point in looking this good if I can't get as many people as possible to see me?* She pouted. *I guess the features in the local newspapers and The New York Times make it not a total loss.* She loved that there was finally a legitimate reason for the whole world to revolve around her. Three whole months of talking about the wedding till the eleventh of March! I can't wait to marry George, but I am sure going to miss the attention, she confessed to Tanya while she was trying on her bridesmaid's dress.

"You seem really sure in your decision to marry him," her friend remarked. "No second thoughts or anything?"

"Not one. Why?"

"No reason except, it seems just yesterday you were still hung up on James. I didn't think you'd move on so quickly."

"Some women are just better at knowing what they want, which saves them the trouble of wasting too much time on the wrong guy. For something other than sex that is," Sylvia pointed out, indifferently.

The event planning and coordination was so overwhelming that even the anticipated meeting with her in-laws didn't throw Sylvia off her hectic schedule. One chilly autumn weekend she arrived with George in the quiet town of Salem; his father had preferred to stay at their colonial house rather than move to Concord after he was sworn into office. Sylvia was immediately drawn to the waterfront estate located on a small cove, with its private dock and sandy white beach, as well as to the way she was warmly welcomed into the home and hearts of these people. It was obvious the mere fact their son had chosen her for his wife was a good enough reason for them to already have the highest opinion of her. Still, Sylvia had never been worried about meeting her partner's parents. Getting under people's skin was her specialty. Her enticing vulnerability and delicate femininity instilled in men the unconscious desire to protect and guide her, and predisposed women to confide in her as they didn't feel threatened. Mothers adored her. It was something she had been trying to teach Tanya for years. "The deal can be sealed only through the mother," she often told her. "Of course, he needs to be on good terms with his. Then again, you don't want to have anything to do with anyone who has mommy issues, because these translate to women issues later on in life. It should never be your job to pick up the pieces of a broken man or to housebreak one. There are far better things you can do with your time."

Sylvia walked into the house on Shore Drive with all her arsenal of tricks to dazzle the family of her to-be-husband, but she didn't even have to try. They immediately clicked. She fell in love with the refined nobility these people emanated. George's mother Jacalyn was as delicate and collected as her son, and his father Thomas was authoritative without being threatening or overbearing. *They have all of my parents' qualities, but without any of their irritating provincial streaks,* she observed, pleased, sipping tea with her soon-to-be-mother-in-law one early evening in the living room. All the family had gathered around the lit fireplace, enjoying the magnificent view of the pond through the floor-to-ceiling windows. Mrs. Huntington smiled graciously at George, and delicately put her hand on Sylvia's arm.

"We are so happy to be part of your special day, my dear. Thank you for accepting our suggestion for a venue."

"How could we say no? We're so grateful for all your help with putting the wedding together. Everything feels overwhelming at times."

"That's what we're here for. Every bride should sit back and only worry about enjoying her most special day while her family turns it into a reality."

"I just wish my mother was as collected as you are. She's been running around Fargo, looking for a cake for the past month, but she can't decide on a design or taste," Sylvia winced.

"I wish you would've told us that earlier!" Jacalyn exclaimed with disappointment. "We could've spared her the unnecessary worries, as we already asked Sylvia to make the cake for your wedding."

"Sylvia?"

"Sylvia Weinstock. You must've heard of her! She's a dear family friend," Mrs. Huntington explained.

"You got *the* Sylvia Weinstock to make *our* wedding cake?!" She looked at George, all aflutter. "I don't know what to say. This is too good to be true!"

"We're happy to make your day as special as can be, my dear." Jacalyn held her hand. She gazed down at the sparkling jewelry on her finger and touched it. "I don't know if George has told you of the history of this ring. It goes back to the sixteen hundreds, and it's been in our family for generations, with the eldest son being the one to give it to his betrothed."

"George told me how much your family values traditions, but I don't think he fully communicated the extent."

"When all is said and done, the only thing that remains are those invisible bonds that drive us forward while holding us together," George's father joined the conversation. Sylvia looked at him with respect. She used to look down on people who thought so highly of outdated customs and over-hyped bonds, but the soft-spoken rigor of this man won her over. The model of this family with a clearly-defined hierarchy provided the security she needed and had looked for her entire life.

"Do we have a final number on the guests yet?" George asked.

"Two hundred and twenty three," his father replied.

"It went up again? I thought I'd made it clear we wanted a small wedding. Nothing over the top." Sylvia made an effort to hide her satisfaction *No, love. YOU wanted a small wedding. I want to be seen by as many people as possible on MY day.* She looked at his father, awaiting his reaction.

"Inviting people to your wedding is a gesture of respect and recognition for people whom you hold in high regard. It is not about you, George," he pointed out sternly.

"I'm aware of that. I didn't mean to sound disrespectful. It was just my impression that all these people would've come to less than a hundred," his son was quick to explain.

"Yours and Sylvia's former classmates and colleagues together with her relatives make about half of the total. The rest are old family friends, some of my classmates from Yale and other respectable people."

"Whatever you deem fit. Will we able to accommodate all of them?"

"I already spoke to the wedding coordinator at The Granite Rose and they assured us it won't be an issue," his mother commented.

"All right then," George nodded.

"You worry too much, my dear. Like I said, you and Sylvia just need to leave everything to us," she added.

"Point taken, and please know how much we appreciate all your help and support." He smiled at his mother.

"Please, darling. What are families for?"

Winter flew by in a daze of family reunions and trips between New York, North Dakota and New Hampshire, with Sylvia counting down the hours to the anticipated day. The introduction of the two families went without serious incident, as everyone was extremely careful to avoid any topics that could cause issues on a personal level. *Or no one wants to rock the boat, knowing their offspring cannot possibly marry into a more suitable family,* she concluded as she observed her father and Mr. Huntington discussing politics in the den one evening. *After all, it's about everyone's best interests, isn't it?*

Just as she had anticipated, people who had left her life long ago suddenly re-appeared on the horizon after news of her engagement graced the wedding sections of various newspapers, but Sylvia was mostly interested in James' reaction. Predictably, there wasn't one and she took his silence as the ultimate proof that he had heard, and wasn't indifferent to the news. "Thirty years and still the same trying-not-to-give-a-fuck pose. Cute," she told Tanya while out picking the centerpieces with Jacalyn one early day in January.

"I thought you didn't care what James thought anymore," her friend remarked.

"No. I said I didn't care what he *wanted* anymore. There's a difference," Sylvia pointed out, irked. "Anyone who tells you they don't care about the opinion of an ex is a liar, and not a very good one either. It's a constant competition and that's just the natural order of life."

"Competition?"

"Yeah. The who's-gonna-die-miserable-and-alone competition. Why else does everyone keep tabs on their exes through every possible source? And thank God for social media, which has been making it considerably easier for the past ten years."

"So we never really move on with our lives, do we?"

"Of course we do. As long as we're better off than our exes we're fine," Sylvia winked at Tanya, then turned around and nodded at the Lily of the Valley centerpiece. "I want this one. It's simple and classy."

"What are the flower types?" Mrs. Huntington turned to the shop-assistant.

"This arrangement is white gardenias, stephanotis, lily of the valley, polo roses and peonies. We arrange them in small groupings so the lilies are not overwhelmed by the bigger flowers. It's the perfect combination of various flower types without it seeming too piled," the girl explained.

"Perfect. That's the one we pick. It's very bridal and delicate," Jacalyn agreed, pleased with her soon-to-be daughter-in-law's taste.

As they were making arrangement about the centerpieces to be assembled and delivered to The Granite Rose, Tanya pulled Sylvia away and continued interrogating her.

"But *how* can you know if you're better or worse than an ex?"

"Oh please! That's like the easiest thing to find out! Reality check; are you the one trying to get in touch with him and bitch about your current partner or is it the other way around? The answer to that is the answer to your question."

"And in your case that person is…"

"Don't make me state the obvious." Sylvia rolled her eyes.

"Well, congratulations, Sylvie. Looks like you really *do* have it all."

"I know."

She turned to Mrs. Huntington, who gently held her arm as they left the floral stylist boutique. Tanya skipped alongside.

"What if no one is trying to get in touch with anyone as both are busy living their lives away from each other?" she demanded as they waited for the driver to open the door.

"Then you just haven't waited long enough. Looking up the ex will happen eventually, whether it's for supposed closure, making amends, for reassurance in the choices made, or for boosting someone's self-esteem," Sylvia pointed out, pulling up her sunglasses.

"Why?"

"It's the quickest and safest way to get feedback on yourself without having to invest in a whole new relationship or risk anything in your current one," she explained before getting in the car.

March came with its foggy, cool mornings and warm, sun-lit days. The contrast seemed to reflect that between the life Sylvia was leaving and the one she was on the verge of starting. Standing in front of the mirror in the bridal suit at The Granite Rose on the morning of her big day, she examined her reflection with satisfaction. *This dress is the most flattering thing I've ever worn*, she observed, pleased with how calm and collected she felt. No amount of oohing and aahing had managed to get her overly emotional. *Funny*, she thought, *it takes a guy to get a girl excited about marriage just as it takes one to make her indifferent to the concept of "till death do us part"*. One last twirl, and she left the room, confident in the calculated realization that becoming the future Mrs. Huntington the Third was the deal of a lifetime for her. She felt the closest to happy that she could get, clutching onto the bouquet. The air was saturated with the sweet aroma of the lilies of the valley arranged throughout the venue.

Walking down the aisle, she could see the same restraint in George's eyes. He intently followed her every movement, but there was nothing beyond mild excitement and proud delight on his face. This gave Sylvia the reassurance she needed. *If he feels the way I do about him this is obviously a right decision. No one is head over heels in love; no one is burning with passion or withering with desire. We're just two people attracted to each other, aware of our best interests. That is the recipe for a happily-ever-after,* she thought as she laid her hand on top of his.

The ceremony was short and concise, tasteful and moving without added fluff. There were no self-written vows or romantic testaments to make the guests acutely aware of the newlyweds' overwhelming love. Everything bore the mark of clean and classy simplicity, the trademark of George's style that was part of his effortless and strong presence of power. Sylvia looked at the custom Chopard white gold band he placed on her finger; hers had an added subtle diamond circle that sparkled in the light.

She breathed a sigh of relief on hearing, "I now pronounce you husband and wife", and raised her head. The most daunting thing Sylvia had had to master during their short time together was mimicking George's refined and powerful demeanor together with his temperate taste. Overcoming her provincial mindset of the more the better was her single greatest achievement, although deep down she still hadn't experienced a true change of heart. She was still going through a process of transformation. As they moved to the rhythm of the music in front of hundreds of gazing eyes in their first dance as a married couple, she looked around triumphantly. George guided her confidently and firmly across the dance floor, and Sylvia noted with delight that his grip on her waist was stronger than usual. There was an unfamiliar look of severity in his eyes that gave her a newfound sense of security and comfort. She gazed at their matching bands and rested her chin on his shoulder.

The evening was a surreal blur of lavish partying, and a seemingly unending stream of powerful and wealthy friends, conveying their good wishes to the couple. Sylvia and George basked in the attention with her particularly enjoying being the centre of it. She was introduced to people she had read or heard about, but never dreamt of meeting in person. The sheer number of guests present and introduced as the Huntington's old family friends was overwhelming, and Sylvia couldn't help but feel like she had been granted entry to a very exclusive social club.

It was nearing midnight when the lights were dimmed and all eyes turned to the magnificent 7-tier ivory wedding cake, which rose several feet above the groom's head. George's mother had confided in Sylvia Weinstock's otherworldly talent, leaving the design entirely up to the reigning confectionary diva. As the bride approached the dazzling creation she saw three of the layers were embellished with hundreds of small flowers, amongst which she could make out elaborate tiny roses, lilies of the valley, ivy leaves, white heathers and myrtle. Pinned to barely-noticeable strings, hundreds of fondant butterflies created the illusion of fluttering around the flowers. Everything was highly ornate and beautifully arranged without appearing cluttered. She was unable to hide her awe, and glowed with excitement as she placed her hand on George's and they cut through it. *I've seen her cakes before and she clearly knows her craft, but this time she's outdone herself!* Sylvia thought, as they barely made it through one tier with the knife. Everyone had their eyes on the spectacular creation, although George's and her classmates seemed far more impressed by the Veuve Clicquot fountain they had gathered around. While George had invited all of his close friends and year-long acquaintances she made sure the only former classmates she invited were the ones who wouldn't spare the details when spreading the word about her flamboyant wedding.

Later that night, she finally managed to sneak a couple of minutes alone with her maid of honor. Seeing Tanya head to the bathroom, Sylvia, rushed in after her.

"It's been one crazy night, huh?" she commented, closing the door behind her. "Anyone else in here?"

"Just me," Tanya reassured her. "Congratulations, Mrs. Huntington the Third! You've finally arrived." She hugged her friend.

"I know! Can you believe it?! I mean, I've always known my life would turn out pretty well, but this is just too fucking awesome!" Sylvia grinned at Tanya in the mirror. "George makes all other men I've been with seem like… well, boys; stupid, adolescent boys."

"Even James? I was surprised I didn't see his name on the guest list. I know you've been dying to rub it in his face," her friend teased.

"Naturally. You think inviting him would've done the trick? On the contrary. He'll hear of this; you can be damn sure of it. Why else are Pauline, Beth and Nicole here?" Sylvia chuckled.

"I wondered about that. You were never close with any of them. You and Beth hardly spoke to each other," Tanya remarked.

"True. But remember how they knew everything about everyone? These three are like a fucking tabloid agency. They know stuff before it's even happened. How they do it is beyond me, but I can be sure a detailed description of tonight will reach James. Not to mention the bonus of the extra fluff added to the story every time it's passed along! Ah, the joys of having the same social background as your ex!" Sylvia giggled.

"I thought you were over him."

"Of course I am. This is purely for entertainment and evening the score purposes."

"I understand."

"Do you really?" she asked, unnerved. "Why do I always have to spell it out for you? It's never about how you see yourself. That's irrelevant. We're never fully satisfied with the *status quo*; things can only be appreciated in the light of their absence and that's when it's usually too late. To avoid all that shit all you need to do is look for your life's reflection in the eyes of the people around you. Particularly in the eyes of those who have a whole lot of reasons to despise, be angry with or dislike you. Their opinion is the only objective one."

"Then I shouldn't even bother telling you that you've got yourself a wonderful family and an amazing man beside you."

"This means nothing to me, coming from you that is. There is no higher affirmation than an ex's. And I'm *this* close to mine." Sylvia held up her hand, showing with her thumb and index finger.

"How can you be so sure?"

"Last time we met in Fargo it was *him* who suggested we go back to my place. And it's been *him* calling me for several months, *asking* that I drop by."

"Asking, suggesting, are you sure it's James we're talking about?" Tanya joked.

"I know. It's eerie seeing this change in him. Kinda sad too," Sylvia remarked as she fixed one of her curls with a pin. "Apparently all men turn into pathetic whining slobs when you cut them off for good; you know, taking away what they're used to thinking of as rightfully theirs. Years of convenience, lust and devotion suddenly gone. Men hate insecurity even more so than women. Put them in a situation where they don't know where they stand and you've got yourself a whole new game to play. It's empowering. Of course, someone has to pay the dues. But that's life."

"The next girlfriend?"

"In James' case, his current one. God, I don't even wanna picture what the poor girl must be going through. He was always one to perform quite poorly under stress, and he's prone to losing people he took for granted. That must've shaken up his world quite a bit."

"That seems unfair."

"Collateral damage is always an added bonus when you're trying to even the score with someone," Sylvia pointed out, indifferently.

"That's a bit cold-hearted," Tanya remarked.

"Oh, I'm sorry. I forgot I'm supposed to watch out for *everyone else's* feelings, needs and wants every step of the way," Sylvia mocked her.

"I'm just saying it doesn't hurt to be more respectful and considerate towards other people, especially those who have nothing to do with a situation they've wandered into. It's not their fault."

"It's everyone's fault. We're in this shit collectively, and thinking it's up to you to spare someone the hurt and humiliation you've endured at some point in your life is just delusional. Worse even – you think you're doing good, but you're actually rubbing in their faces how much better and morally superior you consider yourself to be. Who do you think you are? Mother-fucking Theresa? Is it *your* responsibility to redeem someone else's sins?"

"That's not how I mean it."

"But it's exactly how it comes off. People dislike martyrs, Tanya, and you're not going to do anyone any good, let alone yourself, by offering yourself as one. It's not your job to try and save others. By doing that you're only reminding them of their flaws and misdeeds. Women wonder why men don't kiss the ground beneath their feet when they take care of them, pick up after their lazy asses, wash their shirts, cook meals and stay up late while the ungrateful slobs are out fucking some girl they picked up at a bar. But what they fail to see is that depravity is way sexier than innocence and purity."

"I think you're wrong. It's possible to build a relationship based on trust, mutual respect, appreciation, friendship, intimacy, all those things you mock," Tanya argued, disheartened.

"You know what? You're right! How was your date with Paul by the way? Did you get a call back?

"No. But you said he wasn't that interested anyway," Tanya stammered.

"Correction – he *had* every chance to be interested, but you didn't take any of them," Sylvia pointed out, amused.

"How is that then?"

"Perception, my dear. It's all about perception."

"I'm not sure I understand."

"Let me give you an example. When James and I fuck, I wrap my arms around his shoulders and hold him tightly, burying my nose in his neck. He thinks it's a sign of passion and uncontrollable desire. I do it, so I don't have to look at him during. It's distracting. It's much easier to masturbate with another person without the awkward moment of accidentally locking eyes. Otherwise you have to acknowledge it is an actual *person* lying on top of you and that complicates things. My orgasm is all that matters, but he doesn't need to know that. It's all a point of perception."

"I'm still not sure I understand what you're getting at."

"I know you don't. You will eventually. Every woman starts out as you. Then she's given a choice – she can either evolve and save herself, or waste away, trying to save others. I sincerely hope you'll give up on the latter concept eventually."

"We all have our own path in life," Tanya disagreed.

"Typical words, spoken by a person too afraid to take matters into her own hands. I know it's easier to sit back and watch as your life passes you by, experiencing it as a viewer rather than play the lead part. However this type of thinking won't get you anywhere good."

"I think you're wrong to assume everyone is as bold and sure of themselves as you, Sylvie. I just don't have that level of confidence. What am I supposed to do?"

"Fake it till you make it."

"Does it work?"

"You have no idea," Sylvia grinned.

"Shall we?" Tanya walked to the door. "Your betrothed must be wondering where his better half is." She hesitated, and stopped before turning the knob. "So, are you happy now? Got everything you hoped for?"

"It couldn't have turned out better," the bride laughed.

"So you're in love with him then?" Tanya demanded.

"That's a bit naïve, don't you think? After a certain age love falls behind to give way to more important things," Sylvia remarked.

"Such as?"

"Security, companionship, sexual fulfillment, social stature, comfort, mutual respect… Do you need more?"

"Doesn't it bother you that you'll have to spend the rest of your life with someone you're not in love with?"

"Love alone is worthless. It cannot sustain a relationship, any relationship. Holding hands and gazing at the stars and each other's eyes gets old quickly. And once that initial period of lust and infatuation wears off you realize you need a partner by your side, not a horny adolescent who's only good at writing poems and playing love tunes to impress the girls."

"Wow. Between you and me, how did you manage to convince George you're a worthwhile partner to have?"

Sylvia stared at her friend intently. *Kudos for the cockiness. A question so blunt deserves an honest answer,* she thought.

"It's simple, sweetie. I know my worth, which is why I always go for guys who would, otherwise, be considered out of my league. Confident people always get the better deal of everything because they refuse to settle. George knows I'm the right woman for him because I play the part. I fit his social status," she stressed.

"You do make a good-looking couple. I mean, the two of you, you just fit."

"Thank you for stating the obvious. Let's go." She ushered her out of the bathroom.

As she made her way through the guest-filled room, her eyes fell on George, who was talking to Sarkis near the cut cake. He stopped, smiled at her and held out his arm in an invitation for a dance. Sylvia hurried to him and sank into his arms. The music started and everyone circled them in awe and silence. He leaned in and buried his lips in her hair.

"You look beautiful, Mrs. Huntington."

Surprising to herself Sylvia felt a flutter in her stomach. "Thank you, Mr. Huntington," she blushed. *Maybe Tanya has a point. It's all right to care, with the right person,* she reassured herself.

CHAPTER THIRTEEN

James was sitting at the kitchen table, staring grimly at the newspaper when his father walked in the room. He barely glanced at him, and lit up a smoke.

"Who's the slut that's got you moping around this time?"

"Doesn't matter."

"Yeah. I can see," his father remarked.

"Just a wedding announcement of an old friend."

"And by 'friend' you mean a broad you used to do," he clarified.

"Yes, that's exactly what I mean."

James held his head in his hands. *Fucking great. Came here to get away from everything and it's Relationship Trivia all over. Could've stayed in New York just as well. Would've at least saved myself the trip fare.* He looked over at his father, who was stepping out on the balcony to smoke, indifferent to the angry glare of his son. *Why did I even bother coming here? It's nothing like it used to be,* James thought with regret. Everything was becoming too much for him to deal with: Karen; work; his friends' and former class mates' personal and professional achievements; his family's never-ending expectations of him; even his own continuous belief that the success he was destined for was just around the corner. Coming back to the spacious, empty and unkempt apartment he once so fondly referred to as "home" was particularly difficult for James. It was the only place where he had no choice but to face the dreaded reality that stared him in the face. Even the knowledge of his former classmates – all settled down with careers and on their way to personal happily-ever-afters – wasn't as disheartening as the notion of facing his former self; an image trapped between those four walls he had to deal with every time. Anywhere he looked, he was surrounded by bits of what used to be and what he had lost that caused him excruciating pain. Somewhere on the dusty shelves, shoved between a biography of one of his favourite musicians and an old algebra text book, Her picture still lay around. He didn't have to look for it; he knew it was there. He kept coming back to immerse in the tranquillity and stillness of a past long gone, but all he found were stories of people moving on, whose ghosts he still held onto. There was nothing for him here. Especially now. *Particularly now,* James sighed, crumbling the newspaper into a ball and tossing it aside.

Over the years, he had kept convincing himself she was something on the side. *Then why the sudden feeling of abandonment?* he wondered, throwing a cursory glance at the smiling couple on the creased page. But he knew the answer. He felt it. He stood up and looked outside. The sun had started to set, casting its last rays on the top of the buildings across the street. Soon he'd be able to wander aimlessly under the convenient cloak of anonymity the dusk provided. James enjoyed these long silent walks. In his typical self-destructive manner, he spent them reminiscing about a time long gone. He walked slowly past places and people, never stopping even for a minute in a faint effort to escape his past. Somehow, he didn't realise holding onto people from it was the thing that was making it impossible.

The town seemed emptier than usual. Or perhaps it was the notion that Sylvia would no longer come running if he called; her or anyone else. They had all moved on. His back-up plan. His safety-net. James felt betrayed. *We've known each other for over ten years, most of which she claimed she was in love with me. I've helped her out so many times. I treated her well when we lived together in Schaumburg. She was the one who always stayed. Why is she leaving now? And worse even, why do I care so much?* The thoughts rushing through his mind were scaring him, together with the realisation that things with Karen would have been far better if he had the comforting notion of Sylvia being there to turn to. It was the stability of their unspoken rule to not be exclusive, but always have each other present that had made it possible for James to go on with his life after several heartbreaks. He suddenly stopped, overwhelmed by the acute emptiness of having lost something important. *It doesn't matter anymore, but I came to love you, became fond of you, grew attached to you, as I had promised myself not to do when we first met. It's not because I saw myself in you, but because you were always there when I needed you, when I needed someone, anyone. It was always you, Sylvia. And for a short while, being with you brought back my old self that I miss so much sometimes. I felt alive like I haven't felt for the longest time since She left years ago, in a past lifetime. Living had a point. I could take on the world again and keep on fighting. Love was the fuel of my engine; art was the smoke blowing out of it, dark and smothering. And you were the only one who stayed to witness it, to appreciate it, to walk me through the dark labyrinth of my obsessions, my insecurities, my pain. Just remembering that feeling erases all the pain and sorrows of the years passed, the obstacles encountered, the pure hardship of just keeping on living.* Stills of him lying in bed next to her, reaching out to caress her cheek and play with her hair flooded his mind.

For the first time he wanted her to know what she meant to him.

Looking around, he felt an overwhelming feeling of helplessness. *Just as with every other thing in my life, I'm realizing too late that I've lost you, Sylvia. If it would make a difference, I'd thank you for the time you spent loving me. It will soon be seven years since I've felt remotely as happy as when you lived with me in Schaumburg. I wanted so much for you to come back after you went off to college at the end of summer. It was insane, but I don't think I've ever wanted anything more. I didn't want to say a word out of fear of spoiling everything, but I guess I did spoil it anyway. It is true that in this life it doesn't matter who loves you, but who you end up loving. I couldn't show that side of me to you; after all, the only thing that kept you coming back was my indifference, right? It's what drives you women crazy with desire. Truth is, I was so angry at you for choosing him at the time that I convinced myself I didn't want anything more, but now I see I've been fooling myself. You were holding everything together. Now I can't even hold onto Karen because she sees my weakness. Women hate that, don't they? They want to be taken care of; not the other way around. They don't want to look after a wreck, a pathetic remnant of a person. Or maybe she just sees right through me and knows I can't be bothered with this fucking charade anymore.* He started walking again. Suddenly, he felt tired. He looked up at the dark window in the building across the street; unknowingly he had walked in a direction towards Sylvia's apartment. *What's the point of it anyway?* he wondered. *If I'm losing people I never tried holding onto, what's my chance of making it work with Karen — even if I have feelings for her? She'll leave. They all do, eventually.*

James pulled out his phone and stared at the screen. Scrolling down to Sylvia's name, he hesitated and opened up a window for a text instead. *All or nothing,* he thought, as he started typing Karen a message. He pressed send hastily, so as not to give himself the chance to rethink it and back down.

"You feel like home. This place doesn't."

He briefly stared at it as he had a habit of re-reading all his messages and e-mails.

He then turned around and hurried back home. His father saw him walking down the street from the balcony and flicked his cigarette butt down into the street next to him.

"You disappoint me," was the first thing he said when James walked through the door. "No woman is worth the loss of sleep; let alone these mindless adolescent stunts at such hour."

"Thanks for the encouragement," his son snarled. "Get in line. Apparently I've disappointed quite a few people. Might as well form a club, or something."

"Don't go all touchy-feely on me now. You know darn well what I mean. Since when are you one to chase after some dumb broad's pretentious ass when there's more fish in the sea than ever! And they keep getting better by the year!"

"Who said I was chasing after anyone?"

"Why are you moping around then?"

"It's not like you'd understand."

"Try me." His father pulled out a chair and looked at him patiently.

"Karen... Let's just say we're having some disagreements because there was a somewhat misfortunate incident. I tried my best to make sure this didn't happen, but an ex called one night and Karen picked up. Anyhow, long story short, she knows we're still seeing each other and is severely unhappy about it. I can appreciate her situation and understand why she found it hurtful, but I don't see what the big deal is."

"Run for the hills and don't look back. This girl is toxic."

"What makes you say that?"

"A woman intimidated by an ex is a huge red flag. It shows a lot of skeletons in the closet, or *emotional baggage* as you kids call it these days."

"Such as?" James insisted.

"Low self-esteem, insecurity, clinginess, jealousy, possessiveness, emotional instability, to name a few. None of these are a problem on their own, but together... Problem is that suddenly it's the man's job to keep her fragile personality from falling apart at the seams and before you know it, she's turned you into a pathetic slob, who's watching everything he says and does, so he doesn't upset the manic depressive psycho."

"I thought you always said low self-esteem was a good quality in a woman."

"It is if you wanna get her in bed. It's not for a long-term relationship-sort-of-thing. That's what you want with this Karen girl, right?" he asked, rolling another cigarette.

"Yes. At least I thought I did. I'm not so sure anymore," James shrugged. "She's insisting I stop with the potentially detrimental behaviour."

"By which she means?"

"Keeping exes *on call*; having back-up plans. She says it's the same as cheating."

"How's it the same? It's good sense, is what it is!"

"Thank you! I can see her point though; I'd be offended if I knew she was doing it."

"Yeah, but it's different for women. It's not like they spend too much time mourning the end of a relationship. All it takes is one stroll down the street in a skanky outfit and they've got their tight little asses back in the game and off the market. It's a whole other thing for a man, who has to spend months mending his bruised ego, dealing with the rejection and all."

"*Thank you.* She doesn't see it that way, though. That's another thing I like about her, she's so naïve. Her inexperience is priceless. She has other nice qualities too. In many ways she *gets me.*"

"You're trying to convince yourself there's a future. That's a sign you're balls deep in shit, my boy. I'm telling you, get out *now* when there's still time to cut your losses and move on with minimum collateral damage," his father frowned.

"You know, I think I'm gonna stick it out just this once. I mean, I'm not twenty anymore. It's not like my options increase with the passing years. And to be perfectly honest, I'm tired."

"Tired of what?"

"The game. Even in the most superficial relationships the struggle for power is fucking draining. I can't keep up anymore. The rules, the acting, the constant keeping of score. With Karen it's easier. She *actually* believes couples *are* on the same team and it's not a matter of getting the other one to submit to *your* needs and wishes. This would be endearing if it didn't remind me of how effing stupid I used to be for thinking the same," James laughed.

"Good to see you haven't forgotten everything I've taught you," his father remarked.

"Yeah, well, I'm not like you. I can't be fifty and starting anew with yet another woman. Down the line, aren't they all the same? Same stories; same fears; same insecurities; same needs and expectations you have to pretend to live up to… It got old for me at some point I guess. With Karen I have it pretty good. The sex is decent. She's great at cooking and the general having-someone-to-take-care-of-you-stuff. She's a bit more withdrawn than I would like but still…"

"Don't know, you lost me at 'the sex is decent'. What the fuck is that? Sex is decent?! That's the only thing sex is *not* supposed to be with two people who want to make a life together!"

253

"You're putting too much emphasis on it. I've had my fair share of sowing wild oats; been there, tried everything. So she's putting up a little less than adequate performance in that department. It's not something to burn bridges over."

"To each his own I guess. If you're OK with it what can I say?" His father shrugged and stepped out on the balcony again, lighting another cigarette. He stood there for a couple of minutes, then popped his head though the door. "Whatever happened to that wild plaything of yours, Sonya-something?"

"Sylvia?" James corrected him.

"Yeah, that's the one! God, I can't believe my son was fucking the mayor's daughter! I still tell the guys about it, you know!" his father laughed.

"I know. The *one* thing I specifically asked you *not* to do, remember?"

"Come on, you gotta understand your old man. This is the type of stuff that makes you proud of your offspring!"

"Right, and it's exactly the sort of stuff that turns your offspring into a social outcast," James snarled.

"You seemed pretty content in that relationship," his father continued, ignoring his comment. "I never understood why you didn't take things further with her. She was crazy about you; used to wait around like a dog for you to come home from university; called days ahead to make sure you were coming. And from what I recall, you never referred to sex with her as 'decent'." He patted James on the back, winking at him.

"Yeah. No, it was anything but," he agreed. "You just don't get it, though. The whole point of what I had with Sylvia was that it wasn't exclusive. That kept our so-called relationship going from the start. It's what fuelled her efforts to please me and tolerate my being a total asshole to her. *That* and a lot of unresolved self-esteem issues but still. The moment I so much as entertained the idea of something even remotely serious with her she ran for the hills, And into the arms of the son of the governor of New Hampshire."

"Ah, yeah. I thought I read something about their wedding in the paper. Is *that* why you were moping around earlier?"

"Not quite," James hesitated. "I can understand her moving on. I can appreciate the fact that after a certain age a woman has to go with the odds and settle down with the most prospective candidate, the one who's willing *and* able to offer stability, partnership and the whole lot. But I can't understand her cutting me out of her life like that. Fourteen years! Fourteen years of 'I love you'; of going out of her way to please me; of taking it so far up the ass she could barely squirm just because I wanted to see what she'd let me do. That was the deal. You do what you will, but never turn your back on the other one. I thought we were friends. I trusted her. It's hard not to get too comfortable around someone who's always available, you know? Every time I felt horny all I had to do was call her up and fucking boom, she'd materialise at my doorstep within hours, not to mention the fact she'd let me do whatever the fuck I wanted with her body and played my dick like a fucking violin. The dynamics of that relationship were ridiculously great – it was all about *me* and *my* needs. I guess I thought where all the rest left, she would be the one to stay. Obviously I was wrong. She was just pretending to *care*. Now I can't even recognise this stuck-up cunt who can't even be bothered to pick up her phone, let alone gag on my dick like she loved to do."

"Didn't she live with you for a while?"

"Live might be pushing it. She stayed for the whole summer in between semesters back when I was in Chicago."

"What happened there?"

"We got bored of each other pretty quickly I guess. Meeting up to fuck is one thing; trying to build a relationship on top of *that* and nothing else can be challenging."

"The opposite is also true. Try building one without quality fucking. It's doomed from the start. So when did she start acting up?"

"Right around the time she met the upstate prick, I'm guessing. A woman so high-maintenance as her? Come on, she must've wet herself at the sight of a guy who can afford to buy Egyptian cotton toilet paper for her spoilt, slutty ass."

"Were you willing to offer her anything other than your on-going deal?"

"I might've hinted at the possibility. But that doesn't mean I started trying. You know me. I don't like working at it."

"Seems to me like she made the smart choice, the one every woman's faced with at a certain age. Sounds like your friend had sufficient self-confidence to be able to move on and latch onto the better prey."

"Then why did she keep coming back to me months after she had started going out with Prince Charming?"

"Nostalgia. Women can be very sentimental. Never underestimate the power of a pity fuck, which makes for about 90% of women's collective dating history. They always feel guilty when they've emotionally moved on from a guy; especially when they see him struggling or still hung up on them. It's a sort of subtle, *I'm-letting-you-down-gradually-so-you-have-time-to-warm-up-to-the-idea-of-dying-alone* sort of thing."

"How noble!" James growled. "I don't know. I just don't get it."

"Well, you said it yourself. You were always a dick to her."

"That's what got her interested in the first place; that's what kept her coming back for more."

"You should be very attentive of the way you win a girl over. The way you get her interested in you will also be the way you'll lose her," his father remarked, blowing out a puff of smoke.

"Could've told me that sooner."

"How did you get Karen?"

"Lying."

"Well there you go. Things are coming to their logical conclusion."

"What if I don't want them to?" James looked up. "I am still not willing to give her up. I won't be 30-something, picking up the pieces after yet *another* failed relationship. Now, when even my safety net has moved on, what other options do I have? I've *got* to make this work. I just have to!"

"Good to see your level of commitment to the job."

"Sarcasm isn't helping. If you don't have anything constructive to say…" James frowned.

"Look. I know denial is men's preferable comfort zone, but it's a well-known fact you get one shot per woman in a lifetime. A single fuck up and you're out – plain and simple as that. Don't stay and wait to see just how much you've fucked up. Just don't."

"I'll think about it."

James finished his beer, picked up the newspaper and left the room, shutting the door behind him. His father stared after him for a brief moment. He knew him well enough to be certain that his son would do the impossible to make a bad situation even worse. *Everything that boy touches turns to shit,* he observed. *It's like a gift or something.* He shrugged, lighting another cigarette. The years had taught him it was useless to try and talk any sense into him. James seemed to enjoy complicating his own life.

One of the few things that remained unchanged about his returns to this place was the almost palpable feeling of solitude and peace in his room – books, clothes and memorabilia remained in their old places, bearing only the mark of time having passed. Nothing was rearranged or thrown out. Stepping into his old room almost made James feel like his old self again. Or at least it reminded him of where it had all begun. Somewhere between the books on the shelf lay the creased giveaway of the reason for his frantic wandering and chronic unhappiness. He reached for it, summoning the courage to look into Her eyes after all these years. *Maybe I could find some answers. Although it would've been easier if She had just given them to me,* he thought. Holding the picture with a trembling hand, he looked away at the stuffed teddy on the desk. "What's this thing doing here?" he asked out loud. He remembered throwing it away in a garbage bin the second he turned around the corner and hid from Sylvia's sight. At least he thought he did. *Could I really have kept it?* he wondered. He pulled one of the drawers and went through it frantically until he found a picture of a young, puffy teenage girl, smiling suggestively at the camera. Putting it next to the one he was holding in his other hand, James tried recreating the sense of shame and embarrassment he first felt when he started going out with Sylvia, but was unable to. *Man is a funny creature – there isn't anything he's not capable of getting used to*, he shrugged. There was nothing even remotely similar between the two women. They were light years apart when it came to looks, character, charisma, demeanor, importance to him, even…Yet time and consecutive events had somehow managed to erase most of the striking differences and bring them closer in terms of the role they had played in his life. This realization frightened him. Startled, he sat on the corner of the bed, the same bed where he'd made love to both of them for the first time. Their images intertwined in his disturbed mind, where there was an unbreakable bond between the woman that had broken his heart and the one who had persistently put the pieces back together. But it was just when he was forced to be weaned from her presence that James realized Sylvia was the only thing keeping him from falling apart at the seams.

Overrun with thoughts and emotions, he looked around. The past was relentlessly beginning to reclaim him. *Not that it has ever loosened its grip*, James smiled bitterly. The feelings of loneliness and disappointment were almost palpable. Everything he had lost was making itself known in a physically painful way. He reached for the bottle of gin and took several long sips before putting it down. Sliding down the familiar slope of alcoholic delirium brought the much-awaited, if temporary, reassurance that the life he thought he had lost never had existed in the first place, at least not for him anyway. James found peace in that thought. He flipped though the newspaper in an attempt to distract himself with something, anything, but his eyes fell on a picture with a familiar face in it. He read the headline a first, then a second time: "Mayor Watson's daughter announces engagement to New Hampshire senator's eldest son." Staring at the happy faces of the couple, he studied their body language. *That sort of intimacy is not an indication of any gaps on the sexual front. I can't believe I bought the "no blowjob" story. I was too busy jacking off my ego to the thought of being the last guy she's felt "comfortable enough" to do it with I guess.* He threw the paper aside and held his head with his hands. "I'm such an idiot," he muttered.

Sitting there, listening to his alcohol-infused thoughts, he felt exhausted from trying to hold onto so many ghosts from his past. *Right now they're out there, getting married, having kids, living their lives, not knowing I'm stuck re-living our time together in an endless agony of trying to find someone who is just as damaged as myself, so she won't judge my pathetic attempts at being a normal human being.* Just like a person overboard he reached for the first thing in sight that offered any possibility of consolation and salvation. Looking for a substitute was what he did, the only thing he really knew. Her name unconsciously slipped through his lips. "Karen." James looked up. *If there's any chance for me, any chance at all, it's through her. She's my angel; she can help me. There's no one else to turn to. She knows the taste of pain and humiliation; she'll stick with me through the dirt.* He instinctively reached for his phone. He closed his eyes. Thoughts of her dark beauty, her wonderful mind and the enchanting sound of her voice started rushing in. He craved seeing her candid smile; feeling the touch of her long white fingers; burying his lips in her unruly long hair and breathing in her ethereal scent. An almost pressing need to call her and tell her he was sorry overwhelmed him, but if there was something the years had thought him it was to be as silent as possible and allow for these things to slip into oblivion on their own. His usual cynical self crumbled under the soft yet piercing look of her warm eyes. She always looked at him like a medical officer diagnosing him with something he hadn't even known he had. James felt uneasy around her. She was too sensitive, too intuitive, too intelligent for him to successfully pull off any of his usual tricks. *If I am to have any chance of making it work, I'll have to throw everything I know out the window and learn from scratch. There's still time. The damage is repairable if we just let it go and move on as quickly as possible.* Reassured by these thoughts, he laid his head on the cool pillow and closed his eyes. Her inexperience and weirdness only added to his certainty things could work out. *I'm such a lucky bastard,* was the last thing that went through his burdened mind before he passed out.

In the weeks that followed James surprised himself by finding it in him to be particularly attentive and caring in ways he didn't think were possible. This only made him feel all the more hopeless and agitated. Despite his best efforts, things were progressively falling apart, with his frequent trips to Fargo only adding to an already tense situation. Karen had become more withdrawn and distant than usual, something he found extremely irritating as he had no idea how to deal with it.

"I'm telling you, she's more absent than she used to be!" he complained to Lyle. He had started hanging out at his place more often now that things were sliding downhill at an alarming pace. "If she yelled or cried, or even threw something at the wall I'd be fine with it: those are all normal reactions of a human being not completely devoid of sentiment. But Karen, nothing gets through to her."

"Have you tried provoking her?"

"Several times. The most I get out of her is a sarcastic remark or two."

"I don't know what to tell you. I'd say you were warned, given where the two of you met, but I'm guessing you're already aware of that."

"What do you mean?"

"Well, online hook-ups are like…" Lyle hesitated, "buying something from a charity shop. The stuff on the shelf is outdated and damaged, but you convince yourself you'll find something worthwhile if you look hard enough. I mean, come on. It's virtually impossible to come across a woman on the normal dating scene who hasn't got at least one barely tolerable flaw and a decent amount of emotional baggage, but *online*?! It's like scavenging through other people's collective rejects."

"Well put. Still, she seemed pretty nice at first."

"Don't they all?"

"What are you suggesting I do then?"

"Personally, I don't see any reason why you should prolong this remote resemblance of a relationship. OK, so you bet on a poor hand. Pull out while you can still cut your losses. You have your apartment, right?"

"No. I ended the lease two months ago."

"You're a fool. So you have nowhere to go?"

"I was thinking…"

"Can't stay here!" Lyle interrupted him.

"Thanks for the support, mate. Really appreciate it."

"I *am* supportive. I'm not a charity."

"Well I can't just pick up all my stuff and leave! And God knows I've no time to look at apartments. I barely have time for myself as it is," James frowned.

"Looks like you're gonna have to suck it up for the time being."

"Or I could ask Sylvia about her place. She's probably not using it now that she's married, and I know she's not renting it out." His face lit up at the thought.

"How can you be so sure?"

"Because she doesn't need to."

"It's not a question of need, but of pure common sense to put something to work for you instead of having it lie around vacant," Lyle commented.

"Yeah, well, she never had to worry about things like common sense."

"Choosing that politician guy over you seems like pretty good sense to me," he laughed.

"Pile it on," James snarled.

"Come on, you know I'm kidding."

"Whatever. It's just, everything's such a pile of steaming shit. For once I thought I had met the right woman and things would fall into place. But no, there just *has* to be drama."

"That's a little easy, don't you think?" Lyle remarked.

"Why?"

"First of all, there is no *right* person; with sufficient effort and perseverance you can make it work with pretty much anybody. Second of all, did you just meet *you*? What did you expect? You've always been one to fool around and keep your options open. Did you think with the *right* girl you'd magically get the uncontrollable urge to settle down and plan for a happily-ever after with 2.4 kids, white house with a picket fence and a dog named Shep? It doesn't work that way."

"Really? You don't say. How *does* it work then?"

"Save the sarcasm for the ladies. They seem to love the whole asshole thing you've got going on. Plus, I already told you. Every relationship requires a little thing called *effort* – something you're well known for avoiding at all cost."

"Yeah, well, after a while it gets tiring to put up with all the drama that goes hand in hand with the women you date."

"It's kind of a package deal, but you're being way too judgmental. It doesn't get tiring for them to put up with your shit 24/7? And, believe me; you've got a *lot* of it."

"No one's forcing them to. Women are instinctively drawn to men with emotional baggage. Haven't you noticed the groupies lingering on at every gig no matter how good or bad the band is?"

"True. I never understood what that was about," Lyle said.

"It's an ego thing. The only thing that validates a woman is other women's opinion of her – her looks, her clothes, her hook-ups, her dating record. Bagging an emotionally unavailable guy with severe commitment issues is like entering the UFC of the female world, where only the hottest, coolest and sexiest babes get to compete in trying to tame the wild bloke, un-break his heart, and get him to commit to a life with one woman. See, because where all others failed, she came first, figuratively speaking, of course."

Lyle laughed. "I see. That's like straight out of a textbook for mental conditions."

"Female logic, or the lack of it, is fucking scary. You should never try to understand a woman. It's a waste of time."

"Whatever you say, you're the dating specialist. Keep up the good work with Karen." Lyle gave him thumbs up.

"I like her a lot; in many ways she's like the perfect woman. But she's really starting to piss me off with her unnecessary paranoia and unjustifiable suspicion."

"Unjustifiable? Seriously?"

"As far as she's concerned there are no reasons to be suspicious."

"But there are."

"She doesn't know that."

"I wouldn't be so sure, man. Women have a radar for shit like this. Everything you're hoping she never finds out will eventually be laid out for you in detail one day. That's why I always go with honesty. If you know there's nothing you'll be able to hide, why shoot yourself in the foot?"

"Yeah, well, we'll see." James finished his beer and tossed the can aside. "Anyway, I've got to be smart here."

"You've got to set your priorities straight is what you need to do, and figure out what exactly it is you want. You're a fool to continue making the same mistake time and again and expect to get away with it."

"What mistake is that?"

"You're trying to juggle incompatible things. If you want it to work out with Karen or whoever, drop everything else you might or might not have with other women and concentrate on *that* relationship. You want to retain your freedom and mess around till you're in your fifties, do *that*. But don't lead the poor girl on, lying to her that she's got no reasons to feel insecure."

"That's some solid piece of advice you hope to hear from your best friend. You might wanna tone down the feeling of compassion for the girl I'm currently fucking. You're supposed to be on *my* side, remember?"

"Look. James." Lyle paused and stared at him. "All I'm saying is, you keep this up and you won't have a side. Think about it, all right?"

James sat down and leaned in, waiting to hear what Lyle had to say. "Were not twenty-one anymore," he continued. "Sure, I've had my fair share of bed hopping and ex-file storing, but there comes a time when you've got to ask yourself – do you want to grow up and continue with your life? Or do you want to linger on in a perpetual state of stunted adolescence? And no matter how cool and fun the latter may appear to you *now*, trust me, it won't be nearly as fun when you wake up one morning to find everyone has moved on but you. All your friends, all your hook-ups, every single person from your Big Black Book you kept on call in case you felt so lonely and desperate late at night that any human warmth would do. Look around you, James. Everyone's moving on. Even Sylvia, who used to be your main back-up. If *that* doesn't tell you something, I don't know what will."

James just sat there, staring in front of him. "Say what you will about my relationship with Karen, but don't comment on things you know nothing about," he pointed out, agitated. "Sylvia hasn't moved on from me. She can't. A woman never moves on from her first. Basic rule of marketing. All that matters is to be the one who pops her cherry."

"Ah, right. The first rule of marketing according to James. Except, in the cold light of reality, men, for the most part, are the ones that romanticize their first love and entertain the idea of marrying their high school sweetheart, while women always outgrow their partners at some point in time. There's nothing easier than getting an inexperienced woman interested in you. Keeping an emotionally mature one is the real trick. Do you *actually* know of a woman who's stayed with her first? I sure as hell don't, and I'm assuming neither do you. It's about time you gave that concept up," Lyle mocked him. He shook his glass pensively, and continued. "Not sure about you, but I'm at a place in my life where I don't feel like bragging about the women I've gone to bed with, but rather the one I wake up every morning to."

The doorbell rang and startled James. He looked up. "Sean," Lyle replied, seeing the questioning look in his eyes. "He's bringing over a couple of his friends for a quick poker game. You can stay if you want."

"I'm not really in the mood. I'll talk to you later." He stood up and looked around for his jacket.

"K," Lyle followed him. "And James?"

"Yeah?"

"Sort your shit out, mate!"

"Will try. See ya."

"Don't close the door on your way out. I can hear Sean and the guys coming up the stairs."

James bolted from the apartment, hurrying towards the elevator and pressed the button nervously. He didn't want to run into Sean when he was feeling down. *He always seems to pick up my failures like a fucking blood hound*, he thought, listening to the sounds of the voices getting louder and nearer. The elevator door opened and he rushed in with a sigh of relief.

It was long past midnight when he closed the door and stepped into the dark apartment. *So much for leaving the light on for me,* he thought, going into the kitchen. Although the darkness made him feel unwelcome, he couldn't help but notice his dinner covered on the counter as always. It was the thing he hated most about Karen – all the mixed messages she was sending him. If he was sure she didn't want to have anything more to do with him James would have no problem packing up his bags and leaving, especially since she was going out of her way to show she wasn't overly excited about him being in her life. She had stopped confiding in him, stopped initiating any form of intimacy, and stopped coming to him for anything whatsoever. At the same time, she remained as available and soft-spoken as usual, always there for him whenever he approached her. James had never felt more out-of-place and unnerved in his entire life.

He finished his dinner and put the plate in the sink. He slowly walked towards the bedroom, anticipating that he would trip over one of the cats, rubbing on his legs as they liked to do. Closing the door behind him, he turned around and saw their silhouettes curled up in a ball at Karen's feet on the bed. *But of course. Where else would they be?* James thought, annoyed. *Everyone needs to feel the warmth of someone next to them. For her that someone just isn't me, that's all. Replaced by two cats. That's a first.* He had tried negotiating a no-bed policy, but she had been unusually adamant about it remaining a free zone for pets to roll around in. It was one of the things that bugged him the most, as he took it very personally. *A testament to the lengths to which she'll go just to find more things to put between us,* James observed.

He slipped under the covers and listened to her even breathing. She was eerily still, which meant she was still awake. Karen was a light sleeper, and James knew she would always wake up at the slamming of the front door when he came home. Every time, he made sure he slammed it hard enough, so there wouldn't even be a possibility of her not having heard it. At first he did it because he hated the idea of coming home to a silent house, *the opposite of the whole point of living with someone,* he thought, observing her trembling, closed eyelids. Lately, however, he had started doing it out of pure spite. It was his way of showing he wasn't too happy with her either. But mostly it was James' way of trying to provoke a reaction. *Any reaction.*

He watched her pretend to be asleep. He reached out to caress her face, but his hand hung in the air halfway. The face he had gazed at so many times; the lips he kissed; the cheeks he touched; everything that was once so familiar was now more distant than ever. The body next to him was cold and strange. Yet James still desired her, maybe even more so than before. He felt the need to take, to make that body submit once again; but most of all, he wanted to subdue the invisible matter within it.

In a sick way he felt like the universe was punishing him for all the unreturned calls, all the broken promises and all those countless times the woman next to him in bed lay awake at night, trying to find a way into his heart and into his life. *So this is what it's like in the loser's corner?* James thought. He felt deserted, but for the first time he realised with certainty that he didn't want to lose Karen, as there was something about her that brought him a strange sense of peace. She was breathing faintly now, a sure sign she had fallen asleep while pretending. *There's gotta be a way in. She trusted me once, she'll be able to trust me again if I say and do the correct things. I will need some help to get it right, though,* James thought as he slipped out of bed as quietly as he could. One of the cats lifted her head and peered at him with her pale eyes in the dark.

Stepping out on the balcony, he closed up the door behind him and dialed Sylvia's number. He was almost certain she wouldn't pick up, but it was worth a try; he just *had* to talk to someone who would understand and appreciate his situation. He remembered how he used to call Karen in the middle of the night when they were still chatting online, or the times in the very beginning when they would stay up late and talk about anything. It struck him that now he couldn't even bring himself to wake her up and seek closeness and comfort, even though he needed them more than ever.

"Hey."

"You sound unusually cheerful for someone awake at four in the morning," James noted.

"It's noon here."

"Where's 'here'?"

"Lankanfushi."

"Is that even a real place?! Where the fuck is that?"

"In the Maldives. What do you want?"

"What are you doing there? Are you coming back any time soon?"

"I'm on my honeymoon." He sensed the growing irritation in her voice. "I won't be back for another two weeks. What do you want?"

"Talk to me."

"Where's the loving girlfriend? Isn't that her job?"

"She's asleep. Not that she'd want to talk if she were awake. We've been growing further apart."

"I'm sorry to hear that, but I don't have time to listen to your love troubles right now."

"Wow! Do you hear yourself? You've come a long way since the girl that used to call me every day begging to come over just so I could fuck her."

"Is there a point to this conversation? Because I don't recall ordering a flashback call?"

"I just felt the need to talk to a friend. Excuse me for thinking you were one."

"K, fine. I'm here. Talk to me. What's up? Things not working out as planned?" Her voice softened.

"She's… I'm… I guess it didn't go as expected. Ever since you two had that little chat she's drifted away. I don't think she trusts me anymore. How do you build or mend a relationship with someone who doesn't trust a single word you say? God knows I'm trying, but she's just making it too damn hard. It shouldn't be this hard," James grunted.

"So leave."

"That's another thing. I don't have a place to stay at right now, so I'm kinda stuck. You're not using your apartment, are you?"

"No, George and I are moving into a new place downtown when we get back. His mother is redecorating it while we're away."

"Awesome. Bonding with the in-laws, good for you. Back to my problem, though. Can I stay at your old place till I figure out what to do?"

"I don't know, James," she paused. "I really need to discuss it with George."

"Why do you need to discuss it with him if it's your place?"

"We're married now. I can't just make these decisions by myself. I need to take into account his feelings on subletting my apartment to old boyfriends. It's called being considerate – something I don't expect you to understand."

"So, when you said before that if I ever needed a place to crash that yours would always be available, you didn't mean any of it?"

"Of course I did, love. But things change. You've got to appreciate my situation."

"Sure I do. And what about my situation? If things continue to progressively go down the shitter I will literally be left to live on the streets!"

"I'm sure you'll figure something out. What about Lyle? He's your friend. He won't leave you high and dry."

"Don't even get me started on him."

"Look, I'm really sorry you're in such a predicament, but I can't help you out. I wish I could, but it's not just up to me anymore. If leaving is such an inconvenience for you at the moment, perhaps you should try and work harder at your relationship."

"You know me, like *that's* an option."

"I'm serious. You said it yourself back in Fargo, you get older, you start thinking about settling down and God knows you have to work at everything in life. You've found a woman willing to put up with all your nasty shit. Why not make the minimal effort to not fuck it up further?"

"I get the feeling it's gotten to a point, where it doesn't matter what I do as it's already fucked up beyond repair."

"There's a very easy way to determine that. You still fuck, right?"

"Sure."

"How often does she cum?"

"How is that relevant?"

"Just answer the question."

"Every time, I think."

"You think or are sure?"

"K, I'm sure."

"Great! She's faking it! That means you still have a shot at making it work!"

"What the fuck?! How do you know she's faking it?"

"No woman can cum *every* single time just from plain intercourse. If she does, it plain and simple means she's putting up quite a dedicated performance. Then again this should tell you that she still cares for you. We don't fake unless we want the man to feel good about himself and his worth as a lover. If she cares at all about how you feel you still have a chance with her."

"You sure? Some women are more sexual than others and just know their bodies better. You came every time we fucked," James argued.

"Sure I did." There was a brief moment of silence before she continued. "And I'm guessing it's really sexy and hot when she's cumming."

"Yeah, so? It always is."

"No, that's not what I mean. I mean it looks and feels somewhat… movie-like."

"Aha?"

"There's a slight difference between a woman who wants you to think she's enjoying herself and one who's actually enjoying herself. The first will religiously imitate what she thinks a normal, attractive person's orgasms look and sound like, while the latter won't be bothered at all with how sweaty, sloppy, loud or unattractive she seems."

"Kind of like you when we fucked." James grinned.

"Right. Exactly."

"You wouldn't lie to me, right?" he asked, hesitantly.

"About what?"

"Cumming every time we fucked. That thing you told me about George and the blowjobs…"

"Why would I lie to you? We've known each other for more than ten years, most of which I've had very strong feelings for you. You'll always have a special place in my heart, love," Sylvia said slowly, deliberately.

"Thank you."

"There's nothing to thank me for. Look, I really can't talk anymore right now, but call me towards the end of next week when I'll be back in the city, k?"

"K. Wait, one more thing," he hesitated.

"Yeah?"

"Her faking it; should I be worried? I wouldn't stay with someone if she was unable to make me cum."

Sylvia chuckled. "You've nothing to worry about, love. It's different for men and women. Women's most pleasant sexual experiences are related to feeling a connection with someone. Scratch marks on the back, sore muscles and bruised hip bones won't get you into a woman's heart or mind. Gentle whispers and holding her hand will."

"Got it. Thanks for talking to me. I really appreciate it."

"Anytime, love. Bye."

"Bye."

James hung up and leaned on the parapet, gazing at the dimly lit streets and the dark windows of the buildings. Although Sylvia's blunt refusal to sublet him an apartment she wasn't using and didn't need left him feeling disappointed, it didn't bother him nearly as much as he thought it would. Ordinarily, he would consider this a betrayal by a trusted friend, but now James saw her reaction as common sense and was actually impressed by how practical and sane she had become. *In a weird way she actually did help me. Now I have no reasons not to put all my efforts into this relationship. No more back-up plans and safety nets. It's all or nothing. And that's exactly where I feared I would end up. The weird thing is, it's kind of reassuring to know exactly where I stand and what I need to do.*

Lost in his thoughts, he didn't notice the figure in the dark behind him, slipping back into the bedroom.

For the first time in his life James felt like he was losing it. He was so used to the girl bending over backwards to try and please him that he had no idea what to do when the tables turned. Everything he did or said was either taken out of context or straight-on used against him in all the conversations he had with Karen. The woman being more affectionate and suggestive in a relationship was the norm in his opinion and experience, but it was furthest from reality in his current one. This drove James to the point of stretching himself beyond his means. "I knew she was introverted and withdrawn, but this is unbearable," he complained to Anthony, a colleague he occasionally talked to about personal things when they were particularly bad. "It's like nothing I do is ever good enough or able to change her opinion of me. She's constantly observing, studying, like she's sure I'll fuck up again. And if she's so sure, why should I bother cleaning up my act at all?!"

"Not knowing the specifics of the relationship, all I can say is that from my experience all women seem to be exactly the same, it just takes them a while to shed off that camouflage cover they used to attract a compatible mate. If it were me, I personally see no reason in maintaining anything that fucks up with other aspects of your life like self-esteem, plans, confidence and the whole lot. What are prostitutes for? Call 'em up when you're horny, pay 'em and have them leave as soon as possible afterwards. No drama, clean and simple," Anthony pointed out, faithful to his practical nature.

"Yeah, well, while *that* has it benefits I, sadly through experience, have found out that it's just a bit too degrading paying a stranger to have sex with you. And while the dating game is just as brutal and costly, it's something I'd still avoid," James shrugged.

"Enjoy the drama then."

"She's not all bad. It's just that side of her I don't like, her being too in control. Once she stopped trusting me there was just no reasoning with her. A woman's mind is your biggest ally. If I can't get her to believe my words my hands are tied. It's a total mind fuck for me."

"That's why I don't date smart women. Get 'em young while they're as naïve and inexperienced as can be."

"That's partly how she got me to fall for her," James explained. "But like you said, they all put to use the same effective tricks when they wanna dazzle. Not sure if this speaks bad about them or about us for falling for this shit every time."

"I know, right!?" Anthony laughed. "At least now you know. Dump her bitchy ass."

"The thing is, I'm not sure I want to. In many ways she's like the perfect woman. She's serious, down-to-earth, gorgeous, candid, sincere, wildly intelligent and fun to be around. She's challenging, yes, but that's what makes her so interesting."

"Dude, you're describing a woman, not a mare. You make it sound like you've gotta spend the rest of your life taming her, and that's *not* what relationships are about." Anthony shook his head.

"Nah, didn't mean it like that. It's just that she's not your average take-me-to-the-mall, hand-me-your-credit-card Mary Jane you're so used to seeing since consumerism took over. It's a breath of fresh air."

"Well then you're just gonna have to will yourself to put up with her shit. There's a price to pay for everything we want. Just make sure it's worth it, because if the bill doesn't add up, it's just a very expensive live-in maid and hooker service."

"I guess you're right," James agreed, pensively. He looked up and saw several hours had slipped by unnoticed since they had finished playing and he still hadn't started to put away his gear. Slowly, he rolled up the cables and shoved them in the case. He dreaded and anticipated going home at the same time; as much as he loved being around Karen, he feared her piercing look, her constant observing of his every move and word. Nothing went unregistered and James wasn't known for being particularly careful at watching his act. Despite his efforts in the last couple of weeks, Karen remained as distant as before. It was almost as if she was avoiding him, albeit in her usual delicate and polite way. *Which is weird, because as far as she's concerned there's nothing going on that should alarm her*, he wondered as he got in the car.

She was sitting in the dark, barely aware of the fact that she was just staring into nothing when the sound of his steps in the corridor startled her. Karen switched on the light, rushing into the kitchen. The last thing she wanted was for James to notice something was wrong. She had gingerly tried to maintain her usual demeanor for days now, going out of her way not to raise his suspicion. At this point, all she needed was to stay as far away as possible from his explanations, excuses and arguments – things she knew every man resorted to when faced with the undeniably ugly truth of his actions; especially when there was actual proof of the same. Never being one to spy on or generally overstep the boundaries of personal space of others, she felt a wave of shame and insult sweeping over her the night James stepped out on the balcony and she stood in the darkness behind him, listening to every word. Some time after he had came back and slid in bed next to her, she'd had an opportunity to quietly look through his call and message logs, uncovering rather personal and explicit proof of him staying in touch with various exes. The moment stretched endlessly, as she faced the painful realization that she had just learned more about James then she had in all the time they had spent together. Standing in the dark, reading through his messages,

Karen felt embarrassed for the both of them. But worst of all, it was then and there she knew, without the slightest shadow of a doubt, just how unnecessary she was in his life. *Holding onto her doesn't leave any room for me. Although in a way I should be grateful he made me aware of where I stand, even if he did it behind my back,* she thought, looking up from her laptop and smiling at James as he walked through the front door.

"How was your day?" Karen asked him breezily.

"The usual. Yours?"

"Same. Your dinner's on the counter."

"K."

They had mastered the art of having short generic conversations in an effort to avoid any confrontation whatsoever. As unhappy as James was with this he had no way of calling her on it, as he wasn't exactly the talkative type either. It still seemed unbelievable to him that he had found a woman who was more prone to keeping things to herself than the average man. *This is either extremely good or extremely bad,* he thought, unable to chase away the feeling it was the latter. Obviously, something was wrong, and obviously he had to bring it up if he wanted to make any progress out of the awkward stagnation into which their relationship had sunk. He had hoped to find a way to do it without the dreaded "we need to talk" moment, but at this point this seemed more and more impossible. James went into the kitchen and picked up his dinner. He was surprised Karen was even up this late. *Just like in the beginning when she would wait for me every single night,* he observed with hope. He walked back in the living room, sat next to her and started eating in silence. She kept on working without acknowledging his presence. When he finished and she still hadn't so much as looked at him James threw the fork on the plate and glared at her.

"Something you wanna tell me?" he insisted.

"What do you mean?" She looked away from the monitor.

"Lately you've been very cold and distant. Is something wrong?"

"I'm not sure. I guess it depends on what your definition of *wrong* is," she said slowly.

"And what is *your* definition of wrong?"

"Oh, you know, pretty standard stuff: living with a person who sneaks out in the middle of the night to have conversations with his ex, whom he still has feelings for, about the possibility of staying in her apartment," Karen explained.

There was silence – unrelenting, awkward, permeating silence. A couple of minutes later James managed to peel his eyes off the floor and stared right into hers. She had never disrespected him in any way until now and the undisguised sarcasm in her voice caught him completely off-guard. Obviously there was no point in denying anything and faithful to his no-apologies policy he decided this wouldn't be the moment to break it. *After all, playing the guilt trip card has rendered such amazing results in the past*, he reassured himself. "You heard that, huh? Oh well, can't blame a guy for being practical. It's basic common sense to look for other options when you're living with a woman who's a closed book. I never know what's inside your head."

"Of course you do, that it's incredibly rude and inconsiderate to continue doing behind my back what you promised to never let happen again," Karen pointed out softly.

"Now you're mixing two completely unrelated subjects. I did follow up on our deal. Yes, I might have had feelings for Sylvia when you and I started living together, but I assure you they're long gone. The only reason I asked *her* is because I know she's got an empty apartment in the city. That's all. I have to protect myself," James explained unnerved.

"Right. And by long gone you mean less than several months ago, and by unrelated you mean that there can't possibly be a connection between plotting your exit strategy with your back-up plan and disrespecting your current partner in any way?"

"I'm not interested in having a debate with you. I'm pretty sure you'll win since women are so good at twisting facts to fit their demented version of reality and that's fine, but don't expect me to sit here and fuel your need for drama."

Karen stared briefly at him. "You know what strikes me as the most interesting? How you always succeed in twisting our conversation in a way that always makes it appear as if it's *my* fault or happening *all* in my head. That's impressive, I'll give you that!"

"It *is* your fault. Do you even stop to think how this makes *me* look? Being forced to call my exes, asking about a place to stay in case you wake up with your panties in a twist one morning and decide you wanna kick me out? Don't worry about me, love, because it's not *at all* degrading to phone people you haven't spoken to in a while and ask for a favor."

"Oh, I do feel for you, *believe me*," she smiled bitterly. "It must be tough resorting to every number in your Black Book in an almost chronic need to shred to pieces every relationship that potentially may turn into something long-term *every* single time, and then continue bitching about the fact you're still single and alone. Must be *tough*."

"Sarcasm isn't helping. What's your point?"

"My point is, James... I can't continue carrying your emotional baggage for you. I've got plenty of my own."

"Oh, I know you do," he snarled. "You think you're so perfect, nice and serene all the fucking time? Guess again! Keeping your mouth shut, tip-toeing around the man you're living with, leaving him cooked meals in the kitchen is *not* being nice and loving. I don't need a roommate, I need a *woman* who wants to spend time with me, who enjoys my company and worries when I'm not home by midnight. You know? Stuff that *loving* girlfriends do?"

"*Loving* girlfriends? Excuse me, I was just giving you space; the thing you asked for, remember? Why should I call you? For all I know, you could be somewhere, making good use of your much needed space," Karen pointed out annoyed.

"See? You can't even tell the difference. That's how fucked up you are!" James laughed "I can't help you if you think that's what I expect from you. Obviously you haven't got the slightest idea what a relationship between normal people is?"

"Normal people?" Karen repeated slowly. "And do these normal people also have back-up plans they incessantly put efforts and time into rather than, say, working towards making their current relationship work? You know, the one they claim they're so bent on keeping?"

"Oh, what-the-fuck-ever!" James grunted. "It's not my fault you're so insecure you can't open your fucking eyes and see the bigger picture. That's why it's called a *back-up* plan, because it's not your main one! If I had any, even the slightest, interest in making it work with her more than I did with you, I'd be over at her house right now, wouldn't I?"

"Except that it's not possible."

"What?"

"She's with some other guy, right? So you settle for what you can get."

"You think *that* is the reason I'm with you?!" he asked, stunned.

"You spent an awful lot of time defending your right to personal space and her right to be in it; that's all I'm saying. It doesn't look good from where I'm standing," Karen pointed out coldly.

"Everyone's entitled to their own opinion. But only I can know what you mean to me and what she does," James said indifferently.

"Right, no, I know. But somewhere in the course of you trying to find out what exactly it is that you want I realised what *I don't* want."

"And what is that?"

"I'm tired of having to fight for our relationship. I've been doing so from the start," Karen explained, looking him in the eyes.

"So what are you saying? Are you bailing on me?" James demanded.

"It shouldn't be a constant struggle. And that's all that this is."

"Makes sense. When the ship starts sinking the only ones to get rescued are the women and the children. The rest are royally fucked."

"This ship didn't even pass production safety tests, let alone make it to water. Everyone had a pretty good chance of saving themselves from the start; which apparently they did."

"Ugh, again with the back-up plan crap. Are you, at all, capable of letting go?"

"Isn't that what I am doing now?"

"No, you're bailing. There's a huge difference."

"I have no interest in standing here, arguing over semantics. Fine, it can be whatever you want it to be. In fact, make a note of it on your Facebook, Twitter page or wherever else you want to put it up and I'll sign your version, so the whole world can know how the mean girl screwed you over. How's that?" Karen's voice was trembling with anger.

"Well, I would assume I get to do that, keeping in mind it's *you* who gets to walk away scot free, being the woman and all. All you ever get to do is break a guy's heart, trash his entire life and move on to the next poor bastard."

"Yes, that's *exactly* what we do. Not to mention bend over backwards and going out of our way to pick up and stitch together pieces scattered around by your lover's former partners, all the while listening to 'I can't', and 'I don't see a point anymore', because living up to the memory of The One That Walked Away is not an ungrateful task *at all!* Giving someone everything you're capable of in exchange for being regarded as the ungrateful bitch after you decide you don't want to drown with that person anymore."

"How come you decide so suddenly? You wake up one day and fucking poof – instead of good morning it's 'I don't want to see your sorry ass ever again?' That's fucking mature!"

"This is everything but a sudden decision. In fact, it's a very unnecessarily prolonged and painful process, but since you only get to see the final result you think it's out-of-the-blue and unexpected. Ignoring the warning signs was *your* choice," Karen explained.

"How convenient."

"Is it? It seems to me it's everything else but convenient," she replied with sadness.

They both stared blankly at the floor. It was one of those moments of realization that both had said too many truthful things to be able to take back any of them or undo the damage. All that was left was to sit and watch as things further

crumbled to the ground. *Funny thing about love and friendship –
what takes the most time in building up is the easiest to break apart,*
Karen sighed, glancing at him from across the couch. For the
first time in what felt like ages she realized she didn't feel
angry, hurt or disappointed. *We took a gamble and we lost. Does it
really matter who fucked it up and who's unable to let it go? Bottom line
is it's time to cut the losses and do the smart thing.*

"Listen, James," she began slowly and he stared at her
intently as she rarely called him by his full name. "It was
difficult for me to admit this at first, but the truth is there's no
room for me in your life. You're still far too hooked on the
past and, more importantly, on certain people from it. It's not
fair to ask someone to fight the battles with your own daemons
for you. The more I stay the more I feel I am starting to hate
you and I don't want that. You're bad for me. Do you
remember what I told you once before? I need to be with
someone who wants me to be fully present in his life? And this
has nothing to do with his right to personal space whatsoever.
I just need to feel wanted and needed, not selectively allowed
into certain areas of his existence, where he thinks it's safe to
have me. Love is unconditional, and doesn't respond well to
boundaries and restrictions. You're possessive of me, but you
want me far from your own inner world; that leaves me
hanging high and dry in a very unstable middle. I can't live like
that." She moved closer to him and took his hand in hers. "But
since I still love you and am unable to let you go, I'm asking
you to do it. *Please.* Cut me out of your life instead of leaving
me in it like something obsolete you continue using out of
comfort and utility rather than uncontrollable desire."

"Karen, you've just turned twenty-five and you're still
talking like a schoolgirl. I've read my fair share of romantic
novels, but it's time to drop all this corny crap and realize
you're living in the real world. You were never a princess and I
was never destined to save you from the dragon. People meet;
they get together; they make mistakes; they move on and that's
that. Everything else is just remnants of a prepubescent
masturbatory fantasy." James pulled away his hand. "Stop
expecting things I never promised," he added.

Karen stared motionless in front of her. She felt a cold shiver down her spine. "I didn't mean to make it sound like I was expecting anything from you or that it was *your* responsibility to fix any of this. All I'm saying is I need someone in my life I can fully rely on and feel safe in doing so."

"So do it. It's your conscious choice not to rely on me."

"I wish it were that simple. I just can't anymore."

"Right, because you choose not to."

"No, because you screwed me over."

"Oh, boo hoo, get over yourself. Seriously! More psycho-babble-bullshit that is getting us nowhere. Just pipe the fuck down and let's move on with our lives."

"There's just one problem with that. I don't feel safe with you."

"Why not?"

"Because I know you're not fully committed to *us*."

"Look, I won't deny there was such a time in the beginning, but that's not valid anymore. Anyway, you have to understand I was in a position where I had to be smart and moving in with a girl I barely knew and had only talked to online for a while was a hasty decision and a wild gamble. Let's focus on the *here and now* where you've proven to be trustworthy and reliable; *now* I'm fully committed to you *and us*."

"That's the thing," Karen shrugged. "While you were busy proving to yourself *I* was reliable and trustworthy your actions proved to me *you* weren't." Pausing for a minute, she continued reluctantly "Everyone has a breaking point and different things can push us over the edge. From my experience, it's preferable to walk away than to sit and explain to someone why and how they've hurt you. The pain of other people rarely invokes a feeling of compassion, especially if we're somehow responsible for any of it."

"I gotta say it wasn't hard at all," he remarked.

"What wasn't hard?" Karen asked confused.

"Pushing over a breaking point. Pushing you beyond yours wasn't hard at all," James clarified, mockingly.

Karen smiled softly. "I'm glad I haven't troubled you," she said quietly. James shook his head disapprovingly. She felt an overwhelming feeling of helplessness as she glanced at him. *It's just pointless. We're lights years apart in what we want, what we need, what we believe in and what we find important,* she concluded with regret. *What am I to say? How to explain to him just how unfair it is to ask me to stay in this relationship? And how impossible it is for me to do so? How to tell him that what happened is him tearing me to pieces, then putting me back together and demanding that I love him wholesomely while complaining that I do so partially? For him this would be the teary-eyed, overly dramatic gibberish of a girl who's read too many fairy-tales.*

Karen looked around the apartment and breathed in the familiar scent. She had worked so hard at making this into a home for her and James; at building a life for them, but she sensed that they were at the end of the line. *Men. They always start putting every effort towards making a relationship work when it's far beyond salvation or repair. Kinda sad to witness every right action and hear every right word too little too late. There was a time when I needed your support and love, James, right around when you were too busy crafting back-up plans to protect yourself. So I adapted and learned to live without them. Why are you offering them now? What use do I have for your love and support now? I'd have to learn to live with them from scratch if I decide to accept them. I don't think I have time for that anymore.* Karen couldn't lie to herself. She knew she still had feelings for James, but for the first time in her life she was starting to acknowledge the voice of her self-preservation instinct and it was telling her to get out now. She had nothing more to give; no more efforts to try and carve a place for herself in someone else's life when she clearly wasn't wanted there. Or, rather, she was wanted like a bedside dresser – something useful to stuff with emotional baggage and skeletons from the past. *Life's too short to hurt for people who never allowed you into theirs,* she concluded, sitting silently just a step away from the man she had loved selflessly. Summoning the last bits of her courage, Karen looked up and stared at him. He was visibly withdrawn and absent-minded. She felt less in realizing James had never really been there with her.

"I don't know what you expect me to say," he finally broke the silence. "I *am* trying, but I have nothing else to give you."

"I know. You don't have to explain yourself," she replied softly. "We just didn't get it right and there's no one to blame. It happens sometimes."

"That doesn't mean we can't make do. So our relationship is damaged. Who has it picture-perfect?"

"Is that what you really want your life to be? Making do? Living with a person when the closeness is gone?"

"I've lived through worse. You know what they say, man is a disgusting being, he can get used to anything."

"This is hardly comforting."

"Actually it kinda is." He moved closer and took her hand in his. "I want to hear you say it."

"Say what?"

"That you don't want to be with me."

"You know I can't say that. But we *have* to split up. I just don't see how we can make it work, James." She laid her head on the couch.

"No, I don't care what *has* to be done; all that matters is what we *want*. I don't *want* to end this. If you do you're gonna have to say it to my face; without any arguments or excuses. Just point blank, that you don't want to see me ever again. Say it!" he insisted.

"I don't want to lie to you."

"Then we'll just *have* to stick it out. It's *that* simple."

"Why?" Karen asked exhausted of arguing.

"Because you *must* be the one."

She glanced at James, confused. The conversation had worn out her defenses, making her realize she only thought she was ready to move on without him. But just like many times before, when it came to men, Karen often overestimated her abilities to outmaneuver them. She listened to herself, trying to determine if she felt more moved by his comment or just plain surprised, but she couldn't read the fine difference between the two – the exact unfamiliarity with herself that James continued to rely on. Logic and reason were her only allies and in one final attempt at saving herself she reached for them.

"How can you know that?"

"Because all the rest weren't," James shot out without thinking.

"But I *know* you still think of Her," she insisted.

"I don't."

"And I know you want Her more than you want me."

"I didn't. But you've made me believe it."

Karen shook her head in disagreement, but she had no strength to accuse him of sending her on yet another guilt trip. *Perhaps he's right*, the thought crept into her mind unnoticed and completely broke her down. There was something enchantingly disarming about his ability to shed every protective layer off of her until he reached her bare skin, leaving her helpless, vulnerable and painfully aware of his touch. Then he would become attentive and gentle in a strangely vicious way – one that would fool her she was being caressed when she could actually feel herself bleeding under his rough handling. The inexperienced and hopeless romantic in Karen saw this as an undeniable connection of two souls that were entwined in some inexplicable way. James, being far more knowledgeable on the topic, acknowledged this as the typical assertion of the power balance in a relationship that relied solely on submission and dominance.

"You want me strong; you want me forgiving, understanding and 'above things'. Afterwards you're angry that I fight you on everything," she uttered as he ran his fingers through her hair. She could feel the pressure of his strong palm on her neck. It was giving her a strange sense of comfort and security.

"I'm not your enemy, Karen. I'm not the one you should be fighting with."

"I fight with everyone. And everything. I want to be weak sometimes. But I dread being weak with you. Although I need to…" She pressed her cheek against his palm and closed her eyes. "I want to lie in your arms, with you knowing that you're my everything and there's nowhere else I'd rather be, without seeming foolish or pathetic; or having you ridicule my need for romance. I need to not be afraid to show you just how important you are to me. Being weak means to just give up and love you again. I want to."

James was watching her intently. "Then do it," he urged her, pulling her hair back and bringing her down on the couch as he pressed his lips against hers. He could feel her giving in under his caress, twisting and pressing herself against his palm. James stopped the kiss; his touch became rougher.

CHAPTER FOURTEEN

The two cars pulled over and stopped in front of the building on East 26th street. As the driver got out and walked around to open the door for them, Sylvia leaned out of the window and glanced at her home-to-be. George helped her out and they walked through the entrance of the Grand Madison followed by the two chauffeurs, who were carrying the luggage.

The doorman led them into the elevator and pressed the 5F button. Sylvia was pleasantly surprised her anticipation and excitement were growing by the minute. Her life ever since she had said "I do" had quickly escalated into an unending stream of lavish experiences and she was delighted to observe the tendency was to remain unchanged. George's parents had insisted on purchasing the property as a present to the newlyweds, with Jacalyn personally taking on the daunting task of its renovation.

The concierge was waiting on their floor to lead them inside. They walked into a luxurious apartment where timber floors, delicate fabrics and top-of-the-range appliances were carefully combined to create an elegant and spectacular setting. The six arched windows revealed a panoramic view of Madison Square Park and the large terrace in front was alluringly inviting with its tranquillity. Sylvia instantly fell in love with the way the whole place was flooded with natural light; it created the illusion it was even bigger. She turned around and saw that the chauffeurs had left the baggage near the entrance and gone. George nodded at the concierge who excused himself and promptly left too. He then turned to her and pointed invitingly to the master bedroom. She smirked and followed him into a spacious room with a large private terrace with views of the Empire State and Chrysler buildings.

Sylvia had never felt so turned on in her life as she observed George pulling the drapes. She could feel herself getting wet just at the thought of rolling around in the king-size designer bed behind her. The feeling of having nothing left to look forward to in anticipation had given way to the calm realization that this was everything she had dreamed about, hoped and wished for since she was a little girl. She let out a murmur of delight as George picked her up and carried her to the bed. As much as she enjoyed having sex with him, her mind often wandered off during, and she had to make an effort to concentrate on the here and now. But this time it was different. For the first time she was fully present and aware of what was going on. Sylvia was no stranger to years of unsatisfactory sexual encounters and unfulfilled promises that had left a mark on her that it took George quite a while to erase. She could feel herself having reached a place where reality was finally better than what she pictured in her head, so she was able to fully enjoy every single minute of her life.

Hours later, she stepped out onto the terrace and breathed in the scent of the coming summer. The park was unusually quiet, surrounded by the vibrant lights of the town; there was something calming about the contrast. Sylvia smoothed out a crease on her floral Reem Acra dress and switched on her phone. It beeped with the sound of several new messages and she glanced uninterested at the sender's details. All were from James. *How predictable.* Barely ten minutes after switching on her phone, it started ringing. It was him. Sylvia looked around and picked up after seeing that George was conveniently preoccupied with his laptop in the den.

"Yes?"

"Good, so you *can* answer your phone," he sounded as edgy as can be.

"This isn't a good time for me so if you're gonna take that tone…"

"Sorry. I'm pissed, that's all. You said you'd be back a week ago and when you didn't answer your phone or return your messages I just flipped," he explained frantically.

"We passed through London on our way back. What's up? More love troubles?"

"It's all gone in the shitter. I honestly don't see a point in putting any more efforts into it."

"Then don't. It's *that* simple."

"Can I see you?"

"Why?" She waited for his answer with bated breath.

"I want to talk to you."

"We're talking right now, aren't we?" Sylvia replied, slightly disappointed.

"I have to see you. Do you think the husband-figure can spare you for a night?"

A smirk lit up her face. *Bingo,* she thought. "Not a chance, love. But it's nice to see you're capable of some human emotions. I've always known you're not as indifferent as you try to appear."

"Yeah, well, where's the benefit in that?" he muttered. "So you're gonna be faithful now?"

"I will surely try," she giggled.

"Why don't you cut the act and save us both the time and energy."

"I think you have more pressing concerns than lecturing me how I should or shouldn't live my life," she pointed out, irritated. "Try focusing on *your* relationship and making one work for a change."

"Ouch. Low blow, Mrs. Huntington. Low blow. And considering the situation I'm in is *your* fault to begin with!" James grunted.

"My fault?! Wow. Just, wow. I guess some things never change. How exactly is it *my* fault?"

"If you hadn't phoned me that night and if she hadn't found all those texts I wouldn't be in a position where the woman I love doesn't trust a single word I say!"

"Do you even hear yourself? Always blaming others for your own mistakes. You've always defended religiously your right to cheat and fool around while in a relationship; is it *my* job to remind you messages are to be deleted immediately after being read and phones are to never be left lying around if you expect a call from someone other than your significant other? After all, it's *you* I learned all these things from," she stressed.

"Either way, the damage is done and I don't see any way it can be fixed. If you can't meet to talk can you at least tell me if there's anything I can do at this point?"

"To be perfectly honest I don't think there is. You've not only screwed up big time; you've done it on various occasions and you continue to."

"How so?"

"By talking to me. Bitching to the ex about problems in your current relationship? Seriously? That alone will make her run for the hills if she found out."

"Women and their logic. Why? What's wrong with confiding in a friend and asking for advice?" he asked, irked.

"First of all, we're *not* friends. You can't be *just* friends with someone you've stuck your dick into. There would either always be residual attraction and high-esteem or mild hatred. Neither makes for the foundation of a friendship. Secondly, to a woman this constitutes the act of ultimate betrayal. Going back to the ex for whatever – sex, advice, a friendly chat. It just goes to show that you favour the other person over your current partner. That's extremely hurtful and humiliating."

"Is there any way she could've *not* taken it in the way you described?"

"Let me put it this way. Every time she looks at you now, she sees *me*." Sylvia stressed the last word with extreme satisfaction. "Assuming you left around pictures for her to be able to put a face to the voice that is," she added.

"Oh, there were pictures," he admitted sombrely.

"I don't know what to tell you, James. I never thought *you*, of all people, would find yourself in such a predicament."

"You don't have to sound so fucking happy about it."

'I'm not. I'm back from my honeymoon, enjoying the view from my Upper East Side apartment. The last thing I will take pleasure in is your misfortune. I have plenty else to be happy about," she pointed out.

"Congratulations. Sounds like you're getting wet just by listing the qualities of your new nest," he grunted.

"Oh, I am. You know me so well!" she chuckled.

"When will you find the time to meet up then?" he insisted.

"I'll be quite busy the next couple of days, but I might be able to get away for an hour or so. I'll call to let you know, k?"

"Please do." His voice was soft and filled with anticipation like she had never heard it before. "I'm in Fargo till next week so you can call me anytime."

"I will. Talk to you later."

Sylvia hung up the phone before he could say anything else. For a brief moment towards the end of their conversation she had felt compelled to utter that most dreaded phrase, "I told you so", or its equally detested version, "I knew this would happen", but she knew James too well to even bother. Besides, she didn't think it was her job to open his eyes. She had known him for more than a decade, long years in which she had stood and watched him make the same mistake with different women over and over again, each time hoping for a different result. *I can't believe I used to be one of those women,* she pondered, turning around and looking lovingly at her husband sitting in the den. Sylvia perceived George as the walking, breathing testament of her personal growth as a woman. Fortunately, she had moved past the feminine necessity of fixing someone.; of gluing the pieces back together; of being there for people who were never, in return, there for her when she needed them. Once outside the vicious circle of perpetuating dead-end relationships with men, who couldn't give her anything even if they wanted to, she could fully appreciate that she had gotten out just in time.

Looking around, Sylvia hesitated for a moment, then unlocked her phone and started going through her contact list. She deleted James and Stephen and briefly stared at the screen as if to verify she had actually done it. Burning bridges was a concept she wasn't fond of or accustomed to, but she had learnt to go with her instincts and so far it had always worked for her. She looked around again and smiled contented. *Yes, it definitely worked out,* she reassured himself.

After a week of lying low and killing time at his father's apartment in Fargo, James started feeling restless, so he caught the first plane and returned to New York. He was coming back more anxious than he had left. Sylvia hadn't called as promised, which only added to his frustration with the fact that he was getting nowhere with Karen. Neither of them was answering their phone or returning messages. *Fucking princesses,* he thought. *They think the world revolves around their asses. They're lucky there's still someone willing to chase after theirs. For now.* The thing that bugged him the most was that he was well aware that Karen had every right not to trust him. He was all out of excuses and justifications for his behaviour. Everything Sylvia had told him over the phone was true, but he felt no motivation to make an effort to try and correct anything. *Sure, I'd probably feel like shit if it was the other way around, but it's different for men and women,* he tried convincing himself, as he put the key in the lock.

He walked in and immediately sensed that something was off. Although the apartment was as quiet as usual, this time the undisrupted silence that filled it was unsettling. Storming in and out of rooms, James frantically tried to pinpoint what was wrong, but everything was in its place. It took him a while to realise that the cats that annoyed him so much were missing, along with all of their accompanying shit that had been lying around. For a brief moment he felt jubilant. *Bitching excessively finally pays off,* he grinned. *She's gotten rid of the stupid critters.* With that thought in his mind, he checked the balcony for a litter box and when he didn't see it in its usual spot, he returned to the living room reassured. He sat on the couch and turned on the TV in an attempt to distract himself, but he still couldn't chase away the feeling that something was wrong. He looked around the room. Then he jumped off the couch, running to the bedroom. He started pulling out drawers of the dresser one by one. All nine were empty. Feeling weak in the knees, James sat down on the bed, shocked at the realisation of just how easy it had been for Karen to pack up and leave. There had been virtually nothing in that apartment to keep her there. He had lived under the false impression that they had made a life for themselves in the small place in Woodside. "Sure, not a perfect life, but it was still real…" He held in a moan. Faced with the relentless realisation that she was gone from his life, painful recollections of their time together started flooding his mind: weekly trips to the grocery store they both enjoyed so much; afternoon strolls in the park the late walks in the small hours of the night down the empty quiet streets. He frantically pulled his phone from his pocket and dialed her.

"Where are you?" James almost cried out at the sound of her picking up.

"Close," Karen answered. "But far away," she added.

"What about me?" he asked weakly.

"What about me?" she repeated softly.

Suddenly he understood everything. She had left her own home because James hadn't taken any of her hints and done so himself. They had had several conversations; he vaguely remembered Karen telling him things couldn't go on as they did and he had ignored all of them, thinking she would eventually adapt to *his* lifestyle. He had brushed off all of her complaints and disappointments as a clash between reality and the sugar-coated expectations of a girl who had watched too many romantic flicks. And he had even been very careful in hiding all traces leading to people he wasn't willing to give up just yet; but the one thing James was realising just now he had failed to do, was to listen to what Karen was actually trying to tell him. She hadn't just given him signs. She had told him straight up what was coming, but his over confidence in his abilities to brush real issues under the rug had led James to royally screw himself.

"Don't you love me anymore?" he made one last attempt.

"I do."

"Aren't you going to miss me?"

"I'm used to you not being here."

A sense of sadness and abandonment overwhelmed him. This time, he knew, without a shadow of a doubt, that this was the end and there was nothing he could do or say to change her mind. *And there you have it*, he thought wearily. Recollections about all the moments he had wasted away lying and fooling around behind her back started rushing through his jaded mind. *I could've spent that time just loving her*, he sighed regretfully, painfully aware of her absence. It was coming as a surprise even to him how much of a mark Karen had left on his life in the short time they were together. He stopped tossing his phone around and started going through the contact list. When he came to Sylvia's name he felt a wave of reassurance. *I bet a back-up plan doesn't seem like such a bad idea now, does it?* He laughed at himself. *Sure, she might be deep into her Stepford wife act now, but it will pass. It's not like she can stop being a slut.* He sat back, reassured at the thought. It was time to cut his losses and he reached for the first thing he used to keep calm and carry on, the notion that what had ruined yet another relationship was also the very thing that would get him through the hard times. She had always been there for him. *She'll be there one more time.* James sat back on the couch, exhausted.

Karen hung up and wiped the phone screen, staring blankly at it. One of the cats was rubbing itself against her feet. She stood up and looked around the small studio, the only thing she was able to find on such short notice. The lack of space had prompted her to leave most of her stuff behind, something she saw as a clear sign to move on with her life. She had loved James deeply and selflessly and had gone out of her way to guide him through the remnants of infatuations, which were as destructive as his obsession with relationships that were far from over. At least for him. It was just now that she was realizing how worn out she felt from battling ghosts that were not even her own. It never mattered what she did. James was trapped in a hell of his own making and she could no longer martyr herself for him. There was no point. Their life together was a constant game of waiting; waiting for other people's power and influence over him to wear off. And just as she was starting to believe they could make it work, something always arose to send him back into the same circle of obsession and wandering, looking for answers and comfort in relationships that were out of place and time.

Looking out the window at the grey rooftops, Karen sighed with sadness. Her regret for walking away from something she believed could've been truly meaningful was overshadowing her relief of saving herself. And despite the fact that she could physically sense her life having taken a turn for the better, there was still a great deal of hurt for the way she had left things with James. It was surprising to her that she didn't feel any joy or satisfaction from his reaching out to her to make her stay. All she felt was compassion and sadness. *The last thing I want is to add to his already significant count of ghosts of past girlfriends,* she thought, realising she had nowhere else to look for the reason for their falling out but in herself. *Time and again expectations ruin everything.* She remembered Mia telling her something about relationships long ago. *What was it?* Karen tried recalling. *Ah yes: with relationships it's like getting in a car – you have to be sure the person before you has vacated the seat before you can get in. Oh well. My bad.* For months she tried directing her anger and disappointment towards his ex until she realised it was misplaced. *People don't change. They think they do, but they don't. How can you not hate or feel threatened by someone, when you're convinced that the man you're with was better to her than he was to you? I'm sure she was just more patient than me,* she concluded, and returned to the bathroom.

The pregnancy test was sitting on the edge of the bath tub where she had left it. Karen looked down at her watch and picked it up with bated breath. Mocha was rubbing against her feet. A smile lit up her face as she glanced at the result. *It's not like he ever gave me anything else...*

James kept checking his phone, e-mail and Skype accounts for messages, awaiting something that would bring the much-needed closure. On a purely intellectual level he was aware it was over between him and Karen, but he had never been emotionally capable of letting go. His days and nights blended into one seamlessly unending blur of alcoholic delirium and midnight chat sessions with former girlfriends or random acquaintances. *Things fell back into their usual pattern*, he observed indifferently as he poured yet another gin and tonic into an unwashed glass. *It's good to have constants in life.* It came as a surprise to him that he didn't hurt as much about Karen's absence from his life as he thought he would. His anger with her walking away quickly overshadowed any other residual feeling. *One of these mornings*, he caught himself thinking, *and I'll be gone.* He couldn't chase away the random recollections of their time together that lit up his face in an unconscious smile; same as he couldn't bring himself to stop putting up an extra pillow on her side of the bed. James could swear he could still pick up her elusive scent lingering on where she used to sleep. Late in the night, returning from the bar, jaded, he would unlock the front door with bated breath, expecting for a fraction of a second to see her sitting on the couch as always, working with her laptop on her knees. While they had been together he had never been entirely sure whether he had loved her or just enjoyed being loved. Now he knew for sure. *But just as with everything else, knowledge comes when it can no longer serve you any purpose in that relationship. Maybe in the next. Who's to say?* he concluded, filled with regret. He even missed the way she observed him intently, making him feel uncomfortable to his very core, *as though she knew everything I left unsaid.*

The more time passed, the more unjustifiable and unfair her leaving him appeared to be, and he could not find a way to explain what could've driven her to make such a final decision. His mind conveniently blocked out everything that didn't add up, and James started forgetting all the conversations and mutual dissatisfaction that had dragged on for months. This was the only thing that kept him going through his loneliness and disappointment. This, and the thought of the one person James knew he would eventually resort to in a moment of need as he had so often before. It was strange for him that he didn't immediately feel the urge to call Sylvia as he had before. The first several weeks James immersed himself in his solitude and for a brief time he actually discovered unexpected joy in it. When the days started blending into weeks and the weeks blended into months his restlessness began to grow. And when every other contact he had kept at hand in an effort to fill those nights of palpable loneliness stopped answering, he knew Sylvia was the only person left to reach out to. After all was said and done, they were both aware of the driving force behind their constant need for holding onto one another. Her marriage didn't bother him at all as he perceived it for what it really was, *a desperate attempt of a woman nearing thirty to gain some sense of security and comfort while waiting for the man she's loved all her life to be ready to settle down.* James glanced at the time on the screen and picked up the phone.

She reached for the vibrating phone on the nightstand and sleepily gazed at the time. It was nearing three in the morning. Sylvia turned around and glanced at George, who was deep asleep. She hesitated for a moment, then unlocked the phone to read the message, instantly recognizing the sender's number.

She had waited years for this moment. Strangely enough, it brought none of the emotions she thought it would. It was just now that Sylvia was realising what she had known for some time – *James is no longer in a position to validate anything for me anymore.* She looked even for a fraction of satisfaction in knowing he had finally come to understand just how important she was to him, but she couldn't find anything other than regret at how late he was. *It's not like it matters now anyway…*

Sitting up in her bed, Sylvia looked over at her sleeping husband. She reached and ran her fingers through his hair with a newfound tenderness that surprised her. After years of emotional backlash, she had come to believe James had trained her to be immune to such things, but with George she felt like she was awakening from a prolonged slumber, rediscovering the joy in the simplest of things. *Looks like James has finally found love. Too bad it's in the hopeless place that his heart is,* she thought, as she re-read the message, switched off and put back the phone on the nightstand.

She slipped under the covers, entwining her body around George's. It had been years since she had felt the need to cuddle. The past was gradually falling behind to give way to a reality and a future that were much more palpable. The figure of the man who had shaped her relationships, her beliefs and fears was strangely losing its importance and power over her. Fading away, James was taking his rightful place amongst the many other equally irrelevant men in her life, whose sole purpose had been to prepare her for meeting the one who would be good enough for her – that same one whose body was resting next to hers.

King high wins the hand, Sylvia concluded pensively, breathing in the scent of the man next to her. *And it's always a good idea to quit the game on a high note.*

www.ingramcontent.com/pod-product-compliance
Lightning Source LLC
Chambersburg PA
CBHW060538180626
46817CB00002B/630